HUNGARIAN LIBRARY

MÓR JÓKAI

THE
DARK DIAMONDS

CORVINA PRESS

Title of the Hungarian original:
FEKETE GYÉMÁNTOK
(First published 1872)

Translated from the Hungarian
by
FRANCES GERARD

The translation has been revised by
MARI KUTTNA

Jacket design by
MÁRIA HODOSSY

Second edition

© Corvina Press, Budapest, 1968
ISBN 963 13 0465 5

CONTENTS

INTRODUCTION

Mór Jókai was the greatest novelist of the romantic tradition in Hungary; even now, more than seventy years after his death, he is one of the country's most widely read authors. His fame and popularity transcend the boundaries of language: no other Hungarian writer's works have been as widely and as frequently translated into as many languages as Jókai's. On one occasion, Zola, the greatest of all naturalist writers, whose approach to the novel was diametrically different, called Jókai 'the Homer of the nineteenth century' even though he had read only a few of Jókai's works, and in very inferior translations.

Various critics have at times attacked Jókai for his lack of realism. But his readers were never deterred. The critics have been forgotten; Jókai was read and is still being read; his novels are filmed again and again, and many of his heroes still live in the popular imagination as unsurpassed examples of noble and ignoble conduct.

During the eight decades of his life (1825–1904) he witnessed and several times actively participated in the historical process by which a backward, long-oppressed Hungary finally embarked on the road to becoming a bourgeois society, trying to cover two hundred years of evolution in one generation. He was twenty-three years old and just reaching his first literary success when the Hungarian revolution flared up in 1848 under Kossuth's leadership. Then came the War of Independence, which was defeated after a year and a half of heroic struggle. Hungary came to lose even her formal political existence: for eighteen years she remained one among many oppressed, exploited, silently suffering and nearly despairing Habsburg principalities. None the less, by 1867 Vienna was forced to relent. The march of history could not be stopped: feudalism was coming to an end, even in Hungary, and an urban middle class was developing at last. The stubborn, unrelenting resistance of the Hungarian people to Austrian rule continued to be a threat to the Habsburg empire. The Hungarian landed aristocracy were ready for a compromise with the Austrians, and they had a following in the new middle classes who were economically dependent on them. By these, the Austro-Hungarian Monarchy was established; a piebald federation united in foreign affairs, defence and finance, but still remaining as two sharply divided and ever antagonistic nations. Although Hungary continued in this semi-colonial state until the break-up of the monarchy in 1918, the development of Hungary, however much it still lagged behind, could none the less follow European trends after 1867.

This great upsurge of the nineteenth century soon brought Hungarian literature in line with the Romantics of Western Europe. The long period of political oppression and the retarded social development of the country prolonged our Romantic era: before 1848, romanticism had offered inspiration, from 1849 to 1867, it brought comfort and from 1867 to the turn of the century it formulated the ideals of the new middle classes. After all, in any country where a middle class is in the process of establishing itself, the purpose of the arts is not realistic social criticism, but the romanticising of middle-class virtues. Romanticism was the literary equivalent and often the expression of liberalism in politics. It was this which made the great English and French romantic poets and novelists so popular in Hungary. Walter Scott, Byron, Dickens, Victor Hugo and Dumas père were the favourite reading of a public that had been growing from a thin crust into a vast class. They served as models to a fast-growing Hungarian romantic literature, and they were so deeply absorbed into Hungarian popular culture that Walter Scott, Dickens and Victor Hugo have remained to this day at the head of lending-statistics in libraries.

By the time the young Jókai, studying law, painting and literature simultaneously, appeared on the literary scene of the 1840's, there was already a Hungarian literature, mainly poetry, but also novels betraying the influence of Sir Walter Scott and poetic drama modelled on Victor Hugo. Jókai had learnt much from his predecessors, and even more from their models, but his limitless imagination, visual perception, gripping narrative technique and his unusually wide and many-sided intellectual interests soon showed his to be a truly original talent.

His family belonged to the lesser nobility, living in middle-class circumstances (his father was an advocate, too) and he had absorbed at home a liberal, democratic spirit which made him join the revolution, and remain its champion to the end. He was an active revolutionary in 1848, and was in hiding, under an official death sentence, after 1849. Later he became an influential journalist and in the years of the Compromise, a member of parliament. After the Compromise of 1867 he believed, like many others, that the country's progress could proceed from where it had been interrupted in 1849. As he grew older, he became more and more aware of the realities: that feudal abuses had survived, and that the people were miserable and helpless under a surface gloss of national independence and middle-class progress. Disillusion came slowly: it was hard for him to admit disappointment. But a critical tone crept into his novels again and again, though paralleled by an even greater romantic enthusiasm for escaping reality. His stories were becoming more far-fetched and more critical at the same time. In his old age, he began to formulate hopes of a Utopian socialism, though socialism remained incomprehensible, basically, to his fundamentally liberal mind, just as the soul's bitter despair was ever unknown to his Olympian good humour.

By the prime of his life, he had achieved unparalleled contemporary fame in his country, and his renown had spread through the continent. Jókai's novels and tales are always delightful reading: they express man's finest aspirations, and his unforgettable characters—even if they are dramatic exaggerations or psychologically one-sided—symbolize the basic patterns of human behaviour, while his heroes represent all the magnificent qualities which self-respecting men seek to achieve. Such an ideal, guiding example, such an envied and emulated model is Iván Berend, the hero of *The Dark Diamonds*.

Of Jókai's life-work, which exceeds a hundred bound volumes, the best originated in the years after 1867, but before his disillusion had set in during the middle 1870's. In these years, he wrote hardly any historical romances: the memory of 1848, the ever present recent past excited his imagination. He who could conjure up such splendid warrior heroes now created the prototype middle-class hero, sorely needed by the Hungary of the day. Iván Berend of *The Dark Diamonds* (written in 1870) was the most perfect embodiment of the bourgeois ideal. His past was exemplary: he had been a cavalry officer in the revolutionary forces. In the present-time of the novel, he managed his medium-sized capital assets with faultless wisdom; as a natural scientist, he was brilliant and respected; expert in the tricks of the Stock Exchange, but at the same time, able to hold his own with the aristocracy: a reckless duellist, a heroic gambler, and it would be difficult to imagine a more successful lover. Could there be a man who would not wish to be like him?

And the story of this outstanding career, the political, economic and amatory adventures which surround it, the angelic or satanic figures who none the less resemble people, are all set in a romantic, yet scientific, vision of man's relationship with the earth—not the soil, but the geology of the earth's crust. A crisis of nature and a brief phase of Hungary's history in the still oppressed years preceding 1867 come together in the intricate plot. The conclusion brings the reader to a Utopian society, where the class-war ends in the love-match between the surpassingly humane capitalist and a girl from his mine, who had miraculously retained her purity in the midst of physical dirt and moral corruption.

The hero and many of the incidents were closely modelled on various contemporary men and events, and Hungarian critics have argued much about whose character was most closely portrayed in Iván Berend, and which contemporary scandals were reflected in the plot. But for the reader, this has long since become unimportant; it no longer matters much, even in Hungary, and even less abroad. The work has outstripped by far the sources of the story and its romance has thrilled each new generation. The protagonists are known to thousands of readers, and loved like personal friends; and Iván Berend remains for ever an object for envy among men and among women, an object for daydreams.

Géza Hegedűs

Chapter I

A BLACK LANDSCAPE

We are in a deep cave, underground. It is bad enough to be under the earth, but here we are surrounded by complete darkness; the ceiling is black, so are the walls; they are made of coal. The floor is a single black mirror, some kind of lake, polished like steel. Over this polished surface glitters the reflection of a solitary light, the light of a safety-lamp shining through a wire net.

In a narrow boat a man is rowing over the lake. By the flickering light of his lamp he sees tall pillars, which rise from the depths below and reach to the very roof of the cave—slender pillars, like the columns of a Moorish palace. Only up to a certain height are they coal black; above that, they are light-coloured.

What are these pillars?

They are the trunks of pines and palm trees. Such gigantic stems are quite at home on levels above the coal-mine, but how have they come down here? They belong to another world—the world of light and air. The coal layers overhead sometimes catch fire, and the fire, being intense, has loosened the hold of these giants and pushed them down.

Coal-pits often kindle by themselves, as every novice knows, but in this case someone extinguished the flames. Who? That is the question.

The solitary occupant of the rough-made boat, or canoe,

1

moves restlessly back and forth, up and down. He is a man of about thirty, pale, and **with** a dark beard. His thin lips give him a hard expression of strong, decided will; while his forehead, which is broad with large protrusions above his eyes, shows that he is a serious thinker. His head is not covered, for the air is heavy in the cave, and his curly black hair is so thick, that he needs no headgear.

But what is he doing here?

He rows his boat over the black mirror of the lake; round and round he goes, searching the black walls anxiously, his lamp raised in his free hand. Does he expect some secret to be hidden here? Does he think that by touching a spring, and saying 'Open, Sesame!' some treasure hidden for hundreds of years will appear?

In fact, he does find treasure. Here and there, a piece of rock breaks loose from the black wall—weakly constructed in places by the hand of Nature; on it, the impression of a leaf from a long-extinct species. A wonderful treasure, this! In other place he comes upon unknown crystals, to which Science has not as yet given a name; or a new conglomeration of quartz, metal, and stone—a silent testimony to a convulsion of Nature before the world was.

The pillars, too; over them, the waters of the lake have left an encrustation of crystals, small, but visible to the naked eye.

All these finds are meaningful to him.

The lake is in itself wonderful. It has an ebb and flow: twice a day it empties itself; twice a day it fills. The water rushes in leaps and bounds, joyously, tumultuously, into this dark vault; fills it higher and higher, until it reaches the point on the pillars where their colour changes. There it remains, sometimes for two hours, stationary, smooth and still as glass. Then it begins to sink, slowly, evenly, until it vanishes into the secret hiding-places whence it came. Curious, mysterious visitor! The man in the boat knows the ways of the water, he has studied them. He waits patiently, until, with a sudden gurgling sound, as if la-

2

menting the necessity, the last current of water vanishes behind a projecting mass of coal. Then he quickly takes off his coat, his shoes, his stockings; he wears only his shirt and trousers. He fastens a leather pouch round his waist with a hammer and chisel; he takes his safety-lamp and fastens it to his belt; and, so equipped, he glides into one of the cracks of the black rock, following the vanishing lake.

He is a brave man to take on this task, for his way lies through the passages of the palace of death. It needs a heart of steel to be alone here, in this terrible silence—to search for the secret which lies beneath seven seals, the treasure which Nature has concealed for thousands of years. But this man does not know fear. He stays there for two or three hours at a time.

If he had anyone—a wife, a sister, even a servant or a dog, who knew where he was, what dangers he was risking, their souls would go out in agony of fear of all that could happen.

But he has no one; he is alone—always alone. There is no one to weep for his absence or to be glad of his coming; his life is solitary, in the clear light of day as well as in the depths of the earth.

The vanished lake is as capricious as a flirtatious girl, full of tricks and moods. Sometimes it does not show itself for three or four hours; at other times it comes skipping back in a minute, and woe to the unfortunate who is caught by it in the straits of the cave! But this man here knows the moods of the water; he has studied them. They are old acquaintances; he knows signs on which he can depend, and he knows how long the interval lasts. He can gauge its duration by underground winds. When they whistle through the clefts and fissures, then he knows that the water is nearing. If he waited until the shrill whistle ceases, he would die.

A ghostly sound is heard in the darkness—it is like a long sigh, the far-away sobbing of an Aeolian harp; and immediately the shimmer of the lamp is seen coming nearer and nearer, and in a minute the mysterious explorer of hidden secrets appears.

3

His countenance is paler than before—death-like; and drops of sweat run down his forehead and face. Down below the air must be heavier than in the cave, or the nightmare of the abyss has caused a cold sweat. He throws his well-stuffed pouch back into the boat, and gets in again.

Just in time. He has hardly sat down when a gurgling is heard, and out of the cracks in the rock comes a gush of black water, shooting out with a loud gurgle. Then a few minutes' pause follows, and then another gush of water. The cave fills up rapidly. Soon the watermark shows itself on the smooth surface of the wall. Clear as a mirror it rises, silently, relentlessly until it reaches the black line on the pillars.

The boat, with its silent, watchful occupant, floats on the water like the cave's ghost. The water is not ordinary water; it is heavy, like metal. The boat moves slowly, only now the rower does not care to look into the depths of its black looking-glass; he pays no attention to the mysterious signs on the walls. He is occupied by observing the air, which is growing denser every moment, and he looks carefully at his safety-lamp, but it is closed securely—no escape there.

There is great mist round the lamp. The air in this underground abyss takes on a blue colour. The man in the boat knows full well what this means. The flame of the safety-lamp flares high, and the wick turns red—evil signs, these! The angel of death is hovering near.

Two spirits live in these subterranean regions—two terrifying evil spirits. The pitmen call one 'Firedamp,' the other 'Chokedamp'; and these two evil spirits haunt every coal-mine, under different names. 'Chokedamp' steals upon its victim, lies like a thick vapour on his chest, follows the miner step by step, takes away his breath and his speech, laughs at his alarm, and vanishes, when it has reached its height, just as suddenly as it came. 'Firedamp' is far more cruel and frightening. It comes like a whirlwind; it sets everything aflame, kindles lumps of coal, shatters the vaults, destroys the shaft, burns the ground, and dashes human beings to pieces. Those who work for their daily bread underground can never tell when they may meet the one or the other of these fell spirits.

The secret of 'Firedamp,' how it comes, when it rises, has not yet been discovered. Perhaps it rises from the contact of hydrogen gases with the acid gases contained in the open air, and 'Chokedamp' needs only a spark to turn into 'Firedamp.' The thoughtless opening of a safety lamp, or the striking of a match, is sufficient to fuse two evil spirits into one.

The solitary man, whom we have been following, watches with increasing anxiety, as the air becomes increasingly opal-coloured.

It is already enveloping him in its thin cloud. He does not wait for the water to rise to the highest point. As the boat reaches the spot where a simple landing-stage has been made, he jumps out, pulls the boat in by the chain and moors it fast, and then, going up the rough-hewn steps to a strong iron door, he opens it with a key, and, closing it behind him, finds himself in a passage which leads him straight into the pit.

Here he is in a busy world, very different from the solitude he has left behind. The cuts, which are narrow and close, are full of miners hard at work with their pickaxes. The men are nearly naked, the boys who push the wagons are completely so. There is no sound except the incessant hammering. In the mine there are no cheerful songs, no laughter or friendly greetings. Over the mouth of each miner a thick cloth is tied, through which he breathes.

Some of the coalseams are so narrow that the miner has to lie on his back to get at the coal with his pick. When he has loosened it he drops it into the little wagon, which the naked boys, crawling on their stomachs, push to the opening.

The man who has come out of the dark cavern is dressed the same way as the others. He wears clothes, certainly, but they are covered with coal-dust, his hands are just as coarse, and he carries a pick and a hammer on his shoulder. Nevertheless, they all know him; there is a rough respect in the tone of each miner as he answers the greeting:

"Good evening. Chokedamp is coming."

This word is repeated all round.

It was true. Chokedamp *was* close at hand, and these men and boys, who quietly come and go, hammer, shove the wagons, lie on their backs, all know, as well as the convict who is awaiting the execution of his sentence, that death may be near.

The heavy, damp fog which lies on each man's chest, and which fills the mine with its unwholesome smell, needs only a spark, for those who are alive and moving, to die, buried underground, while overhead a hundred widows and orphans would weep for their lost ones.

And yet, knowing this, the miners continue their work calmly, as if they were quite unconscious that the Angel of Death is hovering above them.

The man is Iván Berend, the owner of the mine. He himself fulfils the offices of overseer, director, surveyor, and bookkeeper. He has enough to do; but we all know the saying, and, if we are old enough, have tested its truth: 'If you want a thing well done, do it yourself.' Moreover, it encourages the worker, to see his employer shoulder to shoulder with him at work. Therefore, when the master greets all his workmen with the words, 'Bad weather is coming,' they all know that the master does not consider *his* life of more value than theirs; he does not run off or leave them in danger, though he is the owner and collects the profits.

Quietly, with perfect composure, he gives his orders—the ventilators are to be opened, a change of cool air at once to the heated coal; and the workers are to go off after three hour shifts instead of six. He gets into the bucket, covered with buffalo skin, and lets himself down to the bottom of the shaft to see if the new openings are dangerous. With an iron bar he turns over carefully the coal-dust, to test whether any of it is hot, or whether there is gas concealed, which might cause an explosion. Then, as the ventilators below and the air pump above begin to work, he takes his place at the anemo-meter. This is a tender little machine, something like a child's humming-top. Its axle turns on a ruby, and the spring sets a wheel with a hundred teeth in motion; the velocity of this wheel shows the strength of the air current in the shaft. It should neither be stronger nor weaker than the motion of the 'bad weather.'

He has now seen to everything; he has taken every precaution, he has left nothing to chance, and, when all the miners have left the pit, he is the last to ascend in the basket to fresh air and daylight.

Fresh air—daylight!

In Bondavára the sun never shines, the shadow of smoke hangs like a thick cloud over the land; it is a black country, painted in soot. The roads are black with coal-tracks; the houses are black from coal-dust, which the wind carries from the large coal warehouses; the men and the women are black. It is a wonder that the birds over there in the woods are not all black.

The mouth of the Bondavára pit is on the slope of a hill which has a fine view over the whole country. On the other side, in the valley, are the tall chimneys of the distilling converters. These chimneys are busy night and day, vomiting forth smoke, sometimes white, but generally coal black; for here the sulphur, which is a component of coal, is distilled.

Metal can only be melted like this. One of the principal customers of the coal-mine is an iron-foundry in the neighbouring mountains, and from its five chimneys smoke rises incessantly. If the hammer throws up white smoke, then the oven distils black smoke, and vice-versa. The two factories, both working, cast a continuous veil of cloud and smoke over the valley, through which even the sun looks brown and dingy.

From the foundry there flows a rust-red stream, and out of the coal-mine another, black as ink. In the valley these two streams meet and flow on together. For a while the rust-red

7

tries to get the better of the ink-black, but soon it is overcome and the black rivulet flows triumphantly through the black meadows.

It is a depressing landscape, and it is sad to reflect that in such a place men grow from childhood to middle age, from middle age to old age, and never see green fields or the blue of God's heaven.

But Iván Berend, when he came out from the pit into the open air, found little difference between ground-level and underground. Below, there was the stifling smell of gas; above, a suffocating fog: below, the black vault of the mine; above, the murky vault of the sky: and the same men.

It was evening; the sun had set, and for the moment even the vile smoke could not take away its final glory. The towers of Bondavára Castle in the distance were touched with the gleam, and the chimneys of the distilleries were aglow with the crimson light. Miners were standing about idly; the women and the girls, employed in shoving the wheelbarrows, sat gossiping together, as is the habit of their sex. One of them, a young girl, began to sing—a simple little song, with simple words. It was a Slav folk song—a sort of ballad. A mother is taking leave of her daughter, a bride of a few hours; she recalls to the girl her childhood days and her mother's care, in these words:

'Say, when I smoothed your hair,
Showed I not tender care?
Say, when I dressed my child,
Was I not fond and mild?'

The melody was touching, with the sad strains of all Slav music, as if composed of tears; and the voice of the girl who sang was melodious and full of feeling. Iván stopped to listen to the song, until the singer and her companions disappeared behind the houses.

At this moment, it seemed to him that there was, after all, a great difference between life underground and life in the open air.

The song still echoed in the distance; clouds had passed and extinguished the light of the setting sun, enveloping the landscape in total darkness. No star, no white house; only the light from the windows of the foundry lit up the night: and the smoke of the distillery rose from the chimneys, and threw yellow circles on the sky.

Chapter II

THE SLAVE OF DARK DIAMONDS

There is nothing startling or new in speaking of 'dark diamonds' when we mean coal. That beautiful, brilliant stone, the diamond, is made of carbon. So is house-coal—the only difference being, that the one is transparent, the other dark; and the first is a demon, the latter an angel.

Coal animates the world. The spirit of progress derives from it; railroads, steamboats draw on it for their miraculous strength. Every machine of this age is based on coal. It makes the Earth habitable; it gives the great cities their mighty blaze and splendour. It is a treasure, the last gift presented by Earth to extravagant man.

Thus we call coal 'dark diamonds.'

Iván Berend, the owner of the Bondavára coal-mine, was in a different position from his men. He had seen God's heaven, and knew that in happier lands life was bright, careless, sunny as the cloudless sky itself. But Iván would not have cared for an existence which was all play and no work. He had inherited the coal-mine from his father, who had also left him a heritage of strong will and inflexible perseverance.

No trifle, nor even a great obstacle, could stand in the way of Iván's desires, and his desire and his pride was to work the Bondavára mine without any other help but of his pitmen. It was his ambition—perhaps a foolish one—to have no company behind him, no shareholders to find fault, no widows and orphans to be involved in possible ruin; the mine was his, and it should be his absolutely.

And so it was a quiet business. The foundry and the inhabitants of the nearest town consumed the yearly output at an uncommonly low price. It could never become a great money-making business except at an enormous outlay, as the mine was too far from any of the great industrial centres. Nevertheless, it earned a steady income, especially as Iván had no unnecessary expenses, and was, as we have said, his own manager and his own accountant. He kept an eye on everything that went on, he understood his own business perfectly, and he took pleasure in looking after his own affairs; and these three qualifications, as any businessman knows, ensure ultimate success.

It was lucky, however, that he enjoyed such good health, and that his superabundance of vitality kept him always busy, and so, naturally, he was never bored. There was no denying that it was a solitary life for so young a man.

When he unlocked the door of his small house, and closed the door behind him, he was alone. He did not even have a dog to come and greet him. He waited on himself; and he was a great man at this. He looked on eating as an unnecessary waste of time; nevertheless, he ate a great deal, for his muscles and mind needed nourishment. He was not delicate in his appetite. He ate every day at the same tavern as his pitmen, and his food was very little better than theirs, the only difference being that he avoided strong drink. They worked only with their bodies; but he had to bring a clear intellect to his work, not a sodden one. His bed needed no making. It was a wooden plank, with a mattress over it, covered with a sheepskin rug. There was no point in brushing his clothes; they were always permeated by coal-dust.

Any one who would offer, by way of a service, to clear out his room, would, in fact, have done him a fatal injury. It was full of every kind of thing—new books, half cut; minerals;

11

scientific instruments; plans; pictures; reports. Not one of these could be moved from its place. There was order in his disorder, and in the heterogeneous mass Iván could find what he wanted. In one corner was Lavoisier's pyrometer; in another Berard's gas food-warmer. Over there a wonderful sun-telescope; against the wall Bunsen's galvanic battery, together with every conceivable invention, every sort of chemical apparatus for analyzing and exploring the mysteries of Nature.

Amongst these things Iván spent his long nights. Any other man, tired as he must be after his day's work, would have flung himself upon his bed, and would have sought in sleep some compensation for the labours of the day, or if not tired enough for this, would have sat in front of his door to breathe a little fresh air, which was free from smoke and coal-dust at night. But this student of the unseen withdrew into his inner room, lit his fire, made his lamp blaze high, and busied himself breaking lumps of coal, boiling liquids, developing deadly gases, a breath of which would be enough to dispatch a man into eternity.

What was he searching for? Was he seeking the secret of the philosophers' stone? Did he sacrifice sleep to find out how to make diamonds from coal? Did he strive to extract deadly poisons, or was he simply pursuing the *ignis fatuus* of knowledge—trying out experiments, grubbing about in darkness until, in the hopeless endeavour, his overstrained brain would give way, and there would be only the wreck left of what was once a noble intellect?

Nothing of the sort. He had a purpose: to learn a secret which would benefit mankind infinitely—at least, those who are buried in the pits and caverns of Earth. He wanted to find out how fire could be extinguished in burning pits. To discover this he spent his nights, and the years of his youth and his manhood. It was not a thought born of today or yesterday; it had been his only desire for many years.

He had seen so much misery, such heartrending scenes enacted in front of the pit mouths—these monsters that swallow

12

human life like the Juggernauts of old. He wanted to lessen the amount of sacrifice—a sacrifice never considered by those who profit from the work of the victims, whose very blood is spilt to keep others warm. It was possible that this fixed idea might drive him mad, or that he might lose his life; but the knowledge, if he ever found it, would be worth the loss. After all, what is the loss of one life against saving millions? There was no tinge of self in Iván Berend. And he had certain joys in his search. 'Joy' is hardly the word. Whenever he had even a small glimpse of what he wanted, his ecstasy was superhuman. These moments were worth all the pleasures the world could offer, and if we can bring our minds to understand this, then we shall comprehend how a young man preferred to be shut up in a cave, in danger of losing his life, or in a stifling room, trying risky experiments, rather than spend the night with lovely girls or among pleasant friends, drinking, dancing, or making love. There is a charm in Science for those who know her which far surpasses carnal pleasures.

Tonight, however, Iván's experiments fell a little flat. Either because he was tired, or for some other reason. Could it be possible that a girl's song—? Yes, such was the humiliating hindrance. At the moment when he least expected it, the song had unexpectedly returned to his mind.

With an effort Iván lit his lamp, and laid the fire in his furnace. His experiments, however, were a failure. The girl's song kept running through his head, and the words—how did they go?

> 'Say, when I smoothed your hair,
> Showed I not tender care?
> Say, when I dressed my child,
> Was I not fond and mild?'

It was very pretty, and the voice was wonderful—sweet and clear and melodious. Tomorrow evening she might be at the pit's mouth again, and then he might discover her name. Even

13

if she were not there, the other girls would know; there were not many among them who sang.

'Say, when I smoothed your hair,'

Oh, he could settle down to nothing with this tiresome song running in his head!

'Showed I not tender care?'

He wished he had seen her face, merely to know if it matched the voice. Very likely not. She would be hard-faced, like the others—bold, unfeminine creatures; beauty and modesty were rare gifts in Bondavára.

The next day, Iván arrived early at the pit. The opening of the ventilator had done its work; there was only a small fraction of hydrogen in the pit's air. The ventilators could be shut and Iván was able to spend some time outside.

At the noon-tide bell, as the girls came off the wheelbarrows, he heard again the clear young voice singing the same song. He had not been wrong about the voice; it was fresh and lovely, like a blackbird, uneducated and unspoilt, but full of natural charm, tender and joyous. He caught sight of the singer—a very young girl, hardly more than sixteen. The ordinary blue bodice she wore showed every undulation of her virginal figure, untrammelled by fashionable corsets. Her short skirt, tucked up on one side, and fastened to her waist, revealed her even shorter shift, which only reached to her knees, so that her legs were uncovered. They might have been modelled for a statue of Hebe, so perfect were they in shape—the ankles small, and little feet beautifully rounded, like a child's. The girl had wound a coloured cloth round her head and she had tucked her hair under it; her face, like those of her companions, was blackened by coal-dust, but even this enemy to beauty could not disfigure her. Her features were regular, her eyebrows thick and dark,

14

her lips red. There was a mixture of earthly dirt and other-worldly beauty in her; moreover, she had assets that even coal-dust could not conceal or dim, her eyes—her large black eyes—shining like diamonds, and lighting up the darkness like twin stars.

As these wonderful eyes met Iván's glance, it seemed to him that these diamonds were cutting away a part of the glass case in which he had preserved his heart, kept it hitherto untouched. But he did not know that this was only the beginning; that his protecting glass would soon lie in fragments all round him.

The girl made a little curtsey to her employer, and accompanied this small act of duty with a smile which showed two rows of beautiful, pearly-white teeth.

Iván felt like an enchanted knight in a fairy-tale. He forgot what had brought him here, and what he wanted to say; he remained rooted to the spot, gazing blankly after the girl's retreating figure, and her companions. He hoped, without exactly defining it, that she might look back. That little action would have broken the charm under which she had placed him. But she did not look back, although one of her companions called her by her name, 'Evila.' Iván could see them talking to her, whispering, no doubt, about him. This did not seem to rouse any curiosity in her. They had now reached the open shed, where they sat down on the ground, took out of their pockets pieces of black bread and crab-apples, and ate their dinner.

Iván wandered back to his house. For the first time in his life it struck him how lonely it was. It was his habit to keep a sort of log-book, in which he entered his personal notes upon all his workers. This was a practical necessity: he knew that a skilled, reliable workman is far more useful at a high wage than a lazy good-for-nothing who would come for half the wage. At the footnote by the name 'Evila' he read:

'A young orphan; supports a crippled brother younger than herself, who walks on crutches, and whose tongue is paralyzed. She is very steady, and does not go into town.'

15

He was quite sure that he must have seen this child earlier, but had paid no attention to her. Each Saturday he paid wages to every workman, every girl and lad in the pit; then how had he escaped noticing those wonderful eyes? He did not know, educated though he was, that there is a bond between two souls destined for one another. It is like an electric shock, this sudden birth of love; but Iván scoffed at this idea. Love? Nonsense! He in love with a girl from the mine? Ridiculous! It was compassion, pity for a pretty child who was left without either father or mother to watch over her at this tender age, and still worse, with a deformed brother to care for and provide with food and medicine. No doubt she gave him the best of everything, while she had to be content with black bread and crabapples, and all the time she remained an honest, steady girl. She never even turned her head to look at him. There was nothing but pity in his heart for this coal-black Naiad; it was only pity which made him wish to cover those tender little feet with proper shoes; it was only a proper regard for the weakest amongst his work-people, which would cause him to make inquiries about this poor forlorn child. Oh, self-deception, what a large part you play in the hearts of men!

The following Saturday the workers came to receive their weekly wages. Iván, who always paid the money himself, remained at his desk until the last one came. On this occasion Evila was the last. Iván sat at a table with the money to be paid laid out, which was regulated by the amount of work done as registered in the day-book.

When the girl, who was still dressed in her blue bodice and red skirt, came, Iván said to her with the kindness of superior generosity:

"My child, I have decided to increase your wages; you shall have double pay from now."

The girl opened her large eyes, and stared at him in surprise. "Why?" she asked.

"Because I am told that you have a crippled brother, whom

you have to keep out of your pay. You cannot have enough to clothe and feed both him and yourself. I have also heard that you are a good, honest girl, and therefore it gives me pleasure to reward you by giving you double pay."

"I cannot take it."

It was Iván's turn to be surprised.

"Why not?"

"Because I know what the others would say. They would tease me about your being my lover, and I should have so much trouble that I could not stay here any longer."

Iván was so confused by this naive, simple and unembarrassed explanation, that he could not think of any answer. He counted out her usual week's wage, which she stowed away in her bodice without any coquetry, wished him good night, and went on her way.

He was left with all his thoughts in a jumble. In all his experience—and he had had a good deal, even besides his reading, he had been about in the world, and he had known many women—but he had never known a woman like this one.

'She is afraid that they would say I was her lover; she is afraid they would tease her so much, that she may have to go away! Has she, then, no idea that once I, the master, became a girl's lover, she would not need to push a wheelbarrow any longer? Does she even know what a lover is? She knows full well that she must guard herself against one. Poor child! How earnest she was, and yet she laughed, and she did not know why she laughed, nor yet why she was grave.'

He got up, locked his desk, and turned to leave his office; then sat down again, thinking.

'She is unlike every other woman, I doubt if she knows how beautiful she is, or the worth of her beauty. She is Eve, a perfect copy of Eve—the Eve of Scripture, and the Eve of Moses. She is Eve, in not knowing why she should blush for her own nakedness—the model of loveliness in its primitive state, unwashed, savage, with her hair undone, who wanders through the garden,

17

fearing nothing, and even plays with the serpent. With men she is a woman, by herself she is a child, and yet she displays a motherly care for her little brother. Her figure could serve as a model for any sculpture, her face is full of spirit, her eyes bewitching, her voice melodious; and yet her hands are hard with the barrow-poles, her mind is troubled with sordid cares for her daily bread, her face is covered with coal-smut, and she has learned her songs in the street.'

'The worse for her!' and, after a pause, Iván added with a sigh, 'and the worse for someone else, too.'

In his mind, a total revolution had taken place. Intellectual inspiration deserted him for once, and others had taken its place, those demons which the blessed Anthony had fought with such good effect in the desert.

When poor Iván tried to banish these tempters by burying himself in his books, the form of Evila came between him and his current experiment, just as Marguerite appeared to Doctor Faustus in his laboratory; her voice sounded in his ear, her eyes glowed among the coals, and when he tried to write, he found himself drawing a maiden in a blue bodice and short red skirt. It was the same with everything he began. Some mocking demon seemed bent on tormenting him.

Abandoning his experiments, the poor man took to reading a volume of light literature. What did he light upon? A book on the loves of great and nobly born men for lowly born and inferior women. Thus Lord Douglas fell in love with a shepherdess, and became a shepherd for her sake; Count Pelletier took to wife a gipsy girl, and went about the streets turning an organ; Bernadotte, the King of Sweden, sought the hand of a peasant girl, who minded a flock of geese for a farmer; Archduke John married the daughter of a postmaster; and another Austrian duke raised an actress to the position of Grand Duchess; the consort of Peter the Great was the daughter of a peasant; a Buonaparte married a washerwoman, who had been his mistress.

And why not? Are not beauty, sweetness, fidelity and true

worth to be found under a wool dress as well as a silk one? And, on the other hand, do we not find sinners enough in the best circles?

Dit not Zoraida kill her own children, and was she not a born princess? Faustina took money from her lovers, although she was the daughter of an emperor; the Marquise Astorgas ran a hairpin through her husband's heart; Semiramis strewed a whole churchyard with the corpses of her mates; King Otto was poisoned in a grove by his queen; Joanna of Naples treasured the ribbon with which the king, her husband, was strangled; Jeanne la Folle tormented her husband to death; the Empress Catharine betrayed her sovereign and consort, and connived at his murder; and the Borgias, Tudors, all had wives who became notorious, for entwined in their crowns they wore the girdle of Aphrodite.

And do we not find the most exalted virtues in what is called low life? The actress Gaussin, to whom her wealthy lover gave a blank cheque, with *carte blanche* to write a million or more on it only wrote that she would always love him; Quintilla, another actress, bit off her tongue, rather than to betray her lover, who was implicated in a conspiracy; Alice, who undertook to fight a duel for her husband, and was killed; and many others, who have suffered silently, and died for love itself.

Philosophy and history both conspired against Iván. And then came sleep.

A dream is a magic mirror in which we see ourselves as we would be if our own wishes and inclinations were all-powerful. In his dreams, the bald man has hair, and the blind can see.

By the end of the following week Iván came to realize that he had lost the use of his understanding. The more he tried to force his mind back to its original groove of abstract theory, the more the demons ranged themselves against him. One evening, in his absence of mind, he overheated one of the retorts and it burst in his face, and small glass particles cut his nose and face. He was forced to bind his wounds with pieces of sticking-plaster. It did not occur to him that strips of black diachylon

19

placed obliquely across his nose would not improve his appearance. He was, however, very angry at his own folly—a folly which went still further, for he began to argue with himself in this way:

'It would be better to marry this girl than to go mad for her. Marry her? Who ever heard the like? A pit-girl! What *a mésalliance!* And who cares? Am I not alone in the world? Am I not my entire family? And do not these recurring thoughts of her come between me and my work? If this goes on any longer I shall be ruined; and as for the *mésalliance*, is there a single soul within six miles who would understand the meaning of the word? Not one; and if there should be one, he would have to look for me in the pit, and he would find my face black with coal-dust; no one would ever see me blush for the shame of it.'

At the same time, he did not seek out the girl. He waited for Saturday, when he knew she would come for her weekly wages. She appeared, as usual, as the last, for she was the youngest, and she stood before him as he sat at his desk. But this time, when Iván had put the money into Evila's hand, he kept the little fingers in his firm clasp. The girl laughed—perhaps at the plasters, which still ornamented his face.

"Listen to me, Evila. I have something to say to you."

Evila looked uneasy; she stopped laughing.

"Will you have me for your lover? Nay, my child, I mean you no harm; only one must talk of love before one talks of marriage."

The girl nodded; and then shook her head. "It is not possible," she said.

"Not possible! Why not?"

"Because I am already engaged."

Iván let go her hand. "To whom?"

"I am not going to tell you," said Evila, "if I did, I know very well that you would do something. You would fire him, or you would hold him back, and we cannot be married until he is taken on as a regular pitman."

"He is, then, a daily casual worker?"

"Yes."

"And do you think more highly of this simple fellow than you do of me, your employer?"

The girl shrugged her shoulders, and bending her head a little, she threw a look at Iván which made the blood rush to his head. Then she went on, quietly:

"I gave him my promise before mother died, and I must keep my word."

"To the devil with your father and your mother!" cried Iván, beside himself in baffled hope and rage. "Do you imagine I care what you have promised to a fellow like that? I ask you again, will you give him up and come to me?"

Again Evila shook her head. "I dare not. My bridegroom is a wild, violent man; he would think nothing of doing you in, and setting the pit on fire into the bargain when gas was on. Good evening!" And then, she ran away quickly, and disappeared among her companions.

Iván threw down the day-book so violently that the pages flew from one end of the room to the other. A common creature, a wheelbarrow-girl, a half-savage, had dared to cross his wishes and refuse his offer. And for a dirty, miserable miner—a mere mole!

Iván had a hard battle to fight when he was once more alone in the solitude of the night.

Beware of the man who professes to be above human passion, who glories in his iron will and his heart of ice; avoid him and the quiet, holy, studious man with a soft tongue, who turns his eyes away from women, and shuns what others enjoy. It is on these that outraged human nature takes its revenge; and once the inner demon breaks loose, he plays a great game to indemnify himself for all the restraint he has suffered. The love of the worldling is a lapdog; that of the hermit is a lion.

With this wild beast, which he had suddenly unchained, did Iván, the man of science, spend the long night, now walking up

21

and down the narrow room, now throwing himself on his bed, a prey to the most horrible temptations, his heart beating with a thousand passionate desires, his thoughts running in as many evil directions. Evila's opposition had stimulated his passion, and also roused his native pride. The master of the Bondavára mine was a man of fiery temper, kept in check by his strong command over himself; but this command seemed now at fault. He no longer had any power to lay this demon which had taken possession of him, tempting him from all sides. With his powerful fist he struck himself a blow upon his chest, near to his throbbing heart.

'Will you be silent? Who is master, you or I? Do your duty, slave. I am your lord, your king. Your duty is nothing but keeping my arteries going, in pumping air into my lungs, in forcing blood to flow. When you stop, your atrophy is my end; but you cannot be my master, for my will must be supreme.'

And as Iván had struck his breast, it seemed to him as if he saw in a magic mirror a reflection of two forms—himself and another Iván, locked in deadly combat. It seemed to him that this other self had robbed him of his shape and features, to perpetrate in his name the most odious sins, and as he hit out against this horrid image of himself, it slowly vanished; and then Iván, falling back on his pillow, cried out aloud: 'Never return, fiend; never come into my sight again!'

In another hour, pale and exhausted, Iván was sitting quietly at his desk. It required a heroic effort on his part to begin his prosaic calculations, to add up the long columns of figures; but he forced his weary brain, his tired fingers to the job, and the slave obeyed its master, the body submitted to the mind.

Chapter III

THE MAN-EATER

The morning light found Iván still seated at his table. As daybreak and lamplight did not agree, he put out his lamp, threw his papers on one side, and gave himself a moment's rest.

He had conquered; he was himself again. All the fire of passion had died out, the sinful images had vanished, and in his breast a profound peace reigned. He had resolved upon his course; an angel had been at his side and inspired him.

It was Sunday morning. The engines which work the distillery were at rest. On Sundays the enormous water-basin, or trough, which fed the steam-pump, was utilized to remove the week's grime from the miners. From six to seven the basin was reserved for the women, from half past seven to nine, for the men. The keys of the great pump-house were handed over each Saturday night to Iván by the machine superintendent, so that no curious or peeping Tom should hide himself there, and see these Venuses bathing through the small window, which gave upon the basin, and which was put there mainly to allow the stoker to check that the level of the water was not disturbed while the pumps were at work.

It had never once entered Iván's brain that he could play Tom if he liked. But on this Sunday morning he took the key from its nail and put it in his pocket: and he did so, not between six and seven, but shortly after eight o'clock: it was the men he wanted to see bathing, without being himself seen.

And why? Because he knew that it was the custom in coal-mines, that when a couple become engaged, it was usual to tattoo the name of the girl upon the man's naked body. Where the miners have got this Indian and savage habit is hard to say. There is a certain tenderness in it, and tenderness is more often found with the savage than the civilized man. The lovers tattoo themselves with a needle, on the arm or shoulder, and then rub in a corrosive acid, either red or blue. Such a testimony is irradicable. Sometimes some poetic temperament adds two hearts transfixed by an arrow, or a couple of doves; or it may be the signs of the miner, the mallet and the pick. It occasionally happens that the relationships change, and that a lover would be glad to remove the name of the fickle one from his album. This can be done by placing a plaster over the name, and eventually the writing vanishes, together with the skin; a new skin grows, and upon this a new name can be written. Many are not so discreet. They punctuate a fresh name beneath the old one, and they allow the list to grow, until sometimes there is hardly a single empty spot.

It did not give Iván much trouble to find the right man. As soon as the water washed off the black soot from the bodies of the bathers, he saw the name of Evila on a shoulder, the letters in blue, two hearts in red. His rival was an intelligent, hard-working labourer; he was called Péter Saffran, and his comrades had added the nickname: the man-eater. Péter had never taken umbrage at this misnomer. He was a particularly quiet man, and when they teased him, he took no notice. He never complained of anything, and never went either to church or to the tavern. He had a remarkable antipathy for children. If a child came near him he drove it away, grinding his teeth, and throwing anything he had in his hand. This peculiarity was so well known that the mothers always cautioned the little ones against the man-eater. Apart from this, he was on good terms with everyone.

Iván, having found out what he wanted, left the pump-house,

and returned home, placing himself in front of his door, so that he could see the people as they passed him walking in groups towards the church in the neighbouring village. He noticed that Evila was among them. He examined her critically and in cold blood, and he came to quite a scientific conclusion as to the peculiar style of her beauty, which showed a mixture of racial characteristics. The small hands and feet, the slender figure, the narrow forehead, the finely cut nose, the silky black hair, all spoke the Indian or Hindoo type; but the short upper lip and the long, serpent-like eyebrows, were probably derived from some Slav ancestor. The starry, seductive eyes were decidedly Eastern, the chin and the colouring recalled the Malay race, and the quick, sudden rising of the red blood to the velvet cheek, the Caucasian—for only Caucasian people can blush readily, owing to the cellular texture of their skin being fine almost to transparency.

Iván pondered on all this as Evila passed him; he also wondered why her lover was not with her, as would be the established custom in Bondavára. Péter, however, evidently had no mind to follow the rules of courtship; he was lounging on one of the benches in front of the ventilation-oven's gates, close to the pit mouth, his head in the air, his chin in his hand.

Iván went up to him. "Good morning, Péter. What are you doing here, my good man?"

"I am listening to the wind that's coming up from down there."

"Why don't you go to church?"

"Because I never pray."

"And why not?"

"I do nobody any harm. I neither steal nor kill, and if there is a God, He knows better than I do what is good for me."

"You are quite wrong there, Péter. In these matters there is an immense difference between educated people and those who are called the children of Nature. I have my science and thought to fall back on—my intellect is my guide, and preserves me from

25

temptation; but with you, and men like you, it is otherwise. Those who have no other knowledge but what concerns their daily labour have a need of faith, of hope, of consolation, and of forgiveness." As he spoke, Iván sat down by him, and laid his hand upon his shoulder. "Is there something on your mind, Péter?"

Péter nodded. "There is something."

"Does it weigh on your soul?"

"On my soul, on my body—everywhere!"

"Is it a secret, Péter?"

"No, it is not. If you care to hear it, I will tell you."

"Is it murder?"

"Worse than that."

"Don't you think you had better not tell it to me? It may place you in danger."

"There is no danger for me. If it were written up—on the Market Cross, the law could not touch me; besides, most people know it. You would hear it from someone else, if not from me."

"Then tell me."

"It is a short story. When I was only a boy, not quite twenty, I went to sea to seek my fortune. I was taken as stoker on board a Trieste steamboat. We sailed with a cargo of meal to Brazil. Our voyage out was lucky. On our return, we brought back coffee and wool. Just above the Equator we met a hurricane, which broke our engine, smashed our mainmast, and drove the vessel against a sandbank, where she foundered. Some of the passengers took to the life-boat; they went only a short way when it turned over, and they all drowned. The rest of us made a raft from the planks of the sunken ship, and had to trust this frail thing on the open sea. We were thirty-nine in all, including the captain, the helmsman, and a merchant from Rio de Janeiro, with his wife and a three-year-old child. There was no other woman or child, for the rest were lost in the life-boat. We thought them unfortunate, but now I think they were the happy ones. It would have been better, far better, if I had died then.

26

Out of our thirty-nine, soon only nine remained. Oh, how I wish I had been one of the dead! For eight days we floated on the water, buffeted here and there, or in a calm, nailed, as it were, to the ocean, without a single drop of water to quench our thirst, or one morsel of food. Ten of us had died of hunger.

"For days we had never eaten, and the ninth day came, and no hope of rescue. The sun was burning us up, and the water reflected the heat, so that we were between two fires. Oh, the horror of that terrible time! That evening we decided that one of us should be sacrificed for the others—that is, that we should draw lots who should be eaten. We threw our names into a hat, and we made the innocent little child draw for us. The child drew his own name.

"I cannot tell you, sir, the rest of that ghastly business. Often I dream of the whole thing again, and I always wake at the moment when the miserable mother cursed all those who ate of that horrible meal, invoking Heaven that we might never find a day's peace. At the recollection of her words I jump out of bed, I run into the woods and wait to see whether I shall be turned into a wolf. It would serve me right.

"I am the only survivor of that cursed meal. The thought haunts me; it burns into my very soul. With my own blood, the blood of another human being runs in my veins. Dreadful thoughts pursue me. The piece of human flesh that I have eaten is in me still; it has taken away all my wish for other food. I can now understand the pleasure of cannibals. I can never see a rosy-faced child without thinking what a delicious morsel his little rounded arm would be. When I behold a sickly, pale baby, the idea at once occurs to me—Why let it live? Would it not be better—"

He shuddered, and stood up. He hid his hands in his blouse, and after a pause, went on:

"Tell me now, sir, is there any relief for what I suffer? Is there a doctor who can cure me, or a priest who will absolve me? I have told my story to both priest and doctor, and one has told me to fast and to chastise myself, the other to drink no brandy and to have my blood let. Neither of them is worth a pin, and such advice only makes the matter worse."

"I will advise you," said Iván. "Get married."

Saffran looked at his employer in surprise, and a weak flash of a smile appeared on his face.

"I have thought of it myself. Perhaps if I had children of my own, this horror would disappear."

"Then why don't you marry?"

"Because I am too poor. If two beggars mate, then you have a pair of paupers, instead of one. One must have something to live on first."

"That is true; but you are a hard-working man. I have long wanted to make you a first-class pitman, but I waited with your promotion until you got married. It is my rule to give the best places to married men. I have found that the single go to the dogs as soon as they get higher pay. One can depend better on a married man; he won't leave his place just for a whim. So think it over. After the first Saturday when you can tell me that your banns have been called in church, you will have the pay of a pitman, and I shall give you a house to live in."

A tear appeared in the worker's eye. He nearly fell to the feet of his benefactor; he almost sobbed as he stammered out his thanks.

"Now," cried Iván, with friendly encouragement, "it is Sunday today. Does this make you think of anything, my friend?"

The man sprang to his feet, and wiped his eyes.

"Service has not started yet," went on Iván. "People are still on their way to church. I think there would be time for you to catch up with your bride, and go with her to the priest."

Péter said nothing, but he started to run; his legs were long, and he was soon out of sight. He was bareheaded; he had left his hat on the bench. Iván saw it, and took it home to keep for him. He stood, looking after the running man until he disappeared behind the corner. Then he went inside, with Saffran's hat in his hand.

'How happy he is!' he thought, and sighed.

Back in his room, he entered in his daybook that from the following day, Monday, he had engaged Péter Saffran as a first-class pitman with the usual wages, and that in his place another day-labourer should be taken on. As he closed his book, his heart whispered:

'My cruel master, are you satisfied now?'

But Iván had his misgivings, and answered his heart:

'I don't believe in you, since I have seen how easy it was for you to take me onto thin ice. I must watch out in the future. I am not sure of the purity of my motives, even now. God knows what lies under my apparent abnegation. Perhaps you think that as a young wife, she will still be lovely and perhaps more attainable . . . But I shall watch you closely, my treacherous heart; you shan't lead me into any more dangers.'

Again he consulted his account-book, and found that the increase in the year's income allowed him to take on an overseer at a very fair salary. He wrote out the proper advertisement, and despatched it that very evening to various foreign papers.

In that way, he would not be thrown into daily contact with his workers.

Chapter IV

THE COINER

A fortnight after Iván sent his advertisement to the foreign papers, one morning, and again it was a Saturday morning, Péter Saffran came and told him that two gentlemen had just arrived, wishing to see the mine.

"They must be foreigners," he added, "since they spoke French to each other." Péter's life as a sailor had given him some knowledge of the French tongue.

"I shall be with them immediately," said Iván, who was busy pouring a green liquid through a pointed sieve. "Let them get into a miner's outfit in the meanwhile."

"That's been done; they are ready for you."

"Very good. I am going. And how are you getting on, Péter?"

"With the wedding? Everything is going fine; tomorrow our banns will be called for the third time."

"And when will you be married?"

"It is Advent just now, and the priest will not marry us; but we shall have the wedding on the first Sunday after Twelfth Night. I don't really mind the delay, for I have to save up a little money. When a man marries, he must have all sorts of things—furniture and the like; and something laid by for the winter as well."

"And have you put by nothing from your wages?"

"Yes, sir; I had over a hundred and fifty florins laid by. I had denied myself everything—food and drink, and even a smoke—

to get together this money. Then, what should the devil do, but bring the recruiting commission down here, and I had to pay all my money into the greasy hand of the examining doctor, so that he might report me as being unfit for service because I squint. It's a trick I have. I can squint for a quarter of an hour together, although my eyes are straight; on this account I was let off by the doctor, but my hundred and fifty florins are gone. I shall have to squint during the wedding, for the priest will only marry me because I am unfit for service."

"Well, Péter, you may count upon some help from me."

"Thank you, sir, but I don't like loans; that is like eating one's supper for dinner."

By this time they had reached to where the strangers were waiting.

"Ah," cried Iván, "it is you, Felix!" holding out his hand with gladness to one of the visitors.

The old friend whom Iván greeted as Felix was a man of about his own age. His soft complexion, carefully waxed moustache, short beard, his fine, dark-blue eyes, and particularly the shape of his head, and the way it was held on his shoulders, taken together with his elegant dress, which the rough miner's blouse could not quite conceal, betrayed the man of the world. When he spoke, his voice was almost feminine; its tone was clear and ringing, like a singer in the Vatican.

Felix hurried to set his friend's mind at ease about the trickiest part of the meeting.

"I hope you will forgive us for putting up at the inn. I was sure you would have made us welcome, but you are a busy man, and you would not care to be troubled with the bother of entertaining us; besides, like all men of business, you live, I dare say, a little in the rough, and the inn is really very comfortable. May I introduce my travelling companion, Gustave Rauné? He is a mining engineer."

Iván was well obliged for his friend's forethought in the matter of not requiring hospitality; not that he would not have made him welcome as far as he could, and there were unoccupied rooms in his house which could have accommodated the two men—but his way of life would have been disturbed. He had never for a moment thought of having guests.

"My house," he said frankly, "is not fitted for receiving my friends, and, indeed, none come; but the inn also belongs to me. I trust you will consider yourselves my guests while you are here."

"We accept your offer," said Felix lightly; "especially as we have come in fact on your business. I read your advertisement some days ago. You say you require an overseer?"

"I do." Iván looked doubtfully from one gentleman to the other.

"No, no; it is not for me," laughed Felix. "I know nothing of your business; but Rauné might be inclined to join you, if he finds your outfit worthy of his talents. Rauné is an old friend of mine. He learned his business under Erenzoter. You know the firm of Erenzoter? He is an extremely well qualified man."

Rauné said not a word, all the time, perhaps for the best of reasons, that, being a Frenchman, he did not understand the language in which the others spoke. He was a small man, thin, with penetrating eyes, a sharp profile, and a frighteningly long, pointed beard.

To this gentleman Iván explained in fluent French that he would be glad to show him every part of the Bondavára mine in person.

Then they went down together into the pit. Two experts were soon convinced that they were testing out one another's knowledge of the whole machinery and workings of a mine. And each became convinced that the other knew his business. Sometimes they held different opinions about certain systems, and in the discussion or even argument which would arise, each disputant soon realized that the other had nothing to learn.

Rauné displayed his extraordinary quickness and knowledge in valuing the coal stratum. Even without looking at the geological maps, he was able to decide upon the probable profit, as also upon the probable extent of the layer or stratum beyond the actual ground covered by Iván's pit. His valuation agreed in almost every particular with that already made by Iván. By mid-day the inspection was over, and they went to the inn for dinner, having first given some time to washing and changing clothes. A visit to a pit is by no means clean fun.

The afternoon was devoted to the inspection of the distilling ovens, and in the evening they went over the foundry. When they returned from the foundry, Felix went back with Iván to his house, while Rauné returned to the inn.

Iván led his old acquaintance into his workroom, where, in truth, a wonderful disorder prevailed. He cleared a chair, full of maps and books for his friend and told him to light his cigar at a new type of chemical lamp.

"You always had an inquiring mind, Iván. I well remember how you out-distanced everyone at college. As for me, I was a dilettante compared to you. Now, tell me truly; have all your knowledge, your industry and your physical labours made you a rich man?"

Iván laughed. "This mine gives me an annual income of ten thousand florins."

"In other words, it produces nothing, or, at least, next to nothing. You are your own director, overseer, cashier, engineer, secretary, book-keeper, and transport; and you receive, at a rough calculation, just what you would have to pay such employees if you did not unite all their different functions in yourself. In other words, your work, your talent, your studies, your zeal, your expenditure of thought and strength upon this mine of yours, only bring you in the miserable return which any owner would pay the man who filled even one of these jobs. In fact, you don't gain a farthing from it."

"The mine is not to blame, and neither am I. It is the result of a very small demand. In consequence production cannot be increased endlessly."

"I will tell you in two words where the fault lies. In the present day strength is to be found only in co-operation. In the political world the smaller states go to the wall; they are forced to tack themselves on to larger ones, and form unions. It is the same in the commercial world; small tradesmen must give way to larger combines: and it is better for them to understand this, and become a part of a company."

"There is no danger of our foundry closing; our iron and our coal take first place, and could not be crushed."

"An additional reason for developing my idea—an idea which, I may as well tell you, was what had brought me here. You have already guessed, I imagine, that I am not such a good fellow as to undertake the journey solely to save Rauné's getting bored on the way. He could have found the place himself. I have a great plan in my head. I intend to make you a very rich man, and naturally, I shall make a profit myself at the same time."

"How so?"

"I do not know where I once read this short synopsis of how different nations acquire money: the Hungarian seeks it, the German earns it, the Frenchman wins it, and the American makes it. It is a most characteristic description. You have only to watch the Hungarian, how he looks under every bush for his money; the German will work with the sweat of his brow, till he gets his reward, that gold piece; the light-hearted Frenchman will win the last gold piece his victim has; but the Yankee sits in a corner, gnaws his finger-nails, and makes his pile. Yes, gold lies in undiscovered millions, only waiting to be made. And it lies in the opportunities of life, in bold undertakings, in treasures concealed in the earth, which require development, and the outlay of capital; in new discoveries, in the extension of the means of communication, in the increase of luxury, in the follies of mankind, in the exertions made by scientists; and especially in the money-box where small capitalists keep their gold, which should circulate through large channels to be of use.

34

The small holdings should be thrown into one large concern, and with such credit every coin would bring in three times its value. This is a fine art; this is how one can make piles of gold. It is a splendid art, an honest art, and it seems to make those who practise it thrive."

When he had concluded his rather long-winded exhortation, Felix threw himself back in his chair with an air of one saying: 'Are you not dazzled with the brilliance of my conception? Is not Felix Kaulman one of the greatest financiers of the day? Surely you must be convinced that he is.'

As far as this went, the name had a fair reputation indeed. The Kaulmans had always been in finance, and they were well-known bankers. Of late, since Felix had inherited the business from his father, the firm was even more in the public eye. Iván knew his old school-fellow well; he looked at him now quietly.

"How do you propose to make a pile out of my pit?"

"I have a very big scheme in mind."

"But the whole pit is hardly very big."

"So it appears to you, because you don't see it from my point of view. You have looked for diamonds in the mine, but it has never occurred to you that there may be iron ore. This pit produces, you tell me, a profit of ten thousand florins; that is the interest of two hundred thousand florins. I can show you a company which will buy the whole place outright for two hundred thousand florins."

"But I would not part with my pit for any price. I am in my element here, like the mud-worm in mud."

"You need not leave it, certainly not; on the contrary, if you wished to go, I would keep you chained down if necessary. The company will start with a recognized capital of four millions; we will form a large business, which on one side will ruin Prussian coal, on the other side will drive English iron from the market. You shall be the principal director of the business, with a yearly salary of ten thousand florins, and two shares in the business; besides which you will be allowed to take, if you wish it, a portion of the purchase-money in bonds at par, and these will bear interest at twenty per cent. You will enjoy an income of thirty thousand florins and, on top of all, do a sixth of the work you are doing now."

Iván listened to this proposal without interrupting the speaker. When Felix had finished, he said in a calm voice:

"My dear Felix, if I were to propose to a company which has already a capital of four millions, the sale of a business which up to the present had only produced ten thousand florins profit, and which could never realize more than eight hundred thousand florins in the future, do you not think I would be a despicable crook? If, on the other hand, I put my own money into such a company, I should be just as big a fool."

Felix burst into laughter at such a re-stating of his proposal. Then, passing his pliant little walking-stick behind his back, he placed both his hands on its ends, and said with an air of profound wisdom:

"You have not yet heard my whole plan. It has not altogether to do with your settlement. You know well that your pit is only a small portion of the giant coal deposit of the entire Bonda Valley. I intend to buy up the whole region; it can be had for a song now, and when it is worked properly, it will be worth millions—millions earned honestly. No stealing or taking unfair advantage of anyone. We only raise a treasure which lies at our feet, so to speak, which is there, ready for us, or for anyone. It needs only sufficient strength for those who try to pick it up."

"That's quite another matter. Now I can understand your scheme. I will not contradict your assertion that it is lawful and generous; but it is just because it is so that it is full of pitfalls. It is quite true that the treasure which lies concealed in the Bonda Valley is immense, and it is possible that it represents millions; but this treasure cannot be discovered, for the property is not for sale."

36

"Really!"

"I will tell you why; because at this moment it belongs to Prince Bondaváry, who is one of the richest men in this country."

"I should imagine that no one knows better than I just how rich he is."

"Richest or not, he is one of our proudest aristocrats, to whom I, for one, would not venture to make a proposal for turning his old family property—the cradle, we might say, of his line—into a mine to be worked by a company."

"Oh, as far as that goes, we have seen many an ancient line glad of a little commercial dirt. The King of Italy is a crowned king; and, nevertheless, he has sold Savoy, the place from which his family took their name."

"Well, even supposing the old prince were inclined to sell the property, he could not do so while his sister, the Countess Bondaváry, is alive. Their father left the castle and the surrounding land to his daughter, who is now nearly fifty-eight, and may live another thirty years yet. She has grown up in the castle; she has, to my knowledge, never left it, not even for one day; she hates the world, and no human power would induce her to part with her beloved Bondavára to a coal company, not even if the world's last remaining stratum were to be found under the castle, without which the world would perish."

Felix laughed, then answered with an air of ineffable conceit:

"I have overcome greater difficulties than this; and for that matter, women's hearts are seldom locked with Bramah locks."

"Well, let us suppose," said Iván, good-humouredly, "that you have overcome the prejudices of the prince and his sister, and that you have actually established your monster company. Then all the technical difficulties will begin, for what is the first necessary to an undertaking of the kind?"

"A sufficient supply of money."

"By no means. A sufficient supply of workmen."

"Where there is plenty of money, men are pretty sure to gather."

"Between men and men there is a whole wonderful difference. This is a subject on which one can easily deceive oneself. Even we here have a shortage of first-class workmen."

"We could get men from France and Belgium."

"But those who would come from France and Belgium would not work for the wages we give our men. They would ask twice as much. In such a commercial undertaking, the first false step would be to raise the wages above the old system, for I am convinced that every industrial enterprise, to be safe, must expand within the limits of its own internal capacity. We should measure our strength according to the circumstances in which we find ourselves, and we should educate our own workmen; tie them to us by growing together. The trade should extend slowly, but safely, by small experiments."

"You are too cautious. I can convince you of the contrary. For instance, a steam-engine of a hundred-horse power needs the same labour to work it as a four-horse power engine, and a small business requires as many account-books as a large one, and small undertakings, even if they are in themselves lucrative, will eventually be swamped by the larger ones if they lack the means to increase their activity, for without growth all trade dies by itself."

"Nevertheless, there is less danger of sudden collapse in a small business," said Iván reflectively. "I like security."

"And what is your security? Suppose, just for the sake of argument, that one bright morning the Austrian Minister of Trade listens to a petition from the English iron masters, and that the free import of raw iron is allowed. Your neighbour over the hill will at once close his foundry, and you may go and sell your coal to the local blacksmith, eh, Iván?"

"I have gone into all that. Our raw iron can compete with the English, and there would be . . ."

"Your ideas are *rococo*; they belong to the last century. If America had worked on these lines she would not have grown to overshadow Europe."

"That is as may be. But I maintain that foreign workmen are a bad investment. Those who come to us are, for the most part, men who cannot get on in their own country; restless fellows, always wanting a change; members of secret societies, socialists and atheists; and as soon as they get in among our men they begin disseminating their vicious doctrines; and the next thing is a strike for higher wages."

"Have you ever had a strike here?"

"Never!"

"How do you prevent it?"

"That is my secret, which is impossible to tell in a few words. However, I am convinced of one thing; the first obstacle a company would have to contend with would be the price of labour, and the second difficulty would be to secure the services of a really capable overseer; one who would understand the technique of the business."

"We could easily get one from abroad."

"That might be; but I, as a private individual, could get one easily if I had sufficient money to pay him, for I could choose the best for my purpose, and could give him what I choose, as far as his merits deserved."

Felix laughed at Iván's description. "That's it exactly, just as if you were reading it from a book; and just for this reason I intend to give the complete direction of the business to a man who understands it to a T, and this man is you."

"That would be an absolute mistake. I do understand the working of my own small business, but I am quite ignorant of the ways of a great concern. Like many other small men, I should be a child in the hands of big speculators, and I should probably wreck the whole concern."

"You are too modest. On the contrary, I think you would outwit the big speculators."

"Well, suppose all went according to your wishes, or rather, according to your imagination. The great business is in full swing, delivers goods at moderate prices, and in sufficient quantity. Now comes the real objection—a topographical impediment. The Bonda coal-mine is twenty miles from the nearest railway, and twenty-five miles from the nearest river. On your way here you must have noticed the state of the roads. During four months of the year we can send no freight to any distance, and at any time the cost of transporting our coal and iron adds so much to the price that it is impossible for us to compete with either Prussia or England."

"I know all that," said Felix, stroking his beard with the coral head of his stick, "but a narrow-gauge railway would soon settle all this. We could run it from Bonda Valley to the principal distributor." He spoke as if running a narrow-gauge railway were a mere trifle.

"A railway through the Bonda Valley!" returned Iván, in a tone of suprise. "And do you really believe that with a capital of four millions you could construct a railway twenty miles long?"

"Certainly not. That would be quite a separate affair."

"And do you think you would find people ready to advance money for such an uncertain return as freight traffic alone would offer to the shareholders in such a railway?"

Felix moved his stick from his beard to his mouth, and began to suck its knob.

"And why not," he said at last, "when the State would guarantee a certain rate of interest on the advance?"

Iván opened his eyes still wider, and placed a heavy emphasis on each word.

"The State to give a guarantee of interest to this railway! You will excuse me, but that is not likely."

Felix answered, after some thought: "There are certain keys by which the bureaux of even Ministers of State can be opened." After this oracular speech, he was silent, pressing the knob of his stick against his lips, as if to restrain his words.

Iván opened the drawer of his writing-desk, and took from it a piece of black bread.

40

"Do you see this? People who eat such coarse stuff don't dance attendance upon ministers."

Felix threw back his head with a scornful laugh, and twisted his stick impatiently between his fingers.

"*Allons, n'en parlons plus*," he said. "You have plenty of time to make up your mind, for what I have once resolved to do, I do. I am quite ready to bet you that I shall secure the Bonda Valley property from under the nose of the old prince and the crazy countess, and that the largest factory in the kingdom shall be established here, and the trade carried on with the outside world. This will all come to pass, as sure as my name is Felix Kaulman."

"Well, I wish you every luck in your undertaking, but for my part, I will have none of it."

The arrival of Rauné interrupted the conversation. The Frenchman explained that he had thought over Iván's offer, and was ready to agree to his conditions, and to take up the job at once. Iván shook his hand, to signify that their agreement was settled. Then he handed him the books and the strongbox, the former with the complete list of pitmen, labourers, girls and boys engaged in the mine; the latter with the money which was paid to them for their week's work, and he asked the new overseer to appoint a room at the inn, where he was going to stay, as the place where the miners should come to be paid.

As it happened, this was a Saturday, and therefore on the very evening the overseer would begin his new duties.

The inn was opposite Iván's house. Groups of pitmen had gathered on the open ground between the two houses. Iván went to the window to see how the payments would be made by the new manager. Felix also amused himself with his lorgnette, staring at all the women.

"Ah!" he exclaimed suddenly, "that little Cinderella over there in the red skirt wouldn't be a bad model for a statuette. I should like her to teach me to say 'I love you' in Slav."

41

"Take care," laughed Iván; "her betrothed is nicknamed *man-eater*."

Just then Péter Saffran came out from the pub. He had collected Evila's wages with his own, and offered it to her. She, however, refused to take it, and the couple went off, looking happy together. The young girl's hand was upon Péter's arm, and as she passed the window they heard her singing.

"*Saperlot!* What a voice!" exclaimed the banker. "Why, she beats Thérèse. If she were in Paris—" Ivan lit a cigar, and sat down silently in the corner.

Chapter V

THE DOCTOR

The next day was Sunday. Iván took Felix and Rauné through the workmen's settlement, to show them their houses, which were clustered together like a village. This village had been built by Iván's father. The district had been formerly occupied by the very poorest, who live only on potatoes; but now the miners were well fed and well lodged. Each pitman had his own cottage and orchard.

When the three men came to the house in which Evila lived they stopped and looked into the little yard behind the fence. They felt drawn to do so, first, because the gate stood open, and secondly, because of the scene in the yard which they could watch unseen.

Péter Saffran was beating Evila. The lover held his betrothed by her long black hair, which fell over her shoulders, nearly to the ground. He had the rich tresses gathered up in his left hand, and wound round his wrist, while in his right he had a thick plaited cord with which he struck the poor girl's shoulders, neck and back. As he did so, his eyes expanded until nearly all their white was visible, his eyebrows almost touched one another, his face grew white with rage, and through his open lips his white teeth looked like those of an infuriated tiger. At each blow of the rope he growled:

"So you will have your own way, will you? You will defy me, will you?"

43

The girl did not cry, and she did not beg him to spare her. She pressed her apron to her lips, and looked at her cruel persecutor with eyes full of divine compassion.

"What!" cried Felix. "Cinderella and her lover!"

"Just so," replied Iván, indifferently.

"But you should interfere; you should not allow that pretty child to be tormented by that savage."

Iván shrugged his shoulders. "He has the right; she is his betrothed, and if I were to interfere, he would beat her even more. Besides, don't you see he has been drinking? It would be useless to reason with him."

"Well, I shall reason with him to some purpose," returned Felix. "I am not going to stand by and see that pretty creature beaten."

"You will do no good, I warn you. Miners have no respect for men in silk coats."

"We shall soon see. Do me the favour to call out 'doctor' as soon as you see me take the fellow by the arm."

As he spoke, the elegantly attired Felix rushed across the narrow passage which led to the yard, and confronted the furious savage.

"You brute!" he cried. "Let go that girl. Why do you beat her?"

Saffran answered phlegmatically, "What's that got to do with you? She is engaged to me." His breath indeed stank of brandy.

"Ah! so you are thinking of marrying, are you?" returned Felix, looking at the Hercules, whose shoulder he could hardly reach. "And how is it that you are not doing military service, my friend?"

The cord slipped from Péter's hand. "I could not pass," he said in a low voice. "I have it in black and white. I am not fit."

"Could not pass—not fit—when you can use your arms so well? Who was the upright doctor to give you such a certificate in black and white? Such muscles—" He touched with the tips of his grey gloves the startling muscles on the brawny arm.

"Doctor!" called out Iván.

When Péter heard this exclamation, and felt the pressure of Felix's fingers, he released his hold of Evila's hair. She was free.

"You just wait till to-morrow, young man," continued Felix, shaking his cane under Péter's nose, "till to-morrow, and you shall have a second examination. I shall be curious to see what secret impediment makes you unfit to serve your country. That's my business here."

Péter suddenly began to squint.

Felix burst out laughing. "Two can play that game, young man," and he, too, fell to squinting. "I shall pay you a visit to-morrow."

At this, Péter took to his heels, and making a rush for it, was soon across the yard wall and never stopped running until he reached the wood.

Iván was astonished to see the result of Felix's interference. He, who was twice as strong as this effeminate, town-bred man, would have been routed easily, while the weakling in his grey gloves had chased the savage from the field, and was the master of the situation! He felt annoyed, yet he wished to conceal his vexation. He saw Felix calmly conversing with Evila, whose saviour he had been. Iván was not going to stand there open-mouthed, admiring the hero of the moment.

"Let us go on," he said to Rauné. "Herr Kaulman can follow us if he wants to."

But Herr Kaulman was not inclined to continue his walk. A full hour later, when they were returning, they met him again. He said he had been looking everywhere for them, without luck.

Finding himself alone in the yard with the girl, he had spoken to her with sympathy.

"My poor child, what did you do to that brute, that he should use you so cruelly?"

The girl dried her eyes with the corner of her apron, and made an effort to smile. It was a piteous attempt, tragic in its effort to hide her suffering.

"Oh, sir, the whole thing was only a joke. He only pretended to strike me."

"A nice joke! Look at the welts his blows have left."

He took from his pocket a little case, which held his pocket-comb and a small looking-glass, which he held before her eyes.

Evila's face and neck reddened when she saw the disfiguring marks of her lover's affection. She spoke with some anger in her voice:

"Sir, you have been very kind, and I will tell you all about it. I have a little brother, who is a cripple. As soon as my father died, Mother married again. Her husband was a drunkard, and when he was tipsy, he would beat us and tear my hair. Once he threw my brother, who was only three years old, down from high, and he has been crippled ever since. His bones are bent and weak, and he moves on crutches; his breath, too, is affected; ha can hardly breathe from asthma, and this was stepfather's doing. But that did not soften him; on the contrary, he persecuted the poor baby, and it was ten times worse after Mother died. I had to bear many blows and glad I was to get them, if I could only save the child! At last my stepfather fell from the shaft; he was drunk, and he broke his neck. A good thing it was, too; and we have lived alone since then, and what I earn does for us both. But now I am going to marry Péter, and Péter hates my poor crippled brother. He says he must go out and beg; that an object like him on crutches could stand at the church door on Sundays, and in the market on week-days, and get pennies enough to support himself. Oh, it is shameful! And today we had another quarrel about it. He came to take me to church, where our banns were to be called for the third time. I was nearly ready, but I said I should first give my little brother some milk, and I went to get it. The boy was sitting on the doorstep waiting for it.

" 'Warm milk!' cried Péter in a rage. 'I will give him what will make him fat!' and then he struck the child, and tore at his ear, as if he would tear it from his head. The child is peculiar

—strange for a child—he never cries, although you might beat him to death. He opens his eyes and his mouth, but says nothing, and gives out no sound. I implored Péter to let the poor thing alone but this put him in a terrible rage.

"'Then let the dwarf go packing!' he yelled. 'Give him a beggar's sack, and let him beg from door to door; there never was an uglier cripple; so let him bring us home something for his keep, the scarecrow!'"

The tears ran down the girl's face as she recounted all this.

"How can he help being so ugly and crippled?" she went on. "It was not God who made him so, it was my stepfather; and so I told Péter, and that I would rather he would beat me than that he should touch the child.

"'And I will beat you,' he said, 'if you say another word,' and then he took hold of the child and kicked him. 'Get out of my sight, you little ugly monster!' he said. 'Go to the church door and beg, or I will eat you.' And he made such a horrible face that my poor little brother shrieked with fright. I could not stand seeing him tormented in this way. I took him, and would have held him safe in my arms, but he ran and hid himself in the chimney. I was very angry.

"'If you torment him like this,' I said, 'I shall break our engagement.'

"Then he seized me by my hair, and fell to beating me, as you saw. Now he will do it every day."

"No, no," returned Felix. "The fellow will have to serve his term; a muscular boy like him cannot get out of military service. If everyone did that, who the deuce would defend the country and the emperor? It cannot be winked at . . ."

"Then are you really a doctor?" said Evila, doubtfully.

"Of course I am, if I say I am."

A faint reflection of pleasure crossed the girl's face.

"Then, perhaps, you can tell me if my little brother could ever be cured?" she said eagerly.

"I can tell you. Bring me the child."

Evila went into the kitchen, and with some trouble persuaded the little cripple to come out from his shelter in the chimney-nook. This poor victim of cruelty was a miserable object. He looked as if nature had exhausted the stuff of which he was made; not one of his limbs fitted the other, and his will seemed to have no power over his body.

Evila took the sick boy on her lap, and kissing his cheek, withered like dried parchment, told him not to be afraid, for the stranger was a kind gentleman.

Felix examined the limbs of the cripple with all the attention of an experienced surgeon, and then said with a professional air:

"The injury could still be cured; it requires only time and care. There is an orthopedic institution in Vienna especially for such cases; cripples are treated there and grow up strong, healthy boys."

"Ah!" cried the girl, taking Felix's hand. "Would they take Jánoska there? But it would cost money, which I haven't got. I might get employment at this institution where cripples are made straight again. I would serve them well if they would cure my little brother."

"I don't see any reason why he shouldn't be admitted," returned Felix, seriously, "especially on my recommendation. I have great influence, and a word from me . . ."

"You will say it, won't you, and God will bless you for ever!" cried the girl, throwing herself on her knees, and covering the hands and feet of the counterfeit doctor with kisses. "I will serve them; I will work for them day and night. They need not keep a dog; I will be their dog, and guard the house for them, if they will make Jánoska straight, so that he need not beg at the church door. Is it far to Vienna?"

Felix laughed, "You don't think you could carry the boy to Vienna, do you? I will arrange the journey for you. When I have made a promise, I keep my word. I have my carriage here; I will, if you like, take you both to Vienna."

"Oh, I will sit by the coachman, with Jánoska on my lap."

"Very well, my child," returned Felix, with the air of a patron. "I am glad to help you. If you have resolved to take your brother to Vienna to have him cured, I shall give you the opportunity. Be ready to-morrow morning when you hear the sound of the post-horn. That rough fellow who beat you just now will be recruited next week, and he will have to serve his four years. Now, here is some money for you, that you may buy some warm clothes for the boy, for the nights are cold, and I travel through the day and night."

The sum of money he placed in the girl's hand took her breath away, and left her no voice to thank him. Two bank-notes—a fortune to a poor girl. The gentleman was a great nobleman; he was a prince. He was, however, already on his way before she could speak a word, and it would not do to run through the streets after him.

Evila then gave way to her joy like the child she still was. She laughed, ran about the room carrying the boy, set him on a bench, knelt down before him, kissing and hugging his ema-ciated body in her arms.

"We are going away, Jánoska, my heart's darling, in a coach to Vienna. In a coach with four horses all hung with little bells! And Jánoska will sit in my lap. Jánoska will have good medicine and good food, and his feet and his hands, his back and his chest will grow straight. He will be a big fellow, like other boys. Then we will come home, not in a coach, but on our feet. We go in a coach, and we come back on our two feet without crutches!"

Then the poor little cripple began to laugh with her. Evila ran off to the store, and bought a warm winter jacket for the child, a cap, and boots; still, she could not, even with such stupendous purchases, spend half the money. She was deter-mined to return to the gentleman the sum she had left over.

By now it was high time for church. Her friends wondered on seeing her come in alone. They asked her where Péter was? Evila said that she had not seen him that day. It went against her conscience to tell a lie before Mass, but then, when one is placed in a situation where one must lie, what can be done? A woman or a girl who has been beaten by her betrothed or her husband must deny it. God pardons the lie, and society demands it.

Péter Saffran was nowhere to be seen in church. Evila felt terribly ashamed when the priest from the pulpit read out for the third time the banns of her marriage. And there would be no marriage! Tears came into her eyes, and sorrow filled her heart at the thought that she was leaving her home, her bridegroom, her friends, all the places she knew, the things she was accustomed to, and was going out into the world alone. These thoughts preyed upon her all day, until she was obliged to go out and look for Péter Saffran. She had a suspicion of where she would find him.

In the depths of the wood, at the bottom of a narrow valley there was a cottage, or hut, where, at the time of the recruiting, the men and boys who wanted to avoid conscription would hide for a few weeks, until the recruiting officers would have passed on somewhere else. No one betrayed their hide-out. Evila went blindly through the thicket. The night was dark, the wood still darker. The growling of the hungry wolves came from the mountain. The girl trembled with fear, but went on all the same, resolved to find her betrothed, although she was sure he would beat her again. On the path she picked up a stick, and as she went along she shook the bushes, crying, 'Go away, wolf!' But her heart beat wildly when, with a rustling sound, some beast fled through the brushwood. She was getting deeper into the wood, and it was growing darker with every moment, still she kept on her way.

At last, through the darkness she saw the glimmer of a light in a window. This was the hut. Her breath came shorter as she neared the house, from where came the mixed sound of bagpipes and shouting. They were merry inside. She stole softly to the lighted window, and peeped in. They were dancing. Evila knew the girls who were there; they were not her own sort: she and her friends used to cross the street when they met them. The piper sat upon the pig-trough, and when he blew, his instrument grunted like so many pigs.

Among the men, Evila saw Péter Saffran. He was in high spirits, leaping so high that his fist struck the ceiling as he danced. He danced with a girl whose cheeks wore two spots of red paint. Péter had both his arms round her waist; he threw her up and caught her again, kissing her painted face.

Evila turned away in disgust and hastened back through the woods, unmindful of the cries of the wolves, and the howling of the wind. She no longer even had her stick; she had dropped it, and she had no means of beating the bushes.

That evening Felix Kaulman came again to Iván.

"I want to have your last word," he said. "Will you join my speculation?"

"I don't change my mind so quickly," returned Iván, coldly. "My answer is the same as it was this morning—I will not."

"Very well. I have acted as your friend in this matter, and now I tell you frankly that, as you do not choose to join me, I shall start the company alone, always leaving it open to you to rescind your decision, and to join me if you wish. I cannot say fairer than this, and I trust we shall always be good friends. You will forgive me if I try to pick up some of the diamonds which are scattered hereabouts."

"I leave you perfectly free to do what you can."

"I shall avail myself of your permission, and the day will come when I shall remind you of your words."

Iván's forehead contracted as he thought: 'What could he mean? What can he take from me? Not my coalmine; that is my possession, and the law protects me. The cut on the neighbouring mountain? So he may! What I have is enough for me.'

"Good luck to your company!" he said aloud. "And many thanks to its director."

So they parted. Early next morning Iván was roused from his sleep by the post-horn which sounded the note of Felix Kaulman's departure. Iván wished him a happy journey, then fell asleep again.

Later, as he was coming out of his house, he met Péter Saffran at his door. The miner presented a sorry figure. His features bore the marks of a night's dissipation, his eyes were bloodshot, his hair ragged, his dress in disorder.

"Now, what is it?" asked Iván, angrily.

"Sir," said the man in a hoarse voice, "that doctor who was with you yesterday—his name?"

"What do you want of him?"

"He has carried off Evila!" burst out Péter. In wild agitation he snatched the hat off his head, tore his hair, and raised both his hands to heaven.

In the first moment Iván was conscious of feeling a cruel satisfaction.

"It serves you right, you brute!" he said. "Serves you right! What business had you to ill-use the girl—your promised wife—on the very day that your banns were called for the third time?"

"Oh, sir," cried the miserable man, his teeth chattering, and beating his head with his hands, "I was drunk! I did not know what I was doing; and, after all, it was only a few blows with a light strap. What's that? With us common people it is nothing. A woman likes a man the better when he beats her. It is true; but to leave me for a gentleman . . ."

Iván shrugged his shoulders, and went on his way. The miner caught him by the tail of his coat.

"Ah, sir, what shall I do? Tell me, what shall I do?"

Iván, however, was not in the mood for giving him advice; he was angry. He pushed Péter away, saying harshly:

"Go to hell! Run to the tavern, drink brandy, then pick out another bride from the girls whose company you frequent, who will be only too glad if you are drunk every day in the year."

Péter picked up his hat, put it on, looked Iván in the face, and said in an altered voice:

"No, sir, I shall never drink brandy again; only once in my life will I taste the accursed thing—once more! You will remember what I say, and when I smell of it, when I am seen coming out of the pub, or when you hear that I have been there, then stay at home, for that day no one will know how, or when, he will die."

Iván left the man, and going back into his house, shut the door behind him. His first satisfaction at the news was passing. This miserable peasant, who had dared to be his successful rival, had lost the treasure which he himself had coveted. The fool had the pearl in his keeping, but he didn't know how to value it, and he had let it fall. That was good; but where had it fallen, this pearl so white and lovely in its purity and innocence? His soul was full of sorrow as he thought how in his eyes it had lost all its value. The girl who had seemed to him so virtuous, who kept her troth so faithfully, whose simplicity had been what he really loved—she had fallen for the first words of a cad. She refused her master, who had honestly offered her his house, his honest name. But he did not have the gifts of the other; he was not a dressed-up fellow, with town manners and seductive ways; he had not the tongue of a seducer, he had not promised her jewels and fine clothes. It was the same story with all women, and Mahomet was right when he denied them their souls, and their place either on earth or in heaven.

Chapter VI

COUNTESS THEUDELINDE

The mistress of Bondavára was fifty-eight years old at this time. Iván had not overstated her age in revealing it to Felix; nor did this indiscretion matter. Countess Theudelinde had long since given up the world. The renunciation had cost her very little; she had never been in touch with it.

Until her fourteenth year she had been growing up in the house of her father, the prince; at that time her mother, the princess, died. Theudelinde's governess was beautiful, the prince was old. The countess—only the first-born can have the princely title; the younger children are all counts and countesses—could not, for various reasons, remain under the paternal roof; she was sent away to finish her education at a convent. Before she went, however, she was betrothed to the Marquis Don Antonio di Padua, only son of the Marquis de Calomirano, then eighteen years of age. It was settled between the two fathers that when Antonio was twenty-four and Theudelinde twenty, she should be fetched from her convent, and they should be united in wedlock by the holy Church. This arrangement was carried out as far as Theudelinde's spending six blameless years in a highly respectable convent. She was then brought home, and the marriage bells were set ringing. But, horror of horrors! when the girl saw her affianced husband, she screamed and ran away. This was not the man she had promised to marry; this one had a moustache! (This was natural, as he was an officer in the Hussars.)

54

Theudelinde had never seen a man with a moustache. Six years before, when she was at home, all the distinguished guests who came to her father's house, the noblemen, the ambassadors, were all smooth-shaven and so were the men-servants, even the coachman. In the convent there was only one man, the Father-Confessor; his face was like glass. And now they proposed to marry her to a man all hair! Impossible! The saints and the prophets of old wore beards, that was true; some of them had a good deal of hair, but none wore it only on their upper lip. The only one she could remember with this adornment were the wicked servants of Pilate in the Stations of the Cross, which, to a pious mind like Theudelinde's, was conclusive. She would hear no more of the marriage; the engagement rings were returned by both sides, and the alliance was at an end.

After this, the countess avoided all worldly amusements. Nothing would induce her to go to a ball, or to the theatre. Nevertheless, she did not seem inclined to take the veil; she had strong leanings towards the wicked world, only she wanted it to be different. She desired to create an ideal out of the general chaos, and this ideal should be her husband. He should be tender, faithful, ascetic; a man with a smooth face, a pure soul, a sweet-sounding voice; a gifted, sympathetic, patient, amiable, soft, romantic, domestic, pious man; prudent, scientific, literary, distinguished, well-born, much respected, covered with orders, rich, loyal, brave, and titled. Such a *rara avis* was impossible to find. Countess Theudelinde spent the best days of her life seeking a portrait to fit the frame she had made, but she sought in vain; no husband appeared for her.

When the countess had reached thirty, there came a halt. Her ideal was as far off as ever. She was anxious to come to terms with the world, but the world would have none of her. Her heyday was past; she had no right to any pretensions. She found herself in the position of having to choose between utter renunciation, or an acceptance of the world with all its wickedness. At this critical juncture the old prince, her father, died, leaving the countess the property of Bondavára, together with the castle. Here Theudelinde retired to nurse her ideal, and mourn over her shattered idols. Here she was absolute mistress; her brother, to whom the property would revert, left her to her own devices.

The countess carried out, therefore, her theories unmolested, and her dislike of beards and moustaches had free play. The growers of these enormities were banished from her presence, and, as was only a natural consequence, as time went on, her hatred of the male sex increased. She suffered only women around her—not only in her house, but outside. The garden, the conservatories, were attended by women—unmarried women all. Matrimony was a red rag to Theudelinde, and no one dared to mention the word in her presence. Any girl who showed any inclination to wear the matron's cap was at once dismissed with contempt. Even the 'coachman' was a woman, exceptionally a widow; and for the reason that it would not have been fitting to sit upon a coachbox in woman's clothes, this female Jehu was allowed to wear a long coachman's cloak, a man's coat, and also a certain garment, at the bare mention of which an Englishwoman calls out, "Oh, how shocking!" and faints straightaway. Truly, at the time this history was written, in our good land of Hungary, this very garment played a serious part, since it had become a shibboleth and visible sign of fidelity to the governing powers, and of submission to the mediators, whether the trouser-leg was worn inside or outside the leg of a highboot. So it came to pass that Frau Liese wore this thing, the only one of the kind to be seen in the castle. Liese, also, was allowed to drink wine, and smoke, and, needless to say, she did both.

Fräulein Emerenzia, the countess's companion, was, so to speak, the exact counterpart of her noble mistress. The Countess was tall and slender; she had a white skin, her features were sharp, her nose almost transparent, her lips, scarlet in colour, were shaped like a bow; her cadaverous form bent forwards; her eyelids fell over her lack-lustre eyes, her face appeared to have two sides, which didn't belong to one another, each half having a totally different expression; even the wrinkles didn't correspond. She wore her hair as it was worn in the days of her youth, as it was worn when Carolina Pia was married, and as it is likely that it will be worn again. Her hands were fine, transparent; they were not strong enough to cut the leaves of a book with a paper-knife. Her whole being was nerveless and sensitive. At the slightest noise she would scream, be seized with a pain, or go off in hysterics. She had certain antipathies to beasts, flowers, air, food, motion, and emotion. At the sight of a cat she was ready to faint; if she saw a flesh-coloured flower her blood grew excited. Silver gave everything an unpleasant taste, so her spoons were all made of gold. If any of her women crossed their legs, she sent them out of the room. If the spoons, knives, or forks were by accident laid crosswise on the table, she would not sit down; and if she were to see velvet on any of her attendants she was thrown into a nervous attack, from the very thought that her own hand might come in chance contact with this electric and antipathetic substance.

Fortunately for her household, her nervous fears kept her quiet at night. She locked and doublelocked the door of her room, and never opened it until the morning came—no, not if the house were burning over her head.

Fräulein Emerenzia was, as we have before said, the exact counterpart of her mistress, in so far that she affected a close imitation of her ways, for in her appearance she was a direct contrast, Emerenzia being a round, short, fat woman, with a full face, the skin of which was so tightly stretched that it was almost as white as the countess's; she had a snub nose, which was addicted to the vice of snuff-taking in secret. Her dress and her manner of doing her hair were identical with the countess's only that the stiff-set clothes acquired, on her small body, a comic look. She affected to be as nerveless as the countess; her hands were as weak—they could not break a chicken-bone. Her eyes were as sensitive to light, her antipathies were as numerous, and she was as prone to fainting and hysterics as her patroness. In this direction, indeed, she went further. As soon as she observed that there was any cause for emotional display, she started trembling and screaming, and so got the start of the countess, and generally managed to sob for a minute longer; and when Theudelinde fell fainting upon one sofa, Emerenzia dropped lifeless upon another; likewise, she took longer coming round than did her mistress. At night Emerenzia slept profoundly. Her room was only separated from that of the countess by an ante-chamber, but Theudelinde might tear down all the bells in the castle without waking her companion, who maintained that her sleep was a species of nervous trance.

One man only was ever allowed entrance into the Castle of Bondavára. What do we say?—no man, no *masculinum*. The language of dogma has defined that the priest is *neutris generis*, is more and less than a member of the male sex; bodily he can be no man's father, spiritually he is father of thousands. No one will read here any attacks on the priesthood. Father Mahók was a brave, honest man; he said mass devoutly, baptized, married, buried when called upon, would get up in the middle of the night to attend the death-bed of a parishioner, and would never grumble at the sacristan for waking him out of his first sleep. The priest wrote no articles in the *Church News* and he never read one. If he wanted a newspaper, he borrowed the daily paper from the steward. When his clerk collected Peter's pence, Father Mahók sent it with an additional florin or two to the office of the Chief Priest; but this did not prevent him sitting down in the evening to play cards with the Lutheran pastor and the infidel steward. He believed in having a good cellar; he had a whole family of bees in his garden, and was a successful fruit-grower. In politics he was a loyalist, and confessed he belonged to the middle party, which in the country means no more than, 'We vote for the tobacco monopoly, but we smoke contraband tobacco because it is good, and we have it.'

From this account, anyone can see that during the course of

this narrative this excellent gentleman will offend no one. We would, in fact, have nothing to say of him were it not that he came every day, punctually at eleven o'clock, to Bondavára Castle to hear the countess's confession, and that being done, he stayed to dinner, and in both functions he earned his small honorarium honestly. There was a general air of satisfaction in his appearance, in his double chin, in his fresh colour, in his round, shining face.

On this day, Father Mahók was punctual. The countess, however, was not. Just as eleven o'clock struck, the holy man knocked at the door of her sitting-room. Only the voice of Emerenzia answered: "Come in!"

The smile of greeting on the visitor's countenance was reflected on that of the companion. It was the meeting of two full moons.

"The countess is still in her room," Emerenzia said in a whisper, as if afraid that her voice could penetrate into the third chamber.

The priest showed by a movement of his hand and an elevation of his eyebrows that the sleep of the just was not to be disturbed. The good man was not aware that it was the toilette of the just that was then in progress. These mysteries were conducted by the countess in private. No one, not even a faithful maid, was admitted until Theudelinde was fully clothed, and for this reason all her garments were made to do up in front.

The priest made use of this unexpected delay to search in the pocket of his coat, and to draw from it a mysterious something, which, after first casting a look round the room, to make sure no one was spying on him, he pressed into the fat hand of the countess's companion, who hastily concealed this surreptitious something in the depths of her pocket, expressing her gratitude by a friendly nod, which the priest returned by a courteous move-ment which expressed, 'No thanks are necessary for so small a service.' Then Emerenzia, turning away, half shyly drew the something carefully out of her pocket, and peering into it, held it close to her nose, drinking in the scent of the something, turning her eyes up to heaven, and again to the priest, who, on his part, expressed by the motion of the thumb and forefinger of his left hand, 'Excellent—special brand!' Then, no longer able to restrain her feelings, the companion took from the mysterious packet between the thumb and forefinger of her right hand something which she placed in both nostrils, and sniffed up in silent ecstasy. It was the priest's pleasure to fill Emerenzia's snuff-box with the very best mixture. This was the platonic bond which existed between them—the mutual desire of two noses for one ideal.

Yellow snuff is not an unattainable ideal. In the ordinary way of business a quarter of a pound can be procured for a few pennies; but common snuff was as different from the priest's mixture as cherry brandy is from Chartreuse. This is easily understood by those who take snuff. How is it that a clergyman always has the best tobacco? How does he prepare it? Does he get it prepared? These are wide questions that a man of liberal mind dare not broach. Even if he knew, it would not be advisable to make use of his knowledge. One thing is certain, only the best tobacco is used by the Church. A bishop, who died not long since, left behind him a hundredweight of the most heavenly stuff, two ounces of which fetched a ducat.

The quiet *tête-à-tête* between the two snuff-takers was disturbed by the sound of a bell; then a metal slide in the door of the countess's room opened, and a tray with an empty teacup was put through. This was a sign that the countess had breakfasted.

Every door in the castle had sliding panels, some large, others small. The slides were made of copper, the doors of strong wood, with brass locks and fasteners. The door of the countess's bedroom was made of solid iron, covered on the inside with a tapestry curtain. Since no man was allowed in the house, it was necessary to have a system of defence against any possible attack. This system included some cleverly-constructed machinery, by means of which the countess, by pressing her foot,

60

could raise the flooring, and precipitate any bold invader of the sacred precincts of her bedroom into a cellar without light or exit. From the alcove of her bed, an electric telegraph was connected to the firetower, so that by raising her finger the alarm bell could be set ringing, and in case of danger the masculine inhabitants of the adjacent farmhouses and hunting lodges could be summoned without a moment's delay. In Emerenzia's room there was a similar communication with this electric apparatus. The different signs by which the countess expressed her wishes were affixed to the door. The cup signified that the chambermaid was required, a book would have meant that the companion was needed.

Emerenzia, therefore, sent the girl to her mistress. When her work was finished the bell rang again, the book appeared, and the companion went in to the countess. After a short time she returned, and opened the door for the priest, while she whispered to him softly:

"She has seen the spirits again; she has much to tell you."

We will follow the priest into his penitent's room; but no one need be afraid that he or she are about to listen to the lady's confession. When the priest had closed the door behind him, he came to the countess, who sat in a large armchair, looking pale and exhausted. She beckoned to the priest to sit in an armchair opposite.

"Have you seen them again?" he asked.

"I have," said the countess, in an awed whisper. "It all happened in the usual way. As soon as the clock struck midnight, there rose from below, perhaps out of a vault, a frightening chorus of voices intoning the *De Profundis*. It was a ghostlike, terrible sound. I could distinguish the solo voice of the celebrant, the antiphone, the chorus; and between them loud laughter, diabolical words, the shrieks of women, and the clatter of glasses. I heard satirical songs accompanied by wild howls; then, again, the soft, pious hymn which was again succeeded by the wild disorder. I pinched my arm to see, did I dream. Here:

61

you can see the mark. I was not dreaming. I got up; I wished to convince myself that I was awake. I took my pencil and notepaper, and when a distinct tune reached my ear I wrote it down. Here is the paper. You understand music."

The priest threw a hasty glance over the ghostly melody, and recognized a well-known Hungarian folksong, 'Dark-eyed maiden let me taste your lips.' Unquestionably, an unclean song to issue from the family vaults at midnight!

"And, gracious countess, have you never heard the peasants singing this in the fields?"

The countess drew herself up with dignity. "Do I frequent the places where peasants sing?" she answered; and then continued her story. "These notes are sufficient proof that I was awake; my nerves were too excited to allow me to sleep again. Moreover, I was drawn by an invincible desire to go down to the place from whence the sound came. I dressed myself. I am certain that I took out my grass-green skirt of Gros de Naples, with a cashmere flounce. I did not call any of my servants; every one in the house was asleep. An extraordinary courage woke in me. Quite alone, I descended the steps which lead to the family vault. When I reached the door both sides opened by themselves; I entered, and found myself in the presence of my departed ancestors. The monuments were all removed, the niches empty; their occupiers sat round the long table which stands in the vault, in the same dresses in which they are painted in the portraits in the hall, and by which their calling in life is shown. My great-uncle, the archbishop, in full canonicals, was celebrating Mass before the requiem altar; my grandfather, the Chancellor, had wide parchment documents before him, upon which he was fixing the State Seal. My great-uncle, the field-marshal, in armour, and with the marshal's baton in his hand, gave orders. My ancestress Katherine, who was a court lady, and of remarkable beauty, rolled her eyes about, and in her whole face no feature moved but those glittering eyes; and my aunt Clementina, the abbess of the Ursuline Convent, sang psalms with my uncle, in which the others from time to time joined."

"But the laughter, the tumult, the satirical songs?" asked the priest.

"I am coming to that. At the other end of the table sat some of my more distant relatives—my young cousin Clarissa, who danced herself to death; and a cousin, who was a celebrated flute player; and my great-uncle Ottó, who was devoted to French hazard, and now rattled dice into a copper goblet, and cursed his luck when he made a bad throw; also another cousin, who died on the night of her marriage, and still wore a faded wedding wreath; finally, my uncle Ladislaus, who was banished from the family circle early in the century, and whose frame hangs in the picture-gallery empty, his portrait being removed."

"How did you know him, then?" By this question the priest hoped to check the flow of the countess's visions.

Theudelinde, however, answered that her uncle Ladislaus, being a rebel and a heretic, had not alone been declared a traitor, but had incurred the ban of excommunication. He was taken prisoner and beheaded. "And therefore," she added, with an air of conviction, "it was easy to recognize him by his death's-head. Likewise, during his lifetime he ignored the king's expressed command, and was the first to introduce tobacco-smoking into the country, and on this account, at his execution, he received the punishment awarded to the smoker, of having a pipe-handle run through his nose. Last night as he sat at the table he held between the teeth of his monstrous death's-head a large meerschaum pipe, and the whole vault smelt of tobacco-smoke in the most dreadful way."

This remark convinced the priest that the countess had been dreaming.

"Between both my cousins," she went on, "the nun and the bride, there was an empty chair. There I felt obliged to seat myself. The bride wished to hear of the fashions; she praised the stuff of my Gros de Naples dress, taking it between her fingers, which, when they touched mine, were cold as death itself. The upper end of the table was covered with green cloth, the lower end with a yellow silk table-cloth, embroidered with many-coloured flowers. At this end every one laughed, talked, sang noisy songs; while at the top the psalms were intoned, and the antiphone was sung. Both sounded horrible in my ears. The dishes contained cooked partridges and roast pheasants, with the feathers sticking in their heads; sparkling wine filled the cups. I was pressed to eat and drink, but neither the food nor the liquor had any taste. Once the bride, my cousin, as is the custom with very young girls, offered me the pheasant's wishbone saying jokingly, 'Break this bone with me, and we shall see which of us two gets a husband first.' I seized hold of my end of the bone; I tugged and tugged, and at last broke it. The largest half remained in my hand. The bride laughed. 'Theudelinde shall be the first married!' she cried. I blushed; it seemed to me terrible that the spirits of my dead ancestors should be so frivolous."

The worthy priest said nothing. Nevertheless, he was inclined to agree with his penitent. He could not imagine why blessed souls, or even condemned ones, should occupy themselves breaking pheasant-bones with an old maid, of all people.

"What gave me most offence," continued Theudelinde, "was the outrageous behaviour of my cousin Ladislaus. One minute he shrieked, then laughed loudly, sang horrid songs. Then he broke out into fearful curses, insulted the saints, the pope, the Sacraments, made jokes that brought a blush to the faces of the ladies, and blew all his tobacco-smoke over me. I shook the skirt of my green silk to prevent the horrid smell sticking to it, but I felt this precaution was of little use. My cousin Ladislaus then began to tease me, and said I had concealed the prophetic bone in the pocket of my green dress. My face glowed with shame, for it was true. I denied it, however. Whereupon he began to swear in his heathenish way, and to thump with his fists on the table until the vault resounded with his blows. My

64

other cousins put their hands over his mouth. Then he spoke through his empty eye-sockets. It was terrible! He cursed all the saints in the calendar, and the Emperor. My great-uncle, the archbishop, stretched out his hands and damned him; my great-grandfather, the Chancellor, sealed the sentence; and my great-uncle, the field-marshal, drew his sword and cut off my cousin's death's-head. The head rolled over, and fell at my feet, still holding the pipe between its teeth, and blew its filthy breath over me. Then I arose and fled."

The priest had now made up his mind that the whole story was nothing but the dream of an hysterical woman. It was strange, however, that the countess should have the same vision so often, and that it should always begin in the same manner.

As she now concluded her recital with the words, "As I took off my silk dress it smelt horribly of tobacco-smoke," a brilliant idea came to Father Mahók.

"Will you excuse my asking you where your green dress is?" he asked gravely.

The countess betrayed some embarrassment.

"I do not know. My wardrobe is in the care of Fräulein Emerenzia . . ."

"Allow me to ask you the question, did you not take the dress off in this apartment?"

"I no longer remember. Emerenzia has been here since; she may know."

"Will you grant me the favour, countess, to send for Fräulein Emerenzia?"

"Certainly. She will be here in a minute."

The countess pressed her finger twice on the electric apparatus, and the companion entered.

"Fräulein," said the countess, "you remember my green Gros de Naples silk, bordered with a trimming of fur?"

"Yes; it is a pelisse of peculiar cut, with hanging sleeves, and fastened by a silk band and buckle."

"That is the dress," returned the countess. "Where is it?"

65

"In the wardrobe. I hung it there myself, first putting camphor in the sleeves, that the moths might not get at the fur."

"When did you do this?"

"Last summer."

The priest laughed slyly to himself. Now, thought he, the countess must be convinced that she dreamt the whole scene she has so accurately described.

"Have I not worn it since last summer?" questioned Theudelinde.

"Not once. The open-hanging sleeves are only for the hottest weather."

"Impossible!"

"But, Countess," put in the priest, "it is easy to convince yourself of what ma'mselle says. You have only to look into the wardrobe. Who keeps the key?"

"Ma'mselle Emerenzia."

"Do you command me to open the press?" asked the companion, with a discomfited look.

"I do," answered the countess, nodding to the priest to follow her into the next room.

Emerenzia, her face puckered into an expression of annoyance, drew her bunch of keys from her pocket, and placed one in the lock of an antique and highly ornamented press, of which she threw the doors open. At least fifty silk dresses hung there, side by side.

The countess never allowed any of her clothes to get into strange hands; no man's eye should ever rest upon what she had worn. Through this museum of old clothes Emerenzia's fingers went with unerring certainty, and drew forth the oft-mentioned green silk dress with the fur trimming.

"Here it is," she said shortly.

The priest felt triumphant, but the countess, whose nerves were more impressionable than those of ordinary mortals, grew suddenly pale, and began to shake all over.

"Take that dress down," she said in a whisper. And Emerenzia, with a jerk, tore it from its peg. What, in Heaven's name, had come over the priest and her mistress?

The countess took it from her hand, and held it, while she turned her head the other way, across his nose.

"Do you smell it?" she said. "Is it tobacco-smoke?"

Father Mahók was astonished. This fine silk dress, straight from out of a lady's wardrobe, smelt as strongly of the commonest tobacco as the coat of a peasant who had passed his night in an alehouse. Before he could answer Theudelinde's question, she was ready with another. From the pocket of the green Gros de Naples she now drew forth a broken pheasant bone.

"And this?" she asked. But here her strength was exhausted. Without waiting for a reply, she fell fainting on the sofa.

Emerenzia, sobbing loudly, fell helplessly into an armchair. The clergyman was so upset by the whole thing that, in his embarrassment, he opened the doors of three more wardrobes, before finding the door which communicated with the sitting-room. Then he summoned the servants to attend to their mistress. Some supernatural witchcraft was indeed at work.

Chapter VII

THE COUNTESS'S ALBUM

The worthy Father Mahók was of the opinion that the mystery of the countess's dress smelling so strongly of tobacco-smoke could not be accounted for by any law of Nature, and judged, therefore, by the light of his priestly office, as well as from his worldly experience, that these diabolical visions were matters worthy of deep consideration on his part. They occupied his mind during dinner, which he partook of in company with the countess's companion, but of the subject of his thoughts he spoke no word to her. They were alone at the table. The countess remained in her room, as was her habit when she suffered from what was called 'cramps,' and her only refreshment was a little soup. After dinner she sent for the priest again.

He found her lying on the sofa, pale and exhausted; her first words referred to the subject which filled both their minds.

"Are you now convinced," she said, "that what I told you was, indeed, not a dream?"

"Doubtless there has been some strange work going on."

"Is it the work of good or bad spirits?" asked the countess, raising her eyes.

"That can only be ascertained by a trial."

"What sort of trial, holy Father?"

"An attempt to exorcise them. If these spirits, who every night leave their graves, are good, they must, by the strength of the exorcism, return to their resting-places, and remain there till summoned by the angel's trumpet to arise on the last day."

"And in case they don't return?" inquired the countess, anxiously.

"Then they are bad spirits."

"That is to say, damned. By what signs can you know that?"

For a minute there was a struggle in the priest's mind; then he answered boldly:

"This night I shall keep watch in the castle."

"And if you hear the unearthly noises?"

"Then I shall descend into the vault, and scatter the ghosts with holy water."

The countess's face glowed with fervour as she exlaimed:

"Holy Father, I shall accompany you."

"No, countess; no one shall accompany me but my sacristan."

"The sacristan! A man! He shall not set foot inside this house!" cried the countess, excitedly.

The priest explained to her in a soothing voice that his sacristan was almost as much a part of the Church as himself; moreover, that he was absolutely necessary on this occasion for the performance of the exorcism; in fact, without him the ceremony could not take place, seeing that the sacred vessel containing the holy water, the crucibulum and lanterns, should be carried before him to give all due effect to the religious rites.

Under these circumstances, countess Theudelinde gave her consent, on the condition that the obnoxious male intruder should not enter the castle itself. Further, the priest promised to hold his vigil in the greenhouse after the castle gates were locked.

According to these arrangements, when it grew dark, Father Mahók arrived, bringing with him his sacristan, a man of about forty, with a closely shaved moustache, and a very copper-coloured face. The priest left him in the greenhouse, and pro-ceeded by himself to the dining-room, where the countess was expecting him for supper. No one touched a morsel. The priest had no appetite, neither had the countess, nor her companion. The air was too full of the coming event to allow for such a gross thing as eating.

After supper the countess withdrew to her room, and Father Mahók went to the greenhouse, where the sacristan had made himself comfortable with wine and meat, and had built up the fires in the stove. The servants had been kept in ignorance of what was going on; they had never heard the midnight Mass, nor the wild shrieks and infamous songs of the inhabitants of the vault, and the countess would not allow the ears of her innocent handmaidens to be polluted with such horrors. Therefore, everyone in the castle slept. The priest watched alone.

At first, Father Mahók tried to pass the long hours of the night in reading his prayers, but as his habitual hour for sleep drew near, he had to fight a hard battle against his closing eyelids. He was afraid that if he slumbered his imagination would reproduce the countess's dream, to which, be it said, he did not give credence; at the same time, he did not completely doubt her. Generally, he found that his breviary provoked sleep, and now he thought it better to close the book, and try what conversation with the sacristan would do to help him keep awake.

The clerk's discourse naturally soon turned on ghostly appearances; he told stories of a monk without a head, of spirits that appeared on a certain night of the year, of hobgoblins and witches, all of which he had either seen with his own eyes, or had heard of from persons whose veracity was unimpeachable.

"Folly, lies!" said the priest; but he could not help the creeping sensation which was coming over him. If he could at least smoke, perhaps it would have strengthened his nerves; but smoking was forbidden in the castle. The countess would have smelt it, as the giant in the old fairy-tale smelt human flesh.

When the sacristan found that all his wonderful tales of ghosts and hobgoblins were discounted as lies, he decided it was no use tiring himself talking, and as soon as he stopped, he began to fall asleep. Seated upon a stool, his head leaning against the wall, his mouth open, he slept profoundly, to the envy, if not the admiration, of the good priest, who would have followed his example willingly. Soon some very unmusical sounds made themselves heard. The sacristan snored in all manner of keys, in all variations of nasal discord, which so jarred on the priest's nerves that he several times shook the sleeper to wake him up, with the sole result that he fell asleep again in no time.

At last the clock on the castle tower chimed twelve. Father Mahók struck a good blow on the sacristan's shoulder.

"Get up!" he said. "I did not bring you here to sleep."

The clerk rubbed his eyes, already drunk with sleep. The priest took his snuff-box, to brighten himself up with a pinch of snuff, when suddenly both men were roused from any torpor of sleep. Just as the last beat of the clock had finished striking, the unearthly Mass began to be intoned in the vault below. Through the profound silence of the night, the voice of the priest was heard singing the Latin Mass, with the responses of the choir, accompanied by some instrument that sounded like an organ, but which had a shriller tone, and seemed to be its parody.

A ghostly shiver crept over the whole body of Father Mahók.

"Do you hear it?" he asked the sacristan, in a whisper.

"Hear it? Who could help hearing it? Mass is being said somewhere."

"Here, under us, in the vault."

"Who can it be?"

"The devil! All good spirits praise the Lord," stammered the worthy priest, making the sign of the cross three times.

"But it seems that the evil spirits praise the Lord as well as the good ones," rejoined the clerk.

This assertion was soon contradicted, however. The next psalm was rent by a diabolical chorus and the air resounded with:

71

'Come, dearest, come to me,
Come, I am at home;
Two gipsies play for me,
And here I dance alone.'

Shrieks of laughter followed, in which the shrill cackling of
women mingled with the hoarse laughter of men, and in the
wildest discord, as if hell itself was let loose.

The poor priest, who had trembled at the pious psalms,
nearly collapsed at this pandemonium. He broke out in a cold
sweat; he realized that the countess was right, and that this
was, in truth, the work of the Evil One.

"Michael," he said, his teeth chattering with fear, "have you
heard . . ."

"I must be stone deaf if I didn't—such an infernal din!"
replied the other. "All the spirits of hell are holding a sabbath . . ."

Just then, a loud bell tinkled.

The tumult subsided, and the voice of the celebrant was once
more heard intoning Mass.

"What shall we do?" asked Father Mahók.

"What shall we do? Go down into the vault, and exorcise
these evil spirits."

"What?" cried the priest. "Alone!"

"Alone!" repeated Michael, with religious fervour. "Are we
alone when we come in the name of the Lord of hosts?
Besides, there are two of us. If I were a priest, and if I were
invested with the stole, I should go into the vault, carrying the
holy water, and with the words, *Apage Satanas*, I would drive
before me all the legions of hell itself."

The worthy priest felt ashamed that his ignorant sacristan
should possess the greater faith, and show more courage in this
combat with the powers of darkness, than himself; still, fear
dominated over his shame.

"I would willingly face these demons," he said, in a somewhat

72

hesitating manner, "were it not that the gout has suddenly seized my right foot. I am not able to walk."

"But consider what a scandal it will be if we, who have heard the spirits, have not pluck enough to send them packing."

"But my foot, Michael; I cannot move my foot."

"Well, then, I will carry you on my back. You can hold the holy water, and I will take the lantern."

There was no way out of this friendly offer. The priest commended his soul to God, and taking heart, resolved to challenge the demons below, armed with nothing but the holy insignia of his office.

"You will be careful, Michael; you will not let me fall?" he said in a somewhat quavering voice.

"Don't be afraid, Father," returned the sacristan, as he stooped and raised the priest on his shoulders. "Now, forward!" he cried, taking the lantern in his hands, while Father Mahók carried the vessels necessary for the exorcism.

A cold blast of air saluted them as they issued from the greenhouse and crossed the large hall of the castle, which the glimmering light from the small lantern illumined only faintly. Half of it remained in darkness; but on the side of the wall where the portraits of the armed knights were hung, an occasional gleam showed Father Mahók the faces of the countess's warlike ancestors, who had done good service against the Turks in their day. They looked at him, he thought, somewhat contemptuously, and seemed to say, 'What sort of man is this, who goes to battle pick-a-back?'

Michael stopped in front of a strong iron door in the centre of the hall. This was the entrance to the subterranean vaults and cellars under the castle. And now the priest suddenly remembered that he had left the key of this gate in the greenhouse. There was nothing for it but to retrace their steps. Just as they reached the threshold, however, Michael suggested that something very hard was pressing against his side. Could it be the key which was, after all, in his reverence's pocket? This suggestion proved correct, and once more he had to run the gauntlet of the old crusaders and their contemptuous superiority.

The key creaked as it turned in the lock, and a heavy damp smell struck them as they passed through the iron gate.

"Leave the door open," said the priest, with an eye to securing a safe retreat.

And now they began to descend the steps, Father Mahók remarking that his horse was not too sure-footed. He tottered in going down the steps so much that the priest, in his fright, caught him with his left hand tightly by the collar, while he pressed the other more closely round his throat, a proceeding which Michael resented, calling out in a strangled voice:

"Reverend sir, don't squeeze me so; I am suffocating!"

"What was that?"

A black object whizzed past them, circling round their heads. A bat, the well-known attendant upon ghosts!

"We shall be there in a few moments," said the clerk, to encourage his rider, whose teeth chattered audibly.

While they were descending the steps the noise in the vault had been less audible, but now as they came into the passages which ran underneath the hall, it broke out again in the most horrible discord. The passage was long, and there were two wings; one led to the cellars proper, the other to the vaults. Opposite to the steps there was a passage crossing, at its end, by ascending some seven or eight steps, a passage through a lattice door led into the open. This lattice served also as the means of ventilating the passages, and on this particular night there was such a strong current of air that the light in the lantern was in danger of being blown out any minute. It would have been well if that were all. The sacristan hadn't taken three steps in the direction of the vault before a terrible sight was revealed to both men.

At the end of the passage a blue flame was burning, before the flame there stood, or sat, or jumped, a dwarfish figure all in white. It was not three feet in height, and, nevertheless, its head was of monstrous size. As the sacristan, with the priest, drew near this horrid apparition, the blue flame suddenly flared up, throwing a bright, whitish light all over the passage, and by this light the terrified spectators beheld the dwarf stretch itself out, and grow taller and taller—six, eight, twelve feet—and still it grew and grew. Its shadow danced in the light of the blue flame on the marble floor of the passage like a black serpent. Then the fearful apparition raised its head, and the vaulted roof rung out with its howls and shrieks.

Michael's courage suddenly disappeared. He turned, and, burdened as he was with the weight of the priest on his back, he ran back as fast as he could. In the middle of the passage, however, he took a false step and fell with Father Mahók, flat upon his face. In the fall he broke the lantern, the light went out, and left them in the dark. Groping along with outstretched hands, they missed the steps which led up to the iron gate, but after some time found themselves in the crossing passage, and saw the soft light of the moon shining through the lattice window. They made at once for the door. At first there was some difficulty in opening it, but Michael managed to force it, and, to their great joy, they were once more in the open air. Over the stubble, through the thorn bushes they flew, never pausing to look back. Singularly enough, the gout in the priest's foot in no way affected his speed. He ran quite as fast as Michael, and in less than a quarter of an hour was in his bed, as was the sacristan, whose fright produced an attack of fever, which kept him imprisoned there for three days.

The next morning Father Mahók, with many inward qualms, went up to the castle. His was an honest, simple mind; he preferred rather to believe in the wiles of the devil than in the wickedness of human nature; he credited what he had seen with his own eyes, and never sought to penetrate the dark veil which shrouds many supernatural mysteries. He believed firmly that he had to do with damned spirits, who at their midnight orgies cracked pheasant bones to see who should be married first.

He found the countess in a good humour; she was friendly, lively, and received her visitor with a smiling face. This change did surprise Father Mahók. He was accustomed by this time to the caprices of countess Theudelinde. One day she was out of humour, the next all serenity.

The priest went straight to the kernel he had to crack.

"I watched last night," he said.

"Oh, Father, thanks, ten thousand thanks! Your mere presence has been sufficient to banish the evil spirits which have haunted the castle for so long. Last night all was peace; not a sound did I hear."

"Not a sound!" cried the priest, rising from his chair in his astonishment at such a statement. "Countess, is it possible that you did not hear the noise?"

"Profound repose, Arcadian peace reigned in the house, both upstairs and below."

"But I was there, and awake. I did not dream it. And, moreover, I can show you the bruises and abrasions on my elbow; they witness to the fall we had, to say nothing of Michael, the sacristan, who is this moment in a high fever in consequence. No, never did any one hear so demoniacal, so terrible a noise as echoed through the vault last night. I was there myself, Countess, in my own person. I was ready to encounter the wicked spirits; I would have met them armed with all the terrors of Mother Church, but the courage of my weak-kneed sacristan failed. I have now come to tell you that my knowledge is at an end. This castle is bewitched, and, Countess, my advice to you is to leave it without delay, and to take up your residence in a city, where your family ghosts cannot follow you."

The countess placed the middle finger of her left hand upon her breast, and spoke with haughty dignity:

"I leave this castle because the spirits of my ancestors dwell here! Your advice, Reverend Father, shows how little you know me. To my mind, it is a powerful reason for remaining. Here the spirits of my forefathers, the ghosts of my ancestors, surround

76

me. They know me, they claim me as theirs; they honour me with their visits, with their invitations, and you counsel me to abandon them. Never! Bondavára is dearer to me than ever; the presence of my ancestors has doubled its value a hundredfold."

It was on the tip of Father Mahók's tongue to answer: Well, then, remain here by all means, but for my part, I tender my resignation; provide yourself with another confessor. He restrained himself, however, and said quietly:

"Will you tell me, Countess, how it happens that if you have these close relations with your ancestors' spirits, you heard nothing of the witch's sabbath they kept last night?"

At this bold question the countess's pale cheeks were suddenly enflamed by two carnation spots; her eyes fell before the sharp look of her father confessor, and striking her breast with her hand, she sank slowly to her knees, whispering in great agitation:

"Father, I have sinned. There is something which I have never confessed to you, and which lies heavy on my conscience."

"What is it?"

"Oh, I fear to tell you!"

"Daughter, fear nothing," said the priest, soothingly. "God is merciful to human weakness."

"I believe that; but I am more afraid that you will laugh at me."

"Ah!" and the priest leaned in his chair at this strange speech, smiling to himself.

The countess rose from her kneeling position and went to her writing-table; she opened a secret drawer, and took an album from it. It was a splendid book with an ivory cover, chasings of gilt enamel, and clasp of the same.

"Will you look through this album, Father?"

The priest opened the clasp, took off the cover, and saw a collection of cabinet photographs, such as are generally to be found on drawing-room tables. There were portraits of eminent

77

statesmen, poets, actors, with whose likenesses all the world is familiar. Two points were remarkable in this gallery—one, that no one was included who had any scandal connected with his name; secondly, it was only clean-shaved men who had a place in the volume. Father Mahók recognized many whom he knew either by sight or personally—Liszt, Reményi, the actors Lendvay, Szerdahelyi, and others, together with many foreign celebrities, who wore neither beard nor moustache. Another peculiarity struck the priest. Several of the leaves, instead of portraits, had pieces of black crape inserted into the frames. This circumstance made him reflect.

"It is a very interesting volume," he said, closing the book, "but what has it to do with the present circumstances?"

"I confess to you," said the countess, in a low voice, "that this book is a memorial of my folly and weakness. A picture-dealer in Vienna has for many years had an order from me; he sends me every photograph that comes out of clean-shaved men, and I seek amongst them for my ideal. I have been seeking for many years. Sometimes I imagine I have it; some one of the portraits takes my fancy. I call the man whom it represents my betrothed. I place the photograph before me; I dream for hours looking at it; I almost fancy that it speaks to me. We say to one another all manner of things—sweet nothings, but they fill my mind with a sort of ecstasy. It is silly, I know, and something tells me that it is worse than silly, that it is sinful. I have been for a long time wondering whether I should confess this as a sin, or keep silence about such foolish nonsense. What is your opinion, Father?"

Father Mahók, in truth, did not know what to say. It was true in the Scripture some words were said about sinning with the eyes, but photographs were not named. He answered vaguely:

"Anything else, my daughter?"

"After I had for some time been silly over one of the portraits, I have seen in a dream the man it represented. He appeared to me as a beautiful apparition, we walked together through fields and meadows, arm-in-arm; a sort of heavenly halo surrounded us, flowers sprung up under our feet. We were young, and we loved one another." The poor lady wept bitterly as she related her dream, and she sobbed as she said: "Is not this a sin, Father?"

Father Mahók had no hesitation in answering. He had found the name of the sin—it was witchcraft; but the form the penance should take puzzled him. The countess, however, helped him to a decision.

"Ah," she said sadly, "I thought it was some demoniac possession; and for these visions, sweet as they were, I must now do penance. Is it not so, Father? Will it extenuate my sin if I burn in the fire the portrait of the man who appeared to me in my dream, and fill the empty space in my book with black crape?"

This remark explained the many frames filled with crape. The priest thought that the penance was well chosen. Nothing could be better then a burnt offering.

Theudelinde continued: "During these visions, I lie in a profound slumber. My soul is no longer on the earth; I am in the paradise of lovers. No earthly feeling chains me here below; I am a glorified spirit, consequently no sound reaches me. I am as deaf to this world as if I were already dead."

"Therefore the ghostly tumult never reached you last night; you were wandering in your dream world."

"I confess it was so," whispered the countess, covering her face with her hands.

Now, here is a nice state of things! thought the priest. The dead ancestors play all manner of pranks in the family vault, while their descendant projects herself out of her human body to make love in some other region. They are, indeed, an extraordinary race. A poor man daren't even think of such extravagances, and how can I, a poor parish priest, deal with such queer goings on? I only know how to settle with the everyday penitent, who commits the usual sins.

79

This complication, in truth, of the ghosts below and the be-witched countess above, was too much for a man of his calibre to deal with. It required a superior genius to exorcise the spirits and to calm the hysterical mind of Theudelinde. In the difficulty it appeared to him better to temporize.

"My daughter, the penance you have imposed upon yourself is well thought of. Have you already committed to the flames the portrait of the last demoniacal appearance?"

"No," answered the countess, with all the hesitation a young girl would have in speaking of her lover's picture.

"And why not?" questioned the priest, almost sternly. He was glad to find some tangible fault.

"It would be wrong, I think, to throw this particular portrait on the fire."

"And why would it be wrong?"

Before she replied, the countess opened a concealed pocket in the album, and drew forth what it contained.

"Ah!" cried the priest as he took the photograph, which he at once recognized as the Abbé Samuel, the head of an influential order with many different branches.

"The photographer in Vienna had my orders to send me the photograph of every clean-shaven celebrity. He, therefore, has made the mistake of sending me the portrait of this eminent priest. The fault is mine, not his."

"And in your dreams, have you wandered arm-in-arm with the original of this?" asked Father Mahók, still holding the photograph in his hand.

"I am guilty!" stammered the countess, laying her hands upon her breast.

"Then," said the priest, "Heaven inspired you not to throw this portrait, like the others, on the fire, for in this man you will find a physician able to cure your sick soul. It is really providential that this portrait should be in your hands, for the others were idle, foolish dreams. Here you have found your ideal, under whose guidance you may hope to find health and salvation. He will lead you, not in a dream, but in reality, to the blessed regions of peace and true piety, where alone, my daughter, real happiness is to be found. This man possesses strength of mind and elevation of character sufficient to exorcise all the spirits which haunt your castle, and to banish from your mind those temptations which spring from the same source as the more visible demons which we call ghosts."

Chapter VIII

THE EXORCIST

Acting upon the advice of Father Mahók, the countess resolved to lay all her troubles before a new physician for her soul. That very day the priest wrote to Abbé Samuel, who was then in Pest, inviting him to come to Bondavára Castle.

The abbé was a man of high calling; one of those priests who are more or less independent in their ideas. He was on friendly terms with many great personages, and the initiated knew that articles which appeared with the signature 'S,' in the opposition's paper, were by his pen. In society he was agreeable and polished, and his presence never hindered rational enjoyment. He shone in intellectual circles; his lectures, which were prepared with great care, were attended by the *élite* of society, and, as a natural consequence, the Ultramontane papers always came out strongly against him. Once, even, the police had paid him a domiciliary visit, although they themselves did not know why he had given rise to suspicion. All these circumstances had heightened his reputation, which had lately been increased even further by the appearance of his picture in a first-rate illustrated journal. This won the general public for him. His air was stately, with his high, broad forehead, manly, expressive features, well-marked eyebrows, and frank, fearless look, with nothing sinister or cunning in it. For the rest, there was little of the priest about him; his well-knit, robust, muscular form was more that of a gladiator. He was well known as the independent priest through the whole of the country, who dared to tell the government his true opinions.

For this reason, the worthy Father Mahók had the greatest respect for him. He, as an insignificant parish priest, could do little for his country. It was true that, many years ago, he had fought more than twenty battles in the Honvéd Battalion; he had preached to his men that they should love their country, and for this he had been sentenced to death, a sentence which had been commuted to ten years' imprisonment; he had passed five of those years in chains, and his feet still bore the marks of the wounds made by the heavy irons. But what were these trifles, which Father Mahók valued little, compared to the bold deeds of the Abbé Samuel, who dared to write independent articles in the papers, and to sign them with his initial. To have fought with Haynau against the Russians under heavy fire, to have been in the galleys, that was a mere joke. To have the dreaded police on your tracks, that was serious. Father Mahók thought most highly of the abbé's capabilities, measuring them by the loss of his own physical and mental energy—for after fifteen years, five of which had been spent in iron chains, a man is not what he was.

After some days the invited guest arrived. The priest related, circumstantially, all that was relevant to the countess, except of course, such matters as were under the sacred seal of confession. He told him about the ghosts, and of his own experiences.

Abbé Samuel received the narration with fits of laughter.

"You may laugh here as much as you like, but I beg of you not to do so before the countess; she clings to her ghosts," remarked the priest, with the air of one who knew what he was saying.

The abbé then asked for information concerning the arrangement of the rooms in the castle, how they were situated in regard to one another. He made the priest describe minutely every particular of that to which he had himself been witness, also how he and his sacristan had made good their escape through the lattice door.

The equipage of the countess came at the usual hour to fetch the two guests to the castle, at some little distance from the village.

It was only natural, all things taken into account, that the countess should lose all control of her nerves on her first introduction to the abbé, and that she should give way to several hysterical symptoms, which could only be calmed by the abbé laying his hand in paternal benediction upon her forehead. Fräulein Emerenzia's nerves, in accordance with the sympathy which existed between her and her mistress, became at once similarly affected, and would have required a similar imposition of hands; but neither of the priests troubled themselves about her, and when the countess recovered from her attack, the companion did likewise.

During dinner, which was served with great elegance, the abbé discoursed upon every possible subject, and made inquiries about the state of the country, the occupations of the people, the age of the servants, and so forth. He addressed a great deal of his conversation to Fräulein Emerenzia, and attended to her wants; when he offered her wine she covered her glass with her hand, and declared she never tasted anything but water, which seemed infinitely to surprise him; also, when he wished to know whether the ring on her finger was one of betrothal, Emerenzia tried to blush, and gave him to understand that, from her own choice, she meant to live and die a maid.

After dinner was over, Father Mahók remained in the dining-room to entertain the Fräulein—that is to say, he seated himself in an armchair, folded his hands upon his rotund stomach, closed his eyes, and during a sweet doze listened to the clatter of Emerenzia's sharp voice.

The abbé followed the countess into her private sitting-room. She sat down on the sofa, her eyes on the ground, waiting with much inward trepidation to hear what sentence so exalted a personage would pronounce upon her demoniacal possession. As he did not speak, she in a timid voice began:

"Has my confessor told you the terrible secret of the castle?"

"He has told me all that he knows."

"And what view would the authorities of the Church take, do you think?"

"My individual opinion, countess, is that the whole thing is a conspiracy by the living."

"By the living!" repeated the countess. "And my visions?"

"Those can be explained by psychological means. You are of a susceptible, nervous temperament; your senses have been made acquainted with the first portion of the history, your imagination works out the remainder. Your dreams, countess, are hallucinations, nothing else. Visible ghosts do not exist; those who are dead cannot live and move, for the reason that their organic powers are at an end."

The countess shook her head incredulously. To tell the truth, she was not pleased. She had expected a very different explanation. If he could only tell her this, it was, indeed, trouble lost to send for him all this way.

Abbé Samuel was quick enough to read from her face what was passing through her mind, and hastened to apply a radical cure.

"Countess, I know you doubt what I say, because you have firm faith in what your eyes have seen, your ears have heard. You are quite convinced that you yourself have been many times in the haunted vault, and have there seen the spirits of your departed ancestors."

"Only last night," whispered the countess in an awed voice, "the tumult was fearful. They told me they would come again tonight, that they would expect me."

"And have you promised to go to them?"

"When day comes the idea makes me shudder, but at night some strange, mysterious power draws me to the vault; I know all fear will vanish, and I shall not be able to stay away."

"Very good. Then tonight I shall go with you to the vault of your ancestors."

At these words a sudden flush covered the pale face of the countess. The living portrait! She should go with him—where? Perhaps into hell. She trembled at the thought; then with a violent effort recovered her composure, and said in a hesitating manner:

"I do not know. I do not think it would be possible. I should have to let my household into the secret."

The abbé understood the nature of the problem, and all the consequences it involved.

"That would not be necessary. On the contrary, your household must know nothing of my visit."

The countess looked at him. She was puzzled, agitated. What could he mean? He could not imagine for a moment that he was to spend the night with her—alone?

The abbé read her thought and answered quietly:

"I shall go away now with Father Mahók. I shall return about midnight, and will knock at your door to announce my arrival."

Theudelinde shook her head. "That is impossible. In winter every door in my house is locked by seven o'clock. To reach my suite of rooms, you would have to pass through no less than seven doors. First the castle gate. This is watched by my portress, an old woman who never sleeps; besides, two giant bloodhounds keep guard there. They are chained to the door with long chains; they would seize you if you tried to pass. Then comes the door in the corridor, to which there are two locks; my companion keeps the key of one, my housekeeper the key of the other, and to open it you must wake both. The third is the door to the staircase; the cook has the key under her pillow, and she sleeps so soundly, that the whole house is up before she stirs. The fourth is the entrance to the secret lattice passage; this is in the keeping of the housemaid, a nervous girl, who, when it grows dark, would not go into the next room. The fifth door leads to the chamber of my own maid, a very

86

modest young person, who would not open the door to a man, were he prophet or saint. The sixth door is that of Fräulein Emerenzia, my companion; she falls into violent hysterics if any one turns the handle of her door at night. The seventh and last door is that of my dressing-room, which is fitted with a peculiar lock, a new invention. I ask your reverence if, under such conditions, you could make your way here at midnight?"

"Permit me, in my turn, to put a question to you. You have given me to understand that you descend constantly to the vault of your ancestors. How does it happen that you pass through all these well-guarded doors?"

Over the countenance of the countess a triumphant smile passed. The superstitious woman could repel the attack of the scientist.

"Oh, I do not pass through any of them. From my bedroom a secret staircase leads to the chapel vault. I go down this staircase."

It would have been only natural if the abbé on hearing this, should have proposed to conceal himself in the library, and there await the countess. But he read the character of his hostess, and knew that such a proposal would have shocked her prudish mind, and have offended her so deeply that, in all probability she would have refused to listen any further. She required the most delicate management; the abbé recognized this perfectly.

"I am still of the same mind," he said calmly. "I shall knock at your door this night at twelve o'clock."

At these words the countess was seized with a nervous shudder, but the abbé went on without taking any notice:

"If you believe that there are unearthly beings who are possessed of mysterious powers, by which they pass through locked doors and make themselves visible to some human beings, invisible to others, then why should I not have this power also? But you imagine that because I am only a man born of dust I cannot infringe the laws of nature. Let me remind you that there is a natural explanation for all that may seem to you incomprehensible. Witchcraft is now no longer a mystery. We do not now burn Boscos and Galuches upon funeral piles. Do not for a moment think that I am a Bosco or a Paracelsus. I repeat that what I promise I will perform: at the same hour at which the ghosts begin their orgies, I will knock at your door with the words, *In nomine Domini aperiantur portae fidelium*—'In the name of the Lord may the doors of the faithful be opened.' Remember, no one but us two are to know anything of my coming tonight. Till then may the blessing of God be with you."

Theudelinde was much impressed by her strange visitor. His confidence infused courage into her weak mind, while his masterful ways acted on her like a spell. He addressed her from such a superior height that she felt it would be almost desecration not to place the utmost faith in his word, and, nevertheless, he had promised to perform the impossible. How could she reconcile the two, unless, indeed, she had to do with a being from another world? She saw from the window the carriage drive away with the two clergymen. She watched them get in; and she remained at her window until the carriage returned empty.

The female Jehu showed to the other servants the tip she had received; it was a new silver piece. It passed from hand to hand. What a miracle! Of the fifteen million inhabitants of Hungary, fourteen million five hundred thousand had never seen such a thing as a silver coin.

The time passed slowly for the countess; the clock seemed to go with leaden weights. She wandered through all the rooms, her mind revolving in what possible manner, by what possible entrance a man could find his way into the castle. When it had struck seven o'clock she saw herself that every door which communicated with her wing was carefully locked; then she sat down in her own room. She took out the plan of the castle, which had been drawn by the Florentine artist who had built it. It was not the first time she had studied it; when she first received the castle as a present from her father, she had made herself mistress of every particular concerning it. The building was three times larger than she intended to maintain. She had, therefore, to choose which wing she would occupy. In the centre there were fine reception-rooms, a banqueting-hall, an armoury, and a museum of pictures and curiosities. This portion was out of the question. Also, from this portion of the castle a concealed staircase led to a subterranean passage. This could be used as a means of escape, and had no doubt served such a purpose when the old castle had been besieged by the Turks. The countess's grandfather had walled up these steps, and no one could now get into the secret passage. The left wing, which was similarly constructed to the one which the countess inhabited, had served as some sort of pleasure-house to her pleasure-loving ancestors. There were all manner of secret holes and corners in it, communications of all kinds connecting the rooms, doors behind pictures, concealed alcoves, and the like. The architect's plan showed these without any reticence. Theudelinde naturally turned away in horror from the idea of inhabiting this tainted wing, so full of sinful associations; she set up her Lares and Penates in the less handsome but more homely right wing, with a few good rooms fitted for domestic life, a library, and the family vault below. It contained only one secret staircase: the one which led to the family tombs. For the rest, Countess Theudelinde had taken care to wall up all the passages which led to either the centre or left wing of the castle, and there was no means of communication between them and her apartments. All the chimneys had iron gates to shut off any possible intrusion that way; every window was provided with strong iron bars. It would have been impossible even for a cat to effect an entrance into this enchanted castle.

The countess, meditating on all these precautions, came to the conclusion that there was only one way by which the Abbé Samuel could introduce himself into the house, and that was by a secret understanding with someone of her household. But again, setting aside altogether the high character of the priest, which would render such an act improbable, the very circumstances attending his visit made this impossible. He had never been absent from the countess for a minute, except during his short walk to the carriage, and then Father Mahók had been his companion. Theudelinde, therefore, dismissed the idea from her mind. She sent her household to bed early; she complained to Fräulein Emerenzia of pains on one side of her head. Immediately, that sympathetic companion complained of pains on the other side of her own head. When the countess thought she would try to sleep, Emerenzia felt the like desire; she wrapped her whole head in warm cotton wool, and snored relentlessly.

Theudelinde shut herself up in her bedroom, and counted the minutes. She tried to play *patience*, but the cards would not come right; her mind was too much disturbed. She took out her Bible, splendidly illustrated by Doré. She looked at all the pictures; she counted the figures of the different men and women upon those two hundred and thirty large plates; then the horses and the camels, till she came to the scenes of murders. Then she tried to pass the time by reading the text. She counted which letter of the alphabet was repeated the most frequently on one side of the page. For the greater part the letter *a* was the favourite, *e* came next, then *o*, also *u*; *i* was the worst represented. This was in the French print. In the Hungarian text *e* had the majority, then *a*, *o* and *i*, and, last of all, *b* and *u*. But she soon wearied of this. Then she sat down to the piano, and tried to calm her agitation by playing dreamy fantasias; but this did not succeed, either. Her hands trembled, and she could not sustain herself at the instrument, she was so tired; and as the fatal hour of midnight drew nearer she gave up trying to distract her mind, and abandoned herself to thinking of the impending ghostly tumult. She found herself completely under the influence of her ancestral spectres, for she was always consumed with *ennui* until the noise began. Then a sort of fever would come to her; she would undress, crawl into bed, draw the covers over her head until she broke into perspiration, and then fall into a deep sleep. The next morning, when she awoke, she really believed that she had witnessed the scenes of which she had only dreamt.

This night she drew forth her talisman, the photograph of the abbé, and tried to find some strength in it. She placed it before her on the reading-desk, and sat gazing at it. Was he really a superior being, at whose command the doors of the castle would fly open, spectres would vanish, and the gates of hell would close upon them? It could not be that such things would happen. The more the night advanced the greater her nervous fears grew. Her heart beat loudly. It was not so much the nightly ghosts that she dreaded, but this new and equally unearthly visitor. What was he? A wizard, an enchanter like Merlin of old, or a saint come to exorcise and banish her tormentors?

The weary, lagging hours went by, until at last the pendulum of the old clock began to vibrate, and its iron tongue struck midnight. The countess counted every stroke. Its vibration had hardly ceased, when, as before, the infernal noise began; from the vault below the tones of the Mass reached Theudelinde's ears. She was, however, listening for another sound, listening with feverish anxiety to catch a stealthy footfall in the adjoining room, to hear the rattle of a key surreptitiously moving in the lock. Nothing! She came to the door, and, putting her head to the keyhole, strained her ears in vain. All was still. It was now a quarter past midnight; the tumult in the vault below was in full swing—the witches' sabbath, as it might be called, with its yells, shouts, songs, prayers; it was as if all the devils of hell had given one another rendezvous in company with the countess's ancestors.

He will not come, she thought, and trembled in every limb of her fever-stricken body. It was folly to expect it. How could a man accomplish what is only permitted to spirits?

She retired to the alcove, and prepared to lie down. At this moment she heard a tap at the door of her sitting-room, and, after a moment, a low voice spoke in firm tones:

"*In nomine Domini aperiantur portae fidelium.*"

It was the signal given by the abbé. Theudelinde gave a shriek; she nearly lost her senses from fright, but gathered herself together with a supreme effort. It was real; no hallucination, no dream! He was at the door, her deliverer. Forward!

The countess ran to the door and opened it. The crisis gave her unusual strength. This might be a trap, and instead of a deliverer she might find herself opposite to a robber or murderer. Under the carpet lay concealed the trap-door; the midnight visitor stood on the very spot. One pressure of the secret spring, and down he would go into the abyss below. Theudelinde had her foot on the spring as she undid the door.

The abbé stood before her. No sign of his clerical calling was to be seen. He wore a long coat, which reached to his feet, and carried neither bell, book, or candle to exorcise the spirits. In his right hand he held a thick stick made of rhinoceros' skin, and in the left a dark lantern.

"Stay where you are," said the countess in a commanding voice. "Before you set foot in this room you shall tell me how you got here. Was it with the help of God, of man, or of the devil?"

"Countess," returned the abbé, "look about you. Do you not see that every door in your castle stands open? I have passed easily through these open doors. How I passed through the court is another thing. I will tell you that later."

"And my household, who sleep in those rooms?" said the countess in an incredulous voice.

"The curtains hang round every bed; I have not raised them. If your household be asleep, they will no doubt sleep as the just do, without waking."

The countess listened, only half believing what she heard; she was growing nerveless again. She led the abbé into the sitting-room, and sank exhausted upon the sofa.

The noise in the vault was indescribable.

"Do you hear it?" she said in a whisper.

"I do hear, and I know whence it comes. I am here to face those who cause this unseemly riot."

"Have you the weapons that the Holy Church has provided for such a task?" asked Theudelinde, anxiously.

The priest for all answer held towards her the strong staff he carried.

"I have this good stick, countess."

"Do you hear above all the noise that strident voice? It is my cousin Ladislaus," cried the countess, grasping the abbé's arm with both her hands. "Do you hear that horrible laugh? It is my cousin's laugh."

"We will soon find the author of that unpleasant cachinnation," remarked the priest quietly.

"Why, what do you propose to do?"

"I shall go down and join the worshipful society below."

"You will descend into the vault? What to do?"

"To pass judgment upon that unruly gang, countess. You promised to accompany me."

"I promised!" and Theudelinde retreated from him, her eyes staring wildly, her hands pressed to her breast.

"It was your own wish."

"True, true! I am so confused; my thoughts are all to pieces. I cannot recollect them. You here, and that fearful noise below! I am terribly afraid."

"How? You who had the courage to go amongst the ghosts by yourself, are you afraid now that *I* am with you? Give me your hand."

The countess placed her trembling fingers in the abbé's hand, and as she felt the firm, manly clasp, an unusual sense of strength and protection possessed her; she ceased to shake and shiver, her eyes no longer saw shapes and fantasies moving before them; her heart began to beat steadily. The bare touch of this man's hand gave her new life.

"Come with me," the abbé said, while he stuck his whip under his left arm, and with the right drew the countess after him. "Where are the keys of the secret staircase, and of the room through which we must pass?"

Theudelinde felt that she could not let go his hand for one minute. She followed him submissively; she knew she would follow him, were it to the very gates of hell. Without a word she pointed to the key cabinet, an antique piece of furniture in which there was a drawer full of keys.

Without a moment's hesitation the priest put his hand on the ones that were wanted. It was no miracle that he should do so, although to the weakened mind of his companion it appeared to be miraculous; on one of the keys there was a cross, the well-known sign of a vault key.

The abbé now drew aside the curtain which concealed the secret passage to the library, and here, at the first step, he was met by conclusive proof against the countess's statement that she was in the habit of descending to the vault: as he opened the door, a mass of cobwebs blew into his face. The countess, however, stood firmly by her hallucination. It is a phase of such nervous disorders as hers to believe that a dream is actual fact; even to small details.

As the countess went down the steps, she whispered to her companion:

"One of the windows is broken, and the wind whistles through it." And as they turned the angle of the steps, there was a narrow slip-window which gave light to the staircase in the daytime, the panes of which were actually broken. She had never seen this. When they came to the door of the library she confided to the abbé that she was always frightened to pass the threshold.

"It is such a haunted place!" she said. "When the moon shines through the shutters of the upper window, it throws white specks on the mosaic of the marble floor, making it look like some mysterious script. In a corner, between two cupboards, there is a glass case with a skeleton, in another case the death-mask of Ignatius Loyola."

Everything was just as the countess related. The moon shone through the upper windows, the skeleton stood in his glass case, the waxen head of the dead saint lay in the other, but the countess had never crossed the threshold.

Maybe in her childhood one of her nurses had told her these tales of the Bondavára Castle, and when she had become its mistress, her first care had been to lock these rooms. Ten years' dust lay on the carpets, on the chairs and tables; cobwebs hung from the ceilings, for no one ever came here.

At the moment in which the countess and her companion entered the library, there was comparative quiet in the vault below. The noise seemed to have abated; there were neither shrieks nor demoniacal songs to be heard. From the mortuary chapel, however, the notes of the organ reached the ears of the two listeners. It sounded like the prelude which is played in church before Mass begins, only the chords of the prelude were all discords; it was as if the organ were being played by a condemned spirit.

The countess stood before the chapel door, her breast heaving with emotion. She caught hold of the abbé's hand with a strong grasp, to prevent him from turning the key in the lock. She trembled in every limb.

"What are those frightful sounds?"

Then came a confused noise, as of many voices intoning the Vespers. One voice, which imitated the monotonous delivery of an officiating priest, began to sing in Latin the words of a hymn:

Bacchus, prepare the libation.

Another voice answered in the same tone:

And hasten, brethren, to drink!

Then a third took up the text in a parody of the *Gloria:*

'*Gloria Baccho, et filiae eius Cerevisiae et Spiritui Vini, sicut erat in Baccho natus, et nunc, et semper, et per omnia pocula poculorum. Stramen.*'

The countess felt her whole body turning to ice; fear mingling with horror. She knew her Latin and understood the impious parody.

The organ accompanied the antiphone.

'*Date nobis de cerevisia vestra; quia sitiunt guttura nostra.*'

'Give us of your beer; our throats are dry.'

Then followed the psalm:

'Brother to brother spoke these words: shall two goblets of beer quench man's thirst?'

'Two, three, five, six are not enough for man's satiety.'

'Blessed be Bacchus, who gave us beer.'

Then followed the Capitulum.

'Brethren, attend, and do as I command ye. Before ye leave the congregation for your own homes, empty every tankard, leave not a drop in any, but tilt them and drain every drop of wine. This do from cup to cup. Stramen.'

The countess felt, as she listened to this profanity, like a damned soul who, for the first time, consorts with devils. But now a hellish chorus broke forth of men's and women's voices, yelling out a parody of a hymn:

'Bacchus, who gave us drink,
Art thou not called the god of liquor?
Grant us all the holy grace,
Strength to drink in every place,
So that, drinking everywhere,
We for glory may prepare
In thy eternal wine-cellar.'

This was followed by the ringing of the bell, and the priest's voice intoned the blessing.

'Bacchus be with you.'

The chorus answered, 'And with thy pint-pots.'

Then came the Oratio:

'Let us eat. O all-powerful Bacchus, since thou hast created this society of ours for thine own honour, grant to us its continuance, and give to us a constant supply of brave topers, who never may cease drinking from cup to cup.'

And the chorus answered, 'Stramen.'

The countess was not able any longer to hold herself up. She sank on her knees, looking at the priest in mute horror, without knowing what she was doing she just gazed in utter despair at his tall figure lit up by the rays of the moon, which played round his head like a halo.

The abbé put the key into the lock of the chapel door. The countess caught his hand; her fright amounted to agony.

"Do not—do not open it!" she cried. "Inside is hell let loose."

With an elevation of his head, the abbé answered proudly:

"*Nec portae inferi*—the gates of hell shall not prevail," and turned the key in the lock. The heavy iron door swung open. Through the open doorway, the entire scene in the vault and chapel could be seen, lit up by candles.

All the candles were lit on the altar and in their light every part of the strange performance, every feature in the faces of the performers stood distinct.

And what a scene! Along a long table, filling most of the vault not the countess's ancestors, but the servants of her household were seated, eating and drinking. The maids, who were so strictly supervised, now were in the company of the men who had been shut out of the house. So, the countess could see that it were flesh-and-blood ghosts which had so long haunted her ancient castle. Each of her hand-maidens had a lover, either the steward, the bailiff, the gamekeeper, or a clerk from nearby. The nervous housemaid, who was afraid of her own shadow at night, was now drinking from the innkeeper's glass; the virtuous chamber-maid was in the arms of the mayor's footman; the porteress, the elderly virgin, was holding a jug in her hand, and performing a clog-dance on the table. All the rest were clapping their hands, shrieking, singing at the top of their voices, and beating the table like a big drum. The shepherd, who was dressed as the countess's grandfather, sat upon the chancellor's monument, his legs round the cross, and played his bagpipes. It was this instrument which had, at the burlesqued Vespers, imitated the harmonium. The beer-barrel was set up on the gravestone of the first archbishop. All the maids were dressed in the countess's silk dresses, with the exception of the female coachman, who, as usual, wore man's clothes, but by way of symmetry her lover, the coachman of the neighbouring brewery, was dressed in woman's clothes. The countess recognized on the head of this bearded fellow her nightcap, and round his body her cloak, trimmed with her best lace. Worst of all, at the top of the table sat Fräulein Emerenzia, on very intimate terms with her neighbour, a young lawyer. She wore the skirt of a favourite dress of Theudelinde's, of flame-coloured brocade; the body would not meet round her corpulent form, so she had her mistress's best lace shawl wrapped round her. Her face was red; she had a large tumbler of wine before her, and she smoked a pipe. The modest Emerenzia!

The men were drunk and noisy, the women screamed in a fiendish way; the bagpipes squealed; the table resounded with thumps and the clatter of the portress's clogs. From the altar came the voice of the mock priest, his arms outstretched in blessing. Through the din the words *Bacchus vobiscum* were heard, and the tinkle of the bell. This mock priest was no other than Michael, the sacristan, who had brought along even the church ornaments confided to his care. He wore the priest's vestments, and on his head an improvised skull-cap. The acolyte was the parish bell-ringer.

The countess was smitten to the heart. The terrible ingratitude, especially of the girls, while she had been a mother to them— more anxious indeed than their own mothers to keep them pure and innocent—wounded the poor lady who had taught them to sing hymns on Sundays, had fed them from her own table, and had never allowed them to read a novel, or hear a bad word spoken. And this was the outcome of her efforts. They insulted the graves of her ancestors, played upon her nervous fears, destroyed her nightly rest, nearly drove her mad with their ghostly noise, wore her clothes at their orgies, and, worse insult of all, she, a high-born lady and a pure woman, had the degradation of wearing the same garments afterwards, defiled as they were with the smell of wine and stale tobacco.

Bitter as such ingratitude was, it counted as nothing compared to the profanation of using the holiest objects of religion, the sacred ornaments of the Church, to carry out these impious rites. 'Woe to them from whom scandal cometh,' says the Scripture, and this woe means pain and suffering that nothing can soothe.

Mortal fear still filled the countess's heart. She was in the presence of those who had no control over their already besotted senses. If these drunken savages found their revels were discovered, what would stop them from tearing her to pieces? Only one man stood between her and them. Theudelinde looked at her solitary protector. His eyes gleamed with such apostolic anger that her timid soul grew fearful of the consequences, to him and to herself, of his just wrath. She seized both his hands, to hold him from venturing amongst the demons. The abbé freed himself easily from the clasp of her weak fingers. In one leap he sprang down the steps, fell upon the false priest as he was in the act of pronouncing his final Stramen; with the butt end of his rhinoceros whip he gave him two blows.

What the countess now witnessed was indeed not a vision. She saw how one man, armed with no more formidable a weapon than a horsewhip, ventured into the midst of the hellish assembly, with one hand seized the table and turned it over. All swept off—dishes, glasses, and wine-cups; with his other hand he cracked his whip in the faces of the guests, who sprang to their feet, like the profaners of the Temple, in all the terror of detection. They were driven towards the vault's door, the abbé's whip falling on their shoulders with impartial justice. They went tumbling over each other, howling and screaming, pressing on while pursued by the strokes of the abbé. The bagpipe player missed his footing in his haste, those behind stumbled over him, and so they scrambled together in a heap. Not one went without some remembrance of the abbé's strong arm, for he spared no one. No effort was made at a reprisal; the criminal who is caught seldom shows fight. The servants, moreover, were taken by surprise, and the clergyman was possessed of extraordinary strength; one man who tried to drag the horsewhip from his hand was dealt such a blow in the face that he too was glad to release his hold and take to his heels.

"Go on! Go on!" whispered the countess, who had no pity for her former servants, now passing by her as they made their way pell-mell to the door. Emerenzia covered her head, not for shame, but fearing her face might get a blow. Almost the last was the sacristan, whose clerical dress hindered his speed, and whose back was so battered by the abbé that the vestment he wore hung in ribands.

After the last guest had departed, the abbé closed the heavy door of the vault and returned to the countess.

His face wore a look resembling glory, it was the consciousness of his male strength. As he reached her, the countess fell on her knees, and tried to kiss his feet, unable to speak, from her tears. The abbé raised her from the ground.

"Compose yourself, countess. Your present situation needs all your strength. You must know that at this moment there are only two people in the whole castle, for I have locked the door which leads to the courtyard. This folly is over. You see now that no wicked spirit had any part in it. You must realize by now that the Evil One can only haunt you in human bodies; and those have been chased away now."

"What shall I do?" asked the countess, forcing herself to speak calmly.

"Take my lantern. I am going down to lock the wrought-iron door, to stop anyone coming in from this side. But you can go back by the way we came, back to your own apartment, where I advise you to make yourself some tea; you are freezing with cold."

"Must I go back all that way alone?"

"Remember the words, 'If God is with me, who is against me,' and you can never be alone. To see ghosts is an illness; the method of curing it must be heroic."

And as he saw that the countess, in spite of her efforts, could not subdue her nervous tears, he took her by the hand, and returning with her to the library, led her to the glass case which held the skeleton, and opened the door.

"Were you afraid of this? Why, it is nothing to fear. It is a standing proof of the wisdom of God. Every limb of this wonderful collection of bones tells us that the Almighty created man to be ruler of the earth. Look at the skull; upon this arched forehead is written the birthright of humanity, in every corner and line of the face the superiority of the white race over all others. This skull teaches us how deep our gratitude should be to an all-seeing Providence who has created us superior to all other beings on the earth. The sight of a skull should cause no shudder in the breast of man; it should give rise to feelings of thankfulness and reverence, for it is the symbol of the great love which our Heavenly Maker has for the creature He has made and chosen from all eternity."

As he spoke the priest laid Theudelinde's cold hand upon the skull of the skeleton. The countess stopped trembling. New life and strength, born of the words of this singular man, seemed to bring new blood to her veins.

"Now go to your room," said the abbé. "I shall follow you soon, but I must put out the sconces on the altar first. We must not have a fire on our hands."

"I am quite ready to go alone," returned the countess. "My foolish fears are cured, but I am now concerned for you. Perhaps those wretched servants of mine are still about, and if you venture into the dark vault they may fall upon you and take their revenge."

"Oh, I am provided with something to scatter such cowards as they are," said the abbé, drawing a revolver from a pocket. "I had resolved to use stringent measures with them if necessary. Now, in God's name, retire to your room, countess."

Theudelinde, without another word, took the lantern, and went through the long library. The priest watched her until she had crossed the threshold, and had passed through the door leading to her own apartment. Then he hurried back to the vault. In the passage he saw a blue flame burning in a tin dish.

"Alcohol and ammonia mixed together," murmured the priest. "This is what frightened Father Mahók." Close to it lay the winding-sheet and mask. The abbé pushed the vessel with the flame into the corner, for he knew that in an encounter with an enemy it would be of little profit to be in the light, and then he went along the dark passage with slow care. No one was there; they had all run away, and were probably running still. The wrought-iron door stood open; he shut it, and barred it carefully; then he returned to the vault, and locked that as well, having first extinguished the candles, except one which he took to light his way back to the countess's room.

He found her sitting composedly before the samovar. She had obeyed him. As he entered the room she rose, and, folding her hands upon her breast, cried:

"Most holy saint and apostle!"

"You must not give me such exalted titles," said the abbé, smiling. "What I have done does not merit such high-sounding terms. I have accomplished no miracle, for I had only to do with mortals. One circumstance which appears to you in a miraculous light is easily explained. I allude to my entering a house where all the doors were locked. But first, will you pour

102

out the tea?—and I shall be grateful if you can spare me a cup, for the occurrences of the last hour have excited me somewhat. Then we will talk over the whole affair."

The countess gave her guest his tea, then sank back in her armchair, and wrapped herself in her cloak; she was still shivering.

"That the supposed ghosts and noises were in no way supernatural was evident to me," continued the abbé, as he sipped his tea, "from the first moment Father Mahók took me into his confidence. I was convinced that the nocturnal disturbance was the work of your own household, and it served their purpose to make it look as haunted as possible. The situation is the result of your over-caution, countess. Your women servants were not allowed to hold communication with the opposite sex; they, therefore, found other means to meet, and to give a cover to these illicit meetings they set up an atmosphere of haunted mystery, by which their goings-on were well concealed. The conspiracy was carried out perfectly. If they had conducted their sinful intercourse along any other lines, you would have discovered them, long since. When the priest told me that he and his sacristan had escaped through the wrought-iron door, I suspected that it was through this door the men found their way into the vault, and that the sacristan must be a participator in the plot, whatever it was. Moreover, I calculated that the women must, of necessity, find their way through the cellar passage, and that, therefore, they would naturally leave every door in the house *open*, so that their return might be conducted without any danger of waking you by the sounds of unlocking the doors. The countenance, the skin-colour, the eyes of your companion betrayed her; it is easy to see that she has always been a sensualist and that, moreover, she drinks. I knew today, at dinner, that she was a hypocrite. She held forth against all alcoholic drinks; that settled her with me. I had no doubt that I should find all the doors open; and I did. In order to make no noise, I came on foot to the garden door. Countless footsteps

103

in the fresh snow showed me that the company had already assembled. From the open garden door the footprints led to the wrought-iron door, and thence to the vault. This door was closed. I pushed it open, and I was in the passage. I turned to the left, up the steps to the cellar passage; the door was open. I could now count upon finding every door open; it was just as I had imagined. The only difficulty lay in passing through your dressing-room, which has no key, but a peculiarly constructed spring-lock. I felt certain that your maids would borrow some of their mistress's silk dresses, and therefore the spring-lock would be arranged so as not to betray by its loud snap the return of the stolen garments to their proper place. On looking closely, I found that this was the case; the lock was kept in its place by the insertion of a penknife. Therefore, countess, you have, night after night, slept in this castle with every door open—in real danger—at the mercy of robbers, or even murderers; all the time frightened to death by ghosts and haunting, which kept you a prisoner to your room, not venturing to call your treacherous servants. Countess, you have been punished terribly."

"Punished!" stammered the countess, her face growing even paler.

"Yes, punished; for you have richly deserved to suffer."

Theudelinde fixed a horrified look on the abbé. "Countess, at your door," said the priest, sternly, "lies the heaviest portion of the sins into which your servants have fallen. You have, in fact, driven them into vice. Your eccentric rules, your bizarre and ridiculous ideas made your women servants liars, and induced their irregularities. Nature punishes those who revolt against her, and the long years during which you have isolated yourself from the world and from society has been a flat rebellion, which has brought its own punishment. You now stand before two judges, Heaven and the world; Heaven is ready to punish you, the world to laugh at you. The wrath of Heaven and the ridicule

104

of the world is equally hard to bear. How do you mean to protect yourself against both?"

The countess sank back, annihilated. Only just recovered from the anxieties, horrors, and dangers of this dreadful night, she was not able to face the denunciations of the priest, which were, in fact, only an echo of her own conscience. This torment was greater than all she had undergone so far. There was silence in the room, during which his words rang in Theudelinde's ears like the tolling of a bell.

"How shall you face the anger of Heaven, and the ridicule of the world?"

At last she thought of a way out of the difficulty, and, raising her head, she said in a low voice:

"I will hide my miserable head in a convent. *There* the ridicule of the world will not reach me; there, kneeling before the altar, I will pray day and night to God to pardon my fault. You, oh most Reverend Father, could you perhaps use your influence with the abbess of some convent—I should prefer a very strict order—and get me admitted. I shall find a living grave there, and no one would ever hear my name. I shall leave this castle, and my fortune, and my savings of the last few years, to your order, with only one condition, that every night at twelve o'clock vespers should be sung in my family vault, which has been desecrated by these abominations."

The countess's voice, started speaking low and breathless, gathered strength as she made this renunciation of her worldly goods.

The abbé rose as she finished, and took her trembling hand in his, while, lifting his head haughtily, he answered:

"That everything may be quite clear, I beg you will understand, countess, that neither I nor my order need, or would accept, a gift of your castle, your property, or your money. It is not our habit to take advantage of a weak person in the moment of her contrition, and to extort from her compensation for sins in the shape of worldly goods. We have no desire to

105

acquire property in such a sneaking and contemptible a manner, and therefore, countess, in the name of my order, I decline to spend the night singing vespers in your family vault, or the day in living on your fortune. You must dismiss this idea from your mind completely."

These words filled the countess with admiration. She had already felt singularly attracted by this man. Such proof of his disinterestedness and indifference to worldly considerations completed his dominion over her mind, and subjugated her to his authority. She listened submissively while he continued his advice.

"As for the rest," he said, "I should recommend you to abandon all ideas of convent life, which is quite unsuited to a person of your nervous, excitable nature. You would find neither peace nor happiness; on the contrary, you would be a prey to all sorts of scruples and disquieting thoughts. There are those who find a refuge and salvation in a cloister; for you it would be a foretaste of damnation, and in all probability you would end like the hermit who fled from the world to pray to God, and instead of praying, cursed Him."

The eyes of the countess glared at this awful prospect, but she murmured to herself, "True, quite true!"

"The recollection of your faults has banished you from the Church, and has robbed you of all power to pray," continued the priest, in a harsh voice.

"True, quite true!" sobbed the countess, and beat her breast. "I can never again enter a church, and I dare not pray." Then with a cry of despair she threw herself at the feet of the abbé, and with feverish strength clasped both his hands, screaming: "Where shall I go, if not to the Church of God? Who shall help me if I cannot pray to Him?"

The clergyman saw it was necessary to soothe her terrible excitement.

"Your proper refuge is in your own heart," he said gently, "and your good deeds shall plead for you."

Theudelinde pressed the priest's hand to her burning fore-head. Then she rose from her kneeling position, and stretched out her arms.

"Command me. Advise me. What shall I do?"

"Return to society, and take the place your rank and wealth entitle you to hold."

The countess fell back a step, and stared at the abbé, her face all astonishment.

"Return to the world! I, who left it five and twenty years ago! I should be the laughing-stock of every one, were I to seek at my age the pleasures which I renounced long ago."

"Countess, you have voluntarily thrown away that part of your life to which the world offers its best gifts; but there still remains to you another half, in which you can acquire the esteem of the world—that is, if you avail yourself of the means necessary for success."

"My Father, remember that in that circle which you wish me to enter, I shall meet nothing but contempt and humiliation. The present generation does not know my name, my contem-poraries despise me."

"But there is a magic circle in which every one is recognized, and no one is despised. Would you wish to enter this circle?"

"Place me in this circle, Father. Where is it to be found?"

"I will tell you, countess. Your country is passing through a crisis; it may be called the battle for intellectual freedom. We are all striving to place this country on an equal intellectual footing with other nations—philosophers, poets, industrialists; men, women, boys, grey-beards, aristocrats and peasants. If they knew how to strive together they might attain their pur-pose, but all are divided; each works for himself and by himself. Individual effort is doomed to failure; but united effort is sure to succeed."

The countess listened in breathless astonishment. She did not see where the abbé was leading her.

"What is needed in this tremendous struggle is a centre. The country has no centre. Debrecen is thoroughly Hungarian, but its religious, Protestant exclusiveness has narrowed its sphere of influence. Szeged is well placed, but it is far too democratic. Kolozsvár is indeed a Hungarian town. The aristocracy can be found there, and a certain amount of culture, but it lies beyond the Királyhágó, and the days of the Bethlens and the Bocskais are over. Pest would be the proper centre; it has every advantage. I have been through the five quarters of the globe, and nowhere have I found such a place. In Pest no man troubles himself about his neighbour, and each man believes that the world is made for him alone. The first look of the city takes one by surprise; the fine embankment along the broad Danube river, the beautiful squares and streets, with the six-storey houses, each in a different style of architecture. Side by side are palaces built in the Roman, Moorish, Spanish, or Renaissance style, with, perhaps, the occasional introduction of a quaint Dutch mansion or Gothic structure. Opposite the Chain Bridge rises a large stone band-box with four towers; this is called the Basilica, but it looks more like a giant scaffold than anything else. On all sides range monster factory chimneys, which spread quantities of poisonous smoke upon the town. Factories, docks, gambling casinos, the Academy of Science, the Municipal Concert Hall, are crowded together. The Academy is placed where it's in the way of the business of the docks, and the noise of the shipping trade disturbs the academicians. The smoke of the steam-engines suffocates every one and the complete conglomeration, says to the stranger, 'Come nearer, friend; this is a new Constantinople.' "

The countess could not help smiling over this graphic description.

"The inner town," continued the abbé, "is a labyrinth of narrow, irregular streets, which were built when the site of the present Town Hall was only a marsh for the pigs to wallow in. In spite of their narrow proportions, these streets contain some of the finest shops in Europe. The contrasts are amazing; the

finest carriages jammed against the over-laden wagons convey-
ing merchandise; the most elegantly dressed women jostling
against beggars in rags. The prettiest women are to be seen in
this quarter, and this in spite of a wind that drives all the dust
into one's eyes. In the suburbs, houses are rising on all sides
with marvellous rapidity, small and large, in every style and
variety, giving more dust for the wind to bring. The whole
place is a wilderness of stone, with a small green oasis here and
there not bigger than a private garden. Around the city lies a
Sahara, the earth of which is constantly dug up, so that the
wind is never in want of dust. This is how Pest looks, a city
which presents the different features of a manufacturing town,
a centre for trade, and a city of arts and science, as well as
those of the capital of a country, where men of all classes
assemble to make their pile, but when they have done it, they
hurry away to spend their gains in other places.

"As far as social conditions are concerned, and these, after
all, concern us most," said the abbé, with a quick look at his
listener, "they are as complicated as the commercial interests of
Pest. Each class is surrounded, so to speak, with a Chinese wall.
Trade and the Stock Exchange are altogether in the hands of
Jews and Germans. This would not really be an evil, were it
not that a great amount of fraudulent speculation goes on, and
at every turn of the money market in Vienna the funds go down.
The Hungarian element is made up of small gentry and artisans;
there are besides these about twenty thousand Slavs from the
hills, who are unskilled workers. Pest is, or should be, the head-
quarters of our national education. It is, however, not fashionable to live there. It should be the centre of science and literature;
it is not, however, considered elegant to cultivate anything but
foreign literature. Pest can boast of very distinguished *savants*,
and of a very haughty aristocracy; but no one is allowed to
enter this magic circle but those who belong to the upper ten
thousand. Society is on a wrong footing, everybody fights his
own battle, bears his own burden; the finest ideas are lost

109

because no man understands another. A common interest is needed. A healthy life is dying out, the freedom of thought and action is being strangled by the iron laws of a short-sighted Government, which forbids discussion of any kind.

"The Parliament and the County Hall are closed. The only open ground left is in Society; but here class prejudices step in. A certain portion of our aristocracy are too indifferent to trouble themselves to do anything for the general good; the rest are too fond of their ease and amusement: they have no aim in life, except their own pleasure. There are some, however, who do know what their duty is, and who would willingly make sacrifices to fulfil it, but during the last ten years they have suffered such a loss of income that they are no longer in a position to bear the expense which would be entailed by opening their houses. There are others, those most fitted by intellect as well as by position to be leaders. Alas! they will never return to Pest; it is too full of tragic memories for them, haunting the houses where they once lived, and where bereavements have banished for ever the laughter from among the walls. So we have arrived at the position, where there is not a single centre where the clever, the worthy, the noblemen and the gentlemen can meet on equal terms; and without this no real good can be done."

"Then let me create this centre!" cried the countess, rising to her feet, with an inspired look and addressing the abbé. Her whole being seemed transformed by this thought, which had been skilfully suggested by the words of the clergyman, and who seemed pleased at his effect.

"Then you understood," he said; "and for you the advantages will be incalculable. Here is the shelter you require. If you come to Pest, if you live there as befits your rank and your fortune, you can collect round you the very cream of society. To your salon every one will come, distinguished not only by birth, but by talent—politicians, artists, poets, nabobs, priests, prelates, and laymen; the aristocracy of the land and the aristocracy of intellect shall each be represented. Your mission will be to further the apostolate of truth, of culture; and by so doing, to assist the progress and development of your own country, thus making your own position most honourable. As hostess and mistress of such a house you will be respected and admired."

The countess seized the clergyman's hand and covered it with kisses, sobbing in her excitement:

"I thank you, I thank you, I thank you!"

"Do you not see, countess, that there is a better vocation for you than convent life?"

"You are a prophet."

"In the meantime, may I ask you a practical question? For the task which you would undertake with such praiseworthy zeal, certain material qualifications are absolutely necessary; the first being a sufficient income. May I ask you to give me your confidence on this delicate subject?"

"I am rich," answered Theudelinde. "My capital is invested at a good interest. From my savings I have bought a fine mansion, situated in the best part of Pest; it is let at present."

"You will now take it into your own hands," said the abbé, "and have it properly furnished, as befits to your rank. As far as your securities go, it may be better to invest your capital differently. We shall see. How much does your yearly income from the Bondavára estate come to?"

"About twenty thousand florins."

"How large is the estate?"

"About nine or ten thousand acres."

"Then the return is far too small. The agent is to blame for this; and this income would be too small to support the position you now intend to hold. Twenty thousand florins would not be nearly enough to keep up an establishment on a proper footing in Pest."

The countess was surprised. She said humbly, "I imagined it was a great deal of money."

111

"So it is for living in the country; but Pest is as dear, if not dearer, than Paris. To keep a proper establishment going, and take a leading position in society, such as it is your ambition, you must command a yearly income of forty thousand florins at least."

"But I cannot do that. What shall I do?" said Theudelinde, greatly distressed.

The abbé's lips parted in a smile. "Oh, we might manage that for you! It will not be difficult. The management of the estate must be overhauled; you must get a better agent, a more enterprising steward. I myself do not understand finance, but I have friends in the inner circles of the Stock Exchange, and one or other of these will undertake to advise you about your affairs when you are settled in Pest. In any case, I am quite certain that your land is let at too low rents; it should bring in double the interest you get from it. I know that much of economics."

The countess was delighted at these words. What a friend to have! Her income to be doubled! Truly this abbé was sent to her from heaven.

"Do as you think best," she said. "I give you full powers to act for me."

"Then, if you will allow me, I shall have your property revalued, and new leases made. This will double your income, and it will only cost you a trifle—a factor's fee, in fact."

Theudelinde was like a child in her joy—like a child in her submission to her spiritual adviser, to whom she looked up as to a father, a counsellor, a true friend.

All this he might be; but it was also true that from the date of this conversation the owner of Bondavára had lost her hold on her own property for ever.

Chapter IX

THE UNPLEASANT FELLOW

Countess Theudelinde was exultant with joy. She ran to her bell apparatus, touched the spring, and the machine put itself into motion.

"What are you doing, countess?" asked the abbé, in some amazement.

"I am going to have my steward to be sent up at once."

"By whom?"

And then, for the first time the countess remembered that there was not one living soul left in the castle.

She grew very grave.

"The real problem is," continued the priest, "how we are to get out of the castle."

"What do you mean?" asked Theudelinde, who was rendered so weak-minded now that she had to have everything explained to her.

"We two are quite alone in this house," returned the abbé. "If I go away to get the necessary assistance for packing up your things and making the arrangements for our departure, I must leave you alone here."

"I would not for all the world stay here alone."

"Then you have the alternative of coming with me on foot to the posting house in the nearest village."

As he spoke, the snowstorm was heard outside beating against the window. Theudelinde shivered.

"Why could we not drive? My horses are in the stables."

"But I can neither harness them nor drive them."

"Oh, I should never think of such a thing!"

Nevertheless, the countess had now to consider whether she should remain alone in the castle, or take the alternative of walking with the priest through the heavy snow.

The two bloodhounds started to bark at the gate.

"Somebody is knocking at the door," said the abbé.

"It must be my steward," returned Theudelinde. "He has heard what has happened, and has come to our assistance."

"But there is no one to open the door. Your portress was one of the ghosts."

"She was the old witch who danced on the table."

"Have you a second key by any chance?"

"It hangs there, on that bunch to the right."

"Then I will take it with me, in case there isn't one in the lock."

"But the dogs, Father; they will tear you to pieces. They are fierce to strangers."

"I will call them by their names, if you will tell me what they are."

"I don't know their names," returned the countess, who never troubled herself about such a common thing as a watch-dog's name.

"Then I must shoot them."

"But, Father, do it as gently as you can." By this Theudelinde did not mean to appeal to his compassion for the dogs, but to remind him to spare her sensitive nerves.

The abbé took his revolver, and went on his mission; he carried no lantern with him, for daylight was breaking.

The watch-dogs lay one on either side of the gate. They were chained so that they could keep clear of one another, but it was impossible to pass between them; if you escaped being bitten by one, the other was sure to tear at you. The abbé, therefore, had to shoot one to get to the door. He then drew

114

the bolt, and saw a man standing before him, with a revolver in his hand, too.

"Who are you? What do you want?" asked the priest.

"Who are you, and what brings you here?" returned the stranger.

"I am the Abbé Samuel, the countess's confessor."

"And I am Iván Berend, the countess's nearest neighbour."

The abbé lowered his pistol, and his tone changed to one of courtesy.

"You must confess that it is rather an unusual hour for you to come," he said, smiling.

"*Honi soit qui mal y pense*," said Iván, putting his weapon into his pocket. "I came at this unusual hour in consequence of a letter which I received this very night, in which I was informed that the castle was in a state of confusion, and the countess was in great need of help."

"The cause of the confusion . . ."

"Oh, I know; it was mentioned in the letter. Therefore, I have come to see what I can do, although I am aware that the countess does not admit men into her house, especially at this hour."

"She will receive *you* most certainly. Allow me first to close the door. There is absolutely no one in the house. Take care of the dog on the left-hand side; he is still alive."

"Have you shot the other?"

"Yes; you heard the shot, and drew your revolver?"

"Naturally. I did not know who could have fired it."

Both men ascended to the apartment of the countess. The abbé entered first, to prepare her.

"We have unexpected help," he said; "a neighbour of yours, Iván Berend."

"An unpleasant person," returned Theudelinde, scornfully. "He is an atheist."

"It does not matter in the present crisis whether he be a Thug, a Mormon, or a Manichaean; we have very great need

115

of his help. Someone told him of your plight and he wishes to see you."

"I will not see him, or speak to him. I beg you to talk with him instead of me."

"Countess, if this man is what you say, a heretic, he may say that he will not confer with one of my cloth."

"Very well. I suppose I must see him; but you will be present?"

"If it should be necessary."

The countess pulled her shawl round her, and went into the reception-room, into which the morning light was breaking. Abbé Samuel thought it necessary, however, to light the candles on the mantelpiece.

Theudelinde, with a cold look, asked Iván to sit down, and placed herself at a considerable distance from her visitor.

"Countess," Iván said, "while I was reading, earlier tonight, someone knocked on my window, and when I opened it, he put this note into my hand. It is written by your steward."

"By my steward!" exclaimed the countess, in a tone of surprise.

"It is written in his style, and quite unfit for you to read. I will tell you what may concern you. The steward says that your entire household have made their escape, and that he is following their example."

"My steward too! But why?"

"He gives a reason in his letter. I suspect, however, that it is only an excuse to hide a more serious crime. I am of the opinion that he has robbed you."

"Robbed me!" repeated the countess.

"Do not alarm yourself; there are many kinds of robbery, as for instance, being an unfaithful steward, exploiting your land, and profiting himself at your disadvantage. This man, I imagine, played this game, and he has now tried to give a humorous turn to his flight, so that the laugh may be turned against you. This is what I think."

The countess was obliged to acknowledge that her neighbour was both a clever and a kind-hearted man.

"In this letter," continued Iván, "your steward states that after what has happened he could never dare to look you in the face again, as he could not convince you that these scandals had gone on without his knowledge in the castle. I do not believe him. I felt certain that you had dismissed your household on finding out how grossly they had deceived you; therefore my first care on getting this letter was to send a messenger on horseback to the nearest telegraph office with a message to your banker in Pest, to tell him that the agent of the Bondavára estate had absconded, and on no account to honour his signature. I thought it was probable he had taken the liberty to draw in your name."

"This was really very practical and thoughtful on your part," said the abbé. "The countess feels most grateful to you."

Theudelinde bowed her head graciously.

"This was one reason to bring me here," continued Iván, "to make sure you approved what I had done; and also to offer you my assistance in case you wish to leave the castle. I will help you to get away, and I will send my people to look after your property till you can make further arrangements."

"This is really most neighbourly and friendly, and the countess owes you a debt of gratitude," repeated the priest, again assuming all responsibility.

"I am merely doing my duty," returned Iván. "And I would add that if you should be in any difficulty about money, which is very likely, as your steward and bailiff have both made off, don't let this distress you for a moment; I can lend you ten thousand florins."

The abbé whispered to the countess to accept this offer in the spirit in which it was meant, and on no account to mention interest.

Theudelinde held out her hand accordingly with gracious dignity to her chivalrous neighbour, who drew the money in

117

bank-notes from his pocket. The countess wished to give him a receipt, but he declined it, saying the money was lent for such a short time that it was not necessary.

"And about leaving the castle," he said. "How soon do you start?"

"The sooner the better," cried the countess.

"Then, if you will allow me to suggest a plan for accomplishing the first stage of the journey, which is the difficult part of the business, it will be necessary to pack up the things you need. Will you be good enough, countess, to select the trunks you mean to bring? When this is done, I will harness the horses, then we must lock and seal the rooms, and my servants will watch them until you send your proper people. This done, we can set out; and as we shall have to pass the steward's house, we can call there, and look for any ledgers he may have for the accounts of the estate. They might be useful."

"I shall not go there; I don't want any accounts."

"Very good. Then we shall go straight to the inn in my village."

"What for?"

"Because there is a posting-inn there. We must get post-horses."

"And why post-horses? Why not drive with my own horses?"

"No."

"And why not?"

"Because they are screws. They would not reach the next posting-inn."

"My horses! Why do you say they are screws?" asked the countess, angrily.

"Because they are in a bad condition."

'An unpleasant man,' thought the countess. 'He speaks to me so roughly.'

"I shall not go into an inn," she said determinedly. "I go nowhere where they serve drink. Could I not wait at your house until the horses are changed?"

"Certainly. I shall be pleased to receive you, countess; only you will find nothing suitable for you. I live alone *en garçon*."

"Oh, that does not matter," returned the countess, with an air of indifference.

"Will you have the goodness, then," said Iván, "to begin your preparations, and select the clothes you mean to pack up?"

Theudelinde gave a strange smile. "My packing will not take long; my luggage will not be heavy. Will you make a good fire while I go to my wardrobe? It is very cold in this room."

In the sitting-room there was a large marble fireplace, and some sparks still lingered in the ashes of the grate. Iván put some wood on the smouldering fire, and a genial blaze soon flared up. It welcomed the countess, who presently returned, carrying in her arms a heap of dresses and clothes of all description.

Iván looked at her in dismay. "You are going to pack all those?"

"Yes, and as many more, which still remain in my wardrobe."

"But, countess, where?"

"Here," returned Theudelinde, as she flung the bundle on the fire.

It filled up the whole fireplace, and as the fire caught the light silks, there was presently a crackling sound, while the old chimney roared again with joy at such a splendid contribution.

The two men looked in silence at this *autodafé*.

Ten times did Theudelinde go to her room, each time returning with fresh armfuls of finery, and when these were exhausted, her linen, boots, shoes, etc., followed; while at each sacrifice the flames in the chimney leaped and danced, and the wind blew the flames up the chimney, where they roared like so many demons.

'Well, this sort of packing makes short work,' thought Iván, but he said nothing.

The clergyman stood with his hands behind his back. The countess's eyes danced, her cheeks were flushed, her activity

119

was relentless. When all was consumed, she turned to Iván with a triumphant air.

"It is finished," she said.

"And may I ask in what your ladyship intends to travel?"

"In the clothes I wear, and my fur coat."

"Then I shall go and get the carriage."

When he was gone the countess, assisted by the abbé, put on her coat lined with sable. She took with her nothing that she had ever worn; in her opinion everything was defiled.

After a few minutes Iván returned, and announced that the carriage was at the front gate. Then they locked the doors, and fixed a seal to each.

When they entered the hall, the sight of the dog which the abbé had spared reminded them of a difficulty. If they left him there, he would starve. The countess thought it would be better to shoot him too. Iván, however, thought that that would be a pity.

"I will chain him to the carriage, and he will follow us."

Theudelinde was certain the hound would bite him; but the dog's instinct assured him that it was a friend who approached. He allowed Iván to chain him, and licked his hand to show his gratitude. All was now set. Iván locked the gates, gave the key to the abbé, who was already seated in the carriage with the countess, jumped on the coachbox, and drove away from Bondavára Castle. They went slowly, for the two miserable nags, though dignified with the name of carriage horses, could hardly drag them along. They were spent with age and starvation, and were only fit for the knocker's yard.

As the vehicle turned towards the coal-mine, Iván noticed a cloud of smoke in the distance. Soon after, they met a group of workers with fire engines, hurrying towards the smoke. On being questioned, they said that the granary of the noble countess was burning, but that they hoped to put out the fire quickly.

"I think it will be easy," Iván said. "The steward probably set it on fire to conceal how much of the crops he had misappropriated."

The countess was indignant at such evidence of human wickedness but Iván remarked dryly that agriculture was only a good business for those who looked after their own interests; not for people who locked themselves up in their chamber.

An unpleasant man!

It was full daylight before the fine coach, drawn by that pair of fire nags, made its way through the heavy snow to the mining village. The wretched beasts were steaming as they drew up at Iván's door. It was Iván's first care to call the postmaster to take them to his stable, and to order a good pair of fresh horses to replace them. Then he led his tired guests into his workroom. All the other rooms were cold, never being heated, so he took them to the only place where there was warmth and light.

In the room everything was in the utmost disorder; it was hard to find a place for the countess to sit. She looked about her with astonishment at the strange objects which encumbered the tables and chairs; every available spot was taken up by some extraordinary, diabolic-looking invention. She cast a look of terror at the chemical laboratory, at the furnace where the coals still glimmered, testifying to the experiment which Iván had been making when he had been interrupted by the steward's tap at the window.

"Cagliostro's workshop," she whispered to the abbé. "There must be mysterious things done here."

What annoyed the countess far more than the evidences of mystery and magic which surrounded her, was the idea that she was the guest and the debtor of this rough, common fellow. She, a rich, well-born, faithful child of the Church, owed her rescue from a very unpleasant predicament to this obscure, godless tradesman. If she could only pay him the heaviest interest for his loan, and had not to say 'Thank you!' And yet she had to swallow even this indignity.

Iván, after an absence of a few minutes, returned, followed by a maid carrying a tray with a steaming breakfast. She laid the cloth, and set out the cups and coffee-pot. The countess would gladly have made some excuse to avoid tasting the food presented by her ungodly host, but the abbé, who was a man of the world, drew his chair to the table, and invited Theudelinde to follow his example, "For," he said, "we shall not get anything to eat till the evening, as there are no inns on the road; and you shall want some refreshment before such a long journey."

When the countess saw that no demons seized the clergyman, and that the coffee of the Warlock seemed innocent of evil, she, too, came to the table and sipped a few spoonfuls, but she found it was execrable stuff; though the milk was not so bad, and she contented herself with that and bread.

Iván began to talk about the weather—a very general subject of conversation; but there was a difference here. Instead of an ignoramus, it was a meteorologist who discussed the subject. Iván assured the countess that both the barometer and his English glass pointed to fine weather, the sun was as warm as in May, their journey would be pleasant. As he spoke, Iván drew back the thick green curtains, and let in the kindly sunshine to enliven the sober room. The first effect of this sudden eruption of light was to show the countess her own face reflected in a large concave mirror, which hung on the opposite wall.

It is an undoubted fact that we all like to see our reflection in a glass; our eyes wander to it naturally, and the most earnest orator, in the midst of his finest peroration, will perform to a mirror suddenly shown to him with more satisfaction than to a crowded audience; but it is a totally different thing if it should be a magnifying glass. What a horrible distortion of ourselves—head large as a cask, features of a giant, the expression of a satyr; a sight too dreadful to contemplate.

"What an awful glass you have there," said the countess, peevishly, as she turned her back on the mirror.

"It is undoubtedly not a toilette mirror; it is a glass which we use in chemical experiments to test the highest degrees of heat."

Here the abbé, who wished to air his scientific knowledge, interpolated:

"As, for example, for burning a diamond."

"Just so," returned Iván. "That is one of the uses of a concave mirror; it is necessary for burning a diamond, or in the flame of a gas retort."

The countess was grateful for the abbé's remark, for it gave her a happy inspiration.

"Do you mean to tell me," she said, addressing Iván, "that a diamond is combustible?"

"Undoubtedly, for the diamond is, in fact, nothing but crystalline coal. With a high enough heat you can extract as much invisible gas or oxide of coal from the patrician diamond costing ninety florins a carat, as from a plebeian lump of coal."

"That is proved by the focus of the magnifier," remarked the abbé.

"I don't believe it," said the countess, throwing back her head.

"I am sorry," returned Iván, "that I cannot prove to you that the diamond is combustible. We do not use such costly things for mere experiment, but have splints for the purpose, which are cheap in comparison. I don't have any of these on hand, however."

"I should like to be convinced, for I do not believe it," repeated the countess. "Will you make the experiment with this?" As she spoke she unfastened a brooch from her dress, and handed it to her host. Its central stone was a fine, two-carat diamond. Theudelinde expected that Iván would return it to her saying, 'Oh, it would be a pity to use this beautiful stone,' and then she would reply, 'Then pray keep it as a slight remembrance,' and in this manner this unpleasant individual would have been paid for his service. But to her amazement, the countess found she had deceived herself.

With the indifference of a philosopher, and the courtesy of a gentleman, Iván took the brooch from her.

"I conclude you do not wish to have the brooch melted," he said quietly. "I will take the diamond out of its setting, and if it should not burn you can have it reset."

Without another word he extracted the stone with a small pair of pliers, and placed it in a flat clay saucer; then he opened the window, which lay in the full blaze of the sun. He placed the saucer on a trivet in the middle of the room, and just in front of the countess; then he took the magnifying glass and went outside, for in the room the sun's rays had not enough power to concentrate on the mirror.

The countess was now certain that the trick would not succeed, and that she would have an opportunity of offering the diamond to Iván on the pretext of repeating the experiment when the sun's rays were more powerful.

Iván, when he had found the proper spot outside the window, directed the rays from the apex of the burning glass straight into the saucer, where the diamond was awaiting the moment of its annihilation. The stone emitted a thousand sparks. As the sun's rays touched it, it threw out as many colours as are in the rainbow; it seemed as if it were to be the victor of the fight.

Then, of a sudden, the fiery rays condensed themselves in a narrower circle upon the doomed diamond, the small room was filled with a blinding light that turned everything into silver; not a shadow remained. Out of the saucer a ball of fire shot like a flash of lightning; the next minute the burning glass ceased to work.

Iván still stood outside the window. He spoke to the countess, who was transfixed with astonishment.

"What is in the saucer?" he asked.

"Nothing."

Iván returned to the room, hung the mirror in its place, and gave her brooch without its solitaire to the countess.

The abbé could not help remarking dryly, "That was a spectacle which only kings can afford to watch."

But now the postilion blew his horn, the countess put on her fur coat, and was escorted to the carriage by Iván. She was obliged to give him her hand, and to say the words, "God be with you."

When the carriage had gone a little way, she said to the abbé, "That man is a sorcerer."

But the clergyman shook his head. "He is far worse; he is a scientist."

"H'm! he is an unpleasant fellow."

Chapter X

HIGHER MATHEMATICS

The counting-house of the firm of Kaulman stands exactly where it was fifty years ago. The entrance is the same, and the very panes of glass are identical with those through which the founder of the house, in 1811, was wont to make his observations—as from an observatory—upon the faces of the passers-by, when a rise or fall in the stocks was expected. He knew that the faces of a crowd make an excellent barometer, and that much can be gleaned by observation; just as a chance word, let fall by accident, often contains the germ of much truth, and is to an experienced man prophetic to a certain extent.

The young head of the house did not set much store by the counting-house business. He had higher aims. He lived on the first floor, in luxurious bachelor chambers; his sitting-room was a museum, and his writing-table was crowded with bronzes and antiques; his inkstand was a masterpiece of Cellini's—or, perhaps, a good imitation in galvanized plaster—his pen was of agate, with a gold nib; he used gold sand for blotting; the sand-sifter was made of porphyry, the pen-holder was a branch of real coral, the paper-weight a mosaic from Pompeii, the candle-shades real crystal, the cover of the blotting-book Japanese. Every article had its own value, from the Turkish paper-knife to the paper itself, which was of all sorts and description, from the thickest vellum to the most delicate straw, perfumed with mignonette and musk. In spite of these elaborate arrangements, no one had ever been known to write at this so-called writing-desk.

The science cultivated by Felix Kaulman did not require the use of pen and ink; it was purely intellectual work. Felix worked night and day; during his sleep, even, he worked, but no trace of his labour was to be found on paper. When he amused himself, dancing, riding, or making love, he always appeared occupied by the task on hand; he was working, nevertheless, all the time. He was aiming at a certain goal he loved, and this alone aroused his interest and his real enthusiasm; he never for one moment forgot the one aim of his life. He had something more to do than to make a pen move over paper; he had to move men.

One day, not long after the events in the Castle of Bondavára, Abbé Samuel was seated in Felix Kaulman's room. They were engaged in serious conversation. Before them an elegant Sèvres set of fragrant coffee, whose fumes mingled with the Latakia, which our friend the abbé smoked from a genuine Turkish pipe. Felix only smoked cigars.

"Well, here is your agreement with the countess. As you wished, it is properly drawn up for thirty-two years. And now I should like to know of what use it can possibly be to either you or your company? It is not enough for the countess to sign it; you need the signature of the prince to make the contract useful to you, for the countess has only a life-interest in the Bondavára property. As soon as she dies, it goes to the prince, or to his grandson, and then your agreement is void."

"I know that," returned Felix, knocking the ash from his cigar, "and for this reason we must take care to keep the old girl alive. Let her have a good time, and she will live to a ripe age. It is very hard to kill an old maid, especially if she has lots of money. Besides, I am not so careless as you suppose. I have looked into the matter; I have seen the will of the old prince, and I know all its provisions. There is a clause that makes me pretty safe. When Countess Theudelinde goes off the

127

reel, either her brother or his heirs are obliged to compensate all those, whether they are tenants, householders, or creditors, who may have erected buildings on the estate. You see, the old prince considered that it would be more than probable that his crazy daughter might, in a fit of holy enthusiasm, build either a church or a convent, and he thought he would give the heirs the advantage of her generosity. It never entered into his head that any one would erect a factory, a refinery, or open a mine. Now you see how useful this clause is to me; the heirs are not likely to be in a position to refund us the two millions we are putting into the property."

"Unless they find another company to advance the money."

"That would not be so easy. First of all, the company would have to go into the very intricate affairs of the Bondavára family; then it would require immense capital, great enterprise, and a certain amount of risk. Besides, I can see as far as my neighbours. I don't sit with my hands folded, I can tell you, and I have not put all my chips on one card."

"Right! By the way, what has become of the little wild cat you carried off from the Bondavára mine?"

"I have put her in Madame Risan's school for the present; she is being educated, for she has extraordinary abilities, though in a general way she is a stupid creature. She has a splendid voice, but she cannot sing, as singing goes nowadays; she has a wonderfully expressive face, but does not know how to make use of it; she is full of feeling, and speaks no language except her mother tongue."

"Do you mean to educate her for the stage?"

"Certainly."

"And then?"

"I intend to marry her."

The abbé raised his eyebrows in some astonishment.

"I should hardly have thought," he said coldly, "that a pupil of Madame Risan's would be likely to make a satisfactory wife, although she might become an excellent actress."

Felix looked at his visitor haughtily, then shrugged his shoulders, as a way of saying that the abbé's opinion on this point did not trouble him. For a few minutes the two men smoked in silence. Then, his face clearing, suddenly Kaulman said, in his blandest manner:

"I want to ask you a question. You know the ins and outs of marriage laws. Is there any way for a marriage to be set aside, without having recourse to the Divorce Court? Divorce always means a lot of expense and a good deal of scandal; and if the other side should be obstinate and malicious, it can drag out interminably."

"I know of only one other method. We will suppose that you are already married according to the rules of the Church in this country. You wish for some reason to dissolve this marriage. Well, you have only to go to Paris, and take up your residence in the banking house your firm has there. Your father was a French subject, and so are you. According to the French law, no marriage is valid that is not solemnized before the civil authorities; therefore the remedy would be in your hands. A short time ago the matter was tried by the French courts. A certain count had married in Spain; the eldest son of this marriage sought to recover his birthright which had been forfeit in consequence of his father's having neglected to be remarried before the registrar in France. The court, however, pronounced the Spanish marriage invalid, and yours would be a similar case."

Felix got up from his seat. "I thank you," he said, "more than I can say. If the recollection of the friendship of our youth didn't remind me that I shall always owe you my *love*, I should certainly feel that I am immensely indebted to you now."

"For what?" returned the abbé, lifting his eyes in some surprise. "It is well for you to remind me of our young days. Was I not then your father's debtor? What did he not do for me? He found me a miserable, over-worked, ill-paid student. He made me your tutor, and so opened my road to better things.

Oh, I can never forget! But let us not talk any more of the past."

"No, for the future is before us, and we shall work together. Now I must ask you, as the countess's representative, to sign the necessary papers. This is the contract, and here is the cheque for the first half-year's rent, and here is another draft on my cashier for the sum of forty thousand florins."

"To whom is this payable?"

Felix answered by pressing the cheque into the abbé's hand, while he whispered in his ear:

"To the fortunate go-between."

The other shook his head with a wounded look. "You mean to offer *me* a present?"

"You do not understand," returned Felix. "This money does not come from me; it forms part of the expenses of the company, and in all such undertakings figures under the head of 'necessary expenses.'"

As he spoke, Felix lit another cigar, and looked slyly at his companion, as if to say, 'You see what a capital fellow I am!' A contemptuous smile flickered round Abbé Samuel's mouth as he tore the cheque for forty thousand florins into four pieces. He laid his hand upon the banker's shoulder.

"My dear boy," he said, "I had the whole Bondavára property in the hollow of my hand; it was mine to do as I chose. I did with it as I do with these pieces of papers." He threw the torn cheque into the grate. "Understand me, once and for all. I am not a begging monk. I am a candidate for high honours; I will not be content with a tithe; I am looking for a kingdom."

The haughty air with which the abbé said these words impressed the banker so much that he laid down his cigar, and stared at his visitor.

"That is a great word," he said slowly.

"Sit down and listen to what I shall tell you," returned the priest, who, with his hands behind his back, now began to walk up and down the room, pausing from time to time before his admiring listener.

"The whole world is in labour," he said, "and brings forth nothing but mice. And why? Because the lions will not come into the world. Chaos rules everywhere—in finance, in diplomacy, in the Church. One man who would have enough brains to see clearly could be master of the situation. But where is he to be found? Fools in motley coats are the leaders; we see a country governed by incapables, who do not even know how to begin. They would force it to submit, but they are afraid to use the necessary means. They oppress it, and at the same time live in dread of what it may do. And this same country does not itself know what to-morrow may bring, whether it shall submit, pay the demands of its oppressors, or call to arms against their tyranny; neither does it know who is its foe, who is its friend, with whom to ally itself, against whom to fight; whether it will go on submitting, whether it shall break out into curses, or wild laughter, at its own follies. The country still possesses one element, which stands, as it were, neutral between the two parties. This element is the clerical; the Church is a power in Hungary."

Felix's face grew darker; he could not imagine where all this would lead. But the abbé had now paused, and was standing before him.

"What do you think, my son," he said, "would be the reward due to the man who could find a way out of this mass of confusion, who could unite the classes, and bring them into conformity with the wishes of the Government? Do you not think that there is anything which would better further your Bondavára speculation than a submissive deputation of priests and people, who would give a promise of fidelity to the Ministry? One hand washes the other; he who brings about such an unlooked-for condition of affairs would be rewarded. Now, do you understand what use this would be to you?"

"I think I begin to see."

131

"And what office do you think should be offered to the man who brings the peasant's smocks into subjection, and elevates the mitre?"

Felix clasped his hands together. That was his answer. The clergyman resumed his walk up and down the room; his lips were compressed, his head in the air.

"The primate is an old man," he said suddenly.

Felix leaned back in his chair. In this position he could see better the various expressions which passed over the abbé's face. He started when the abbé murmured, almost under his breath:

"The pope is older still."

There was a moment's silence, and then the abbé continued, speaking fast and with excitement:

"Dwarfs are at the rudder, my son; dwarfs who believe that their efforts will avert the storm. The Church is in danger of going to pieces, and they make use of the old, outworn supports. Listen to my words. All the efforts of Rome are fruitless; it tries to maintain its dignity with Peter's pence, and has allowed millions to slip through its fingers. Only here in Hungary has the Church any real property left. I know well that in the Minister's drawer there is a Bill prepared which only needs the signature of the State to become law; it only requires a slight pretext, and Vienna will declare war against the power of the clergy in Hungary. Vienna will fight for the liberal principle, and those who oppose will be the unpopular, the losing side. It is only a question of time. The national debt grows daily, the Government is in a fix, the treasury is empty, a loan is impossible. Hence a fight over the budget; or a trifling war somewhere. You know the proverb, 'When the devil is hungry he eats flies.' The clerical property in Hungary is the fly, and Austria will make one bite at it. The Chair of St. Peter and Church property in Hungary are both in danger. How is the danger to be averted? Let us put our shoulders to the wheel; let us be more patriotic than the democrats, more loyal than the prime minister, more liberal than the revolutionists; let us save

132

the Church property from the Government, and the Church itself from the revolution. Let us throw a gigantic loan of a hundred millions into the market upon the property of the Hungarian Church, for the rescue of the throne of St. Peter. What do you now think of the man who could do this thing? What should be his reward?"

"Everything," stammered Felix, his mind confused by this bewildering, yet fascinating, programme.

"I have destined you for this great work," said the abbé, with a solemn, majestic air. "Your Bondavára speculation is necessary, for with it you can make a *coup* which shall bring you world-wide reputation, your name shall be on a par with that of the Strousbergs, the Pereiras, with that of Rothschild itself. This is the reason why I have given you my support. When you are firmly established, then I shall say to you, 'Lend me your shoulder,' upon which I shall climb where I will."

After this Felix sank into a waking dream. Before his eyes gleamed the gigantic loan, and through a golden mist he saw the tall form of his friend glorified.

Chapter XI

SOIRÉES AMALGAMANTES

One winter's morning Iván Berend, to his great astonishment, received a letter from the president of the Hungarian Academy of Science, telling him that the members of the physical, scientific, and mathematical departments had in the last general assembly chosen him as an honorary member and before being elected as a member of the Academy itself, he should, in conformity to the established custom, address the assembly.

Iván was struck by amazement. By what means did this honour come his way? He, who had never written a scientific paper in any periodical; who had no associates or friends in the academical assembly, who was not an aristocrat, and had played no part in political life. He was puzzled; he could not conceive who could have put his name forward. Could it have been, he thought, that in some way his chemical researches had reached their ears? In that case, he told himself, every director of a mine, every manager of a factory, would be considered a scientist and made member of the Academy, for everyone of them possessed as much knowledge as he did. But it seemed useless to think about it too much; the honour had been bestowed on him, and should be accepted. So he wrote to the secretary expressing his gratitude for the unlooked-for honour conferred upon him, and saying that he would present himself in Pest, towards the end of the year, and read to the illustrious assembly his inaugural address. Then he thought about the subject of this address long and carefully, and spent much of his time working it out. It was an account of microscopical crustations, the study of which he had followed closely during the boring of artesian wells, and which he had perfectly mastered during ten years. It took him until late in the autumn to complete his essay.

In places where such scientific research is valued at its proper merit, his paper would have been appreciated, and might have caused even a sensation; but we are bound in honesty to confess that it did not do so in Pest, and that during the sixty minutes allowed by the canon-law of all institutions for such lectures, the microscopical crustations produced an amount of yawning unprecedented even amongst academicians.

After the reading was over, the very first person to greet the neophyte and offer his congratulations was the Abbé Samuel, and then enlightenment suddenly burst upon Iván. He saw now who it was who had discovered his talents, and who had been his patron. It was something of a knock to his vanity; well, it didn't matter. The abbé was doubtless as learned as any one in the assembly, and he owed him his thanks. Little attentions, it is said, consolidate friendship.

Iván decided to spend some days in Pest; he had business to do. During the week several papers noticed his academical address; the most merciful was one which announced he had given an interesting lecture upon the 'Volcanic Origin of the Stalactites.' Iván's only consolation was that in his own country no one read these reports, and that abroad no one understood them, being written in Hungarian. He was wrong, however; some one did read it—but more of this later. One day, as Iván was making his preparations for his journey home, he received from the Countess Theudelinde Bondaváry an invitation card to a *soirée*, to be held in three days' time.

'Aha!' thought Iván, 'another thanks-offering; it is well that it did not come sooner.'

He sat down to his writing-table, and answered the invitation in the most courteous manner, regretting his inability to avail himself of it on account of his immediate departure. He was in the act of sealing the letter when the door opened, and the Abbé Samuel was announced. Iván expressed his pleasure at receiving so distinguished a visitor.

"I could not let you leave Pest without coming," answered the abbé, in his most friendly manner. "I came, not only because I was indebted for your kind assistance at Bondavára, but also because I felt it a necessity to tell you what an honour I count the acquaintance of such a distinguished scholar as you have proved yourself to be."

Iván felt inclined to say that he was neither distinguished nor a scholar; however, he remained silent.

"I trust," continued the abbé, seating himself on the sofa, "that you intend to make a long stay in Pest?"

"I am leaving to-morrow," replied Ivan dryly.

"Oh, impossible! We cannot lose you so soon. I imagine you have a card for the Countess Theudelinde's next *soirée*?"

"I regret that I am prevented from accepting her kind invitation; I have pressing business which necessitates my return."

The abbé laughed. "Confess honestly," he said, "that if you had no other reason to return home, you would run away from an entertainment which would bore you infinitely."

"Well, if you must have the truth, I do confess that a *soirée* would be something of a penance to me."

"These *soirées*, however, are on a different footing from those *réunions* which, I agree with you, are more pain than pleasure, and where a stranger feels 'out of it,' as the saying goes. Countess Theudelinde aims at having a 'salon,' and succeeds admirably. She receives all the best people. I don't mean only the upper ten thousand, but the best in the true sense, the best that Pest affords in art, in literature, in science; the aristocracy of birth, talent, and beauty."

Iván shook his head incredulously. "And how can such a mixed gathering work?"

The abbé did not reply at once; he scratched his nose thoughtfully.

"Until they get to know one another, it is, perhaps, a little stiff. But with intelligent people this stiffness must soon disappear, and each one will do something to keep the ball rolling. You have an excellent style of address; I noticed it the night of your lecture. You could easily find a subject on which to lecture which would interest your listeners by its novelty, surprise them by its profundity, and amuse them by its variety; their intellect and their imagination would be equally engaged."

It was Iván's turn to laugh, which he did loudly. "My good sir, such a subject is unknown to me. I confess my ignorance; neither in print nor in manuscript have I met with it."

The clergyman joined in the laugh.

At this moment a servant brought Iván a letter, which claimed instant attention, so that a receipt might be given to the messenger who waited for it. Iván begged his guest to excuse him while he opened this urgent dispatch. The abbé agreed with a wave of his hand.

As Iván read the letter a remarkable change passed over his face; he grew suddenly pale, his eyebrows contracted, then a sudden rush of colour came into his cheeks. He held the letter before him, read it several times, while his eyes held a wild stare, as if he had seen a ghost. Then all at once he started to laugh. He thrust the letter into his pocket, and returned to the subject under discussion.

"Very well then," he said, laughing, "I shall go to Countess Theudelinde's *soirée*, and I shall give a lecture to her guests such as they have never heard before—that I promise you. Science and poetry, imagination and learning mixed together, with dates and genealogy, so that the *savants* present will not know what to think; I shall give a lecture which will make every geologist a prince, and every princess a geologist. Do you follow me?"

"Perfectly," returned the other; not, indeed, that he saw

what Iván meant, but he wished to encourage him. "That will be the very thing—first rate!"

"What do you say to illustrations by means of an electric —magnetic machine, eh?"

"A capital idea; very amusing. My dear friend, you will have a *succès*."

"May I ask you to convey to the countess my acceptance of her invitation? I shall require a large apparatus."

"I can assure you in advance that the countess will be charmed at your kind offer. As for the apparatus and arrangement, leave that to her; she will be overjoyed when she hears that she can expect you."

The abbé then took his leave, fully contented with his visit. Iván read his letter again, and again, and sat staring into space, as if he had seen a ghost.

People were saying the countess Theudelinde's *Soirées Amalgamantes* would make history. The mixture was excellent; grandees rubbed elbows with poets; academicians with prelates; musicians, painters, sculptors, actors, critics, professors, physicians, editors, sportsmen, and politicians of all shades were gathered under one roof. It was a bold experiment, a brilliant society *in thesi*. Neither was the element of female attraction wanting; all that Pest held of beauty, charm, and grace lent its aid to the idea of amalgamation.

Count Stephen, the uncle of countess Theudelinde, was a great help to her *soirées*, for he was a well-informed and cultivated man, able to talk on all subjects, and especially on the poetry of the world. As for the countess Angela, she was a classical beauty; her grandfather was a political celebrity—a great man, who had a following of all sorts, both bad and good. It was, therefore, quite in the usual manner of society, that when an unfortunate outsider was presented to countess Angela, he should, after the third word or so, mention her illustrious grandfather, Prince Theobald of Bondavára, and inquire after his health. After this question, however, countess Angela never addressed another word to the stranger. She allowed him to speak if he wished, or to retire in confusion. Even the most dried-up specimen in the world of learning felt ill-used by this. His heart could not resist the glance of those heavenly eyes, so sweet and friendly, at first, now cold and haughty. And yet what had he done? The poor man will probably never know; he is not in the inner circle of the Polite World.

Countess Angela was indeed a perfect, ideal beauty; this cannot be repeated too often. A pure, noble face, with classical, well-proportioned features, nose and lips finely shaped, long straight eyebrows, and lashes veiling the eyes of a goddess. When these eyes glowed, or when they were half closed under their downy lids, they looked black, but when they laughed at you, you would swear they were blue. Her hair was rich, of that most lovely of all shades, chestnut brown; her whole countenance betrayed that she knew herself to be charming, that she was aware that she was the centre, at all times, of admiration, and that this knowledge pleased her. And why not? A woman must be very silly not to be aware that beauty is a gift and a power.

But what was the reason of her cold looks at the mention of her grandfather's name? Just what one might expect from a woman with her beauty. All the world—that is, her world—knew that she and her grandfather, Prince Theobald of Bonda-vára, were at daggers drawn. The wily old politician had promised his only and beautiful grand-daughter to a German, Prince Sondersheim. She was to consolidate some political matter, only she didn't see it in that light, and refused to ratify the bargain, not caring for Sondersheim; and for that matter, he cared as little for her. But then, it didn't mean so much to him. Angela had an ideal of married life, however, and so she quarrelled with her grandfather because he pooh-poohed her ideals, and called them romantic folly. Upon this, she vowed she would never speak to him again, and he, in his anger, told her to leave his house, which she did at once, and came to her aunt Theudelinde, who had just set up house in Pest, and was glad to have such a bright and beautiful niece. Since then, Angela had refused all communication with her grandfather. This was why she would not even hear his name mentioned; and it never was, except by ignorant outsiders, or 'know-nothings,' as the Yankees call them.

Abbé Samuel had enough wit to see that the *Soirées Amalgamantes* were not the success they should be. Conversation did not suffice; amalgamation was at a standstill. The young girls sat in one room, the married women in another; the men, herded together, looked glum, but not as bored as the women. Then the abbé, considering what ought to be done, had a happy idea. He introduced dramatic representations, readings, and concerts, all of which were a decided success. Soon conversation became lively, strangers got to know one another; when they rehearsed duets and little plays together, their stiffness wore off. The women seemed different in day dress, free from the restraints of the 'grande toilette'; they grew quite friendly, and later on they found subjects upon which they could chat at their ease. It must be confessed, however, that after midnight, when the reading, the concert, or the representation was over, and the outsiders had gone home to their beds, society began to enjoy itself. The young people danced, the old played whist or tarok, and they stayed till day-break. They would have done the same had the scientists, the poets, the artists stayed among them; they didn't want them to leave, but, naturally, those people felt out of it, and besides, they were not trained to stay up all night like the aristocracy, so they went home very properly; they knew their place.

Abbé Samuel knew well how to manage these things. Whenever the countess was to have a particularly good party, he took care that it should get talked about, and the names of the performers, their parentage and history, together with any interesting circumstance, true or false, should be the town's topics of conversation for days before. In this way he sent round Iván

Berend's name with a great many details as to his interesting life in the mines, his extraordinary cleverness, and the wonderful lecture he was going to give at the countess's next *soirée*.

The abbé knew his world, and how to whet its curiosity by exaggerated reports.

"Is it true that for just one experiment he burned a diamond belonging to countess Theudelinde, which was worth eight hundred florins?"

"The stone weighed four carats, and was worth fifteen hundred pounds."

"We must give him a good reception. See, here he comes, escorted by Abbé Samuel."

The gentleman who spoke last, was countess Angela's cousin, Count Edmund, a handsome young man of about twenty-two. He hurried to meet Iván and the abbé as they entered the door, and introduced himself as nephew to the lady of the house. He took Iván by the arm in the most friendly manner, and led him to Count Stephen, the countess's uncle. The count was a man of intelligence and wide reading; he assured Iván that many in the room were extremely interested in hearing his lecture. After this he was presented by his new friend to several distinguished-looking persons with decorations, who all pressed his hand, and spoke in the most friendly manner. The beginning of the evening was its most agreeable part. The abbé and Iván finally made their way into the next room, where the ladies were assembled, and here they found the countess Theudelinde, who received them, and Iván in particular, most graciously. The young man, Count Edmund, again took hold of him, and, laughing and talking, led him up to the countess Angela, to whom he was introduced with a great flourish. Iván bowed before the lovely vision, feeling somewhat stunned, though not shy or awkward.

"You come very seldom to Pest," said the young countess, with a reassuring smile.

"It is some time since I have been here; but I understand this is your first visit, countess. You have never lived in Pest?"

Angela's face assumed its cold expression; she felt sure he was going to inquire for Prince Theobald.

"I do not see," she said in a sarcastic voice, "of what concern it is to any one whether I have ever been to Pest."

"It is not an uncommon accident," returned Iván quietly, "that a man visits a place where he has never been before; but when many people meet in the same spot, it looks as if there was something more than accident in such a gathering, and in this instance, where so many brilliant personages are brought together, it seems as if Providence had more to do with it than mere chance."

At these words Angela's face cleared. "Then you believe in Providence? You acknowledge there is such a thing as divine ordinance?"

"Undoubtedly, I do believe it."

"Then we shall be friends." She turned away as she spoke, and Iván took this gesture as a sign to withdraw.

After another quarter of an hour's waiting, Edmund came to tell him that everything was ready in the lecture-room, and the company had already gathered there. So Iván ascended the rostrum which had been erected at the far end of a large room, and holding his papers in his hand, addressed his audience. He had a pleasant voice, his manner of address was perfectly unaffected, composed, and winning. From the first moment he held the attention of his audience—his subject was *Magnetism*.

Chapter XII

RITTER MAGNET

When the lecture had concluded, the lights were carried out of the room, and only the candles in the lustre were left alight. Iván then exhibited to the astonished spectators an electric flame. Many of them had never seen such a clear, beautiful light as this ball of virgin-like purity. It looked like a heavenly planet; as if Venus had descended from her place in the firmament, and was shining on the company. The candles in the lustre burned blue, and threw shadows on the wall. Every face lost all trace of colour from the effect of this strange illumination; people whispered to one another, almost frightened. Iván, standing upon the platform, looked like some magician of old, his features chiselled like a statue, his eyes in deep shadow; and what added considerably to the picturesque effect, and heightened the charm of this noble assembly, was the strange colouring given by the light to the splendid national costumes worn by the company, and the enamelled appearance of the jewels on the ladies' necks and arms.

The eyes of every one were directed to two persons, while an involuntary 'Ah!' was whispered about at the extraordinary transformation produced in their appearance. One was countess Angela. The light seemed to have taken from her face that look of pride and self-satisfaction which, although natural in one so beautiful, gave a hard expression to her face, and somewhat marred its beauty. Now she looked like a heavenly vision, with the expression of a glorified spirit who had done with earthly matters and soaring towards her true home in heaven; all earthly passions, joy, sorrow, love, and pride, had vanished. Such was the miraculous effect of the magic light. The other transformation was countess Theudelinde. She was seated in an armchair. The magic light touched her face gently, and gave it a fairy-like expression; the noble features were lightened, her naturally pale colouring became transparent, the diamonds in her magnificent tiara sparkled above her forehead as a garland of stars; she was sublime, and, for five minutes, the loveliest amongst the lovely. It had been many a long year since her mirror had last told her she was beautiful. But round the hall, there were large pier-glasses set into the wainscoting, which reflected the company. Theudelinde, therefore, could see her beautified self reflected in full. She sighed as she thought, 'I look like Queen Mab.'

Suddenly the miraculous light went out, and the room, lit only by candles, fell into darkness by contrast. 'Ah!' was echoed in sorrowful tones through the assembly; people rubbed their eyes, and recognized familiar faces once more. Alas! it was over too soon. There were no more angels, fairies, queens, or heroes; only a group of excellent everyday people, counts and countesses. The face of Angela again wore its proud, vain expression, and Theudelinde was once more pale and stiff.

Iván descended from his platform, and received the company's congratulations and compliments. Some opinions differed, of course, but they were held in private. Every one joined in praising the lecturer to his face.

Iván thanked every one for their approval, but in a cold, reticent manner, and soon disengaged himself from his admirers to go in search of his hostess; he wished to thank her for her kindness.

Theudelinde received him with smiles. Countess Angela was with her, leaning on the back of her aunt's chair. The young girl had just said:

"You looked, auntie, quite lovely—a perfect Queen Mab."

The smile these words had called to Theudelinde's face still lingered round her lips when Iván presented himself. She was indebted to this man for her five minutes of beauty, and was not ungrateful. She gave him her hand, and thanked him in the most gracious manner for the enjoyment he had given her.

"I owe you something," returned Iván. "When you honoured my house with a visit, you gave me a diamond which you allowed me to burn before your eyes. In return for your goodness on that occasion, I give you this diamond which was created before your eyes." With these words he handed her a piece of carbon, which he had removed from the Voltaic pillar, used with his talk.

"As I explained to you in my lecture, coal can be changed by electricity into a diamond, and in this condition can cut glass."

"Ah!" cried countess Angela, her eyes beaming with pleasure, "let us try the experiment now. Where is a glass? Yes, one of the pier-glasses. Come."

Countess Theudelinde was also excited. She stood up, and went with the others to the mirror.

"Write one of the letters of the alphabet," said Angela, watching Iván. She was curious to see the letter he would choose. If he were vain, as very likely he was, he would write his own initial 'I'; if a toady and flatterer, like most people round her aunt, he would choose 'T'; and if he were a silly fool, like so many men, he would write 'A'. In any of these cases he would have seen a scornful smile on the beauty's face.

Iván took the piece of coal, and with its point wrote on the mirror the letter 'X.' Both ladies expressed their astonishment at seeing the coal write, and countess Theudelinde assured Iván it should be preserved carefully, with her other jewels.

Countess Angela stood so near Iván that the folds of her dress touched him.

"I believe," she said slowly, "every word you told us. I beg of you, do not tell me that all your romantic descriptions were but the necessary clothing of a dry scientific subject, meant to make it palatable to your silly, ignorant audience, and to raise in their minds a wish to search further, so that they might in so seeking acquire a taste for knowledge. I do not want to seek, I believe implicitly all you said; but of this world of wonder and miracles I would like to know more. How far does it go? What more do you see? For the magician must know everything."

As she spoke, the young countess looked into Iván's eyes with a strange magnetic power impossible to resist. Such a look had many times dazzled men's brains.

"You said, also," continued Angela, "how fiery and strong are those who live in this magnetic kingdom, but that they have no credit for the virtues they possess; it is due to the working of magnetism. I believe this also. Magnetism has, however, two poles, the north and the south pole. I have read that the opposite poles are drawn to one another, and the homogeneous drift asunder. If, therefore, in the magnetic kingdom hearts are drawn to one another, seek one another, love one another, which is an immutable fact, so also is it an immutable fact that there must be human beings who hate one another with an undying, a deadly hatred, and that such hatred is no sin. Am I not right?"

Iván felt himself cornered; he understood the drift of the countess's question. Here his knowledge of natural philosophy came to his assistance.

"It is true," he said, "that as far as life upon the earth is in question, there must also exist antipathies and sympathies. You have studied magnetism, you have read of the poles, therefore you must know that there exists an equator, or line, which is neither north nor south. This is the magnetic equator, that neither draws the magnet nor repulses it, and here there is an equilibrium, a perfect peace. Just such an equator is found in every human heart, and however a man may be carried away

146

by the passions of love or hatred, his line remains unchange-able, and those who live there dwell in peace."

"And who are the people who live under the magnetic equator?" asked the countess, with curiosity.

"For example, parents and their children should dwell there."

The young girl's face was covered with a vivid blush; her beautiful eyes shot a volley of lightning glances at Iván, who remained quite unmoved under their battery.

"We must talk more of this," she said, with sudden dignity.

Iván bowed before the haughty beauty who turned and left him.

Meanwhile, the lecture being over, a rush had been made for the refreshments. The army of outsiders were the first in the field. If they were of little account elsewhere, they took first place at the buffet, and here the citizen showed his origin distinctly.

Iván mixed with the company, and conducted himself as one accustomed to such society, and quite at ease in it, and he was well received. The men were very civil towards him; he was made one of themselves. It didn't matter much, as he was said to be leaving Pest the next day, and would be lost in the depths of Mesopotamia. Some one said he came from Africa. They tried teasing him a bit, all in a friendly way, and were pleased to find that this pedant, an excellent fellow, who took a joke in good part, laughed heartily at a well-delivered thrust, and returned it with a sly hit, which never offended anyone's feel-ings.

"He is one of us," they said. "This man is up to things; he is a capital fellow. We must give him a good time."

"Is it true that you don't drink wine?" asked the Marquis Salista of Iván.

"Once a year."

"And is to-day not the anniversary?"

"No."

"Then we have drunk enough for one year; let us move on."

Some of the men returned to the drawing-room; these were, for the most part, the young fellows, and those who wished to dance. The ladies, after their tea, had begun to play the piano; quadrilles, and even the *csárdás* for those who liked it.

Count Stephen, however, drew apart the better portion of the men to his quarters, on the second storey of the countess's house. Here he entertained in his own way. His rooms being on the other side of the house, no noise penetrated to the floors below, which was necessary, as the count's champagne was of the very best, and given unstintingly; it flowed, in fact.

Iván, who was one of the party, showed himself in a new light; he drank wine; his toasts were spicy, his anecdotes fresh and amusing, his wit sharp and unrestrained; and although he drank freely, he showed no effects: he was quite steady.

"Brother," hiccuped Count Géza, who was half drunk towards two o'clock, "the captain and I have agreed that when you are quite done up we shall carry you home, and put you to bed; but, my dear friend, my dear Ritter Magnet, the misery is that I don't think I can get up the stairs; I am quite done for. So take your wings and fly, and let the captain take his, and both of you fly home. As for me—" Here the count lay down on the sofa and fell asleep.

Everyone laughed; but the name he had given Iván—Ritter Magnet—stuck.

"Do you care to play cards, my learned friend?" said the Marquis Salista.

"Once every three years."

"That is not often enough."

The marquis could not at this moment explain why it was not often enough, for at this moment Count Stephen informed his guests that it was time for them to depart, as the ball downstairs had broken up, and every one had left. The countess's rest, therefore, might be disturbed by any overhead noise. Every one agreed that this was quite proper.

"Only," said Salista, "there is no need for us to go home. Let us have the card-table. Let us spend our time well. Who is for a game?"

Three players soon presented themselves; Baron Oscar was one of the first. But the fourth? The marquis called to Iván.

"Now, my learned friend."

Count Stephen thought it necessary to inform the stranger, who was his guest, that at the tarok-table the stakes were very high.

"Only a kreuzer the point," said the marquis.

"Yes, but kreuzer points in such a game often amount to seven or eight hundred florins for a loser. These gentlemen have changed a simple game into a hazardous venture."

Iván laughed. "Every day of my life I play hazard against nature itself; every day I speculate all I have on a mere chance, and play only one card," and he rolled his chair to the green table.

The game begun. The game of hazard, as it is generally played, is a game of chance, it needs only luck and boldness; a drunk can almost win by sheer accident. But as it is played in Pest, it is something quite different; what is called luck, chance, accident, is here allied to skill, prudence, consideration, and boldness. The tarok-player must not only study his cards, but also the faces of his adversaries. He must be Lavater and Tartuffe in one; he must be a general who develops at every moment a fresh plan of campaign, and a Bosco who can, from the first card that is played, divine the whole situation; he must, moreover, be generous, and sacrifice himself for the sake of the general good. Therefore the spectators pitied Iván when he sat down to the card-table to play with these three masters of the game.

It was seven o'clock when the players rose from the card-table. As Iván pushed back his chair, the marquis said:

"Well, comrade, it is a good thing for the world at large that you only drink once a year and play cards once in three

149

years, for if you did both every day there would be no more wine in Stephen's cellar, or gold left in Rothschild's bank."

Iván had, in truth, stripped the three noblemen.

"Nevertheless, we must have a parting cup," continued Salista. "Where is the absinthe?" As he spoke, he filled two large glasses with the green, sparkling spirit, of which moderate people, possibly regretting their prudence, never drink more than a liqueur-glass.

Count Stephen shook his head over what he considered a bad joke, but Iván did not shrink from the challenge; he clinked his glass with that of the marquis, and emptied it without drawing breath. Then, with his most courteous bow, he took leave of his host, Count Stephen, who assured him it would always be a pleasure to receive so delightful a guest.

As Iván made his way into the ante-room, his step was steady, his air composed. Not so the marquis; the dose had been too potent for him. He insisted on claiming Iván's astrakhan cap as his, and, as there was no use arguing the matter with a drunk, Iván had to go home in the military helmet of a hussar officer. On the staircase the captain maintained that he could fly; that he was one of the inhabitants of the magnetic kingdom, and had wings. The others had all the trouble in the world to get him down the stairs. When he came to the first floor, he thought of paying the countess Theudelinde a visit, to thank her for her kind reception of his lecture, for he was the lecturer, and he was ready to blow out the brains of any one who contradicted him. He was got with great difficulty into a cab, and was driven to his hotel. When he got there he had to be carried to his bed, where he lay in a deep sleep until late in the following day.

Meantime, Iván, after a short rest, went about as usual, wrote his letters, and paid some visits.

"He carries his liquor like a man," said Count Stephen. And from this time all the world called him the Knight of the Magnet, or Ritter Magnet.

The Knight was to be met everywhere. He had numerous visitors; he was invited to the best houses. He was elected honorary member of the Club; he had been introduced by the abbé. The Club had three kinds of members—the day grubs, the evening moths and the night birds. In the daytime the library, where there was an excellent collection of rare books, was visited by all the *littérateurs* of Pest. From six to eight came the lawyers and the politicians to play whist and talk politics, and from eight until midnight, the men of fashion had their innings. In this way two men might go every day to the Club and never meet one another.

Iván first ransacked the library; then he distributed his time equally. He gave no more thought to returning home. He enjoyed everything and went everywhere, never missing to pay a visit to Countess Theudelinde's box during the opera nights.

In the second week of his stay the countess gave her ball. Iván was invited, and went.

"Shall you dance?" asked Salista.

"I haven't done so for fifteen years."

"It suits men of our years to look on," remarked the marquis, languidly. "No man dances now after two and thirty."

Looking on was pleasant enough. The nameless grace and wonderful agility displayed by the aristocratic, fashionable women was a sight for gods to admire. Countess Angela was surpassing fair to-night. She wore a rose-coloured dress, with a bodice all studded with pearls, in the Hungarian fashion; the sleeves were of lace. She had taken a fancy to dress her hair like peasant girls, in two long tresses plaited with ribbons; it suited her to perfection. But men get tired of everything, even of a sight fit for the gods. After supper one said to the other:

"Let us make use of our time; the young fellows can dance; let us play tarok."

Iván played cards every day. He played most games well; he never argued with his partners. He could lose with good grace, and when he won he was not elated. When he held bad cards he showed no ill temper, and seldom made a mistake. He was looked upon as an acquisition, and for a *savant* he was really a useful man. On this evening he was in exceptionally good luck.

Suddenly Count Edmund came into the card-room in a violent hurry. He said to Iván:

"Throw down your cards. Angela wishes to dance a turn of the Hungarian cotillon with you."

Hungarian cotillon! Strange times, that we should have a Hungarian court, a Hungarian ministry, Hungarian silver and gold coins. That is nothing wonderful; it is only natural, it is fate, and our proper due. But the Hungarian cotillon belongs to the days of revolution. We dance it to the music for the *csárdás*.

Iván obeyed Angela's command. When he came, he bowed low before her.

"You wouldn't have troubled yourself to come near me, if I had not sent for you," she said, in a tone of gentle reproach.

"One doesn't intrude into the presence of a queen, one waits to be summoned."

"Don't try to flatter me; if you do, like others, I shall treat you like them and not speak a word to you. I much prefer your own way, although you are always insulting me."

"I do not remember ever having offended you."

"Because you do nothing else. You know that very well."

Their turn came; they joined the waltzers, and no one would have guessed that it was fifteen years since Iván had last danced.

Meanwhile, in the card-room this new whim of the young countess raised more gossip. Count Edmund, as he shuffled his cards, declared his cousin Angela was bewitched by this Ritter Magnet.

"Ah, is that so?" cried the Marquis Salista.

"Don't you believe him," interrupted Count Stephen. "I know our pretty Angela; she is as full of mischief as a kitten. As soon as she notices that a man has a hobby-horse, she makes him

152

mount and put it through all its paces, caracoling, leaping, *haute école*. This is her trick: once she knows what subject interests a man, she talks of it with such a serious face, such sympathetic eyes; but when he goes away, charmed by her intelligence, and her sweetness, she ridicules the unfortunate devil. This is the way she treated poor Sondersheim, a very brave young fellow, whose only one fault was that he worshipped Angela, and she abhors him. She laughs at everybody."

"That is true; but she praises Iván, not to his face, but behind his back to me, and not because he is a man of science, a geologist, but because he is such a brave man."

"That is another of her tricks; the artful little puss knows full well that the praise which comes at third-hand is the sweetest of all flattery."

"I shall take good care not to repeat a single word to Iván."

"There you show him real friendship," remarked Salista, laughing.

In the ball-room the dancers had returned to their places.

"You were ready to leave Pest," Angela was saying, with a charming pout. "You needn't deny it; the abbé told me."

"Since then, circumstances have detained me longer than I expected," returned Iván, coolly.

"Have you got a family at home?"

"I have no one in the world."

"And why have you not?"

This was a searching question.

"Perhaps you already know what my business is. I have a colliery; I work with the miners, and spend the day under the ground."

"Ah! that explains everything," said Angela, looking at him with tender sympathy. "Now I understand: you are right indeed. It would be unforgivable to condemn a woman to the sufferings a miner's wife must endure. What can be more terrible than to take leave of her husband each morning, not knowing whether they will ever meet again? To know he is in the depths of the

153

earth while she breathes the fresh air of heaven; to fancy that her beloved is perhaps buried alive, and she cannot hear his cries for help; that even if it is not so, that he is surrounded by a deadly atmosphere, that it only needs a spark to become a hell, in which her darling would be lost to her for ever. I can understand that a woman's heart would break under such a daily agony; even to her child she would say, 'Do not run so fast; for a stone may fall on your father's head and kill him.' "

Then, with a sudden change of expression, Angela turned angrily to Iván. "But why do you stay down in the mine like a common miner?"

"Because it is my element, as the battlefield is the soldier's, the sea the sailor's, or the desert belongs to the explorer. It is a passion with me, as it is with them. I love the mysterious darkness of the underground world."

The warmth with which Iván spoke these words kindled enthusiasm in his listener.

"Every passion is absorbing," she said, "especially the passion for creation and for destruction. I understand how a woman would follow a man she loved, not only to the field, but into the battle itself, although the art of war has now become a very prosaic and second-class affair, and has lost every trace of chivalry. I must confess, however, that the heroism of the miner is incomprehensible to me. A man who busies himself with dead, cold stones is like Prince Badrul-Buder in the Arabian Nights, who was turned to stone, and whose wife preferred a living slave to her marble husband. I prefer those who penetrate to unknown regions of the globe, and I envy the wife of Sir Samuel Baker, who had travelled by his side all through the deserts of Central Africa, holding a pistol in one hand, while the other hand clasped that of her husband. Together they suffered the burning heat, together repulsed wild beasts; they appeared before Negro chieftains hand in hand, and what the arm of the husband failed to procure was given to the charms of the wife. I can place myself in the position of this woman, who, alone and deserted in the Mangave wood, sat through the lifelong night with the head of the wounded traveller on her lap, and a loaded pistol beside her. To heal his wounds, she ventured into the woods and found herbs; she contrived to cook his food in the desert. She did this for the only man she loved, whose only love she is, and has ever been. Her name is known and revered in every place where Europeans have penetrated."

Again they had to join the circle of dancers, and when they returned to their place Angela resumed the conversation:

"What I said just now was sheer nonsense; the whole thing was the outcome of despicable vanity. A miserable idea to travel through countries where a woman is hardly to be distinguished from a beast, and that because she walks upright; where the ideal of beauty is to have the upper lip bored into a big hole, so that the nose is visible when laughing—ridiculous! And then to be proud because she was the most beautiful woman, and her husband perforce was faithful to her. A great thing, indeed, to be the queen of beauty amidst monsters of ugliness! No, no; I know of something better, far bolder. A woman, Fräulein Christiany, has accomplished a journey on horseback alone all across the steppes of Asia. What if a man and a woman had the courage to penetrate through the Polenia Canal to the warm seas discovered by Kane? or if a man and a woman had the courage to cast anchor in the regions of the North Pole, and to the inhabitants of that magnetic kingdom boldly say, 'Compare yourselves with us; we are handsomer, stronger, more faithful, happier than you are?' That would be a triumph; and such a journey I would willingly undertake."

As she said these words, Angela's eyes gleamed upon Iván with the splendour of the Aurora Borealis. Iván decided to make a sudden experiment.

"Countess, if you have the passion or desire to visit strange worlds, and to excite benighted natives to a proper emulation of something better, truer, more intellectual than that they have hitherto known, if this is your sincere wish, I can recommend to you a country equally in need of such enlightenment, and infinitely nearer to you."

"Where is it?"

"It is Hungary."

"But are we not in Hungary already?"

"Countess, you are in it, but not of it. You are merely visiting us. You do not know what and who we are. You need not go so far as the Poles or Abyssinia; here is a new world open to you, a large field where your passion for creating and improving can be gratified easily."

Angela opened her fan, and with an air of indifference fanned her white bosom.

"What can I do? I am not my own mistress."

"You are not your own mistress, and, nevertheless, you rule."

"Over whom?"

"Countess, it would only need one word from you to bring the Green Palace and all it contains from Vienna to Pest. Society here requires a leading personality who is lost amongst the crowd now in Vienna, whose existence is spent in aimless inaction. Pest needs the Prince, your grandfather. He adores you. One word from you would give a new meaning to our life, one word from you, and Prince Theobald would come to live here."

Angela ceased fanning herself; with an angry gesture she folded her hands, and turned an angry look upon Iván.

"Do you know that the subject you have just mentioned is so distasteful to me, that any one who has ventured to name it to me has forfeited my acquaintance?"

"I am quite aware of the fact, Countess."

"And why have you dared to broach the subject?"

"I will tell you, Countess. Because of an old connection between our families."

"Ah! that is something quite new. I have never heard of it."

"Possibly not. One of your ancestors was a cardinal, and one of mine was a parson in Patak—a great difference in their relative positions, no doubt; and this difference had a terrible result for my ancestor. The cardinal condemned him to the galleys for life. The parson had, however, only one word to speak, as the cardinal told him, and he would be free. That word was *abrenuncio*—'I renounce,' or 'recant.' He would not say the word, however, and so he went to the galleys. As they were putting the iron shackles round his neck, which holds the chains to fasten the slave to his bench, your ancestor, the cardinal, who was not a hard-hearted man, with tears in his eyes entreated my ancestor to say the word '*abrenuncio*.' The parson, however, not only refused, but called out '*Non abrenuncio*.' In the same way I stand before you and repeat the same words, '*Non abrenuncio*.' This is the *rapport* between us. Would you treat me as the cardinal did my ancestor?"

Countess Angela tapped her fan upon her knee as she whispered between her small white teeth, and with a cruel smile upon her lips:

"What a pity that those days are past! If I were in the place of my ancestor, I would order you to have iron goads driven under your nails."

Iván burst out laughing at this formidable threat. After a minute Angela followed his example, and began to laugh herself.

It was a bold experiment to meet the young beauty's wrath with a burst of laughter, but it was a good answer to her foolish speech. The countess was aware that she had been a cause for laughter; but she was offended, nevertheless, and sat down, giving only a haughty look to the offender.

Iván did not move from her side. A cotillon, even though it be the 'Hungarian,' has its uses. One partner cannot leave the other even if they wish to separate.

In the meantime a young man, one of the many blockheads in Society, came to Iván and whispered in his ear that Edmund sent him to call him back to his game; luck had changed, and the pile of gold Iván had left was lost.

157

"Tell him he has done well," replied Iván; and he took his pocket-book from his breast-pocket, and handed it to the messenger. "Tell him to make use of this," he added, "and lose it, if necessary." And he remained where he was.

Angela never turned her head towards him again. The cotillon went on and on; Count Géza, who led it, wished to show that the Hungarian presented as many opportunities for new figures as the German cotillon, and the demonstration lasted a full two hours. Iván stayed to the end, although Angela maintained her cool silence throughout. When they had to join in the waltz, she leaned on his shoulder, her fingers pressed his, her breath touched his face; when she returned to her place she resumed her coldness, and kept her head averted.

When the cotillon was over, Edmund brought Iván the news that the long dance had cost him a thousand florins. Iván shrugged his shoulders, as if the loss didn't concern him.

'Wonderful man!' thought Edmund. Presently he said to his cousin:

"It seems that you kept Ritter Magnet all to yourself, my pretty cousin."

Angela raised her white shoulder to him, while she said angrily:

"The man has bored me for a long time."

From the moment that these words were spoken by the queen of fashion, the opinion of the world about Iván's merits began to change. He was no longer considered a capital fellow, but as a pushing *parvenu*. Angela did not need to say anything more; this one sentence had conveyed much. Sometimes, the vanity of men of low origin misinterprets the true meaning of conde-scension shown to them by those above their station, and by so doing such men make mistakes which must be punished. Such bold *parvenus* must be taught to curb their ambition. Iván was to be counted as one of these. The foolish man had imagined that a high-born lady, a Bondaváry, because she was patriotic, would, forsooth, stoop to such a one as he; he had mistaken her graciousness for the encouragement she might give to one of her own class. He must be ostracized, and that speedily.

The signal had been given by those words of the countess's, 'He has bored me for a long time.' The first step under such circumstances is to make the offender ridiculous. This can be done in different ways. The victim may notice that his weak points are stressed, that he is never left in peace, that he is perpetually placed in situations which are arranged to make him the laughing-stock. Not that any one is rude enough to laugh at him openly; on the contrary, they are extremely polite to him, but it is a politeness that provokes laughter. He may soon find that he has no friends, no one seeks his intimacy, even though no one actually insults him; but if he is a man of any intelligence, he soon feels that he is not one of Society, and that his best gesture would be to pick up his hat and go.

This happened now to Iván, but his habitual detachment did not desert him; he understood the situation; he was determined to take the joke against himself, and to turn it.

He was invited to take part in an amateur opera, made up of most aristocratic personages. He was given the role of the King. So he sang it for them. His voice was a fine baritone, and though he sang the part imperfectly his voice created a sensation. Angela was Elvira, Salista was Ernani; but the King was the favourite.

"That man's the very devil," growled the marquis. "He has been an actor, I'll bet."

Then, he was invited to a fox-hunt at Count Stephen's splendid hunting-box near Pest. The *élite* of the country round gathered at these hunts which took place in the beginning of the season. It was arranged that Iván should be mounted on a fiery Arab horse. This was planned as a big joke. It would be such fun to see the quiet book-worm in the saddle; he would have to cling hard, for the Arab would hardly allow the owner himself to ride him. It would be rare sport. But here was another disappointment; Iván sat on the fiery racer as if he had been born in the saddle. When Salista saw him mounted, he muttered between his teeth:

"The man's the very devil. I bet he was a Hussar."

Well, there is no saying, these days, what a man might have been in the past.

Countess Angela took part in the first run at Count Stephen's. She rode her horse splendidly: she was quite at home in the field.

About ten sportsmen drew the first cover; the hounds had the fox out of the bushes, and the cavalcade rode after it, when the fox took his course over a slope of a hill, which was divided by a cleft in the rock. At the bottom of the cleft a mountain stream ran. The fox took refuge in this ravine; he probably thought he might find there an empty fox-hole, where he might hide. In any case he might escape by the skin of his teeth, as the horses could not venture to follow him among the boulders, and if the dogs hunted him out of his burrow, he could escape along the right-hand side. The hunt was concentrated on the left.

"Forward!" cried the daring countess Angela, and put her horse to leap the ravine.

It was a breakneck jump. How many will risk their lives to follow her? When she reached the other side, she turned to look back. Only Iván was beside her.

The dogs pursued the fox, who had taken to the stream; the rest of the hunt galloped along to the left of the chasm. Angela gave them as little thought at that moment as they did to her. There was only one thought in every mind—the fox. The countess rode at the very edge of the gorge, taking no heed of the dizzy height, or dangerous depths into which one false step of her horse might throw her. She followed the poor fox, who was seeking an escape, distracted as he was by his pursuers. Suddenly, the fox broke out through the riders on the left bank, and took to the woods.

"After him! Tally-ho!" resounded along the hillside, and

160

soon fox, dogs, and horsemen were out of Angela's sight. At once she turned her horse's bridle; she made for a short cut through the woods, in order to join the hunt without loss of time. She never looked back to see whether Iván followed her, but galloped up the steep mountain-side, sitting on her horse splendidly.

At the turn of the path, a hare broke suddenly from the cover under the horse's hooves. The animal shied, and swerved violently, throwing the countess from the saddle. As she fell, the long skirt of her riding-habit got entangled in the saddle, and tied her to the frightened horse. Her head was hanging down with her hair streaming on the ground. The terrified horse ran towards the ravine, if he dragged his rider down its side, her head would be battered to pieces on the tree-trunks.

Iván just caught the bridle in time. He freed the foolhardy rider from the saddle; she was unconscious. He laid her down on the turf, and raised her head on the stump of a moss-grown tree. Then he saw how the fall had disarranged her dress. The malachite buttons had come off from her habit, and her bodice was revealingly torn. Iván drew his pin from his necktie and closed the countess's dress with it.

When Angela regained consciousness, she was alone. Both the horses were tied to a tree by their bridles. In the distance, against the setting sun, she saw a man coming towards her from the valley. It was Iván, who had gone to fill his hunting-horn with water. The countess rose to her feet at once; she needed no help. Iván offered her the water; she thanked him, but said she was quite recovered. Iván threw the water away.

"I think it would be well if you were to return to the castle."

"I will do so."

"It is not far. I know a short-cut through the wood. We can lead the horses."

"Very well," returned Angela, submissively. But when she looked at her dress and saw how it was fastened, a hot blush spread over her face. When she reached the woods, she turned

161

to Iván, and said suddenly, "Have you ever heard of Julia Gonzaga?"

"No, Countess."

"She was the Lady of Fondi. Barbarossa had surprised Fondi in the night, and carried off Julia. A noble knight came to her rescue, and she escaped with him from the bandit. This was in the night, and she had to ride barefoot, for she had been carried off from her bed. Do you know how she rewarded her deliverer? She stabbed him through the heart with the first dagger that came to her hand."

"She was right," returned Iván. "A stranger should not have seen her naked feet."

"And the man?" asked Angela.

"Ah, poor fellow! he had the misfortune of being too fortunate."

Chapter XIII

ONLY A TRIFLE

The fox was taken. From the woods, a triumphant 'Halali!' was heard, and then the horn sounded to collect the scattered members of the hunt.

Countess Angela and her escort had reached the edge of the wood by this time. Iván sounded his horn in answer to the summons, to signal that they were already on their way home, and they arrived at the castle a quarter of an hour before the rest of the company.

They separated at the entrance and did not meet again until supper-time. The huntsmen were discussing the events of the day, and the ladies were busy with their toilettes.

Countess Angela told her aunt what had happened. She was incapable of any deception. Lies, which come so easily to the lips of some women, were impossible to her. If she did not want to tell a thing she kept silent; but to speak what was not true—never!

She wondered whether Iván would relate to the men what had occurred? It was their habit to talk over the day's sport, and to joke about everything. Why should he not make capital of such an adventure—a rescued lady—a beauty *en déshabillé?*

When supper-time came, every one was struck by the constrained manner of the countess, and close observers noticed that she avoided looking at Iván. She was dressed in black, which was, perhaps, the reason why she looked so pale. She was silent and preoccupied; she was wondering if they all knew what Iván knew.

The gentlemen attempted to amuse her. They were full of the day's run, how the fox had doubled, how they thought they would never catch him, how they regretted that the countess had not been present, how unfortunate it was that she had been on the opposite side of the mountain, though it was far better for her to have lost the run than to have ventured to find a way across the ravine. That would, indeed, have been madness; an accident would certainly have been the result. No one alluded to the fact that she had had an accident; but then, well-bred people never allude to anything unpleasant, which, although otherwise agreeable, has the drawback that one never knows how much or how little they know.

It was a remark of her cousin Edmund that convinced Angela eventually that Iván had kept quiet about her accident.

"Did Berend accompany you to the house?" he asked. No one called him Ritter Magnet any more, nor were there any familiar jokes about him.

"Yes."

"And was such an escort disagreeable for you?"

"What makes you say that?" Angela flared up.

"Iván's manner; he seems rather cast down. He hasn't a word to say to a dog, and he avoids looking at you. Didn't you notice it? You have, I think, made the place too hot for him; he won't stay longer. Have I guessed right?"

"Yes, quite right."

· "Shall I give him a hint to go?"

"Do, for my sake; but do it gently. I would not have him offended."

"Do you think I am a bungler? I have an excellent plan to get him away quietly."

"You must tell me what it is. I am not vexed with the man, only he bores me. Do you understand? I won't have him driven

164

away by any of you; but if he goes by his own free choice, I should be glad if he went to the Antipodes."

"Well, I will tell you. This man is a scholar, a philosopher, as you know. His opinions are very different from ours, who live in the world. For one thing, he abhors duelling. Don't spoil your pretty face by frowning. I am not going to call him out, neither is any one else, as far as I know; that would be a stupid joke. But this evening, in the smoking-room, Salista and I will get up a dispute about some trifle or another; the end of it will be a challenge. I will ask Berend and Géza to be my seconds. Now, what will happen? If Berend refuses, which is most likely, he will have to withdraw from our party—that is etiquette—and we will have nothing more to say to him. If, on the other hand, he accepts, then the other seconds will manage to fall out about the arrangements of our meeting—Salista's and mine—and the usual consequence of such a falling out is that the four seconds challenge one another; then our philosopher packs up, thanks us for our hospitality, and goes back to brew his gas. He isn't going to fight, not he; for I believe, that although it is within the bounds of possibility that even a philosopher, if deeply insulted, may reach for his pistol to punish an offender; but when it is a matter of pure, worldly etiquette, it is only your born gentleman who will stand up in a duel."

"But suppose he does consent to fight this duel?"

"Then my plot has failed. We should then have a sort of court-martial, and it would have to decide that no offence was meant, and none given. We would all shake hands, and the little comedy would be at an end."

Angela yawned, as if weary of the subject. "Do as you like," she said. "But take care. This man can show his teeth; he can bite."

"Leave that to me."

That evening the conversation at supper was purposely turned to duelling, in order to convince Angela that Iván's views on

165

the subject were sound as regarded his own safety. The opportunity offered, for the latest event in fashionable life had been a duel, in which the only son of a well-known and distinguished family had lost his life in some trifling dispute.

"I hold duelling to be not merely a mistake, but a crime," said Iván. "It is flying in the face of God to take the law into our own hands. The appeal to weapons as satisfaction is an offence against society, for it prevents anyone from telling the truth. The man who tells us our faults openly to our face is a benefactor, but by the present custom of society we are bound to challenge him, and to kill him if we can; we have no other course, so it must be false compliments, or the duello."

Edmund continued the discussion. "I take a different view of the matter," he said. "If duelling were not a law of society it would be in a sense a denial of God's mercy, for it cannot be denied that one man is weak, another man strong, and that this is a decree of Providence. The result of this difference could easily be that the weaker would become the slave of the stronger, who could box his ears, insult him, and all the satisfaction the law would give him would be, perhaps, a couple of pounds. This chasm between the law of God and the law of man is filled by the bullet, which makes the strong and the weak equal. The gun is not a judge, for it often decides the cause unjustly. Nevertheless, this unwritten law, and the respect, not to say fear, it generates, has a salutary effect, and makes it impossible for the bully to tyrannize over a man of more education but less physical strength."

"But that it should be so is the fault of society," answered Iván. "A false sentiment of honour has dictated this law. The world has no right to make such a rule; it should honour those equally, be they poor or rich, well-born or humble, who keep the law of the land as it is written. But what does society do? If one gentleman gets a box on the ear from another, and does not immediately demand satisfaction for the insult, and *nolens volens*, make himself a target to be shot at by perhaps a better marksman than himself, what happens? He is at once dishonoured; society ostracizes him. The world, if it pretends to any justice in the matter, should reform this absurd principle, and punish the man who has given the first offence. Then society, and not a bullet, would be judge."

"That is all very fine in theory, my dear sir; but I ask you, as a man of honour, to put yourself in the position in which, for some reason or another, you find it necessary to have satisfaction for an affront."

"I could not imagine myself placed in any such position," Iván answered quietly. "I never offend anyone intentionally, and should I do so inadvertently, I would apologize at once. I give no man the opportunity to asperse my honour, and if he were foolish enough to do so, I would call upon those who know, and I should deem myself indeed unfortunate if they did not clear me of any such accusation."

"But suppose the honour of some one near and dear to you were attacked?"

"I have no one who stands to me in so close a relationship."

This last remark ended the discussion. Nevertheless, before many hours had passed the Marquis of Salista proved to Iván that there was one person whose good name was dear to him.

It was at supper, and Angela was present. The marquis was entertaining her with anecdotes of the Revolution, in which he had taken part. He was bragging about how, as a lieutenant of the Cuirassiers, he had performed prodigies. At the battle of Isaszeg, with only a handful of men, he routed the entire regiment of Lehel Hussars, and he cut the Wilhelm Hussars to pieces, and didn't spare a man.

Not a feature in Iván's face moved. He listened silently to these wonderful tales. Angela at last grew weary of all this boasting and glorification of the Austrians over the degraded Hungarians; she turned to Iván, and put the direct question to him.

"Is this all true?"

Iván shrugged his shoulders. "What can I, a poor miner who lives underground, know of what happens on the surface of the great earth?"

Angela need not feel anxious about him. He is a philosopher, and there is no fear that he will go too near the fire.

After supper the company separated; Count Stephen with countess Theudelinde and some other ladies went into the drawing-room. The moonlight came through the bay-windows. The countess played the piano, and Angela came and spoke to Iván.

"Here is your pin," she said. "You know the old superstition—a present of sharp-pointed instruments dissolves friendship, and those who wish to be friends never give them?"

"But," answered Iván, smiling, "the superstition provides an antidote to break the spell. Both friends must laugh over the present."

"Ah! that is why you laughed when I spoke of the iron goads. There, take back your pin, and let us laugh for superstition's sake."

And they laughed together, because it was a superstition to do so. Then Angela went out on the balcony, and took counsel from the soft summer; she leaned over the balustrade, waiting for Count Edmund, who had promised to bring her the first news of how the plot had worked.

The gentlemen stayed on in the smoking-room; the night is their time for enjoyment, and Angela had a long vigil. The moon had disappeared behind the high tops of the poplar trees before Angela heard Edmund's steps coming through the drawing-room to the bay-window. The ladies were still playing the piano; they could talk unreservedly.

"Well, what happened?" Angela asked.

Edmund was agitated. "Our trifle has turned out to be a rank piece of folly," he said crossly.

"How?"

"I should not tell you, Angela, but under the circumstances

it would be wrong to conceal anything from you. We had it all arranged just as I told you; when we were in the smoking-room we began to play our practical joke. Someone said how pleased you seemed to be with Hungary—"

"Oh, how stupid of you!" said Angela, angrily.

"I know now it was a stupid thing to do. I wish I had seen it before; but it always happens that knowledge comes too late."

"What business had you, or anyone, to mention my name? I gave no permission for it."

"I know, I know; but among men, unfortunately, no one asks a lady's permission to mention her name. It was only a joke. It had been settled amongst us that I, being your cousin, should protest against this gossip in connection with you, then Salista was to say that he knew well that what kept you in Pest was the fine eyes of a certain gentleman, that I was to get angry, and forbid him to say any more, and that then we should get up the mock duel."

Angela was trembling with anger, but anxious to hear more, she controlled herself with some difficulty.

"I never heard of such a childish joke," she said. "It was a schoolboy's trick."

"It would have been better for us all if it had ended as a schoolboy's trick. When I told you that we had prepared a trick, you approved of it, Angela; you know you did. None of us thought for a moment that it would end as it has done. Berend was sitting at the chess-table; Salista was opposite to him, leaning against the mantelpiece. After Salista had said the words, 'I know that a certain pair of eyes keeps countess Angela in Pest,' and before I had time to make the answer agreed upon, Iván challenged. 'That is a lie!' he said."

"Ah!" cried Angela; an electric thrill ran through her veins.

"We all sprang to our feet; the joke had ended badly. Salista grew pale; he had not counted upon this. 'Sir,' he said to Berend, 'take back that word of yours; it is a word that in my life no man has said to me'."

169

"And Berend?" asked Angela, seizing Edmund's hand.

"Berend stood up from the table, and answered quietly in a cold voice, 'It is possible that up to the present you have given no occasion for this reproach to be cast in your face; but tonight I repeat that you have lied.' Then he left the room. I ran after him to try and smooth things down. I met him in the hall. He turned to me and said quietly, 'My dear friend, you know what must now happen. I beg that you will ask Count Géza in my name, and that you and he will be my seconds. You will let me know what is arranged; all is in your hands.' In this way he invited me to play the part which I had destined for him. Now he is the duellist, and I am the second. I tried to drive him into a corner. I pointed out to him that it was not his right to give a challenge for the countess. He answered, 'It is the right and the duty of every gentleman, to protect the lady whose guest he is.' This answer, from a chivalrous point of view, is perfectly correct, but it sounds strange from the lips of the man who a couple of hours ago told us there was no one in the world for whose good name he would fight a duel."

Angela sank back in her chair. "Oh, what terrible folly all this is!" she wailed. "No, no, this duel must not take place. I shall prevent it."

"I wish you would tell me how you intend to prevent it."

"I will speak to Iván Berend at once—this moment; do you hear?"

"Unfortunately that is impossible. When he left me, he ordered to have his horses put to. There, you can hear the wheels. That is his carriage. Géza has gone with him, and the four of us are to follow him presently. One cannot arrange this sort of thing in a strange house; that is done only on the stage. The principals must wait in their own houses to hear what we have decided to do."

"But, my God! I will not let it be done; do you hear? I will speak to Uncle Stephen."

"I have told you everything so that our sudden departure

170

should not surprise you; but I can tell you exactly what Count Stephen will say—that no fuss must be made; let the whole thing be done quickly and quietly. The seconds, too, must act with great prudence, and not irritate the principals by too much delay."

"What do you mean by saying the seconds should act with prudence?"

"As far as they can they must determine the issue of the duel, and either soften or accentuate the conditions. In this case we will soften. Your name will not appear as the cause of the challenge. We will induce Berend to say that he used the word 'lie' in connection with Salista's expressions concerning the Hungarian troops. This plausible ground for a challenge will be accepted as sufficient by both sides, and in this way your name need never be mentioned."

"But I do not care. What does that matter? If anyone is killed for my sake—"

"Compose yourself, my dear cousin; the seconds will be prudent. We shall place them thirty feet apart, and give them worn-out pistols with which, at half the distance, the aim would be uncertain; then we shall not allow them to aim for more than a minute, and you may be sure if they were both as thick as an elephant's hide and protected like robin redbreasts, they couldn't be safer; they may fire away for hours and never hit one another. Now, my dear child, be sensible, I beg of you. When you have a husband, he will have many an affair like this on his hands, and all for your beautiful eyes. But I must be going, the carriage is at the door, and we start at daylight."

And Edmund took himself off with a hasty good-bye.

This little joke had spoiled their sport. The loss of six men made it impossible to continue hunting the next day; therefore every one resolved to return to Pest in the morning. The night was disturbed. Countess Angela's maid, who slept in her room, told everyone that her mistress had hardly slept a wink, that she was constantly getting up and lighting her candle, saying that it must be daylight, and time to set off for the city.

The next morning, at ten o'clock, when all the guests had left, and Countess Theudelinde and her suite were already in Pest, Countess Angela went to her room, and walked up and down restlessly until about eleven o'clock, when Count Edmund was announced.

He came in pale and disturbed, and Angela, who tried to read his face, concluded that something had happened.

"In God's name, what is it?" she asked. "Who is hurt?"

"No one," replied Edmund, dryly; "but the affair is in a worse state than it was."

"Has the duel taken place?"

"Yes and no. It has begun, but is not finished."

"I do not understand."

"I own it is something quite new. I have never known such a thing in all my experience. If you wish, I will tell you all about it."

"Oh, for Heaven's sake, do!"

"As agreed, I called at Berend's house at six o'clock to fetch him; Géza went on with the doctor. When we got to Laszlovszky, Salista was just getting out of his carriage. Iván lifted his cap, and wished him good morning; he probably did not know that this is not usual. The principals never greet one another. Salista did not return his bow, although he might have done so, seeing that Iván was evidently ignorant of the proper etiquette. From Laszlovszky we all drove together to Leopold's Field, where we got out of the carriages, and walked into the forest. When we reached the appointed clearing, we stopped, and the seconds of both sides asked the principals, according to the rules, whether they would not make up their difference. Both sides refused. So we measured the distance, marked the barrier with our handkerchiefs, and loaded the pistols. When this was over, the principals, who had been pulling blades of grass and standing about, took their places. We handed them their pistols; signal was given by Géza clapping his hands. Salista made two steps forward and shot. Just as I expected, he did not hit his man. Iván called out in a loud voice, 'To the barrier!' and Salista advanced to where the white pocket hand-kerchief lay, while Iván went to his barrier. Then said he, ad-dressing Salista,' You did not return my greeting; but if I take my hat off to you, you must do the same.' He then took aim; the half minute during which he held his pistol showed us his nerve was perfect. The pistol went off, and Salista stood opposite his adversary, bareheaded; his hat lay two paces behind him, with the gold rosette torn from its front."

"Ah!" cried Angela.

"This man shoots as well as Robin Hood. We loaded again, for it was agreed that they were to have three shots each."

"Three shots!" exclaimed Angela.

"Yes. We all agreed it was better to have the affair on a proper footing, as far as the conditions went. Thirty steps is a great distance; besides, the pistols were bad. In addition, both men were wrapped up to the chin; one had a black coat, the other a dark grey military cloak, colours bad for hitting; and both had their shirt-collars concealed. There was not a point about either that would serve for a target. But the hat business had changed the nature of the whole affair, and created bad blood. It proved, for one thing, that Berend was a first-rate shot, and this put Salista on his military mettle. The barriers were withdrawn for the second shot. Salista took off his grey cloak, tied back his hussar jacket, so that his red waistcoat and white shirt stood out clearly, and instead of standing, as is usual in a duel, sideways towards his adversary, he presented his full front, blazing in red and white, the best colours, as every one knows, for a mark. Yes, and while we were loading, what do you think he did? But Salista is a madman when he is roused! He took his cigar-case out of his pocket, and lighted one to show his indifference. For the second time it was his turn to begin. He took much more pains than the first time; in fact,

173

he was such a time taking aim that we had to call to him to shoot. Again he missed. The leaves of the branches under which Iván stood fell upon his head; the ball had gone into the tree."

Angela shuddered.

"Iván now addressed his opponent. 'Sir,' he said, 'it is not fitting that at such a solemn moment you should smoke a cigar.' Salista made no answer, but stood fronting Berend; his face was slightly turned to one side, and he blew clouds of smoke into the air. Iván raised his pistol for a second, took deliberate aim, then a sharp report, and Salista's cigar flew out of his mouth."

An involuntary smile spread over Angela's lips, but it was gone in an instant, and her face resumed its immovable expression, as if cut of stone.

Count Edmund went on. "In a fury Salista threw his pistol on the ground. 'The devil take me,' he cried, stamping with rage, 'if I shoot any more against this man! He is Beelzebub in person. He has shot the hat from my head, the cigar from my mouth, and the third time he will shoot the spurs from my boots. He shoots all round me; he is like a Chinese juggler. I will not shoot any more against him, that's flat!' His seconds tried to persuade him in vain; he would not listen; he was furious; he would hear of nothing. He wasn't going to be such a fool as to stand up there to be a mark for a second William Tell, who would not only shoot the apple from his head, but aim right at his heart. If they wanted to have a fair fight, with all his heart; but let it be with swords, then one could see which was the better man. We all talked to him, told him not to play the fool, that he must stand his adversary's fire, no matter where he was shot, on his spur or his head. The duellist has no right to refuse; he is in the hands of his seconds. At last Berend got curious to know what the row was about; he called to me and Géza, and we had to tell him that Salista would not stand another shot, but had demanded that the duel should be decided by swords. To our surprise Iván answered coolly, 'Gladly.

174

Give us the sabres.' 'Do you consent?' 'I consent to fight with scythes if he wishes.' So it was agreed. Salista's seconds heard this discussion with great satisfaction; they were very much put out by his outbreak, it being quite unusual to change weapons in a duel; and there would have been a regular scandal if Iván had used his right of refusing any such change in the conditions under which the duel was to be fought."

"And you have allowed such an innovation to be made?" said Angela, looking at her cousin with drawn eyebrows.

"Certainly, when the challenger agreed to it."

"It was shameful of you!" Angela continued, with suppressed tears in her voice. "Ungenerous to allow such an unequal fight. One man has practised fencing all his life; it is his profession; the other has never had a sword in his hand."

"The fight will be drawn at the first blood," said Edmund, in a soothing voice.

"But you had no right to agree to such a bloodthirsty idea; you have overstepped your duty as second. You should have said to Salista's seconds that the affair should be concluded then or never."

"That is quite true; and we should have done so, only Berend chose to interfere."

"You should not have allowed it; you could have stopped it. When does the duel take place?"

"As we had no swords, they could not fight this morning. It is against the law to have a duel in the afternoon, therefore we have postponed the second meeting until tomorrow at daybreak."

"Before daybreak tomorrow I will put a stop to the duel."

"How so?"

"I shall speak to Berend; I shall explain everything to him."

"If you tell him that this affair arose out of a joke, the result will be that, instead of fighting a duel with one man, Berend will have six duels on his hands."

"I will tell him in such a way that he will not expect to fight any of you."

"Then you will have ruined Salista."

"How so? What has he to do with it?"

"If the world gets wind of a half-finished *rencontre*, and it reaches the ears of the authorities that an officer refused his adversary's third fire, Salista will be cashiered, he will be received nowhere, and he would have to go back to the Pope's army as zouave."

"I don't care if he becomes the devil's zouave! Why should I worry about him? Let him go to the Sultan of Dahomey. He may go to the devil; for all I care, he is halfway there already. But who cares what happens to him? *I* don't. Your duty is clear; you should protect your own principal. Isn't that so?"

Edmund beheld with astonishment the excitement into which the countess had thrown herself; she was trembling, and her eyes gleamed with passion.

"This is quite a new view of the affair," he said. "If you look upon it in this light, I must agree that we have been wrong, and you are most certainly right. I shall go at once and look for Géza; we will both repair to Berend, and tell him our view."

He bowed low before his cousin, and left. In an hour he returned. He found Angela in the same place.

"Well, what is done? Is it all settled?"

"Listen. Géza and I went to Iván. I explained to him that we considered it our duty not to infringe the conditions laid down in such matters, and that we were resolved not to allow the duel with swords to proceed. He pressed both our hands warmly. 'I thank you,' he said, 'for the friendship you have shown me, and since your convictions will not allow you to stand by me in this affair, I shall not try to persuade you. I shall go to the nearest barracks, and I shall tell the first two officers I may meet that I am engaged in an affair of honour to be fought with swords, that I am a stranger in the town, and that I throw myself upon their kindness to be my seconds.' "

Angela, with a despairing gesture, clasped her hands together.

"You spoke the truth," continued Edmund, "when you prophesied that this man would show his teeth. He has the grip of a bulldog when he gets hold of an idea. We told him that Salista was a celebrated swordsman. He took it quite coolly. 'If the devil himself was my adversary, I should face him squarely,' was all he said."

Angela sat down and covered her face with her hands.

"We couldn't do anything but to assure him, that as far as our services went, he was free to make use of us. So it was settled. We call for him tomorrow at daybreak. God only knows how it will all end."

Then Edmund took his leave. Angela did not even notice that he left the room.

That evening, she did not go to bed. All through the long hours of the night she walked to and fro in her room. When fatigue forced her to sit down for a moment, she could not relax. Only did once the thought that was in her mind found expression in words:

"I have treated him as Julia Gonzaga treated the man who saved her life."

When daylight broke, she threw herself, dressed as she was, on her bed. Next morning the maid found the pillow in which she had buried her face wet with tears.

Chapter XIV

THIRTY-THREE PARTS

It must be admitted that our philosopher was acting somewhat inconsistently. He had left his home and his business, where he lived simply, among his own people, happy in the study of the mysterious powers of fire and water; he had abandoned his scientific pursuits in order to join a world to which he was, and must ever be, a stranger, more or less a fish cast on dry land. He had turned into a farce even his scientific knowledge, risking disgrace to it. He had lent himself to lectures and tableaux, to singing operas, and to dancing Hungarian cotillons, to riding the fox at breakneck speed, to rescuing a beautiful lady (mixing himself up the while in the affairs of noble families), to fighting duels with officers for the sake of a lovely countess, and running the risk of being cut down by an intemperate savage! It was no wonder that, thinking about all this, Iván should say to himself: 'I am making a fool of myself. What have I to do with all the nonsense that goes on in this fashionable world of Pest? Above all, what is it to me whether the countess Angela is at war with her grandfather, whether she goes to Vienna, or whether he comes to Pest? Why is it necessary for me to remain here, leading such an uncongenial life, apparently without any point or purpose? And, although I have a purpose, if it were known to the world, I should be considered an even greater fool than now.'

Now, as I have made public Iván's reflections, it is only

proper that the reason of his apparently pointless course should be laid before the reader, so that he or she may be in a position to judge whether he was foolish or wise, or something in between—a man of strong feelings, who acts as his heart commands him. With some men the heart can never be silenced; it claims its dues. We may remember that when the Abbé Samuel paid his first visit to Iván, he found him in the act of writing a refusal to the countess Theudelinde's invitation; that he was, in fact, on the point of returning to Bondavára, and that receiving a letter had changed all his plans, and caused him to remain in Pest. This letter came from Vienna; from a pianist whose name had been for some years included among the leading artists of the day—Árpád Belényi.

Nearly fourteen years before our story, Iván had lived for a long time in the Belényis' house. We shall return later to what he did there. Árpád was at that time a child of five; he was already looked on as a prodigy; he could play long pieces on the piano. At that time, warlike and patriotic marches were all the fashion. One day the bread-winner of the family, the father, died suddenly. The widow was in despair, especially for the future of her orphaned boy. Iván consoled her, promising that he would look after the boy, and provide for his education.

Unexpected circumstances, however, forced Iván a month or two later to leave the family of Belényi somewhat suddenly, and it seemed doubtful if he would ever see them again. At parting, Iván gave all the money he could spare to the widow, and told her to make sure Árpád had a good musical education, to start him on a musical career. He believed that the boy would achieve eminence, and make a living by his art. And here let it be clearly understood that Iván was neither a friend of Belényi nor the lover of Madame Belényi; he was not connected with the family in any way, nor was he bound in duty to do all this.

For years the Belényis heard nothing of Iván, nor he from them. Once, on inquiring about them, he was told that they had

179

lost their house in consequence of a lawsuit, had left the town, and that neither mother nor son had since been heard of. Then, in a few more years, Árpád Belényi's name began to be mentioned in various newspapers, always as a young and astonishingly clever pianist. From this time Iván regularly took a musical journal, and followed attentively his adopted son's career. The latter, however, knew nothing of his kind benefactor until, later, Iván's name also appeared in the papers. His lecture at the Academy led to his discovery by his adopted son, who at once wrote him a letter, beginning: 'My dear father.'

It was a letter full of simple, boyish feeling, though the natural fun and playful humour of the artist broke through it at times. He told Iván everything about himself; how he had travelled in many countries, always accompanied by his mother, and how he had to account of all his actions as accurately as possible, to her. He had already given concerts to the highest and mightiest, and had received several Orders which he was allowed to wear only on Sundays; during the week, they were locked up by his mother. He had earned a good deal of money, but he was not permitted to spend much. Mamma gave him every day a five-shilling piece for pocket-money; the rest she put by to buy back the little house of which 'the old Greek' had robbed her. To make more money, he gave music-lessons, and played accompaniments for artists. This was well paid, particularly of late, since he had fallen in with a young artist, a new singer, who paid very well. She was said to be the wife of Felix Kaulman, the rich banker.

When he came to this passage, Iván's heart began to beat faster. He put the letter down, then picked it up again, and read it with renewed attention.

'This girl is a mixture of muse and Maenad,' wrote Árpád. 'One moment she is a petulant child, the next a wild Amazon; a born artist, full of genius, yet she is not likely ever to rise above the mediocre. She is full of intelligence and life, and yet often as stupid as a donkey. There is no doubt that she could attain an unenviable notoriety, but she shrinks from this: for although she conducts herself like a courtesan, I would swear she is really as innocent as the child she still is. I find her very trying, full of mischief and petulance, and this because I do not treat her with soft manners, but often scold her for being so naughty. If you could only see, dear papa, what a splendid master I am, always serious, no frivolity allowed! Now I have described myself for you, have I not?

'Do not think, however, that I would have scrawled all over my paper this monologue about my pupil, as if I had nothing better or wiser to write about, without a reason. But the subject has a certain interest for you. You must know, this odd little angel confides in me as if I were her confessor. Sometimes she chatters all through her lesson, telling me where she has been, what she has done, everything that happened to her; and she often tells me things which, if I were in her place, I would not talk about.

'Have a little patience, my dear good papa. This lady has thirty-three different *roles*, all of them of different kinds. They are not, strictly speaking, stage parts, but monologues, which are composed expressly for her. These scenes we rehearse together; I play her accompaniment, while she sings and acts.

'I am coming now to the kernel of the nut. I am going to crack it for you. Here are the names of the actress's thirty-three parts:

'Lorelei,'
'Cleopatra,'
'The Queen of the Sun,'
'The Greek Slave,'
'The Bacchante,'
'The Bride,'
'The Matron's Cap,'
'The Bayadère,'
'Claudia Laeta, the Vestal,'
'Nourmahal,'

181

'Amalasontha,'
'Magdalene,'
'Ninon,'
'La Somnambula,'
'Medea,'
'Salome,'
'The Houris,'
'The Despair of Hero,'
'The Phrygian Cap,'
'Turandot,'
'The Peasant Girl,'
'The Mother,'
'Jeanne la Folle,'
'Ophelia,'
'Judith,'
'Zuleika Potiphar,'
'The Market Woman,'
'The Grisette,'
'The Creole,'
'Lucretia,'
'The Will-o'-the-Wisp,'
'Julia Gonzaga.'

'The thirty-third part I do not know; we have not as yet rehearsed it. But why the deuce does she learn all these parts, when she never steps on the stage? It is rumoured, that this lady's talent is much cultivated because she is engaged to sing at the Opera House. This seems even more strange, and I, for one, am slow to believe it. A banker like Kaulman, who is a millionaire, and whose wife pays four thousand florins for her apartment! Besides, she would have to give her singing-master, who would get her the engagement, six thousand, to the leader of the orchestra two thousand, four thousand to the newspapers to puff her, another three thousand to the *claqueurs*, and something else to the men who throw the wreaths and flowers. There would remain for her about a thousand florins; that would hardly pay her perfumier's bill.

'So you see the absurdity of the whole thing. Where are we now? This pretty creature, who wishes to be a famous artist, has several admirers who can easily pay court to madame, seeing that she and her husband live in separate apartments. This is only natural; the banker could not have his thoughts, always full of important speculations, disturbed by constant *solfeggi*.

'There are several persons in Vienna who bear the title of the 'Maecenases of Art'; they are gentlemen of high position, who have great weight in the departmental Government, and whose voices are heard in all social and official capacities. These have had the privilege of being present during the rehearsals of the thirty-two monologues; the thirty-third has not as yet been played to anyone.

'In all this, I can assure you, everything is conducted with the greatest propriety. I am always present, also the husband, who remains as long as the comedy continues. Amongst the company are representatives of the highest nobility, counts, princes, senators, and ministers. They are pleasant people, and call one another Fritz, Puzi, Muke, etc. Amongst others we have two princes, who come every time we have a rehearsal —the Prince Mari and the Prince Baldi; the names they received on baptism being Waldemar and Theobald. Yesterday Eveline —my pupil—was not inclined to work, and without my asking her what ailed her, with her usual frankness, she burst out with her troubles.

'Only fancy,' she said, 'that odious Prince Waldemar threatened me in my box at the Opera last night, that if I did not let him come to our next rehearsal, he would ruin Lixi.' (Lixi is short for Felix, her husband's name.)

'Why don't you admit him?' I asked. 'He is no worse than the other jackanapes who come.'

'Because I can't stand him. I told Lixi what Prince Waldemar

183

had said, and Lixi answered that he would ruin the prince. At the same time he gave me to understand that Prince Theobald must be invited to the rehearsal.'

'All right,' said I, 'he is a fine old gentleman. You can have no objections to him; he is old enough to be your grandfather.'

'The young wife bit her lips, and, with a frown on her lovely face, said:

'I have to ask him to do something. What do you think it is? Oh, you could never guess! It is to give his signature to a certain affair which will cost him nothing, but which will help Lixi greatly. You know that Lixi has a grand speculation on hand, a gigantic coal company, which is to start the business with I don't know how many millions; but the place where the coal mines are situated, the Bondavára property, belongs to Prince Theobald and his sister. The countess has already given her consent, but without his ratification the shares would not be taken up at the Exchange. Prince Waldemar is working against us, and therefore I am to win over the old prince to our side. Lixi says it will be very easy to get round him just at this moment, because his grand-daughter, countess Angela, of whom he is very fond, has quarrelled with him and left him. The poor old man is very sad and lonely, and Lixi says whoever cheers him up will be able to do anything with him; and,' she added with a wise look, 'we are not deceiving him, for the Bondavára coal is the finest in the world.'

'I burst out laughing; I could not help it. Then she pulled my hair and said:

'Why do you laugh, you silly donkey? I think I am competent to judge coal, for I worked for ten years in the mines of Iván Berend.'

'At these words my astonishment was so great that I jumped up from my seat.

'You may stare your eyes out of your head,' she said, laughing at my amazement, 'but it is quite true. I used to shove coal-waggons, and go barefoot, into the bargain.'

'Gracious lady, believe me, I did not jump from surprise at you; I was surprised to hear you mention Iván Berend. What do you know of him? Please tell me.'

'He was the owner of the coal-mine in Bondavára, near which Felix is going to open his enormous works. He was my master; God bless him wherever he goes.'

'Now, dear papa, I have come to the heart of the matter, after, it must be owned, an unconscionably long prelude. With my weak intellect I have thought out the whole thing. Here is my kind friend, my adopted father, the owner of a mine in Bondavára, and alongside him, men with I don't know how many millions behind them, forming a coal company. It would be a good thing to let him know, that he may act in time; for their scheme may be good for him, but it seems to me that it may likely be very bad. Here, the air is full of speculation; you see, I am already slightly bitten myself. Let me know how and in what manner the affair affects you and your interests. I shall write to you of what goes on here, for I shall be behind the scenes; the little fool tells me everything.'

This letter had decided Iván to accept countess Theudelinde's invitation to give a romantic reading at her house, and to enter the society of Pest. He wrote to Árpád, and begged him to give him an exact account every day of what he heard, through Eveline, of the progress of the coal-mine company.

From this time on, Iván received regularly two or three letters a week from Vienna.

'The old prince nibbles at the bait. Kaulman has brought him to the rehearsal of the new piece. Eveline sings and acts enchantingly; that is, when she is within four walls, and has only a few people for an audience. If she acted like this on stage, she would be a celebrated actress in no time; but as soon as she comes behind the footlights, stage-fright seizes her, she trembles, forgets everything, stands there like a block, and, worst of all, sings quite flat. These rehearsals have been given on the pretext that the prince should have an opportunity of

185

judging of her talent, so that he may influence the powers that be, to her at the Opera.

'I know their real object. The prince is a real connoisseur of music, and he understands not only art, but artists as well. He knows that there is a price set on such black diamonds as sparkle in Eveline's eyes. There is the additional incentive that Prince Waldemar is desperately in love with this woman, and Prince Theobald, for certain reasons, will do anything to prevent her falling into his hands. He would even take her himself, rather than to allow such a misadventure.

'A short time ago Prince Waldemar met me, and offered me one hundred ducats for every leaf of the album of the portraits of Madame Kaulman in her character-costumes. You must know, of late, each day that we rehearse one of the monologues, a photographer comes, and takes the *artiste* in her costume. Everything must be finished in the house, and not more than four pictures are allowed to be executed; one of these is for Prince Theobald, one is kept by herself, one she presents to me, and the fourth is for my friend Felix. The negative is then destroyed. I would not sell my photographs to Prince Waldemar, but I send them to you, as they come. Mamma does not like to see such pictures in my room.'

Iván received a photograph with each letter; each portrait represented Evila in a graceful pose. Árpád had not the least idea what an inferno of raging passions were raised in Iván's breast as he looked at the beautiful image of the woman he still loved.

In the first portrait she was represented as Lorelei, the elf, who, above the whirlpools of the Rhine, sings her magic song, and combs her hair with a golden comb, while her left shoulder rises from the waves which partly cover her figure. Her eyes gaze invitingly at the fisherman, whom she entices to his ruin.

In the second photograph she appeared as Cleopatra at Tarsus, displaying her charms to seduce her conqueror, and make him her slave; a rich portrait, in which the lascivious queen was shown laden with splendid clothes and jewels, while the expression of the beautiful face was an admirable mixture of pride, dignity, and weakness.

The third photograph presented the queen of the Sun, Atahualpa, the wife of the last Incas. Her look was haughty and sublime; the sublimity of the expression diverted attention from the uncovered arms, white as marble, round as a child's, which were raised to heaven, offering a human heart as a sacrifice. Her face mirrored the coldness of heaven itself.

The fourth, as the Greek Slave, represented a tortured beauty, who tries to break in vain the chains of shame in which she is bound—a lovely marble statue, equal in conception to any by Thorwaldsen or Pradier.

The fifth was the Bacchante, from a Roman bas-relief representing the procession of Bacchus. A wild, bold, dissolute figure; with startling appurtenances, such as panther skins, floating drapes, cups; an ideal *débauchée*, her limbs moving with a wild freedom.

The sixth portrait was of a bride; a white lace dress, a white garland on her head, her figure concealed by a white veil, an expression of soft emotion on her face at the approach of her happiness, in her eyes tears, on her lips a tremulous smile. With what wonderful charm she stretches out her hand to receive the betrothal ring!

The seventh portrayed a young woman who, for the first time, puts on the matron's cap. Pride, shame, and conscious triumph are all in her face. She feels that the cap upon her head is her well-deserved crown—for which she has sacrificed the garland.

Iván contemplated this picture for a long time; his heart was full of the bitterness of disappointed love. His adopted son's present had been somewhat unfortunate.

The eighth photograph represented Evila as a Bayadère in the artistic dress of an Indian dancer, striking a tambourine over her head. Round her slight figure a shawl embroidered in gold was wound in careless folds, on her neck a chain of gold coins, her small feet bare, and strings of pearls up to the knee.

In the ninth portrait she appeared as Claudia Laeta, the Vestal Virgin, at the moment when she is led to the stake because she has refused the solicitations of Caracalla; on her face an expression of horror, of virginal modesty. With one hand she tries to cover her head with her cloak to escape from the gaze of the multitude.

How was it possible for one woman to play so many parts? Árpád accompanied the pictures with diffuse explanations, so many stabs in Iván's heart. The result of all this posturing was, he said, becoming clearer every day.

'The prince is more and more fascinated; he is falling deeper and deeper into the net spread for him. After each rehearsal he declares that a real treasure has been concealed, a loss to art that must be remedied at once.'

But such treasures are very costly, especially when a man has reached the age of sixty-eight, and has a marriageable granddaughter; then it is necessary to look very closely into his account books to see if it would be possible to provide for his grandchild, and at the same time satisfy the caprices of a beautiful young woman.

Not long ago Prince Theobald had built a splendid palace in the Maximilian Strasse; it was destined for the countess Angela, in case she agreed to her grandfather's wishes regarding her marriage. The palace was furnished with the utmost magnificence. The countess, however, had changed her mind. She broke off her projected marriage with Sondersheim; she had good reasons, no doubt, but she need not have defied her grandfather openly. It was unwise of her to do so, for Evila was weaving her spell closer round the old man's heart, and Angela had best be prudent, and return speedily to Vienna, lest the palace in the Maximilian Strasse should be presented, without doubt, to Madame Kaulman.

Árpád's letters had acquainted Iván with the ins and outs of the whole affair; through them he had learned that the woman he had loved had become the wife of another man, and was likely to be the mistress of a third. The first blow he could bear with a certain resignation; he wished her all happiness; but that she should sink deep into shame, led to it by her own husband, was a bitter thought! No—she should be saved from this degradation if Iván could compass her deliverance. This was why he remained in Pest. It seemed to him that he could pull the strings of this complex drama, and defeat the conspiracy against Evila's honour; for this purpose he went into a world that he despised, affected a manner of life totally inconsistent with his ideas, and cultivated a friendship with the countess Angela, so that his influence might induce her to play the part of a good angel.

Was he a fool to sacrifice so much for a woman who had inflicted on him the severest mortification a man could endure? Those whose hearts are dominated by cold prudence will condemn his folly, perhaps, rightly so; those who also have hearts will admit that he did well in obeying its dictates, and from his point of view, perhaps, he acted for his own ultimate advantage.

If Prince Theobald should be induced to consent to give over his property to the Bondavára Company, Iván's little coal-mine would be ruined. It would be well, if he could while working for another, help himself. A businessman is always a speculator; therefore we say to the warm-hearted and compassionate that Iván acted to save Evila from shame, and to the cold-hearted and unfeeling that it was all in the way of business, to save, if he could, his little property from the monster company ready to devour it.

Árpád continued to send the photographs. They were of all kinds, tragic and comic. Medea, with her murderous revenge and jealousy; the daughter of Herod, with her voluptuous dance to gain the saint's head; the cruelty of Judith, the wild laughter of Jeanne la Folle, the devotion of a holy nun, the coquettish tricks of a *grisette*, a languid Creole, a supernatural

189

Will-o'-the-Wisp—these were the principal representations in which Iván found more of a studied effort at an artistic effect than natural instinct or expression. This was the schooling of Madame Risan, to whom Felix had entrusted Evila's education. Two portraits that came last produced a painful impression on Iván. One represented a mother by the cradle of her child, the other a peasant girl, a coal-carrier, with her hair plaited down her back, and a red frock tucked up above her ankles. It pained Iván deeply that she should profane these two sacred subjects. Why take a mother's love to rouse an old man's admiration? And the girl in the red dress! Ah, that was unpardonable. He could not forgive her; it wounded him to the heart.

One day the pianist wrote to Iván:

'My good patron, Felix Kaulman, is an out-and-out scoundrel. Up till now, he generally attended rehearsals when the prince was present. Yesterday Prince Theobald seemed so excited, that Kaulman noticed it. To his question, the prince replied that he was very happy. He had a letter from his granddaughter, countess Angela, written in the most friendly manner. She wrote that she had met a certain Iván Berend, who had the courage to give her a regular scolding, and had told her outright of the duties of Hungarian nobles towards their country, a duty in which they were wanting, and which Prince Theobald would fulfil if he left Vienna, and came to reside in Pest. If he came, the countess would agree to a reconciliation. The old prince seemed happy at the idea of seeing his grandchild again. Kaulman, however, looked very black, and blacker still when the prince said he was thinking it over; but as the countess had taken a fancy to Pest, he thought he might go there. Inwardly Felix must have gnashed his teeth with rage, but he expressed his satisfaction that the countess had at last broken the ice. It was a sign that she was getting tired of her obstinacy, but if he were in the prince's place, he would try and persuade the countess to come to Vienna, instead of going to Pest. The prince listened to this suggestion; he fell into the trap, and

190

will not go to Pest at once, but will try to bring the countess back.

'In the meantime, we are to have the last two rehearsals. The thirty-second is the representation of Julia Gonzaga, whose story you will find in any library. The most interesting part of this scene is the toilette of the heroine, who appears in a muslin nightdress, with her feet bare. In spite of this rather *risqué* costume, the lady's virtue was irreproachable, for in her hand she held a dagger, and threatened to kill anyone who ventured to look at her feet.

'As I wrote to you, Kaulman has always been present at these rehearsals, but he will absent himself from Julia Gonzaga, as he has to go away for a few days. I believe that my office should be called *garde des dames*.

'As it happens, however, on this occasion I, too, am unavoidably prevented from being present. When I went home and showed Mamma the enclosed photograph, she shuddered, and positively forbade me to assist at a rehearsal in which a woman appeared in such a costume. I must plead illness, or some other excuse, but stay at home I must. I thought over several lies, but at last I decided that I would tell my gracious pupil the truth; so I did.

'Listen', I said. 'My mother will not allow me to accompany you if you sing barefoot. If it really is the point of the piece that Julia must be seen without stockings, then I must deny myself the pleasure of playing on the piano.'

'The silly child laughed very much, and said she would get somebody else. She may do as she likes; I don't care. Mamma is perfectly right in forbidding me to go, and I think that I have done perfectly right to tell my pupil why I refuse to accompany her.'

This letter depressed Iván. For a long time he looked at the photograph, considering it from every point of view. Evila was dressed in a material which showed every movement of her curving limbs; she gathered the folds across her breast with one hand, her eyes had a murderous glare in their violet depths, her long and beautiful hair fell to her feet; in her right hand she pointed a dagger towards a motionless form at her feet, covered by a rug. This was the second time that Iván had heard this story.

The next day he received another letter from Árpád; he found it on his return from his first meeting with Salista.

'Eveline', wrote the artist, 'performed her tableau before the prince without the accompaniment of the piano, and without the presence of her husband. She looked so lovely that all the prince's good principles melted like snow in the sun. He took her hand and kissed it; then the murderous look disappeared from her sweet eyes; she broke out into a ripple of laughter.

'Prince, do you not see that I have a knife in my hand?'

'I can take it from you.'

'The young girl laughed again; and we all know how easy it is to take anything from a smiling woman.

'At this moment an echo of Eveline's laugh resounded through the room; that is to say, if you can call a frog's croak an echo of a nightingale's song. A crippled dwarf crept out of the conservatory, which ornaments one side of the room, supporting himself on crutches. His long head was sunk between his high shoulders, and his white, satyr-like face was distorted by an odious grin as he dragged himself between the prince and his inamorata.

'Prince, we are not alone,' laughed Eveline, freeing her hand from the astonished nobleman.

'In Heaven's name, who is this splendid toad?' he cried with disgust.

'This is my only, my beloved little brother,' cried Eveline, putting her arms round the little monster, and covered him with kisses while she stroked his head. 'My dear, only little brother, my all, my dearest; my ugly, cross, quarrelsome little tyrant, who comes to me whenever he likes.'

'A horrible creature!' said the prince. 'The hobgoblins who

192

kept watch over the gate of the Witch of Endor were cherubims compared to this monster. I beg of you, Eveline, not to kiss his face; it takes away for ever the pleasure one would have in kissing so lovely a mouth.'

'Eveline did not answer, but suddenly turning away, she threw a wrap over her shoulders, put her tiny feet into a pair of slippers, and said demurely:

"Prince, the thirty-second rehearsal is over, and there only remains the thirty-third to complete the course.'

'The prince asked what the title of this last should be, and Eveline whispered that he would know the day after the next.

'And how many more will know it?'

'No one but you.'

'Not this Caliban?'

'Certainly not.'

'The prince was ecstatic when he left, firmly convinced that at the last tableau he would have Eveline all to himself. Eveline needed a day to prepare herself.

'The scene was described to me by the cripple, who likes me very much, and comes nearly every evening to share my supper, for although everything possible for his comfort is provided by Eveline, he is never happy unless he begs. If he were a prince, I do believe the creature would get down of his carriage for alms. He finds supreme pleasure in begging. What pleased him most was the prince's remark about his being a splendid toad. He showed me how he crept out of the conservatory on his crutches, and how he laughed when he saw that the gentleman wanted to take the knife from his sister. You will hear from me again the day after tomorrow.'

The day after tomorrow! These words to a man who might be lying dead by then! They gave Iván a sudden chill; but he said to himself he would not die easily; he would fight for his life.

That night he dreamt a curious dream, in which he saw two Julia Gonzagas, who both wanted to kill him, and yet he had deserved nothing but good from either.

Chapter XV

TWO POINTS

A duel with swords has the advantage over a duel with pistols, that there is no need to conceal it; it is discussed like any other interesting wager the day before. Even in the past, a duel with swords seldom had a fatal ending: thus it is not surrounded with the mystery that attends more serious affairs. For the seconds, likewise, there is far less responsibility. Even if one of the principals is wounded, the surgeon attending declares that the sufferer has not died of the wound, but that there was some organic trouble in the region which would have killed him within the next forty-eight hours anyway. And who, nowadays, would make a fuss over a man who was doomed to die in forty-eight hours?

The duel which was to take place between the Marquis of Salista and Iván was mentioned at the Club with indifference, as a thing that had a foregone conclusion. Salista did most of the talking himself, and at six o'clock the evening before the duel stood at the fireplace, entertaining a select group, among whom were the four seconds, with his views.

The gilded youth of Pest, being in the habit of practising fencing at various gymnasiums, know the most skilful fencers, and are therefore able to predict, accurately enough in most cases, the outcome of duels. Salista had the reputation of a first-rate swordsman; he had already fought several duels, and always won; he had one particular master-stroke, which few fencers could parry; it was a quick thrust in the stomach, which, passing round the point of his adversary's sword, ripped up his abdomen. If the other intercepted the thrust, he was likely to miss a beat, so that his face, being left uncovered, was exposed to a well-delivered cut which would spoil his looks, even if it did not have more dangerous consequences. Some men would have felt that the circumstances connected with the preceding duel required explanation, that the refusal to stand your adversary's fire sounded shady. Others had been rigorously punished for similar offences by having to rusticate for weeks, and sometimes even longer. Salista was, however, a privileged person; his courage was not called in question. He was a cool hand, and carried off his difficult position with the most astounding aplomb. As he now had the carpet, he talked with a good deal of swagger of what would happen on the morrow.

"We shall see what stuff this chap is made of. Sword-play is not like shooting; there can be no mathematics. We will ask him how he construes the under-cut when the sabre cuts his legs under him."

Count Géza rebuked the boaster. "You must remember," he said, "that Iván acted in the most chivalrous manner, when he accepted the sword instead of the pistol, and you must also consider that he is a man of learning, very much respected, and likely to be of service to his generation."

"Very well. You needn't be afraid; I shall not kill him, I shall only slice a piece off his nose, to give him a souvenir of Pest. A scholar like him will not care if his beauty is spoiled; science is not sniffed up like snuff, and his nose is no use for looking through the telescope at the stars."

Here Edmund interfered, and protested hotly against any injury being done to the nose of his principal. At last the marquis had to content himself with a slice of his ear; but Edmund still remonstrated.

"You should be satisfied with a cut on his hand," he said "the whole matter is not worth more."

Count Stephen here made a suggestion, in his quiet way.

"My good Salista, what if this coal-heaver were to cut *you* down?"

"What?" blustered the marquis, standing with his long legs apart in front of the fireplace. "To show you what I think of him, I will give him two points; I will let him have two cuts at my arm, and then I will cut him down. You shall see! You can make your bets. Who takes my wager?" He went on boasting until the discussion ended. His last question was whether the seconds would be quick enough to interfere before he crippled their great scholar.

On the following day the adversaries met. The large ballroom in the hotel had been thought the most suitable place, generally hired for such occasions. The seconds had chalked the floor to prevent the combatants from slipping. In an adjoining room both principals stripped to the waist, then they were led in. There was no need to draw lots for placing, as the room was lined all round with mirrors. Before they were given their swords, the following conditions were read out:

"First blood. Stabbing is not allowed."

Salista protested. He would not hear of first blood. The duel should go on until one of the combatants declared himself no longer able to fight. The seconds tried to persuade him to be more moderate, but he would not give in.

"Give us the swords!" cried Iván, losing his patience. "I am catching a cold, half-naked as I am."

This interruption decided the matter. The paces were measured, the principals placed in position, and given their swords.

Both were naked to their waist. Salista exhibited Herculean muscles, but Iván, too, had a well-developed body. He had certainly less flesh than his adversary, but was bony, had long arms and a vaulted chest. The fight began in the usual manner. They both presented arms, their left hand drawn back, and their heads covered by bent arms. Now and again they crossed their swords dexterously, trying to find a place for a good

196

thrust, and striking one another softly. Each looked at the other's eyes, to read his intentions. Salista tried to give his adversary a thrust which would injure his face. This was very difficult, for the face is always protected by the arm. As for Iván, he endeavoured to give his opponent the double thrust. This requires extraordinary agility; but he succeeded. He tore the top muscle of Salista's right arm. That this blow did not produce blood at once was due to the cellular texture of the muscles.

"Forward!" cried Salista. "No blood."

He now gave up all attempts at injuring his adversary's face, and resorted to his well-known trick, the belly-thrust, which is difficult to parry, and is so often deadly. If it is not parried, the effect is certain, and if it is, the giver can, if he is a good swordsman, give his adversary a terrible cut over the head. Iván did not parry, well or ill. Salista had not forgotten that the duelling sword is shorter than the cavalry sabre; but he forgot, or rather didn't know, that his adversary had arms of unusual length. Iván did not attempt to parry the belly-thrust; he raised his arm, and let the sword-point of his opponent pass at a distance of a hair's breadth of his body, while he aimed straight at the other's arm, cutting him across in the same place where he had before cut lengthways.

These were the two points. Through this crosscut, the difference of strength between the two men was equalized. This last hit filled Salista with fury. With the roar of a wild beast he threw himself on his adversary, and with all his strength made two cuts at the head. He cut as a butcher cuts with his axe; it was a miracle that both their swords didn't snap, for, according to rule, Iván received both thrusts upon the handle of his sword, and before the other could give him a third, he struck a quick forward thrust, with such strength and precision that it came with full force on the head and face of the marquis. Luckily, the sword was a light one, otherwise he would have split his skull in two. Salista reeled under the blow, then raised

197

his left arm to protect his head, tottered sideways and fell, supporting himself on the handle of his sword. His seconds ran to raise him and lead him away. Iván stood with his swordpoint lowered, his face expressionless like marble. His seconds congratulated him.

"Are the gentlemen satisfied?" Iván asked.

"I dare say they are," returned Count Edmund. "Nothing could have turned out better; the affair is settled."

With these words they took Iván into the next room to dress.

When he returned to the hall, he found that his adversary had recovered consciousness; the two doctors were with him, one binding up his head, the other his arm.

According to etiquette, Iván went over to him.

"Forgive me, my friend," he said.

Salista gave him his left hand, and said cordially: "It is not worth the mention; but it was a splendid cut. The other two don't count, because I had said that I would give you two points; the third—ah, that was a cut! But I shall be all right in a week."

Iván asked the doctors if the wounds were dangerous, but Salista answered for them:

"Soldier's luck," he said. "I have given such a hundred times; now it is my turn, and I don't mind. But one thing troubles me: neither arnica nor ice-bandages can cure it; but *you* who have caused it, can help. Confess, now, that you have been in the army."

"Of course," returned Iván. "During the War of Independence I was a Lieutenant of Hussars."

"The devil take you! Why didn't you tell us before? In which regiment did you serve?"

"In the Wilhelm Hussars. Therefore, I am the only survivor and witness of that memorable exploit when you cut us to pieces."

Everybody burst out laughing, no one louder than the wounded man. The doctors reminded him that he must not laugh, for the bandage on his face would slip.

198

"Very good," said Salista. "I shall laugh with only half my face. Comrade, God bless you! I shall not think any more of the cut now that I know it was the work of a soldier, and not of a civilian. Come, kiss me on the other cheek, the one you have left me whole. So, brother, I cannot give you my right hand, for you have given me a cross-cut there that will show a scar for many a day. It was first-rate, that cut, a regular Hussar cut, and, therefore, I don't mind it in the least."

And the combatants embraced one another.

The next moment, his wounds began to bleed afresh, and Salista fainted from loss of blood. Iván held his head on his knees while the doctors bound up the veins, then he helped to carry him to the carriage.

Every one said, 'A first-rate fellow!'

Chapter XVI

GOOD-BYE

Friends and acquaintances of both parties were assembled at Count Stephen's to hear the result of the duel. The seconds had promised to come with the earliest news. All the *habitués* of Society were waiting in hardly suppressed excitement, bets were laid on who would be wounded, and whether Salista would inflict a serious wound, or only a slight scratch, on his adversary. Count Stephen had the courage to bet ten to one that Salista would get the scratch; he also risked even money that only the marquis would be wounded. No one else for an instant imagined that Iván would escape with a whole skin. If they had done so they might have offered a hundred to one, and even then none of the party would have taken it up.

The heralds planted themselves at the windows to be the first to see the carriage of the seconds. When a cab drove up, they called out:

"Edmund and Géza have come."

"Then I have won my bet," said Count Stephen; "the seconds of the man who is least hurt get away first."

Count Edmund went to the countess's apartment to recount what had happened, while Géza went up to Count Stephen's rooms. He rushed in with the triumphant air due to a victorious second.

"He has cut him to pieces!"

"Who? Who? Iván? Salista?" they cried crowding round the messenger.

"Iván has cut up the Marquis."

An 'A-ah!' was the incredulous rejoinder of the others.

"But I tell you he has," repeated the young count; "he has made mince-meat of him."

"And Iván?"

"He is as unscratched as me."

"Ah, you are making fun of us."

"It is no subject for fun. Ask Salista."

"But where is Iván?"

"He will be here presently, and convince the doubting, who will find no wounds into which to poke their fingers. He went home with the doctors, for Salista had two, who at last succeeded in stitching him together."

Then he related in detail everything that had happened. For those who did not clearly understand, he demonstrated with the help of two walking-sticks the course of the duel. He came to the double-cut.

"So Iván parried the stomach-thrust, and gave the fore-cut —the final *a tempo contre coup*, while Salista couldn't harm a hair of his head!"

"Why, he is a wonder!"

"No such thing," protested Count Géza. "He has been in the army—Captain in the Hussars." (He advanced the rank, but captain sounds better than lieutenant.) "He fought through the Revolution; he was in action, nineteen times, and fought the Cossacks besides. He has also received a medal for bravery."

All this the count imagined might be the fact, although he had certainly not heard a word of such a history from Iván. Once a man has scored one success, he is credited with twenty more.

"Truly a wonderful man!" said Baron Oscar. "For three months now he has been among us every day, and has never mentioned his soldiering experiences."

"Now we are really landed with him, like a Sinbad who cannot be shaken off," remarked Baron Edward. "We wanted to be rid of him, and instead we have raised him into the saddle. He will never dismount; he is mounted over us for ever. No one would dare to speak to him now."

"Good God," cried Baron Oscar, "how high the man will carry his nose now! The women will, of course, make a deuce of a fuss about him, and men must have a certain respect for him. *Sacré bleu!* A man who can shoot and fence like this fellow! But I bet anything that it was just an accident."

"I think quite the opposite," remarked Count Stephen, "and I very much fear that Iván will leave us now, thank us for our friendship, and never come near us again."

"Oh, he wouldn't be so foolish! I bet you a hundred to one."

"First pay me the bet you have lost."

Baron Oscar put his hand in his pocket, but before he drew out his wallet, a happy thought struck him.

"How if Géza and his fellow-second were playing a joke on us? They may have made up the whole story. Perhaps the truth is, that in the end the quarrel was made up, and there was no duel, and that they have both come from lunch where no blood flowed, just plenty of champagne."

"If you don't believe me, then drive to Salista's. My cab is at the door. Go and convince yourself."

The baron rushed off. On the stairs he met Count Edmund coming up from the ladies. He asked where Oscar was rushing in such haste.

"He doesn't believe Géza's story."

"That is just the way the ladies have treated me; they won't believe me. They say, 'If nothing has happened to Iván, where is he?' The countess Theudelinde is crying a river full of tears; she berates us all, and declares we have killed her hero. The devil only knows which of the two ladies is more in love with him. Until now I thought I knew, but now I am all confused again."

Baron Oscar returned at this moment. He didn't say a word, but took out his wallet and paid his bet to Count Stephen. It was convincing proof.

"Well, how is Salista?" asked several together.

"He is terribly disfigured."

On this, they all took out their purses and settled their lost bets; they did it with very sour faces. If only the Ritter Magnet had been disfigured!

Just then Iván was announced. Their glum faces changed with marvellous speed to friendly smiles. He was greeted warmly; everyone wanted to shake hands with him. He was the hero of the hour, but he looked tired and serious. Count Stephen was the last to press his hand.

"I am glad," he said, "to see you uninjured."

Two young fellows said to one another: "Old Stephen may well be glad; he has made a good thing of the handicap, and cleared us out fine." But in spite of their losses, they, too, were glad.

They all seemed pleased except, perhaps, Iván. "I thank you all," he said, in his grave voice, "for your warm sympathy; and I thank you, count, in particular, for your cordiality, and for the friendship which you have given to me. I shall always feel grateful for the memory of your kindness. I beg of you, remember me, too, for I have come to say good-bye. I am going home tomorrow."

The count winked with his left eye at Baron Oscar, as who would say, 'Did I not tell you so?' But he did not try to make Iván change his mind. He pressed his hand warmly, as he said:

"You must know that I esteem you highly, and if we ever meet again, you can always consider me an old friend. God bless you!"

Baron Oscar made much more fuss. He took Iván's arm with both hands.

"My dear friend, we cannot allow this. Such a good fellow as you have proved yourself to be cannot slip away from us in this manner—just at the moment, too, when you are going to be the lion of the season. You shan't escape; you belong to us."

Iván laughed; gentle sarcasm, half pain, half irony, unmixed with bitterness, was in his laugh. Then he answered this burst of friendship:

"I thank you, my friend, for the honour, but I am not fit to be Governor of Barataria; I am far better off at home. I will go to get my 'grison' saddled, and I ride away."

(Those conversant with 'Don Quixote' will remember the skit on the island of Barataria, and the affecting meeting between the ass and his master.)

Saying this, Iván made a deep bow to the company, and left the room. Count Stephen followed him, and, in spite of his protestations, accompanied him to Theudelinde's door. He was much moved by Iván's last words.

When he returned, he found the company still in an uncomfortable frame of mind, discussing the scene that had taken place with much annoyance.

"At all events, we have pleased my pretty cousin," remarked Count Edmund. "She wanted him to be sent about his business, and we have done it."

"Oh, is that so?" And Count Stephen smiled sardonically. "*Cherchez la femme*, as Talleyrand said. But I know the dear, capricious sex. When Iván tells the ladies downstairs that he is leaving, there will be a reaction, and your pretty cousin will cry out, 'Then we shall go together.'"

The others laughed, incredulous; only Edmund assumed the air of a Pontius Pilate.

"I should not be surprised," he said. "*Enfin*, there would be nothing disgraceful in it. The fellow is a gentleman; he was a soldier, and is of good birth. His land joins the Bondavára property; his income is something under two hundred thousand florins. Angela is heiress to twenty millions; but then if our beloved uncle, Prince Theobald, lives another ten years, and carries on as he is doing, it may happen that Iván and Angela may be on the same level as regards fortunes. And as far as rank, if the Government continues to play their present game with our rights and privileges, and if under the new parliamentary *régime* the peasant's buskin is to enter the senate, I shall ask to be *raised* to the peasantry."

The countesses Theudelinde and Angela received Iván in their small sitting-room—a mark of intimacy. He came in with a sense of constraint, his paleness, and the feelings he could not hide, added interest to his harsh features.

Theudelinde came to meet him with outstretched hands. She clasped his, and pressed his fingers warmly. Her lips trembled, and she kept back the tears which filled her eyes with difficulty. She could not speak, but nodded to Iván to sit down at a small table, inlaid with a splendid bouquet in mosaic. Theudelinde sat down by him; Angela was opposite. The young countess had not even a flower, usually so becoming to her, in her hair. She was grave, and hardly raised her eyes to Iván.

It was Theudelinde who broke the silence, as soon as she felt able to speak.

"We have been in a terrible anxiety about you," she said. "You cannot imagine what tortures of worry we have gone through in the last two days."

Angela's eyes were fixed on the carpet; she was included in the 'we'.

"I cannot forgive myself, Countess, for my share in causing you pain. I shall do penance for my fault at once, and to-morrow I am going into exile at Bondavára."

"Ah!" Theudelinde's voice expressed surprise. "You are going to leave us? What are you going to do in Bondavára?"

"I will return to my business, which I have neglected too long."

"And do you like to live in Bonda Valley?"

"I can live quietly there."

"Have you any relatives?"

"I have none."

"You have a household?"

"As far as I can, I do everything for myself."

"Are you longing for your friends and acquaintances?"

"I have only my workmen and my machines."

"Do you live a hermit's life?"

"No, countess, for a hermit lives alone, while I have my books and my work; I am never alone."

The countess collected her strength for an important speech. She turned to Iván:

"Please, give me your hand, and stay here."

Iván got up, and bowed low before her. "I shall never forget the kind feelings which prompted your words, as well as the honour you have done me. It is a proof of your great goodness, and I beg you to accept my heartfelt thanks."

"Then you will remain? How long?"

"Until tomorrow morning."

"Ah," cried the countess, with a petulant air, "when I ask you to stay!"

Her disappointment was so transparent, her annoyance so sincere, that it was impossible not to feel sorry for her. Theudelinde looked at Angela as if she expected her help; but Angela never raised her eyes, shaded by long lashes, while her fingers plucked nervously at the petals of a daisy, as if she were consulting that well-known oracle.

"Countess," said Iván, still standing, and with his hand on the back of his chair, "when I answer a friendly invitation such as yours with an apparently uncivil refusal, I feel that I must give you my true reason for withdrawing from your society. I cannot say to you what I would to any stray acquaintance; I cannot make such excuses as 'that I have business at home; that I have been away too long; that I shall return soon.' To you I must confess that I go away because nothing would induce me to remain, and that when I go I never mean to return. Countess, this is not my world; I *could* not live here. I have spent three months as a daily guest in the best circles, living with members of the highest and most cultivated society, study-ing closely their way of life. I quite agree that they have every right to live in any manner they choose; but I, who have been used to a totally different life, who have been taught to consider the world from a different point of view, to revere higher aims, and obey finer instincts, I should be acting a lie and violating my own principles were I to remain in this atmosphere, and live like them. Here, in your exalted rank, you are all solitary rings, while we in the lower orders belong together as links of a chain. You are totally independent of each other, therefore each fol-lows his own inclinations. With us the pressure of life knits us closely together, and we have different names for egotism and generosity. And so I am not fit for your circle. I am ashamed to be proud towards those whom you despise, and I cannot bend to those whom you honour. I do not recognize the gods you worship, and I can't mock at my God, and ignore Him as you do. In this world of yours there is a malicious demon who transforms all the good in a man's nature, and who prompts him to scoff and deny every virtuous impulse. Who tells his friend or neighbour the truth, and who cares for any one who is not present? Close friends race side by side over hill and dale, but if one takes a false step and breaks his neck, good-bye to him, the dear friend is gone. Another may not break his neck, but dissipates his fortune; those who are running with him never say, 'Stand aside, or you are going to founder.' He stumbles, and his fortune and the honour of his ancestors tum-ble into dust. Good-bye to him; his name is struck off the club; the dear friend is no more. It is true, we knew that he was riding for a bad fall, but no one seemed to know it, so we went on with our dear friend to the last. Now all the world is aware of his fall, and so we no longer know him. If a man wants to go his own way, and live a rational life, he is considered a coward, a miser, or a carpet-knight. And how do women fare in this world of yours? What about your family life, and the sweet joys of the home? What tragedies are enacted in those splendid mansions, and outside, how friends and acquaintances mock and gossip! What refinement in sin! What a worship of transient pleasures! And when they are over, what *ennui*, what world-weariness! No, Countess, this life is not for me. I should be poisoned by this atmosphere. You can stand it; you grace it by your presence; but for me, I should go mad if I stayed. So I must go, and the only thing left for me is to ask your pardon for the way I spoke to you. I admit my indiscretion; I spoke bitterly of Society, and yet I still stand on its parquet floor. I have been ungrateful; I have given expression to my dislikes in your presence, you who have been tolerant with my faults and my awkward manners; who have guided me to the fringes of the circle where I have often played a ridiculous part, and yet, have never been ridiculed to my face. But, Countess, I have felt, forced by your goodness to speak these words. You have, with extraordinary kindness, asked me to stay, and I must prove to you that I am forced to leave by a power stronger than myself."

During Iván's rather long speech, countess Theudelinde had risen to her feet. Her eyes lit up, her face assumed a beatific expression, her lips moved as if she repeated each word he said, and when he had finished his last sentence, she seized both his hands, and she broke into saying:

"You speak the truth . . . the truth, nothing but the truth. You speak as I spoke forty years ago, when I left the world as you are doing now. The world is ever the same; it does not change." Here she shook his hands with passion. "Go home," she sobbed, "go back to your solitude, hide yourself under the earth, conceal yourself in your mines, God will be with you wherever you are—everywhere. God bless you! God bless you!"

She did not notice that Angela also rose from her chair, and as Iván took his leave she took a step forward, and said in a firm, decided voice:

"If you go away, you will not go alone, for I shall go with you." Her whole face glowed as she spoke these words.

208

Iván had to be the master of the situation. Standing on such giddy heights, he none the less retained his balance. With great presence of mind, he answered the excited girl:

"You will act rightly, Countess. Tomorrow is your grandfather's birthday, and early tomorrow you can be with him. He is awaiting you with open arms."

Angela turned pale as a statue. She sank back in her armchair, scattering the pink petals round her feet. Iván bowed to her respectfully, kissed countess Theudelinde's hand and left the room.

Not long after Iván had left, Count Edmund called to see the ladies. He was brought by curiosity. Countess Angela was more amiable than usual. When he was leaving, she said to her cousin:

"Go to Salista, and tell him that I have asked after him."

Count Edmund was polite enough to conceal his surprise, but as he went down the stairs he began to hum Figaro's song from the *Barber of Seville*.

The same evening, countess Angela wrote to her grandfather. Iván was right in saying the next day was his birthday, and her birthday greeting was:

"I am not coming home. Good-bye!"

For two days, all Pest spoke of Iván and his duel with Salista; by the third day, he was forgotten.

"Good-bye!"

Chapter XVII

THE LAST REHEARSAL

On the morning of his birthday, Prince Theobald received a letter. It was from his only grandchild, and ended with the word 'Good-bye.'

The prince's birthday had always been a holiday for him. From Angela's childhood to last year's anniversary, each year she had given him a birthday kiss. This day, it had been a bitter salutation.

Amongst his treasures, the old man kept a particular album, handsomely fitted with gold mountings, in which he preserved her birthday presents each year.

There was the posy Angela had given him when she was nine years old; the scrawl she had written in her childish hand on a piece of Bristol board; the bit of embroidery, worked in pearls and gold, which, later, she had done for him with her own hand. To these gifts the prince, with a deep sigh, added her last letter, with its farewell.

Prince Theobald was sensitive, but also easy to anger. Even when he thought about it calmly, he found he had every right to exact obedience from his grand-daughter. Angela owed a duty to him, to his position, to the princely house from which she sprang. If, indeed, her heart stood in the way of agreeing to his wishes, one might, perhaps, excuse her; but Angela, he knew, loved no one. Why, therefore, should she seek to defy him for a mere whim? Prince Theobald went to Eveline's last rehearsal with his mind in a tumult of annoyance and excitement. He could yet cop Angela's farewell!

When he reached Eveline's house, the butler admitted him as a favoured *habitué*, leaving him to wait in the drawing-room. The prince looked round, it was the room where the supposed actress usually gave her representations. The rose-coloured curtains were drawn, one corner was filled with green-house plants; the air was perfumed with the scent of the flowers. In another corner two turtle-doves cooed, while behind a little bosquet a nightingale sang its soft stave of love and sorrow. It was more like the home of a nymph, or fairy, in the depth of a wood, than a drawing-room.

The prince sat down on a sofa, and, taking up an album which lay upon the table, he turned over the leaves. It was a collection of photographs of Eveline in her different parts. He went through it from cover to cover, examining each tempting and seductive portrait carefully, and as he did so there rose before his memory the album in which Angela's letters and embroidery were preserved. His thoughts were so absorbed in these recollections that, with a start, he found himself at the last page in the book before him. He roused himself to look at the beautiful figure in a common stuff frock. How captivating, how simple, how lovely!

The nightingale sang, the doves cooed, the air grew heavy with the scent of orange blossom. The prince wondered in what enchanting form his hostess would appear. And now there fell on his ear, coming from a distance, a forgotten tune. He had heard it once, long ago; but he remembered the air. It moved him strangely. It was a simple folk song, the same with which the nurse was wont to rock Angela's cradle. Some Slovak tune: the words were strange to him.

After a few minutes the song stopped, the door of Eveline's dressing-room opened, and she came in—how? In what new and captivating costume did she appear?

She wore a simple dress of black and white gingham; her·

211

hair was smoothly combed back from her young face, and hung down in a long plait; a white lace collar circled her throat.

Softly, modestly, and yet with the confidence of a child, she drew near to the prince, and when she was close to him, she handed him a little sachet of white satin, upon which was embroidered the kneeling figure of a child. Then raising her eyes, full of tears, to his face, she said in a low voice, which trembled with emotion:

"My lord, will you accept this little birthday gift from me? May Heaven grant you a long life."

This scene was so devoid of acting, it seemed so full of feeling and sincerity, that Prince Theobald, thrown off his guard, forgot himself, and instead of the formal 'madame,' said:

"My child—"

At these words the young girl, sobbing wildly, threw herself into his arms.

"Oh, prince," she cried, "do not take back those words; call me your child. There is on this earth no creature more desolate, more unhappy than I am."

Prince Theobald laid his hand kindly on the head of the sobbing girl, and kissed her gently on the forehead.

"Be it so," he said. "Look up and smile, Eveline. I am serious. You are almost a child, and I shall treat you so. I will be your father—no, your grandfather. Fathers love their children sometimes, but not always; but grandfathers never fail in loving their grandchildren. You shall be my little grand-daughter. When I am sad, you will cheer me with your gay chatter; you will read or sing to me when I cannot sleep; you will care for me, and nurse me when I am ill. I shall take care of you, and provide you with all that you want. In return you will obey me; you will listen to me; you will bear with an old man's whims and his petulant temper; you will try to please me. I promise you that you shall be treated well. You shall be mistress over all I have; you shall have everything befitting the position of my daughter; but I must exact the obedience of a child."

212

Eveline answered by kissing her benefactor's hand.

"Are you pleased by my proposal? Do you think you will be happy?"

Eveline laughed with childish delight. She danced round the room in her joy, then, dashing back to the prince, she cried out:

"Oh, my dear, dear grandpapa!"

Prince Theobald threw himself back on the sofa, and burst into a harsh, bitter laugh.

Eveline drew back, hurt and frightened by the horrid discord of his laugh.

"I am not laughing at you, my dear," said the prince kindly. "Come, my pretty grand-daughter, and sit beside me." (His laugh was at the answer he could now make to Angela's farewell.) He stroked Eveline's hair tenderly. "Now we must talk seriously. Listen to what I have to say, and take my words as commands. In *our* family there is only one master, whom all obey. First of all, there is your husband to be considered. It seems to me he takes the responsibilities of his position lightly. Still, he must give his consent to my adoption of you. I don't apprehend, however, any difficulty in obtaining it; you may leave that to me. After that, you will take up your residence in my palace in the Maximilian Strasse. It shall be yours on one condition—that you receive no visitors without previously consulting me. Kaulman is included in this condition. You must have no intercourse with him, except on matters of business. Will it pain you to be separated from him?"

"I could not mind that. We have always lived apart."

The prince pressed her hand kindly. "Poor child!" he said. "Your husband is a good-for-nothing. He has treated you as one of his speculations, and he has gained his end. One thing, however, you have from him—his name. He cannot take that from you. By-and-by you will learn what an inestimable advantage it is to a woman to bear her husband's name. It is a passport; but I do not think Kaulman meant it in that light. Well, let us talk no more of him, but of your future. I shall

213

arrange an engagement for you at the Opera House. You must have a position in the world. The title of actress is like the mantle of a queen; it gives you the *entrée* to the salons of a certain artistic world. Your future shall be my care. You have talent; if you study, you will succeed. You must rise to the heights of your profession, so that when I die you may be able to support yourself."

"If I could only get over my stage-fright," said Eveline, sadly.

"You will, when you get accustomed to the footlights. You will learn by experience that in this world, and especially on the stage, every one is taken at his own valuation. Any one who makes little of himself goes cheap. Above all, you must be most careful how you choose your friends. This is important, and on this point you must allow me to judge for you. If you feel a preference for any one person you must tell me with frankness, and I shall know whether it will be a safe friendship for you."

"Oh, prince, I shall be guided by you in everything."

"My child, do not promise too much. The promises of a momentary enthusiasm or sentiment are speedily forgotten; but there is one promise I would have from you. There is one man whom you must give your word that you will *never* receive— that you will never open any letter that comes from him; that you will never accept a present from him, never pick up a bouquet he may throw you, never notice his applause. This man must not exist for you; you must take less notice of him than if he were invisible. This man is Prince Waldemar."

"Oh, sir, I already hate him. He is repulsive, dreadful, terrible!"

"I am glad to hear it. He deserves every decent woman's hate; but he is rich, young, and handsome. He is mad for you. Women are flattered by such love, and circumstances may arise to change your ideas. Wealth is a wonderful attraction, and poverty is a great tempter. The time must come when I shall no longer be here. You must swear to me that when I am dead, you would still accept nothing from Prince Waldemar."

214

"I swear it to you by what is most sacred—the memory of my dead mother."

"Now, allow me to kiss your brow. I am going to Kaulman to make the necessary arrangements. I thank you for remembering my birthday. Your little present has made me rich. I came here in a very perturbed state of mind; I go away with a tranquil heart. I shall always be grateful to you. God bless you!"

Some days later, Eveline removed to Prince Theobald's palace in the Maximilian Strasse, where she was surrounded by splendour.

The world supposed that Kaulman's wife was the prince's mistress. The prince imagined that he had a grand-daughter still, and Eveline thought she was fulfilling her duty as a wife when she obeyed her husband's command.

At this time, and as the result of Eveline's obedience, the Joint-Stock Mining Company received the assent of Prince Theobald Bondaváry to the contract already signed by his sister, countess Theudelinde.

And in this manner the Bondavára property passed away from its last rightful owners. If countess Angela had followed Iván Berend's advice, this would never have happened, and the property would have been safe.

Why was the countess Angela so obstinate? Why did she behave so foolishly, so ungratefully towards her kind grandfather?

A word must be said in her defence. This Prince Sondersheim, whom Prince Theobald wished his grand-daughter to take as her husband, was the same Prince Waldemar who has been mentioned. Prince Theobald knew his character well. We have heard what he said to Eveline. The world had the worst opinion of him, and Angela knew what the world thought of her future husband.

Was it any wonder she refused to give herself to such a man? Could she act in any other way? Women are the best judges of this. Men do not have the right to judge.

Chapter XVIII

FINANCIAL WISDOM

The Bondavára Joint-Stock Company was about to issue its prospectus; the speculation had been widely advertised, and now it waited only for a capital of ten millions to begin the railroad which was to put the finest coal-mines in the kingdom within the reach of metropolitan markets. The speculation did not, however, attract the public. Who knows about the value of the mine? said one. Who believes what the papers say? We all know their tricks. The gudgeons held off, and did not rise to the bait.

One day Felix Kaulman brought one of the directors to see Iván Berend, and while these two were in conversation he noticed, lying on the table, a piece of coal from the Bondavára mine. The outline of a plant about the size of a finger was visible on it.

"Is this the impression of an antediluvian bird's claw?" he asked.

"No," Iván replied; "it is a petrified plant."

"Ah, I am making a collection of fossils."

"Then take it for your collection," said Iván, carelessly.

Felix took away the piece of coal in his pocket.

Shortly before the prospectus was issued, in one of the best-known scientific journals an illustration appeared with an article descriptive of the petrified *bird's foot* which had been found in the Bondavára mine. The article was signed 'Doctor Felicius.'

All the *savants* were excited. 'We must see this impression!' they cried.

The discoverer had given to the creature, whose footmark had remained unalterably impressed upon the soft coal, the learned name of *Protornithos lithanthracoides*.

'Ho, ho!' exclaimed the united bodies of geologists, physiologists, professors, philosophers, and artesian-well diggers, 'that is a long word indeed!'

One set of learned men declared the thing to be possible, another denied its possibility.

And why was it not possible? Because at the period of coal-formations neither birds nor any mammalia could exist, or did exist, in the bowels of the earth. There we find only traces of plants, molluscs, and sometimes fish.

And why is it credible? Because these days new discoveries are made daily. Humboldt declared that no apes had ever lived in the antediluvian world, as the fossil of an ape had never been found. Since then, one fossilized ape has been discovered in England, and three of the Ourang species in France.

By degrees, the battle raged in every newspaper; it was taken up in English, French, German, and American publications. At last it was proposed that the matter should be referred to a commission of five well-known professors, to whom the petrified fossil should be submitted, and who should decide the question. Doctor Felicius offered one thousand ducats to anyone who would prove that his bird's claw was not a bird's claw.

The five learned judges examined the fossil with microscopic attention, and after a long sitting brought in a unanimous verdict that the impression was not made by the claw of a Protornithos, but was that of a leaf belonging to the plant *Annularia longefolia;* in fact, there could be no question of a bird, as the specimen of coal containing it was not brown coal, but the *purest* black, in which coal formation it was not possible for a bird even to exist.

Doctor Felix Kaulman quietly paid the thousand ducats, and thanked the whole community of professors for the service they had rendered the Bondavára coal; such an advertisement could not have been obtained at the expense of forty thousand ducats. Let people say that the *Protornithos* was a humbug—who cares? The reputation of Bondavára coal was established, and on the best scientific grounds.

The time had now arrived when the undertaking would be floated on the Exchange. This art of 'floating' is, perhaps, the greatest science on earth. The Stock Exchange has its good and its bad days. Sometimes it is full of life, the sheep frolic in the meadow; at other times they hang their heads, and will not touch the beautiful grass. Sometimes they come bleating to the shepherd to be shorn, for their wool presses too heavily on them; another day they butt their heads, and will not follow their leader. Again, no one can tell why, when the bell-wether starts to run, the rest of the flock run after him; neither the shepherd nor his dog can stop them. The science lies in knowing when the weather is good on the Stock Exchange. On a favourable day men are in excellent humour, there is so much gold in every pocket, everything goes so well that even a company for the excavation and possession of icebergs would find bidders. On a bad day the best and safest speculations do not get a single offer.

It was on one of the fine days that the Bondavára Coal Company made its *début* on the Vienna Stock Exchange. It caught on, and by the day on which the subscriptions should be paid into the Bank of Kaulman came round, it was necessary to have a police cordon across the street, to make the flood of applicants pass in some sort of order. The subscribers had, in fact, gathered at the doors early in the morning; those who were strong trusted their own strength to make their way by elbow-force. In the crush, battered hats and torn coats hardly

218

mattered; verbal insults and personal injuries, pushing and squeezing, were treated as nothing. The street windows of the bank were broken, and an excited man cried:

"I subscribe ten thousand, a hundred thousand, a million!"

When six o'clock struck at last, and the bank doors shut, a stentorian voice called from the balcony to the crowd below:

"The subscription is closed!"

What a disappointment for those who had not been able to place their money in time! They went away dejected.

The Bondavára mine had indeed caught on. Instead of ten million, eight hundred and twenty million had been subscribed. Did subscribers really have all this money? Certainly not. Each one deposited a tenth of the sum subscribed by way of guarantee, and this only on paper; the company did not as yet touch actual money. Those who were part of the vast crowd, who tore the coats from one another's backs, were not blessed with a superfluity of money, neither had they the slightest interest in the production of coal, but today it is fine weather on the Exchange; the Bondavára Company's bonds stand at par. Every one wanted to make a small profit; that done, they cared no more for the bonds, or the company.

However, Providence sees to it that trees should not grow sky-high. Prince Waldemar was the head of the opposition, and was one of the cleverest, most astute men on the Exchange.

To understand, the reader should himself be a speculator. It is carried on something like this; those who want to buy, often only want shares to sell them at once to the first bidder. In consequence, this lowers their value; there is a drop, sometimes a total collapse. If the investment is sound, it recovers its vitality, and the shares go up again. There is, however, a way to guard against this trick. Almost every company maintains a syndicate, for the job of finding out whether applicants for shares are men of straw. Pending their inquiry, the time is then used to employ agents, who receive a gift of, say, five hundred shares. These men immediately start a tremendous ballyhoo; they drive up the shares, they tear the certificates from one another's hands, screaming out the high rate at which they are buying. But the general market sees no shares pass; the experienced know that this is all a well-played farce, and that any one who has ready money need only go to the fountainhead and buy as many shares as he wants, at par. On the other hand, the opposition are biding their time to rush in and cause such a depreciation as will run down the shares to almost nothing. Once they get them at this low figure, they may allow them to rise again.

The only one who loses in this cruel game is the small investor, who has ventured, poor soul, on thin ice, and who has sacrificed his all at the shrine of the golden calf, taken his carefully hoarded savings from his drawer, and has cast it on such unprofitable waters, tempted by tales of a quick return, and such like. All of a sudden the opposition rushes in, the mine explodes, his hopes are blown sky-high, vanished like a dream; his shares are so much waste paper. He goes home certainly a sadder, if not a wiser man. Well for him if he is not beggared.

This is how the Stock Exchange is run.

In the town of X there is a street called Greek Street. It is a crescent of pretty houses, erected by Greek merchants. In the middle of the street stands a church with a marble facade and a splendidly gilded tower, whose bells ring the loveliest in the town. It is said that when those bells were cast the Greeks threw silver coins into the liquid metal with both hands.

Old Francis Csanta was now the last of his race. He had once been a gay companion, a carefree soul; a gallant cavalier among ladies, a reckless gambler among men. But over the years he became a silent, moody miser, avoided the company of his fellowman or woman, and come to hate music and all pleasures. The more he indulged in solitude, the worse his eccentricites grew. As soon as one of his former friends, or relations, or boon companions died, he bought the house in

220

which they had lived. By degrees the whole street belonged to him; only one house remained, the one next to his own. This had been occupied by a connection of his, who had left one daughter. Strangely enough, she had not followed the current custom of spinsterhood, but had married, and was the wife of a music-teacher, who enjoyed the Magyar name of Belényi. This couple had a son in due course whom they named Árpád.

This vexed old Csanta sorely. Why should the last remaining Greek girl have married—above all, married a music-master? Why should there be a son? Why should that son be baptized Árpád? And why should these annoying circumstances take place under his very nose? The house, too, was an offence; the only house in the street that did not belong to him. The church was his; no one went in except himself; the clergyman said Mass for him only. He was the patron, the congregation, the curator, the vestryman; he filled every office; he was everything. When he was dead the church would be closed, and grass would grow over its threshold.

The generation in the next house showed no sign of dying: the boy Árpád was lively as an eel. At the age of five he threw his ball over the roof, and it fell into the old Greek's garden, who, of course, never returned it.

The lad caused him even more bitterness later.

About this time, the country fell on evil days. The Hungarians and the Austrians started shooting each other. Their reason is hard to find nowadays. Historians say that it was all child's play, and that the cause lay in the refusal of the Hungarian sepoys—who are Mohammedans—to bite off cartridges which had been greased with lard—the German method. Or did this happen in India? Nowadays it is all uncertain; what is known about it comes mostly from the songs of the poets, and who would believe them?

What interests us in this old story is that it has to do with Iván Berend, and how he came to stay in the Belényis' house. He had been one of the regiment who repulsed an assault on the town, and he was billeted on the music-master and his wife. He was well liked. He was young then, and of good spirits. One day the poor musician, coming home through the streets, was struck by a bullet, and brought home dead. Such things happen occasionally in times of war. Little Árpád was an orphan, and it was then that Iván adopted him. A short time after this Iván laid down his arms, and retired into private life. Why he did so, and where he went, is quite immaterial. Before he left, Iván gave the widow Belényi all the gold he had, so that Árpád's musical education might be continued. He did not care for money, and he could not have employed it better. If he had kept it, who knows what worthless scoundrel would have got hold of it?

He hadn't been gone long when a Hungarian Government official stood in the market-place of X, and to the accompaniment of much drumming, proclaimed the Government decree that all German banknotes should be brought to the town's great square, and burnt in a pyre. Any one refusing to obey would be dealt with accordingly. Every one knew what this meant, and all who didn't wish *to be dealt with*, hastened to bring their banknotes, which were burned then and there.

The widow Belényi had her little savings, a few hundred florins. What should she do? It went hard with her to see her money thrown into the fire. She went to her rich neighbour, and besought him to help her, and to change her money into Hungarian banknotes. The old Greek at first refused to listen, but by-and-by he relented, and did as she wished. He did even more, for a week later he came to her and said:

"I will no longer keep the money which your father lent to me at the rate of six per cent. Here it is for you—ten thousand florins; take it, and do with it what you can." As he spoke, he paid her the whole sum in Hungarian banknotes.

A week later another commandant arrived in the town; this one was Austrian. The next morning more drumming was heard in the market-place, and it was proclaimed that all who possess-

222

ed Hungarian banknotes must have them burned. Those who refused would be shot or hanged.

The poor widow ran weeping to her neighbour, and asked what should she do. The whole sum he had given her was untouched in her drawer. If it was taken from her, she and her child must beg, or starve. Why had he given her this money? Why had he changed her German notes if he knew that this was going to happen?

"How could I know it?" shrieked Csanta; and still screaming, he lamented for himself. "If you are beggared, so am I—ten thousand times more beggared than any one. I haven't a copper coin in the house. I don't know how I can pay even for a bit of meat. I shall have a hundred thousand banknotes burned. I am ruined! I am a beggar!"

And he fell to cursing both Germans and Hungarians, until the widow Belényi implored him not to shriek so loud, else he would be heard, and, God help us all! hanged.

"Let them hear, then! Let them hang me! I don't care. I shall go to the market-place and tell them to their faces they are robbers, and if they won't hang me I'll hang myself. I am only considering whether I shall suspend myself from the pump-handle or from the steeple of the church."

The widow besought him, for Heaven's sake, not to do such a terrible thing.

"And what's to become of me? Am I to go round with a hat and beg for a penny? Here, these are my last halfpence."

He drew a few coins from his pocket, and began to weep; his tears streamed down his face.

The poor woman tried her best to console him. She begged him not to despair; the butcher and the baker knew him, and would trust him.

"Oh, you will soon see," sobbed the old man. "Come to-morrow morning early, and you will see me hanging from a hook in the passage. I couldn't survive this!"

What could she do? The poor soul carried her Hungarian

banknotes to the commander, and saw them consumed in the market-place.

Oh, it was a funny joke! To this day, when people talk of it, their eyes fill with tears.

For the widow, and many like her, months and years of grinding poverty followed. She had lost all the capital saved by her father; nothing remained except the house. The front rooms she let as a shop, and she lived and eked out her miserable income as best she could in the back.

For a long time she looked with fright towards her neighbour's hallway, expecting to see the old man hanging from an iron hook; but she was spared this sight. The old man had no notion of ending his days. He had certainly lost a few thousand florins, but these were only the chaff; the corn was safe. He had a secret hiding-place to which he could have access by a secret passage underneath his house; the cellar was, in fact, beneath water. A mason from Vienna had built it for him, and the people of the town knew nothing of it. This cellar was full of casks, and every cask was full of silver; the old man's cellar concealed a treasure. By means of some secret machinery constructed in his bedroom, the owner was able to open a sluice concealed in the bed of the stream by touching a spring, and thus submerge his cave in a few minutes. No robber could have penetrated it. All the gold and silver pieces which came into Csanta's hand found their way to this subterranean hiding-place, and never saw the light of day again.

Meantime his neighbour, the widow, suffered in the grip of poverty; she sewed her fingers to the bone to earn their daily bread. She wouldn't have touched the gold pieces Iván had given her, even to save herself from starvation; they were used for their intended purpose—for Árpád's musical education, and musical instruction was dear. The child had genius.

But life grew dearer, work harder to get. The widow was forced to mortgage her house; she asked her neighbour, and he lent it readily. The loan grew and grew until it reached a large sum: and then Csanta asked for it back. The widow was not able to refund, and the old man instituted proceedings, and as he was the only mortgagee, he got it for a quarter of its real value. The amount over and above the debt and the costs were handed to the widow, and there was nothing left but to leave. The poor widow took her son to Vienna, to begin his artistic education in earnest.

The old Greek now owned the whole street; there was no one left to annoy him in his immediate neighbourhood; he suffered neither from children, dogs, or birds. And his treasure increased. The casks which filled the cellar under the water were filled to overflowing, and the contents were always silver.

One day Csanta received a visit. It was from an old acquaintance, a Viennese banker, whose father had been the old man's friend and at whose counting-house he could always get exchange for his banknotes and other little accommodations. The visitor was Felix Kaulman.

"To what circumstance do I owe the honour? What good news do you bring me?"

"My worthy friend, I shall come straight to the point. Time is precious to you, as it is to me. By the authority of the Prince of Bondavára I have been placed at the head of a joint stock company, who have just started a gigantic coal-mine, whose capital has risen from ten millions to eight hundred and twenty millions."

"That is eighty-two millions more than you would require."

"The money is the least of it. What I need is well-known men for the administration, for the result of the whole undertaking rests on the zeal, the ability, the intelligence of the governing body."

"Well, such men are not difficult to find if there is a prospect of a good dividend."

"The dividend is not to be despised. The bonus to each member of the administration will be yearly five or six thousand florins."

225

"Really? What a nice income!—a stroke of luck for those who are chosen."

"Well, I have chosen you for a member, my worthy friend."

"An honour, a great honour for me; but how much must I put down before I am admitted?"

"Neither before nor after shall you be asked to put down anything. The only condition is that every member of the administration must hold one thousand shares."

"That means paying in a deal of money, my young friend."

"I didn't say a word of paying in; I only spoke of holding."

"But, my young friend, although I am only a provincial merchant in a small way, I know that, so far as money is in question, to subscribe is another word for payment."

"With this exception—if both subscriptions equalize one another. Ah, I see you do not like even a question of subscribing. Well, listen. We will suppose that you take one thousand shares in my coal company, and at the same time I give you an undertaking to take over one thousand shares at par from *you;* in this way we are even, and neither of us loses a shilling."

"Hem! But why is this game necessary?"

"I will be frank with you. The world keeps its eyes on the acts of important men; if these move in any affair, others move likewise. If it is known on the Exchange that you, my worthy friend, have bought a thousand shares, a hundred small speculators will immediately invest in shares. In this way you secure a sinecure which will give you five or six thousand florins, and I will secure a splendid future for my undertaking. Now, have I not spoken the truth?"

"H'm! I will think it over. Meet me tomorrow at the restaurant."

Csanta spent the whole morning in the restaurant; he listened to all that was said of the Bondavára speculation, and came to the conclusion that he would risk nothing, since all danger was covered by Kaulman's bond. When Felix arrived he had made up his mind.

"Good! I will take up the shares; but none of them shall be left hanging round my neck, for I don't like paper. Paper is only paper, and silver is always silver."

"Don't be afraid, my friend; I shall keep all the shares. I shall deposit the caution for you, and I pay the instalments."

Felix satisfied the old Greek completely about his pure intentions in the matter, and left him his written pledge to take them over at par.

Now the manoeuvre behind the scenes began. The agents and the brokers rushed in; the Bondavára shares rose rapidly. The syndicate had, all this time, never given a share to anybody. The bears had not yet started their dance. Csanta had begun to study the newspapers. True, his eyes never left the financial column, but that was the tree of all knowledge; it spelt out golden truth. He read with amazement how the value of the Bondavára shares increased every day. The profit grew higher and higher; it went up in leaps and bounds; sixteen, eighteen, at last twenty florins above par. Those who had put down two hundred thousand florins had made twenty thousand in two weeks. A splendid speculation, indeed, to make a fortune in less than a fortnight! Compare it with an honest, hard-working usurer like himself. What difficulties he had to extract twenty per cent interest from his miserable clients! The work was hardly worth the gain; the fatigue of trapping some silly idiot, the odium and hatred incurred by exacting a repayment from some miserable beggar with a family, or taking the pillow from under the head of a dying man; these things go against the grain, yet they must be done, to fill a cellar with silver. And here a wretched, good-for-nothing speculator, by a mere stroke of the pen, makes a fortune in two short weeks. Luck is not meted out to mortals evenly.

The time arrived for Felix Kaulman to demand from Csanta the thousand shares on which he could now make a profit of twenty thousand. No honest man could allow such an iniquitous robbery of his rights, or, at least, not without a struggle. It is only a fool who can be used as a tool. A man may steal for himself; but it is wicked and immoral to rob to fill another man's purse.

When Felix Kaulman came again to the town of X, the old Greek received him with great ceremony and pretended cordiality.

"I hope you bring good news, my dear young friend," he said, clasping Kaulman's hand in his.

"I have come about that little business of the shares," returned Felix, with the air of a man of business. "You remember our agreement?"

"What shares do you mean? Oh, the Bondavára! Is it urgent?"

"Yes, for the first instalment of interest is now due; two florins on each bond, which, as the shares are in my name, will make an addition to my savings."

"Oh, so you intend to call in the shares?"

"But that was our agreement."

"And if I do not wish to surrender more than five hundred?"

Kaulman drew in his lips. "Well, I suppose I should be content."

"And if I do not wish to surrender any?"

Kaulman looked at him uneasily. "Sir," he said, "I thought I was dealing with an honest man. Besides, you forget, I gave you a written agreement."

"My friend, my good young friend, that is true. You gave me a written agreement, and signed that you were obliged to take these shares from me at par; but I signed nothing, and there is nothing to force me to give you these shares. There you have the whole thing in a nutshell."

"But, my good sir," repeated the banker, taking hold of the old Greek's coat lapels, "listen to me. Don't you know that it is one of the laws of commerce that there is no need for a written indenture? If I take shares from you, I have only to make a note in my pocket-book. Surely you know that this is the law on Exchange?"

"What do I know of the laws they make there? I never set my foot in the place."

Kaulman made an effort to laugh. "I must confess I have never been sold down the river like this. I have found my master. Won't you give me any of the shares?"

"Not even half a share."

"Very good. Then you must pay up the agreed sum."

"Certainly. I shall pay down the money."

"I mean the whole sum. Do you understand?"

"Undoubtedly. Don't be afraid; the money is ready; this house is good for more than that. I can pay you in either gold, or in silver."

"Well," cried Kaulman, bringing his clenched fist down on the table, "I would never have believed that I should have been outwitted in this little town."

Csanta suspected that were he to fail paying his first instalment, his shares might be annulled. He, therefore, lost no time in paying the first thirty-five per cent to the bank. But this was not an easy task. It would need several waggons to transport seventy thousand silver florins to Vienna, and not only waggons, but a gendarme escort, and this would make people stare. Well, let them stare!

When the old man went down to his cellar and looked at the casks which contained the sum needed, his heart gave beat. These casks contained all the treasure he had garnered; his solid capital. It was foolish, he knew, yet he could not help tears coming to his eyes as he chose seven casks from the twenty which should be the first to go.

"You shall have no cause to reproach me, you who remain here," he said, "those that are now leaving you shall soon return. They are going on a safe journey, not on a wild, adventurous sea where there would be danger of shipwreck, but on a safe railroad to increase and multiply. Once I have the shares in my hand, they shall not stay a night in my possession. I shall sell them at once, and get back my silver. The profit, too, I shall change into silver. Instead of seven casks I shall return with nine."

In this way did the old Greek miser comfort himself for the temporary loss of his silver pieces. He counted them that night when the day's work was done, and then set about arranging the transport of the consignment to Vienna.

The day before Csanta had decided upon this step, the opposition made its first move. It was, however, only a trial; they only wanted to show their teeth. They started to buy. If silver goes up, paper securities fall. The seven casks from Csanta's cellar arrived opportunely. Two waggons laden with leaden casks, and guarded by armed gendarmes as they went slowly through the streets, attracted enough attention. When it became known that these casks were full of silver, and that all this silver was to be paid as the first instalment of some Bondavára shares, there was considerable excitement. Peru and Brazil were opening their flood-gates. The firm of Kaulman very naturally made as much as possible of the event, a feather in their commercial cap. The delivery arrived, as it happened, during the absence of the chief cashier, which involved an immense amount of running hither and thither in search of him, as it was necessary Csanta should receive his receipt. In the afternoon the shares were handed over, and the silver was counted. All this made much stir and to-do in the Kaulman Bank. Kaulman entrusted the conduct of the affair to his most capable agent. He instructed him how to act, and added that if the old Greek gave him a tip, he was to kiss his hand, and to place himself altogether at his service. This man's name was Spitzhase.

Later in the day Spitzhase brought Csanta his account, drawn up properly, together with the shares, and begged to inform his Excellency 'that he had brought seven hundred florins more than was calculated, since yesterday silver had risen another per cent.'

'H'm!' thought Csanta, 'this is an honest fellow; I shall give him a tip.' And he gave him a fiver.

Spitzhase overpowered him with thanks; then took his hand, and kissed it.

'H'm!' thought Csanta, 'I have given him too much; perhaps one would have been enough.' Aloud he said:

"I made a mistake. Give me that note back; I will give you another." And he gave him a smaller banknote.

Spitzhase thanked him warmly, and kissed his hand.

'H'm! This is really a good fellow—a man after my own heart. Give me back that money; here is another note. I made a mistake.' And he handed him ten.

Spitzhase kissed both his hands, and showered blessings upon him. Csanta was convinced that he had made this man his friend for life.

"If I had brought the silver tomorrow, I could have got even more for it," he said, reflectively.

"No, believe me, today was the right moment; tomorrow silver will fall two per cent."

"How do you know?"

"Oh, I am acquainted with the ways of the Stock Exchange."

"You are? Then why don't you speculate, if you know the ins and outs so well?"

"Because one must have money, and I have none. I can only dabble in trifles."

"Are you well known on the Exchange?"

"I spend all my time there, except when I sleep."

"Then take me to the Stock Exchange. I should like to see it."

Csanta meant to sell his Bondavára shares as soon as he could find a suitable purchaser.

"Can one go in the evening?" he asked.

"That is the liveliest time, particularly on a day like this."

So Csanta was introduced into the temple of Mammon. Even outside, he could hear a strange noise and tumult of voices, and as he stepped inside his head almost reeled at the spectacle. The large hall was full of top-hatted men. Each spoke, or rather shrieked, as if he were quarrelling. They argued with their hands, holding up pieces of paper in the air, making signs and figures on their fingers, and screaming out names and making offers until the noise was deafening.

Spitzhase, who was perfectly at home, led Csanta through the throng. The old merchant was indignant at being pushed about, no one even begging pardon for any rudeness. He would have liked to know what was meant by the words so constantly repeated, 'I give!' 'I take!' His attention, however, was at once riveted by another word which seemed to be in every man's mouth, and which gradually became plainer: 'Puntafar! Puntafar!' It dawned upon him that it must be Bondavár. He stopped and timidly asked one, "Who wants 'Puntafar'? What is the price at which the Bondavára shares are selling?"

"Thirty over par."

Csanta's eyes blazed. "It is impossible; it cannot be!" he said. "Yesterday they were at twenty."

"That was yesterday. Today they are at thirty. If you want to buy tomorrow you will have to pay thirty-five. The whole world is buying the issue. A rich nabob from India has brought all his silver here, and bought Puntafar shares. The Bey of Morocco and a Russian prince, who both own silver mines, have each ordered ten thousand shares. Even the small men who only have a few hundred, are tearing shares from each other's hands; they won't have anything but Puntafar. What will you take?"

Csanta had no idea that he united in his own person the East Indian nabob, the Bey of Morocco, and the Russian prince, or that it was he who had caused this uproar. So far from such an idea crossing his mind, he thought that the man was kidding him.

"Oh, sir," he said, "thirty is too much. I can give you a thousand Bondavára shares at five-and-twenty."

These words caused an uproar such as had never been heard

on the Exchange. Every one crowded on Csanta; he was set upon from all sides, he was mobbed. People fought with one another over his head, and flourished their fists in his face.

"Who is he? Who is he? A conspirator, a thief, an agent! Out with him! Beat him! Pitch him out! Twenty-five will he take? Give him twenty-five blows on his back, and tear up his coat!"

Spitzhase could hardly manage to get him out. He was in a deplorable condition when he emerged, his hat smashed, his clothes all awry, his face pale, his breath short. Once in the open air, his rescuer began to scold him.

"What the devil did you do that for? Just at the moment when the cabal was silenced and trampled in the dust, to come forward as one of them, to run down your own shares!"

"I did not want to run them down; I only wanted to make sure whether such an advance could be realized."

"Oh, that's the way with you," returned Spitzhase, in an aggrieved tone. "Well, I can tell you the Exchange is not a good place to try out your jokes. It is all quite genuine. The Bondavára issue is as sound as ready money. Today it is thirty, tomorrow it will be thirty-two, and so on—always getting higher. If I had the money I would put in my last farthing. I know what I know, and I have studied the weather on Exchange, but what I have learned from Kaulman I cannot tell; my lips are sealed."

Upon this Csanta pressed the clerk very hard. "You can tell me," he said; "I am in it with you. What have you heard?"

"Well," said Spitzhase, lowering his voice and looking round cautiously, "what you say is true; you hold much stock, so perhaps I may give you this hint. *Puntafar has not reached its highest point yet*. Oho! they are very tricky who hold it over. I am in the secret, and there is a plan, the details of which I daren't tell, which drives the shares still higher. In six months one impulse will be given, six months later another. Oh, the world will open its eyes and its ears; but what I say, you will see. In a year's time Puntafar will be at one hundred over par."

"A hundred!" repeated Csanta, falling back against the wall in his astonishment. But he soon recovered. He was angry with Spitzhase for treating him as if he were a fool.

"I tell you what you are," he said; "You are a boaster. Leave me; I shall get home by myself." And he dismissed Spitzhase angrily.

The next morning his first word was to ask the waiter for the papers. His eyes eagerly sought the Exchange column, and there, just as Spitzhase had prophesied, silver had dropped by two per cent. Bondavára stood at thirty to thirty-two, and what is printed, is the Gospel.

"Not one shall I sell!" cried Csanta, clapping his hands.

And then he got up and dressed. Here was a stroke of luck. It was like a fairy tale; a man had only to leave the window open at night, and next morning his pockets were full of gold.

He was swallowing his breakfast when Spitzhase was ushered in, his face beaming with triumph.

"Now, what did I tell you?" he cried, as he put a newspaper in front of Csanta, pointing with his finger to the Exchange column.

The old Greek said not a word of having already read it; he nodded his head as he answered, with great composure:

"Is it really true? Well, that is satisfactory."

"I rather think so; by the evening they will be up to thirty-five. Oh, if I had only some money!"

"Well, here is another note for you. Go and buy yourself a share. There, don't kiss my hand. I cannot allow it." But he did allow it.

"Don't sell the share," he went on, "keep it for yourself. When the next instalment is due, I will pay it for you. For God's sake don't kiss my hand again! I will do more than that for you. If you kiss my hand every time, I shall have no hands left. Remember that I shall expect you to show your gratitude

234

in a more tangible manner. You must let me know first thing if your boss is going to try any tricks with the bonds. You will be sure to give me the first news as to when I should sell. Do you understand me? Good! Now that you have a share yourself, you have an interest in the matter, and if we sell our shares, are we not entitled to a commission?"

Spitzhase kissed every finger of the old man's hand.

"I implore one thing of you," he said; "don't betray me to Kaulman. If he found out that I gave away his secrets to anyone, he would dismiss me on the spot."

"Don't be afraid. You are dealing with an honourable gentleman," returned the Greek, with dignity.

The honourable gentleman believed that he had won over the honest clerk to betray the secrets of the honourable banker, his employer. It was an honourable game all round. We shall see which of the honourable gentlemen played it best.

Chapter XIX

NO, EVELINE!

It was high time that Iván returned to his coal-mine; he was needed. While he was fighting duels in Pest, strange things were happening in Bondavára. Not far from his workmen's colony, enormous buildings rose with almost miraculous speed, as often happens, when price is no object, the only question asked is how soon shall it be done? The shares had not been issued yet, and the company had already spent a million on the undertaking. Everything was pushed ahead at fever-heat. Here was a new invention for making tiles by machine, there a donkey-engine supplied the materials for building the walls. The earthworks were advanced, the chimneys smoked, the roofs were covered, a whole street was already built; a new town was rising as if by magic.

Of all this activity Iván had been kept in ignorance by his assistant, Rauné, who had also kept quiet about another disturbing element which had made its appearance for the first time among his workmen, as dangerous as 'choke-damp' and 'foul air,' and quite as fatal as either. This new element was 'a strike.' A section of Iván's workmen struck for higher wages, or they would join the new coal-mine, which they called 'The Gentlemen's Works,' at nearly double wages. This took place after Rauné had explained to the men that he had accepted the office of director with the new company, and he naturally wished to take with him the best and cleverest of Iván's men, so that they, too, might profit from the new company. Who could resist such tempting offers? Miners are like other men; they have their price.

Iván now realized the folly he had committed in taking into his service, and admitting to the secrets of his business, a creature recommended by the man who was forming a company to bring about his own ruin.

A scientist is not necessarily a good business man. While Iván was studying the probability of animal life in the antediluvian strata of his coal-mines, he was blind to the danger of a rival company close to his own factory. Nay, more; he had allowed himself to be hoodwinked by a lesser intelligence, and had fallen into the trap set for him by his old friend Felix. Iván was philosopher enough to accept circumstances. There was little use, he told himself, in crying over spilt milk; he had broad shoulders, and they should, if it were possible, push the wheel of fortune. But though he said this, he had little hope of succeeding.

On his return, when he got wind of this danger, he called together his workmen.

"Comrades," he said, "the new company offers you wages which, I give you my word of honour, they cannot pay without considerable loss. Up till now, I have worked my mines with a certain amount of profit; I offer you today, in addition to your usual wages, a share of this profit. For the future we shall divide between us what we earn. At the end of the year I shall lay my accounts before you; one of you, chosen by yourselves, shall examine and audit them, and according to the wages of each man, and the work he has done, he shall receive his share. If you agree to this fair offer I shall continue to work. If, however, you think it better for your interests to take the higher wages offered by the other company, I shall not enter into competition with men who have millions to waste; it would be folly on my part. I shall, therefore, sell them my mine, and you may then be certain of one thing, that when they have both mines in their own hands, and find that no rivalry is possible, wages will be lowered again. To those who will stand by me I offer a contract *for life;* the profits of this mine, so long as I live, shall be divided between myself and my workmen."

Many of his men understood his offer, and the new company could not imitate it. More than half his men closed with Iván's offer, and undertook to remain. A great number, however, influenced by the agents, who were sent to stir up discontent, went over to the 'Gentlemen's Works.'

Those who remained had a great deal of annoyance from those who left. Not a Sunday passed without fights taking place between the two parties.

Iván soon heard that his powerful rival had found another way of checkmating him. His customers, to whom he sent large consignments, not only of coal, but also of copper and iron, informed him that the new Bondavára Coal Company had offered the same quality goods at fifty per cent less, and that, unless he was prepared to make a similar reduction, they would not deal with him. Fifty per cent higher wages and fifty per cent less profit means working for nothing. Rauné had Iván's business in the hollow of his hand; he could ruin it, and he meant to do so. Iván saw this clearly, but he did not lose heart. He wrote to all his former customers that it was not possible to give either coal or iron a farthing cheaper, not if it hung round his neck as a dead weight. The consequence was, coal and iron accumulated in his ware-houses; scarcely a single waggon with his name was to be seen in the streets of Bondavára. The mine and the foundry worked for nothing.

Things looked black for the men who had remained true to him. Their former mates jeered at them in the streets. 'Where is the profit?' was a popular cry. Iván tried to quiet the disappointed men; he asked them to wait. By the end of the year, he prophesied, they would be on the winning side. To give things for nothing was not trade, and if the company chose to do it, he wasn't going to follow such a suicidal example.

238

The great buildings of the new works being completed, the directors announced that they would hold an opening ceremony for the undertaking. The principals, directors, managers, and shareholders from Vienna were invited to a banquet.

The largest hall in the factory was fitted up as a dining-room, with tables laid for workmen as well as for the distinguished strangers. It was widely rumoured that the prince was coming. The company had appointed him as president. Both the princes were patrons of commercial and industrial undertakings, but Prince Theobald possessed an extraordinary financial talent; any speculation he entered was sound, it was said; also, that he had taken a million shares in the new company. It was so far true that Kaulman had offered him this million, which was to increase the value of the Bondavára property, but it is needless to remark that the million shares had no tangible existence.

Previous to the inaugural ceremony, a religious service was to take place, and it was only fitting, that it should be conducted by the eminent Abbé Samuel. Before such distinguished guests it would hardly be in keeping to have a man such as Father Mahók, although it was true that he slaved all through the year among the people.

The guests came from the castle, where they had arrived on the previous day. They drove into the town in splendid coaches. That of Prince Theobald came first, with his arms emblazoned on the panels, with two footmen behind in dazzling liveries of scarlet and gold, the coachman on the box in a powdered wig and three-cornered hat. The coach drew up to the church door, the footmen jumped down and opened the carriage door. An old gentleman with white hair, a clean-shaved, soft, friendly face, and a very distinguished air, alighted first. He reached his hand to a splendidly dressed lady in velvet and lace, who descended from the equipage with graceful nonchalance. The crowd saw her shoes of lilac velvet and her embroidered silk stockings.

"What a great lady!" the crowd murmured. "She must be a

princess, for all the gentlemen at the church door took their hats off to greet her."

Only one man, in a rough coat, called out:

"Evila!"

It was Péter Saffran.

The lady heard the exclamation, and turned a laughing face to the crowd.

"No," she said; "it is *Eveline*."

She bowed her head sweetly as she floated up the church steps.

Eveline's vanity had brought her to Bondavára; she wanted to show off her silk stockings to her former friends, who had seen her in wooden clogs and without stockings. It was the vanity of the peasant girl—not pride, note, only vanity. She did not look down on her friends, as some upstarts do; she wanted to do good to every one of them. She was ready to give them money, to earn their grateful thanks, particularly those who had been kind to her in the old days; to those especially she wished to prove that, although she had risen to a high position, she had never forgotten how much she owed to them. She would be good to them now, in her turn.

Eveline had looked forward to seeing her former bridegroom. Most probably he had long since consoled himself for her loss, and married someone. A little present would make *him* happy.

She had also counted on meeting Iván. She remembered his goodness with gratitude, and she was glad to think she had the power to prove her gratitude. She could not give him a present, but she could tell him of the dangers that threatened his property from the large company, and she promised herself to use all her influence to make the best terms for Iván in case he consented to come to terms with his gigantic rival.

Yes, it was indeed the vain desire of doing good that had brought Eveline to Bondavára. She had arranged how and where she would have her first meeting with Iván.

The notables and landowners of the neighbourhood had been invited, in the prince's name, to the banquet which was to inaugurate the works. No one could refuse such an invitation. It was true that when Eveline had proposed to Abbé Samuel that he should undertake the office of intermediary, and call on his learned colleague Berend, and bring him to the banquet, the abbé exclaimed that not for all the world would he propose that Berend should wait upon their excellencies. And when he said this, he knew very well why not.

Back at the church door, as Péter Saffran stood stock still, gazing after the vanishing figure of his former bride, he felt a tap on his shoulder; turning round, he saw Felix Kaulman behind him. Péter's face went white, partly from fear, but more from inward rage. Felix, however, laughed lightly, with the indifference of a great man to what was, in his opinion, only a good joke.

"Good day, my man. Mind you, come to the dinner," he said, as he followed the prince into the church.

Péter Saffran remained gaping at the noble gentlemen as they got out of their carriages, and when the crowd began to move into the church, he followed in the stream. He made his way into the darkest corner, the shrine of a saint, knelt with his clenched hands against the wall, and his head between his arms, and he made a vow, an awful, terrible vow. Those who saw him kneeling with bent head, imagined that he was repenting his sins. When he had finished his prayer, or his curse, he got up quickly, and, without waiting for the end of the splendid service, hastened from the church, casting a wild look behind him as he went, for he imagined that the saint in her shrine was pointing her finger at him, and calling, 'Catch him! He is a murderer!'

The church service being over, the distinguished guests drove to the company's works, and inspected it all. They drove under triumphal arches which were erected in the streets, and were received by a deputation of workmen. The best speaker made a speech which would have been very eloquent, if he had not got stuck in the middle. The young girl who recited some verses was luckier, and her youngest sister presented a bouquet to Eveline, who kissed the child.

"Ah! you are little Marie. Don't you know me?"

The child, however, was too frightened of the beautiful lady to answer.

The guests visited the buildings under the guidance of Rauné, who spared them nothing—the factory, the machinery, the iron-works. They were terribly tired of it all, and glad to get into the large warehouse which had been arranged as the banqueting hall. Here they were received by two bands playing the Rákóczi March. A crowd of guests came to the banquet, invited and uninvited alike—gentlemen, peasants, clergymen and gypsies. Eveline, however, looked in vain for Iván. He had not even sent an excuse. What a rude man—and yet, perhaps he had his reason. If you drink in advance to your victory over your foe, the foe has every right to decline being present at the feast. Péter Saffran, however, came; he was treated as a guest of honour, and given the first place at the workmen's table. This struck even his dulled senses. Looking round, he saw he was the only representative from the Bondavára mine.

The banquet lasted far on into the evening. Gentlemen and workmen were exceedingly merry. Towards the close of the feast Felix sent for Péter, and presented him to the prince.

"Here is the brave miner whom I mentioned to your Excellency."

Saffran felt the blood rush to his head.

"Well, my good friend," continued Felix, "how has the world treated you since I last saw you? Are you still afraid of the 'doctor'? There's a plaster for you; it will heal the scar of your former injuries." So saying, he took a note for a hundred florins from his pocket-book, and put it into Péter's hand. "No," he added, "don't thank me, but thank the kind lady there, who remembered you."

He pointed to Eveline, and Péter kissed her hand, or rather, her beautiful mauve glove.

What a transformation in the man-eater! He had grown obedient and gentle.

"That good lady," continued Felix, "is your well-wisher. At her request, his Excellency, Prince Theobald, has made you the overseer in the new company's works, at a yearly salary of a thousand florins. What do you say to that?"

What could he say? He kissed his Excellency's hand.

Kaulman filled a large goblet with foaming champagne, and handed it to Péter.

"Toss that off," he said. "But first drink to his Excellency, our generous prince."

"And to the health of this dear lady," added the prince, gallantly, at which the trumpets sounded, and Péter Saffran, the prince, the banker and Eveline drank to one another.

This scene delighted the working-men. There was no pride here, the gentlemen clinking glasses with the common miner. This was the right spirit.

Péter Saffran, meanwhile, was wondering which of the two gentlemen was Eveline's husband, and what was the other to her? He emptied his glass, and put it down again, but it did not occur to him to put the question to any of the three, and so it remained unanswered.

The festival closed with a splendid display of fireworks. The sparks from the catherine wheels fell in a shower of molten gold into Iván's mine.

The following morning Saffran came to Berend and told him that he had a job with the company.

"You too?" said Iván, bitterly. "Well, go!"

Péter was paler than ever. He had expected a reproach for his treachery, but as none came, he suddenly burst out with what had been on his mind for some time.

"Why did you call your friend a doctor *that time?*"

"Because he is one. He is a doctor of law."

Saffran raised his hand in a threat. "Nevertheless, it was very wrong of you to call him *that time* a doctor." And then he turned on his heel and left.

Iván's strength of mind was put to the test more and more. Each day brought fresh defections. His best men left him to go over to his enemy, who raised large furnaces which crushed the very life out of his smaller chimneys. His business contacts fell away from him. They thought he was an obstinate fool, carrying on such an unequal fight; but the darker the outlook, the stronger grew his determination to see the affair through to the bitter end. He would not leave his old home, his own little territory; he would carry on the unequal, perhaps the fruitless task of opposing his apparently triumphant adversary.

In the depth of his misfortune one true, reliable friend remained to him, and saved him from utter despair. This friend was the multiplication table. Before he began his calculations, he asked himself:

'Is this Works a company of businessmen? No, a company of speculators. A joint stock company? No, it's a gamble. Is it a factory? No, a tower of Babel.'

And he went on thinking about it. 'Two and two make four, and turn it any way, it makes nothing *but* four; and if all the kings and emperors in Europe, with decrees and proclamations, were to tell their subjects that two and two make five, and if the Pope fulminated a Bull to true believers that two and two make five, and if even the best financial authority was to declare that we should count two and two as five, all these—kings, emperors, popes, and accountants—would not alter the fact that two and two make four. The splendid shareholders of the Bondavára Company are denying commercial facts. The new company builds, creates, invents, contracts, buys and sells without taking heed of the primary rules of arithmetic. It is clear that they are not working for the future, but only for immediate gain. I will outlive this swindle.'

At the end of the year the company gave their shareholders a surprise. The Bondavára shares began to fluctuate between thirty-five and forty florins on the Exchange, although the date of calling in second instalments of capital was near. At such times all early bonds are handed in. Csanta thought this would be a good time for him to bring in his shares, and get his silver back. He was contemplating a visit to the bank when he received a private note from Spitzhase, putting him on his guard not to fall into the mistake of selling. 'This very day the Board of Directors met, and a resolution had been carried unanimously, that at the next general meeting the shareholders should be surprised by a bonus of twenty per cent, upon which the shares would at once rise.' This was a profound secret, but Spitzhase could not allow his good friend to remain in ignorance.

And at the next general meeting, the commercial world heard the same story. The first two months of the Bondavára Coal Company had been such a signal success that, besides the usual dividend, the directors were enabled to offer a bonus of six florins on each share, which amounted (with the usual rate) to thirty-five per cent, an unheard-of profit in two months.

When Iván read this in the newspaper he laughed out loud. He knew, no one better, how much profit the factory could make: but it is easy to manipulate ledgers to present such remarkable results. What do the unbusiness-like, credulous shareholders understand of such matters? The board of directors knew very well how matters really stood; but they had their own ends to serve. The outside world may suffer in the end; what is that to them? There is no court-martial on the Stock Exchange, and no justice for the injured.

Csanta did not sell his shares. He paid his second instalment in silver, rejoiced over the bonus, and blessed Spitzhase's advice against selling his bonds at thirty-five. They had now risen to forty, and continued to rise.

Iván watched this diabolical swindle calmly. He said to himself: 'How long will their game last?'

Chapter XX

RESPECT FOR BROADCLOTH

It was a singular coincidence that at the same moment when Iván said to himself, 'How long will their game last?' Prince Waldemar, meeting Felix Kaulman, beaming with triumph, at the Exchange, asked:

"How long, do you think, will this comedy last?"

"The third act is still to come," replied the banker.

"Yes, the third instalment. Then I shall hoist you by your own petard."

"We will see about that."

The bears could not imagine what Kaulman had planned. That he had a plan was certain; no one knew except Abbé Samuel and Prince Theobald what it was.

The third act was not the instalment; it was the Bondavára Railway. This bristled with difficulties. The Government was angry with Hungary, and in their irritation would not listen to any proposals about railways and such like. Let the country go to the devil; what did they care? And no doubt they were justified in their indignation. Every Hungarian who wore broadcloth was against them. The body of officials, the middle class, the intelligence of the country, preferred to give up their place and government patronage rather than submit to the chimeras which the cabinet at Vienna indulged in by way of government. Good! As far as officials were concerned, it was easy to fill the places others had resigned, for when a feast is spread, guests are never hard to find. The new hirelings took the oath, pocketed their salary, feathered their nests, but did nothing to promote the government's measures. Between the men who had resigned and the newly appointed officials there was only one difference, one set openly declared they would do nothing, while these others pretended to do something, but found it impossible to accomplish anything. They tried to push, but the cart would not move. From those who wore broadcloth among the middle classes, the government could expect nothing, that was evident. Formerly those who wore silk and satin acted as a counterbalance—the high and mighty, the nobles, the lawyers, and the priests—but now all held aloof. The primate remonstrated, the bishops counselled the nobility, the upper classes gathered in Pest and discussed treason.

Flectere si nequeo superos.

Let us turn to broadcloth. Broadcloth is, as every one knows, the commonest garb, only worn by the poorer classes. This cloth was suddenly adopted by the capital of the Austrian Empire. This was no caprice of fashion begun by some high lady who imagined that her elegance could lend dignity to the cheapest materials. It was altogether another matter, inaugurated by the legislative body of the kingdom, who all wore broadcloth. Well, what has any one to say against this? Why not? Don't we all believe in democracy? It is true that these right minded men hardly understood a word of the language in which the debates were carried on, but this had the inestimable advantage that they could make no speeches, and, therefore, could in no way impede the course of government business. Nor did they have any knowledge of the laws of nations, the rights of citizens, the complicated details of finance, or the construction of budgets; and this Arcadian innocence entitled them to universal respect and confidence, for it placed them above suspicion. No one could accuse such honourable members of siding with the Government because they held Government appointments.

247

The man who introduced broadcloth to be worn by the legislative assembly was a man of talent. But in Hungary, too, the fashion should be adopted. Were there not one hundred and eight seats in the legislative assembly waiting for good men? These should not be left vacant. To fill these seats, however, one lever was necessary, and that was the influence of the clerical party.

The clergy in Hungary were such poor creatures, so ignorant and uneducated, that they actually preferred to remain faithful to the traditions of Rákóczi than to adopt new-fangled ideas promulgated at Vienna. Even such an insignificant priest as Father Mahók returned the decree which had been sent to him from the high place, to be read on Sundays to his flock, and stated that it was a mistake; he was not the town crier. If the Government wished to issue a proclamation, let it be done in the market-place, by order of the county judge, and accompanied by drum and trumpet. The pulpit was not the place for government proclamations. A similar refusal came from every priest in Hungary, and, in face of this open rebellion, the ministers resolved that the power of the clerical party should be broken.

"Now is the time to act," said Felix Kaulman to Abbé Samuel.

The primate had been in Vienna; he had been refused an audience; he was in disgrace. The clerical party in Hungary was doomed. The sword was drawn against it; the moment was approaching when it would strike.

The Bondavára Railway was the *gradus ad Parnassum*. If it succeeded, if it was worked properly, the House of Kaulman would rank with that of the Pereiras; then, also, the pontifical loan on Church property in Hungary could be raised. All this in one blow! Worldly rank, political power, influence over the whole empire, success in the money-market, and the triumph of the Church!

Abbé Samuel had entered upon his ambitious undertaking. The first task was to introduce the hundred and eight Hungarian wearers of broadcloth into the legislative body, and thus to secure the Bondavára Railway, a bishopric, and a seat in the Upper House. These three things lay in the hollow of his hand, for he had three strings to pull, which would set in motion the statesman, the financier, and the influential lady.

On one Saturday, Iván, to his surprise, received a visit from Rauné, who stated his business in a few words. The landowners and inhabitants of various parts of Bondavára wished to send a deputation to Vienna, to lay before the Government and Parliament their request for better communications between their mountainous region and the rest of the empire. This matter interested Iván as much as anyone, and it was desirable that he and his workmen should attend a mass-meeting the next day.

Iván refused all co-operation at once. "We live," he said, "under unusual laws, which forbid political meetings. This mass-meeting has a political object, and therefore I refuse to disobey the law."

In spite of his protest, the assembly took place next day, and Abbé Samuel made a brilliant speech. His dignified appearance imposed respect, his proposal was intelligible, and for the general good; its usefulness could not be gainsaid. To ensure its popularity the astute abbé took care not to introduce into his speech the hated word 'Reichstag.' A resolution was carried unanimously that a deputation of twelve men should be chosen to go at once to Vienna, to present the wishes of the people. The twelve delegates were then chosen by the abbé, and his choice was received with loud shouts of approbation. The Bondavára shareholders came forward with unexampled generosity, and presented each member of the deputation not only with the price of the journey, but a broadcloth coat, a hat, and a pair of boots.

Twelve new suits! That made going to Vienna worthwhile. Still, it went against the grain. Peasants are suspicious; they

on't care to break bread with gentlemen; they mistrust presents
that may be dearly bought in the end. If any other gentleman
had made the proposal, it would have met with opposition, but
the advice of a priest, a distinguished priest, can safely be followed; there is nothing to be afraid of when he leads the dep-
tation. All will go well, even though they may have to shoul-
er responsibilities which may some day cause a loss. But what
loss? Ah! Time will tell. Once upon a time twelve men went to
Vienna, and sold the rights of their fellow-country-men to the
evil. God knows what might happen. However, the priest is
with them; there is their safety value.

Nevertheless, all twelve men were made to swear upon their
salvation, before they put on their new coats, to deny that they
could read or write. They were to sign nothing, and if they
were asked who in Bondavára had houses and land, and above
all, sons, they were not to answer.

The deputation set out a couple of days after the meeting,
led by the abbé. Péter Saffran was included among the twelve,
as he was particularly wanted in Vienna.

A day or so later Iván was called before the military commander of the district; he was accused of acting against the
law in denigrating the 'Reichstag' in the eyes of the people, of
preventing the people, especially his own workmen, from taking
part in a legal demonstration, of having insulted members of
the legislature, and of having involved himself with secret
societies. He was cautioned for the future: another offence
would be regarded more seriously; this time he was to go unpunished.

Iván knew well how this denunciation had arisen. It would
be necessary, for the final destruction of his business, to im-
prison him for a year; his innocence would then be established,
and he would be set free. In the meantime his property would
be ruined.

It was lucky for Iván that on this occasion the gaoler's
wife was confined. It would have been necessary to remove

her from the sickroom, which was also the room set apart for suspects before their trial, and so Iván was allowed to go his way.

Ah! It was a great day when the twelve men from **Bondavára**, in their twelve new suits of broadcloth, arrived in the metropolis. Here they are! Here are the Hungarians, the indomitable sons of the soil. A deputation to the imperial council, an acknowledgement of the February proclamation, the pioneers! They deserve three cheers.

The newspapers hastened to welcome them; leading articles of every shade of politics were full of this new and remarkable demonstration.

The minister granted a private audience to the deputation, where the abbé set forth their demand in a well phrased speech, stressing the fact that the people themselves wished to free their country from its present condition, having learned to distinguish their real benefactors from false prophets who would condemn them to evil and ruinous inactivity. The abbé dwelt at length on the intelligence of the men who formed the deputation. In return his Excellency the Minister pressed the abbé's hand and assured him that a bishopric would soon be vacant, and that it would be his care to see that a loyal prelate should fill the seat. His Excellency then began to converse with the members of the deputation, and as none of them understood a word of his language, they were much pleased with what he said. His Excellency, having been told by the abbé that Péter Saffran was the most distinguished of the party, took special notice of him. He shook his hand, and expressed a hope that the members of the deputation would attend the morning sitting; places would be reserved for them—in the gallery.

Péter accepted for his fellows. He could speak German as well as French; he had picked up both during his seafaring days.

All the while, the minister said nothing about the grant to the Bonda Valley railway, and that was the main thing.

At the next sitting of the imperial council the front row of the gallery was reserved for the distinguished guests. They sat in armchairs, leaning their elbows on cushions, and letting their round hats hang over the rails.

His Excellency the Minister gave a discourse which lasted over an hour. The opposition maintained that during his speech his Excellency glanced fifty-two times towards the gallery, to see the effect he was producing upon the Hungarians. One fell asleep, and his hat dropped into the Chamber. It fell on a deputy, and woke him from his sweet nap.

For three days this trivial circumstance gave food to the Government papers; then it became the absolute property of the satirical journals, putting into the mouths of the Hungarians many things which they had never said. Never mind, as the good men couldn't read German, it didn't matter. They stuck fast to their armchairs in the gallery throughout the sitting; they were more comfortable than in their beds.

The last evening of their stay they were taken to the theatre. Not to the Burg Theatre—that would not do for them—but to the Treumann Theatre, where a suitable piece was playing, with plenty of fun, singing, and dancing; and the cream of the joke was that the principal part was to be played by the beautiful Eveline, Frau von Kaulman. Will Péter Saffran recognize her?

It had not been possible to get an engagement at the Opera House for Eveline, for there was an Italian season running. When it finished, there would be an opening for her, if she first learned the technique of acting at some less important theatre, and grew accustomed to the footlights. Therefore she played at the Treumann Theatre.

Her natural gifts and her extraordinary beauty caused a sensation: the *jeunesse dorée* went mad about this new favourite. The piece played in honour of the special guests was a frivolous opera by Offenbach. The aristocratic portion of the audience enjoy these displays more than the poor; it did not, in any case, amuse the guests in broadcloth.

The ballet of lightly-clothed nymphs, their coquettish movements, their seductive smiles, their bold display of limbs, and their short petticoats, were not to the taste of the Bondavára miners. It was true that the girls wore no petticoats in the coal-pit, but then they were working. Who would give that a thought? Chivalry befits the peasant as much as the gentleman; the former indeed practise more of the motto, *Honi soit qui mal y pense*, than do their better educated superiors. But now, as Eveline entered, they felt ashamed. She came on as a fairy, or goddess, concealed in gold-coloured clouds. However, the clouds were transparent. Péter glowed with rage to think all the world could see through this slight covering; he burned with jealous fury as Eveline smiled, cast glances here and there, and was studied through a hundred opera-glasses. Péter forgot that this was only the stage, and that many of the nymphs who played their part on it for an hour or so were virtuous women, good wives and daughters; for what happens on the stage is only play, not reality.

But the ex-bridegroom did not reason like this, he was an uneducated peasant in coarse broadcloth, and his ignorant mind was filled with horror, disgust, and rage. That she should allow herself to be kissed, to be made love to—shame! No, my good Péter, it was no shame, but a great honour. Bouquets and wreaths fell on the stage from the boxes; there was hardly a place where she could put her feet; it was all flowers. The house echoed with applause. This was not shame, but honour—even if not the same kind that would be offered to a saint or a good woman; it was more like worship offered to an idol, and most women like to be worshipped as idols.

Péter comforted himself with the thought that not one of his companions would recognize Eveline. But his heart was sore.

Leaving, he met the abbé, and asked him: "When are we going back?"

"Are you tired of Vienna, Péter?"

"I am."

"Have a little patience. Tomorrow we must pay a visit to a charming lady."

"What have we to do with charming ladies?"

"Don't ask why. If we want to achieve our aim we must try every possible way. We must beg this lady to intercede for us. One word from her to his Excellency the Minister will achieve more than if we said a whole litany."

"Very good; then we had better see her."

Chapter XXI

TWO SUPPLIANTS

The next day, at eleven o'clock, Abbé Samuel came to fetch his followers, and take them to the house of the influential lady, whose one word had more weight with his Excellency than the carefully arranged speeches of priests and politicians.

The carriage stopped at a splendid palace; a porter in a magnificent scarlet livery answered the bell, and between a double row of marble pillars they ascended the steps. The stairs were also marble, covered with a soft, thick carpet. If the schoolmaster at home had a bit of this stuff, he would have made a fine coat of it. On the staircase there were such lovely statues that the poor peasants would have kneeled to kiss their hands. The staircase was roofed with glass, and warmed by hot air, so that the hot-house plants and costly china groups did not suffer from the cold. From the ante-room, servants with silver epaulettes conducted the visitors into the drawing-room.

The sight almost took their breath away. There wasn't a wall to be seen; only panels of sumptuous silk brocade; and curtains of the same material on gold rods. Splendid pictures in rich frames hung on the silk panels. The upper portion of the windows were of stained glass, such as is seen in cathedrals, and opposite the windows was a large white marble fireplace, and on the mantelpiece stood a clock, with a beautiful figure which moved in time to the melodious tick. All the furniture was of mahogany. From the ceiling, on which the gold ara-

255

besques offered another feast to the eye, there hung a chandelier with a hundred lights, whose thousand glass drops reflected all the colours of the rainbow.

The deputation from Bondavára hardly had time to take in the wonders of this fairy-palace, when a gentleman in a black coat and a spotless white tie came out. This grand personage, whom they imagined to be the master of the house, turned out to be an equally important person—the butler. He informed them that the lady was ready to receive them in the next room.

There was no door to this inner apartment, only heavy damask curtains. This second drawing-room was even more wonderful than the first. The walls were panelled in dove-coloured silk. From the ceiling to the floor there were enormous mirrors in china frames, and between each mirror were consoles with marble statuettes representing dancing nymphs. The stone floor was covered with a soft carpet, into which the foot sank as into summer grass. The fireplace was black marble, with a silver grating. The furniture was in the Versailles style; tables and chairs, armchairs and foot-stools of delicate colouring, ornamented with garlands and charming Watteau figures. Every piece was a masterpiece. On the centre table and consoles there were Japanese vases of various elegant shapes. In one of the windows an aquarium had been constructed, full of goldfish and sea-anemones.

The poor peasants hardly noticed any of the precious objects; their attention was fixed by their own reflection in the long mirrors, which, in their ignorance, they imagined were other deputations, headed by another abbé wearing a gold cross. But even this strange spectacle was forgotten in their amazement at the beauty of the great lady, who now came forward to receive them.

She was lovely as a vision. Her violet silk dress was covered with expensive lace, her black hair fell in curls over her shoulders; her face was so beautiful, so fascinating, so dignified, that every man in the deputation was ready to fall at her feet.

256

Péter Saffran was the only one who recognized her; it was Evila.

Now the abbé, bowing low, addressing her in the most respectful way, laid before her the request of the deputation for her powerful patronage to the Bonda Valley population. The lady answered graciously, and promised that she would exert her influence as far as possible. Her heart and soul were in the matter, for she added, smiling:

"I am myself a child of Bondavára."

At these words the deputation exchanged glances, and every one thought she must be the daughter or wife of one of the Bondavára landowners.

Only Saffran felt bitter.

'What is she?' he thought. 'Only last night she was singing, dancing, and acting; her beauty free to the eyes of a crowd, who looked at her through their opera-glasses, while I had to cover my eyes with my hat to avoid seeing her degradation, and here she is today. Like a queen, promising us her influence with cabinet ministers. What is the truth? Was last night a comedy, or is today a clever farce staged by her and the priest?'

Péter Saffran had been in the Fiji Islands, and he remembered how amazed the natives had been when the white man washed the black from his hands, and showed his natural colour; only here it was a matter of the whole body.

The abbé, who seemed highly pleased with the success of the interview, now gave those behind him a sign to move, and bowed respectfully to the lady, who whispered a few words in his ear.

The abbé stopped Péter Saffran as he was leaving the room, and said in a low voice:

"You are to remain; the kind lady wishes to speak to you."

Saffran felt the blood rush to his head. He almost stumbled, and as he returned to the room, he could hardly move. But Eveline hurried forward, holding out both her hands. She had taken off her gloves, and he felt the soft, velvety clasp of her

257

fingers as she pressed his horny hand in hers; he heard the sweet fresh ring of her voice, to which he had often listened.

"Ah, Péter, say a word to me—a kind word." And she patted his back two or three times. "Are you still angry with me? There, Péter, don't be vexed any more. Stay and dine with me, and we shall drink to our reconciliation."

And she put her arm into his, and stroked his cheek with her delicate little hand, which looked as if it had never known what hardship was.

Eveline had religiously kept her promise of always informing Prince Theobald when she expected guests, and the Prince reserved the right of veto whenever he did not approve their reception, for there were among the dilettanti, and even among apparently respectable gentlemen, a few who should not have the *entrée* to the drawing-room of a lady who is not living under her husband's roof.

The prince liked pleasant society, and, if he approved of the company, enjoyed himself all the more when Eveline did the honours for him.

On this particular day Eveline had told the prince she expected two visitors. One was Péter Saffran.

The prince laughed. "Poor fellow!" he said, "treat him well; it will do him good." But when he heard his Excellency the Minister was coming he frowned. "What is this?" he asked. "What brings him to see you?"

"Why, is he a woman-hater?"

"On the contrary, he is a scoundrel, only he wears a hypocrite's coat. Great men, who are at the helm, and guide public affairs, have their weaknesses, but they do not dare to sin openly. A man in his position could no more become a member of the Jockey Club than visit a beautiful actress, unless he had some ostensibly good reason."

"But he has a reason, and a very good one. I asked him to see me."

"You invited him here!" The prince's face grew dark.

"That is to say, I asked him to give me a private audience, and his secretary wrote to say his Excellency would prefer to come here."

"And why did you request an audience?"

"Felix wanted me to."

"Ah, so it is Kaulman's doing! Why?"

"He wants these documents to be signed."

Eveline showed the prince a folded parchment.

The prince glanced at it, and shook his head. "And does His Excellency know that this is why you asked for an audience?"

Eveline burst out laughing. "Oh dear, no! When his secretary first wrote, he asked why I wanted an audience, I answered it was about my engagement at the Opera; and then he said he would come. He knows nothing of this," she added, touching the papers in her hand.

"And Kaulman told you to do this?"

"Yes."

"Then Kaulman is a fool. Do as he tells you; but, believe me, your husband deceives himself if he thinks he can snare that savage with a silk net. You can receive your guest, but I do not think your scheme will succeed."

Eveline put her hand upon Péter Saffran's, and led him into another room, where there was a fine display of silver, and then through a private door into a fourth apartment, wainscoted in dark wood; the ceiling, too, was supported by cross-beams of wood, and finished with painted plaster-work.

The room was empty. Eveline sat down on the sofa, and made Péter sit beside her.

"Listen, Péter," she said, laying her hand on the rough sleeve of his broadcloth coat. "It was the will of God that I should leave you. It grieved me very much because, as you know, our banns had been called three times. But then, you could not stand my little brother; you were cruel to him, and you beat me. I don't bear you any malice now. I have forgotten and forgiven you, but at the time I was very angry with you, though not because you ill-treated me. But I followed you that night to the cottage in the woods. I was quite ready to forgive and forget even then, only I looked in at the window, and I saw you dancing with Manci. I saw you kiss her, and that made me seriously angry."

Péter gnashed his teeth. He felt that the tables were turned, and he could say nothing. It would be different if his wife accused him of such things; he would know how to treat a jealous, scolding wife; but he couldn't take this beautiful lady by the hair, and drag her round the room, and beat her until she begged his pardon.

"But, as I said," continued Eveline, smiling again, "we are not going to talk about bygones. It was all God's will, and all for the best. We would have been an unhappy couple; I am passionate and jealous, and you would have given me cause. Now you can do as you like, and I have the happiness of doing much good. I like to help as many people as possible, and every day some twenty poor creatures are fed in my house. Oh, I do more than that; I get heaps of things done for the poor. I speak a good word for them, and get help from rich people. Also, I mean to be a benefactress of the valley; thousands and thousands of people will bless my name for what I shall do for them. Is it not a happiness to be able to help others?"

Eveline paused for an answer. Péter felt he ought to say something, if it was only to show that he had not become dumb.

"And does all this money come from the Bondavára Company?" he asked.

Eveline blushed scarlet. How was she to answer such a question?

"Not altogether. I earn a good deal by my acting. I get five hundred for a performance."

'Five hundred!' thought Péter. 'That explains it. A good salary indeed! A woman might do without some of her clothing to earn so much. It is money got by work, and not such hard work as carrying coals. She had to show her legs for that, too. But all said and done, that was money honestly earned.'

Péter's face began to clear.

"There, you look more like yourself. Don't look wicked again," pleaded Eveline. "And when you go back home tell every one that you have seen me, and that we had a good talk, and are good friends again. If you know of any one in trouble at any time, send me a line, and if it is in my power, I will gladly help. You must marry, if you are not married already. No? Well, then, you must choose a good girl, Péter. There is Panna, she is just the wife for you, and she was always my friend; or there is Anica, she liked you, I know, and she is a good housekeeper; only, don't marry Manci, you would be very unhappy with her, she is a bad girl. And in case you do marry, Péter, here are my presents for your bride: a pair of earrings, a necklace, and a brooch; and I give you this gold watch as a remembrance. See, Péter, my picture is on the back. Think of me sometimes when you are happy."

When she said these words Eveline's eyes overflowed, and her lips trembled. Péter saw it, and drew the conclusion that in all her splendour she was not happy. A single thought now took possession of him. He paid no heed to the bridal presents. Whether they were of gold or lead was all one to him, no one would ever see them; but what he thought was:

'She has a good heart, she is generous, she gives with a ready hand; but I do not care for her gifts. If she will only kiss me once, I will bless her. What is a kiss to her? Just one out of the many she gives to those fellows on the stage, with their smeared, painted faces.'

Poor fool! he didn't know that stage kisses are only mock kisses, just as stage champagne is only lemonade, or water. Péter believed that one kiss from Eveline would satisfy his thirst; it would assuage the pangs of regret, of jealousy, of rage, that had consumed him since the previous night. All would vanish

261

if he could touch her cool, fresh lips. And, after all, had they not been betrothed once—all but man and wife? Who could object? Only, he didn't know how to express his wish.

"And now let us eat together, Péter," said Eveline, kindly. "I am sure that you are tired of all the fancy food you get every day; you are sick of Viennese cookery. Wait, and I shall cook you something myself—your favourite, Péter, which you often said no one cooked as well as I. I shall make you some cornmeal."

Péter was electrified. A smile dawned over his face, either at the mention of his favourite dish, or at the thought that his hostess would herself prepare it. But how was she to cook? There is no fire, no cooking pots.

"Everything will be here," said Eveline, laughing gaily. "I shall change my dress; I cannot cook in this."

She ran off as she spoke, and returned in two minutes. Actresses learn how to change quickly. She now wore a white embroidered wrapper, and a little cap on her head. She called no one to help her, but laid a cloth on the oak table, filled a silver saucepan with water, and set it to boil on a spirit-lamp. She turned up the sleeves of her dress, and shook the meal into the boiling water with a light hand; then she turned the mixture deftly with a silver spoon round and round until it thickened. Then she took the saucepan by the handle, and emptied it on to a glazed clay plate—yes, actually a clay plate!—and poured cream over the mixture. She fetched two wooden spoons, one for Péter, one for herself.

"Let us eat off the one plate, Péter."

And they ate the cornmeal off one plate. Péter felt a strange moisture fill his eyes; he had not wept since he was a child. The cornmeal was excellent; all the cooks in Vienna together couldn't have given him a meal so much to his taste. There was no wine on the table, nor glasses.

A peasant never drinks during meals; but when they finished,

Eveline fetched a clay jug and asked Péter to drink, after, as is fitting, she took a sip.

"Have a drink, Péter; it is your old favourite."

There was mead in the jug—a very innocent drink—and Péter thought it was his duty to empty it to the last drop. The hell raging in his breast seemed all at once to be extinguished. He said to himself:

'Yes, I shall go back to the church, to the very spot where I made my horrible vow; I shall implore the Holy Mother to allow me to take it back. I shall hurt no one; I shall take no revenge. Let the green grass grow again in the fields, and let her live in splendour, among the smiles of the great. I shall not begrudge her happiness. This day, when she has received me kindly, will drive from my memory the day she left me. But I shall ask her for one kiss, so that I may remember only that.'

However, he delayed too long in naming this wish. The words almost hovered on his lips when the door opened suddenly, and a servant announced that his Excellency was in the drawing-room.

Now, Péter, God help you; you must go without your kiss.

Eveline could hardly say good-bye; she had to change her dress again. The footman showed him out through a side door; there another footman led him down the back stairs, and, opening another door, left Péter in a narrow street, where he had never been before. While he made his way back to his hotel, he had time to think over what he should say to Evila if he ever again had the chance of being alone with her. The recollection of how he had missed his opportunity roused the demon in his mind. The burning lava of hell once more filled his veins, the stream of sulphur which lost souls are ever drinking. He kept repeating to himself, 'The grass shall not grow again!'

By the time he reached the inn he was accompanied only by hatred, envy, rage at his own weakness, horror at his own wickedness, mixed with his political fanaticism; fine company in a man's breast.

Chapter XXII

FINANCIAL INTRIGUES

We can give no authentic account of the interview between His Excellency the Minister and his beautiful hostess. We were not present; nor had we a phonograph.

No doubt he complimented her upon her charming talent, and promised her his high interest, and as in this world nothing is given for nothing, there is every probability that His Excellency hinted at the reward he would expect for using his interest on her behalf; upon which Eveline, like a prudent woman, wishing to have everything in black and white, produced from the drawer of her writing-table the parchment we have already mentioned.

His Excellency took the paper, probably believing it was a petition to grant her an engagement. He held it in his hand while he smilingly assured her the matter was as good as concluded. It is, however, more than probable that when he took a hurried glance at the contents, his face assumed its official expression; he saw it did not refer to an operatic engagement, but to the grant for the Bondavára Railway. Seeing this, it is likely that His Excellency got up at once, and, hat in hand, explained to his lovely hostess how distressed he felt not to be in a position to comply with her wishes, as there were insuperable objections in the way, great oppositions from the Legislative Body, and yet greater opposition in the Upper House, where Prince Sondersheim was working heaven and earth against the Bondavára

Railway, and, therefore, for political and financial reasons, for the state of the country and many other causes, it would be impossible, or almost impossible, to hold out any hope of granting the Bondavára Railway a guarantee from the Government. That then His Excellency made a profound bow and left the room, may be considered a fact. It is psychologically certain that he descended the stair-case with a frown of vexation on his face, and that he murmured between his teeth:

'If I had known that I was going to talk to the *banker's wife*, and not the actress, I should never have come.' As he got into his carriage—and this is a historical fact—he banged the door with such violence that its glass pane was shattered.

While this interview was taking place, a committee-meeting was being held in Prince Theobald's palace, to lay before the shareholders the necessity of paying the third instalment—a critical operation, this attack upon the pockets of the public. The Bondavára Railway now played its part. Felix Kaulman announced he had every confidence that in a couple of weeks it would be established. The deputation from Bondavára had caused a sensation, and besides, the company had the interest of a very influential person, who could persuade His Excellency to do anything, even give the grant for the railroad. The finely cut, aristocratic features of the president did not betray that he knew who this person was.

Kaulman never for a moment suspected that Eveline would tell the prince the names of all visitors who came to her palace in his absence, and who were admitted through the little door.

While the committee was sitting, a note was brought to Kaulman, who recognized Eveline's writing at once. He read the letter quickly, then laid it on the table with a discontented air.

"What is that?" asked the prince.

It was the unsigned document which Eveline had returned.

Kaulman passed him a slip of paper, 'Another hitch in that railway.'

265

The prince said to himself, 'Then his wife has again escaped.' He bent over Kaulman, and laying his hand upon his shoulder, whispered to him:

"My dear friend, one doesn't get everything for a pair of black eyes."

Spitzhase was the committee's secretary. After this little scene he wrote something on a piece of paper, and twisting it up, handed it to Kaulman.

Kaulman read it, then tore it in small pieces, and shrugged his shoulders.

"I know all that," he said. "I don't need any advice."

The committee went away out of humour with each other. It had cost two thousand florins to bring the deputation from Bondavára, and this comedy had been of no use.

The last stake should now be played.

Csanta had determined not to pay the third instalment. He would sell all his shares at the price quoted, and refill his casks with silver.

On the day of the proclamation, however, he received this letter from Spitzhase:

'Tomorrow Herr Kaulman is going to you to offer to buy all your shares at forty-five florins. Be on your guard. I can assure you that the Government have signed a grant for the Bondavára Railway, and so soon as this is public, the shares will rise another twenty per cent.'

Csanta believed in Spitzhase as in an oracle, and with reason. All happened as he said. Immediately upon the issue of the proclamation, and when the shares were a little flat, Kaulman appeared in X, and offered him forty-five florins on his shares. But the old Greek was firm, not one would he sell; he would rather take his last cask to Vienna and empty its contents, than part with any shares.

He was rewarded for his firmness. Two days later he read in

the newspaper that both Houses had generously voted a grant to the Bondavára Railway.

His Excellency the Prime Minister had himself pleaded for the cause in the Upper and Lower House, and had proved conclusively that, from the political point of view, from the present favourable condition of the money market, as also from the side of the landed interest, from every point of view—strategical, financial, co-operative, and universal—the Government guarantee for the Bondavára Railway was absolutely necessary, and, as a natural consequence, the motion was carried. Prince Waldemar, indeed, opposed it vigorously, but nobody minded him.

At the next audit of the Bondavára Company's accounts presented to the shareholders, there appeared under the heading of expenditure this remarkable entry: 'Founding expenses, forty thousand florins.'

"What does this mean?" asked the shareholders.

Kaulman whispered something to the man nearest him; he passed the whisper on, whereupon every one nodded his head, and tried to think it was all right. So it appeared to be, for after the Government grant to the railway the Bondavára shares rose to seventy florins above par. Nothing could be more convincing. Csanta had punch at dinner, and got drunk in his joy.

Later, Eveline met his Excellency in the green room of the Treumann Theatre. The minister thought it was time to press for payment of his services.

"My dear lady," he said, "have I not obeyed your wishes about the Bondavára Railway?"

Eveline curtsied low. She wore the costume of the Duchess of Gerolstein.

"I am eternally indebted to your Excellency," she said. "Next time I shall blow you forty thousand kisses."

At the words 'forty thousand,' his Excellency grew red. He

turned on his heel, and Eveline was relieved of his attentions for ever after; but she could be quite sure that she had lost any chance of an engagement at the Opera House. No matter how well she would sing hereafter, her contract would never be signed.

Chapter XXIII

THE BONDAVÁRA RAILWAY

The Bondavára Railway was being built fast. Prince Waldemar and his followers were crushed—there are always people who are ruined by a good harvest.

Prince Waldemar met his noble relative, Prince Theobald, at the Jockey Club. He confronted the latter.

"You have chosen to become the leader of my enemies. You have done your utmost to trump my best cards. You have allied yourself with Kaulman, though I offered to settle your affairs. I sought your grand-daughter's hand; you promised her to me, and then you sent her away from Vienna. You have invented all manner of pretexts to keep her in Pest, and now the secret is out—she is betrothed to Salista. I had a fancy for a pretty woman, and just to prevent my getting her, you invite her to your palace, and forbid her to receive my visits. Worse than all, you have given over your only unmortgaged property, Bondavára, to a fake company, who want to climb over me; and you have become their president. You have schemed and jockeyed the government into giving the guarantee for a railway that won't pay two per cent. You haven't an idea how deeply you are implicated in these transactions. I pity you—for I have always esteemed you—but take care, for if I succeed in upsetting the pyramid on whose shoulders you stand, the greatest fall will be yours."

Of all this long harangue, Prince Theobald gathered only that

Angela had chosen the Marquis Salista for her husband, and had not written to tell him. She let him hear it from another.

The Bondavára Railway was being built fast. It was nearly finished. There was no further need for a pretty woman's diamond-black eyes. They had done their work.

One day Eveline visited her husband. Felix received her with apparent pleasure.

"I have come," she said, "to ask you a question. Prince Theobald has been terribly sad for some days. Have you any idea why?"

"I have. His grand-daughter, the Countess Angela, is married, and her husband, the Marquis Salista, is taking steps to put the prince under legal restraint, on account of the foolish manner in which he is squandering his fortune."

"And much of this foolish extravagance is spent on me."

"You are really wonderfully sharp, Eveline."

"I shall put an end to his spending his money on me. I shall tell the prince that I must leave his palace. I shall always be grateful to him; he has been a benefactor to me—and so have you. I ought to have mentioned you first. You have had me educated; you have taught me a great deal. I have to thank you for being what I am. I can earn my own living, thanks to you. I mean to become a real artist; but I must leave Vienna. I do not care to stay here any longer."

"I think, Eveline, you have decided for the best. Our minds are really in wonderful sympathy. I was about to advise the very thing to you. By all means leave Vienna; by all means make use of your talents, and take up your work seriously. I shall continue to do my duty as your husband. I shall take you to Paris; I shall settle in my house there, in order to help you. You will make a hit there, I know, and we shall be always good friends."

In spite of her previous experience of this man's character, Eveline was weak enough to be touched by his words, and

accuse herself of having been unjust to him, for it must be a
sacrifice on his part to leave Vienna for her sake. She could
never have guessed that this sacrifice was part of his well-
considered plan for ridding himself of her. She had played her
part in making his fortune, and now she could go where she
chose—to her native coal-pit if she liked. Once in Paris, he
would be able to say:

"Madame, we are under French law here and as no civil
ceremony has passed between us, you are not my wife; you are
at liberty to call yourself unmarried."

Felix had another reason for settling himself in Paris. It was
here he intended to carry out the second part of his plan. Now
that the Bondavára Railway was nearly finished, Abbé Samuel's
castles in the air were beginning to take shape; the next step
should be a gigantic loan in the interest of the Church. This
loan would be another means of aggrandizing the house of
Kaulman. Already Kaulman's name was of European celebrity;
he belonged to the larger stars of the financial world. From
being a baron of the Stock Exchange, he had become a prince.
If he succeeded in effecting this loan, he would be a king of the
money-market, whose name would outshine even that of Rothschild.

The Bondavára Railway was being built fast. A halo was also
forming around Abbé Samuel. The Government had begun to
see that this popular speaker held the people in his hand, and
could lead them as he chose. The people looked on him as their
benefactor, a man whose influence could benefit them. Was not
the Bondavára Railway a proof of this? The twelve broadcloth
envoys were firmly persuaded that the abbé had the government grant up his sleeve.

The clerical party acknowledged him as a rising leader. He
had been lauded in Rome for his zeal in the Papal cause. If he
was made bishop, which was almost a certainty, he would be

271

the first Hungarian prelate to take his seat in the Austrian Upper House. The minister would stare when he found his scheme for the secularization of Hungarian Church property met by another scheme from the new bishop, which, while proposing a gigantic loan on the same Church lands, aimed at enriching the Holy See. The money-markets of France, Belgium, and the Roman State would vie with one another in promoting the loan, and the Pontiff would regard the creator of such a project as the saviour of the Pontificate; his name should be carved in gold letters. In Hungary, the scheme would find favour, as a means of saving the Church property already threatened, for the Government would not dare to refuse this alternative.

Moreover, the Primate was an old man, the Pope was still older. All the wheels were oiled; now the machine could be put in motion.

The day the first locomotive steams out from Bondavára station, the Abbé Samuel might say to himself, 'The way to Rome is open.'

The Bondavára Railway was being built fast. It would be safe to prophesy that Iván Berend's ruin would be complete. The railway would bring the goods of the Joint-Stock Company to the markets of the world, where they could compete with coal from Prussia and England. But, it could be said that Iván had the same chance, his coal was equally good, and the giant of the seven league boots could carry his coal as well as his enemies'. But that which was of use to the company, was Iván's destruction.

The railway was not to run through the valley where his mine was, although that would have been the best and the most natural course to take; instead of which mountains had to be levelled, tunnels had to be dug through the hills to avoid his colliery, and to carry the rails close to the company's mine. In consequence, Iván would be obliged to make a half-day's detour to reach the railway, and so freight costs to the station made his goods five or six per cent dearer than those of the company. For him, the railway was a crushing blow.

In the meantime the end of the year drew near, the time when the miners were to receive their share of the profits. But profit there was none. Neither coal nor iron was sold. The company's low prices had taken all his customers from Iván.

Anyone with ready money can always say, even if he loses, that he has won; the common people call this lying to your own pockets. Iván had a little capital which he had saved up during better days. It amounted, all told, to several thousands, and he calculated, he could hold his own against his giant rival for at least ten years. He forgot that giants were cunning as well as strong, and that they did not despise even the minor gambits.

When the railway directors issued their prospectus, inviting contractors to send quotations for rails, rolling stock and such, Iván thought:

'Now I will have some fun. The shareholders of the Joint-Stock Company offer their iron six per cent below cost. I will offer to the railway directors to deliver iron rails at ten per cent below my cost. I shall lose fifty thousand, but I shall have the satisfaction of punishing my neighbours for their folly in lowering the price of the raw material.'

Simple fool! Just as an honest gentleman imagines that no one would venture to open a sealed letter, so Iván thought that the offers were compared, and that the most advantageous to the company was accepted.

Nothing of the kind!

It is always settled beforehand who is to have the contract. When the proposals come in, it sometimes happens that someone makes an even lower offer than that of the protégé, when the latter is told to take pen and ink, and offer to supply goods half per cent lower than the offer made by the outsider.

This method is well-known, it is only men like Iván, whose minds are occupied, who live in ignorance of such things.

273

The contract offered by the shareholders was half per cent lower than Iván's.

But even this rebuff didn't daunt him. Two and two make four, and those who sin against the multiplication table must come to grief sooner or later.

Iván continued producing iron bars and rails in his workshop, and built up his stores. Their day would come yet.

The Bondavára Railway was being built fast.

Csanta wanted to sell his houses in X, the whole street was for sale. He said he was going to live in Vienna, and become a director of the company. He was to have a large salary, with little or nothing to do. He had changed all his gold into paper —there is no use nowadays for houses, or land, or cattle, or mines; nothing is good but paper, which wants neither grooms, nor manure, nor pay, nor machinery.

Therefore, he wished to sell the whole street. Fortunately, there was so little wealth in X that the inhabitants of the whole town together couldn't have produced enough money to buy a poor little street.

The Bondavára Railway was being built fast. Along the line the navvies laboured like swarms of ants; they shoved wheelbarrows from morning to night; they dug the ground, blew up rocks, bored mountains, plugged streams, hewed stones, and dammed rivers.

In the dark of the Bondavára mine a man stood motionless, always watching the work. His gloomy, threatening face was fixed steadily on the wind-gauge.

It was Péter Saffran. He held a lump of coal in his hand, and as he looked back from the bustle to the fossilized trees, his eyes seemed to say:

'You are the cause of all this tumult, this wealth, this splendour; you are a living power—you!' And he hurled the coal against the wall.

Chapter XXIV

THE POOR DEAR PRINCE

"You have something to tell me. What is it?" asked Prince Theobald, coming to Eveline's drawing-room in answer to a letter, which she wrote after her interview with her husband.

"I want to leave Vienna."

"Ah, this is sudden. And where do you want to go?"

"My husband is moving to Paris, and I am going with him."

The prince studied her face. "Have you grown tired of being under my care?"

"Yes, I am afraid. I live in a gilded cage. I am a prisoner, and I want to see more of life."

"You regret the promise you made me? Well then, I release you; but stay with me."

"I should be too proud to be beholden to anyone when I am so ungrateful. Besides, it would be enough for me to know that you are the master of the palace to take all sense of freedom from me. I don't want to live on kindness any more."

"You wish to become an actress?"

"That, too." Eveline laid a stress on the last word.

"Are you ambitious?"

"I am not sure. If I were ambitious I should be more diligent. But I want my freedom. I don't want my wings clipped. I like to feel I can use them as I choose."

"That is rather a dangerous experiment for any one so young and pretty as you are."

"One never falls so low that one cannot rise again."

"Where did you learn that?"

"From what I see every day."

"You are resolved to leave me?"

"I am—I am—I am!" Eveline repeated these words impatiently.

"Then I had better free you from my disagreeable society as soon as possible," said the prince, taking up his hat. Then with an ironical bow, he added, "Forgive me, Madam, for the weary hours I must have imposed upon you."

Eveline, with an impatient stamp of her foot, turned her back on him. When he had reached the ante-room, the prince found that he had left his walking-stick in the drawing-room. It had been a Christmas present from Eveline, and he would not leave it with her. He went back to fetch it.

He opened the door quietly, and he stopped in surprise. Eveline stood with her back to the door. In her hands, she held the stick he had come for, and was pressing it to her lips, sobbing bitterly. The prince withdrew gently. Everything was clear to him. Eveline quarrelled with him to make their separation easier for him. She pretended to be mean in order that he might forget her more easily. Why did she do this?

The next day the prince found a partial answer to the riddle. His servant brought him the key of Eveline's apartments. The lady had left by the early morning train. The prince hurried to the palace, and he understood why Eveline had left. She had taken nothing; everything was there. She was a pearl among women.

A strand of her hair was wound round the ivory handle of the walking-stick—her beautiful hair, which fell from the crown of her head to her feet.

Eveline arrived in Paris before Kaulman. It had been settled between them that she should stay at a hotel until he arranged where she should live.

Some weeks later Felix came and said:

"Your house is ready for you. Will you come and see it?"

Eveline drove with Felix to her new home, in the Rue Sébastopol, one of the best situations in Paris, on the first floor. As she came into the apartment her heart missed a beat. Everything was familiar to her—the cherry-coloured curtains, the carpets, the dove-coloured panels, the black marble fireplace, the oval china frames, the window overlooking the garden—all as in Vienna. The same pictures, the same silver service, the wardrobes, the jewel-boxes, even the glove which she had left on a table.

Tears came to her eyes as she murmured, "The good kind prince!"

Felix, however, with perfect aplomb, took all the credit to himself, and asked her: "Have I not arranged your apartment to your taste?"

Eveline did not answer. Her thoughts were with the good, kind prince, her best friend. To him she owed her engagement at the Opera House in Paris, the bouquets that were thrown on her first appearance, the carriage she drove every day. All came from the paternal interest of Prince Theobald, who, from the day he called her his daughter, had never ceased to care for her as his child.

Chapter XXV

DIES IRAE

On a gloomy day in the autumn, Iván walked from the forge to his mine, and his thoughts ran in a sad groove on the way. What a curious world we live in; everything goes wrong—at least, for most people. Bread is not for the wise, nor success for the strong, as it was in the days of Solomon. One bad year follows the other, for even Nature has become a stepmother to men. The poor are hungry and beg for bread, and when they have eaten, they forget who helped them. All the great landowners spend their lives without doing anything worth mentioning, either for their country, or their neighbour; the burden of both present and the future seems to fall upon our small, exhausted class. The patriots are hollow; they weep in their cups; they shake their fists, but no one dares to strike a blow.

'It is just as bad in the bowels of the earth. For the last two days we had choke-damp in the mine; the escape of gas has been serious enough to stop the work; there may well be an explosion while I am in the pit.'

Iván's thoughts were as black as the landscape, and suited to its gloom. His road from the forge to the mine led him past the workmen's houses, and, as he passed one of these, a miner came stumbling out of the door. The house was a wine-shop.

The miner's back was towards Iván, who did not recognize him, but he noticed that the man had difficulty in walking straight.

'I wonder who got drunk so early in the day?' thought Iván, hurrying after the man to find out. When he caught up with him, he saw, to his surprise, that it was Péter Saffran.

This struck Iván as odd; he remembered that, on the day Evila had eloped, Saffran had sworn never again to touch the brandy; he knew that Péter had kept his vow. He vaguely recalled that when he said that he wouldn't drink any more, he uttered some sort of a threat. Well, it didn't matter much; if he got drunk, that was his affair. But why did he come to Iván's village to get drunk? Why didn't he go to the tavern near his own works?

Iván called out: "Good morning, Péter."

Péter did not return the greeting. He looked at Iván with wild eyes; he pressed his lips together, and his nostrils extended. He drew his cap down over his eyes.

Iván asked him, "Has the choke-damp got into your pit?"

Péter did not answer. He shoved his cap off his forehead, and, opening his mouth to its full extent, bent his face to Iván's, and let his hot spirit-laden breath blow over him. Then, without a syllable, he turned away, and ran off in the direction of the company's mine.

The heated breath of the man, with its sickening smell of bad brandy, sent a shudder through Iván. He stood still, staring after the runner, who stopped and looked back when he had cleared a fair distance. Iván could still see his face. He looked like a madman; his lips hung apart, like those of a dog with rabies; his teeth gleamed against his red gums. He looked so strange and desperate that Iván touched the revolver in his pocket. For a moment the thought passed through his mind that he would be doing good in freeing the world of such a creature, but on second thought he let him go, and continued his way to the mine to check the ventilators.

In the vault the proportion between hydrogen and air was three to seven. Iván forbade any further work in the pit. He employed his men in the open air, moving the coal, and only

279

allowed those who had to look after the air-pumps to remain below.

He stayed there for the whole day, controlling everything, and keeping a close watch. Towards evening he left the mine, and returned to his house.

It was a foggy, gloomy evening; the weather influenced mind and body alike. When nature is out of sorts man suffers; when the sky is overcast, he, too, is depressed. And when the earth is sick, when worms and mould destroy fruit, when the harvest is ruined by blight, and cattle are decimated by pestilence, above all, when the noxious vapours from coal-mines rise to the surface and poison the very air—then men sicken and die.

All through the day Iván had felt cold shivers running through his body. His limbs were contracted by that unpleasant feeling called goose-flesh, and when he reached home he still shivered, though his room was warm. He was restless and uneasy. He could concentrate on nothing; everything palled on him. The worst of his symptoms was that he could not even work.

When a man refuses food or drink, when he does not care for the company of a pretty woman, when his club bores him, something is wrong; but when he turns away from work, and finds no longer any interest in his usual occupation, then it is time to send for a doctor.

Iván's head throbbed, yet he could not sleep, and to stay awake was torture. He lay down, and with a resolute effort closed his eyes. A panorama of past, present, and future kept dancing before him. Péter Saffran's hot, stinking breath seemed to return to his nostrils, and the very horror brought back to his memory the man's long-forgotten words:

'I shall never drink brandy again—only once more! And when I smell of it, when I am seen coming out of the pub, or when you hear that I have been there, then stay at home, for that day no one will know how, or when, he will die.'

Who cares for the threat of a drunk? Let me sleep. But the drunk would not allow Iván to sleep; his breath was there, it made him sick. His blear-eyed, pallid face was bending over the bed, looking into Iván's with his blood-shot eyes; his open mouth and clenched teeth came quite close to the sleeper, who tried to drive away this horrid nightmare.

Ah, what was that? An explosion like the crack of doom woke Iván; not only woke him, but threw him violently out of bed, to the floor, where he lay stunned.

His first thoughts were: 'The choke-damp has exploded! My mine is in ruins!' This was enough to get him on his legs, and to send him out in the darkness.

Iván stood for a moment, wondering. He felt the earth swaying under his feet; he heard a subterranean grumbling. There! the pitch-dark night was suddenly lit up; a bright pillar of fire rose from the Bondavára Company's mine. At the same moment another fearful explosion was heard, worse than the last. The windows of the house were shattered in a thousand pieces, the chimneys, the roofs fell in. The pressure of the air forced Iván back, and threw him against the door of his house. By the infernal light he could see his own workmen on their knees with a horrified look on their faces. Women and children gathered at their doors, but terror struck, everyone was speechless.

The valley glowed like a volcano's crater. It vomited a rain of sparks, the flames reached almost to the clouds, and rolls of thunder followed on thunder, the like of which had never been heard in the most terrible storm.

Two minutes later the flames died down. The valley was again shrouded in darkness, only a filmy white cloud floated over the company's mine.

"The neighbouring mine blew up!" shouted Iván. "Help! Help!" He forgot that it was his enemy's mine; he only thought that there, in the bowels of the earth, a terrible disaster had happened. "Help! Help!" he cried, and ran to the alarm-bell, and pulled it with all the strength of his body.

His own men came rushing in haste, repeating one another, as if it were something new:

"The neighbouring mine blew up!"

Then a long pause followed. The men with their lanterns surrounded Iván, and looked at him questioningly.

He guessed their thoughts.

Those who drew their breath under God's free heavens were bound to go to rescue those who lay buried, and perhaps still lived. It was no case of friend or foe: they were human beings.

"We must get the ventilators, and the well-buckets," called Iván. "Let each man bring a thick cloth to tie over his mouth. Bring crowbars, cords, ladders, rubber tubes, hoses and pipes. Only the women are to stay here. Come on, men!"

He grabbed an old coat, seized a strong iron bar, hoisted it on his shoulder, and led the way to the company's mine.

It was not easy to enter the works. The proprietors had set up various barricades in order to prevent Iván's carts from using the new road. On the gates there were boards:

'No trespassing. No one to pass without a written order.'

No one minded these notices now. Iván thrust his iron rod through a closed gate to clear a passage, through which his men rushed pell-mell. The miners did not waste time to harness horses to the machines. They harnessed themselves, while others shoved behind, and drove them on over the uneven ground to the mouth of the pit. Like a mad army, the rescuing party rushed through the night, making their way as best they could by the lanterns tied to their belts.

Soon, however, the darkness was illumined. The forge nearest to the pit, and exposed to the fiercest heat, blew up suddenly, and the flames from the furnace filled the air with a red glow. The miners avoided the direction in which it burned, as it would be impossible to guess which way the molten metal would flow.

When they reached the pit, an awful spectacle met them. The ventilating chimneys over the shaft were gone. Bricks and tiles were scattered all over the field. The large cast-iron windlass was thrown far from its former position, and of the conical, bell-shaped buildings hardly a stone was left. Only one wall was still standing; iron girders hung from its side. The pit's northern entrance had fallen in, its handsome stone gates lay in ruins. Stones, beams, iron bars, coals were all mixed, as if a volcano had spat them out.

The air was filled with the laments of weeping women. Hundreds and hundreds of women and children, probably widows and orphans, held up their hands to heaven, and wept. Under their feet their husbands, their fathers, brothers, lovers lay buried, and no one could help.

From recklessness rather than from actual courage a few men had already tried to go down into the pit. They had been stunned at once by the pressure of the gas, and now their comrades, at the risk of their own lives, were trying to drag them out on ropes and slings. Already one was stretched on the grass, the women wringing their hands round him.

Iván began to give orders. "In the first place," he said, "no one is to go near the pit. Wait until I come back."

He took his way towards the directors' offices. He forgot that he had sworn never to hold any communication with Rauné. In any case, he was not to be found. In the next town there was high feast. The directors of the new railway were giving a banquet to honour the completion of the tunnel. Rauné was there. Iván, however, met the second engineer. He was a phlegmatic man, and consoled himself with the reflection that these things happened everywhere.

"The gates must be rebuilt," he said. "The pit roads must be re-made, and probably we shall have to sink another shaft. It will cost a lot of money. *Voilà tout!*"

"How many men are below?" asked Iván.

"About a hundred and fifty."

"Is that all? And what is to be done for them?"

"It will be a hard job to get them out, for they were at work in the new passage, between the north pit and the east, made to improve the ventilation."

"So the only entrance to the pit is the one which has fallen in?"

"Yes; and the eastern shaft is also in ruins. The flames came from there; you must have seen them."

"Yes. And I couldn't understand how it was that the second explosion followed the first after a few minutes."

"That is easily explained. The communicating wall was already so thin that the explosion in the north pit blew it into fragments; the gas in the east pit was probably not kindled by the flames, for they had already gone out, but by the strong pressure of the air, which was heated by the accumulation of coal, and which exploded through the shaft. As when you put sand into the barrel of a gun: the powder bursts the barrel before it throws out the sand."

It was plain that the engineer took a cold-blooded view of the affair. The design for the new stone gate was of more interest to him than the hundred and fifty lives which were in jeopardy. Iván saw there was little assistance to be got from him.

"Before we can attempt to rescue the men buried in the pit," he said, "we must pump the gas out of the opening. Where is your air-pump?"

"Up there," returned the engineer, pointing to the sky. "That is, if it hasn't dropped again."

"Have you no portable ventilator?"

"We never contemplated the necessity for one."

"I have brought mine, if we can adjust it."

"I would gladly know how that can be done. If the ventilator has a copper tube, it would be impossible to push it through all the rubbish and wreckage; if it has a rubber pipe it would be too weak, and wouldn't stand being shoved forward."

"Someone must carry it into the pit."

"Someone?" repeated the engineer, with an air of amazement. "Look; they are drawing up the third dead man who was foolish enough to go down there."

"None of them are dead; they will soon recover consciousness; they are stifled by the gas."

"All the same, I can hardly believe that you will find a man mad enough to be the first to carry a tube fifty feet through all the wreckage."

"I have found the man. I shall do it."

The engineer shrugged his shoulders, but he made no effort to dissuade him.

Iván went back to the men, who had been getting ready for work in the meantime. He called aside the oldest miner.

"Paul," he said, "some one must carry the tube of the air-pump into the pit."

"Good. Let us draw lots."

"We shall do nothing of the kind. I shall go. You are all husbands and fathers, with wives and children to feed. I have no one. How long can a man hold out in that foul air without drawing breath?"

"A hundred beats of his pulse; no longer."

"Good. Fetch me the pipe. Bind a rope around me, and hold the other end. When you see that I no longer carry the pipe, draw back the rope slowly but take care to pull it slowly, in case I faint, and a sudden pull may strangle me."

Iván loosened the woollen sash from his waist, dipped it in vinegar, and wringing it out, wrapped round his face to cover his nose and mouth. He then bound the rope firmly round his waist, took the top of the rubber pipe on his shoulder, and began to make his way through the rubble at the pit's mouth.

The old miner called out: "Count the seconds. Fifty for going, fifty for coming."

Iván vanished behind the rubble. The miners took off their caps and folded their hands. The old man held the fingers of his right hand over the wrist of his left, counting his pulse. He had already counted over fifty, and the other end of the pipe had not moved. It had passed sixty, and was near seventy, when suddenly it was pulled forward. Iván had reached to the deadly atmosphere. The old miner wiped the perspiration from his brow. He counted eighty, ninety, a hundred seconds. They shall never see him again. Then the pipe remained steady.

Now they began to draw the rope. It was slack, and not tightened by any burden. Iván was safe so far; he was still walking, for the rope continued slack. Suddenly it tightened. Be careful now. The rope slackened again; the old miner counted a hundred and sixty seconds. Suddenly Iván was seen coming out of the pit's mouth, supporting himself on the fallen stones of the archway; but his strength failed, and as the men rushed to his assistance, he tottered and fell. His face was like wax.

They rubbed him with vinegar, and the fresh air soon revived him. He sat up.

"I am all right," he said, "but the air down there is awful. How those poor creatures buried below suffer!"

It never occurred to him that those poor creatures were the same men who had deserted him, who had taken service with the company who had sworn to ruin him, who had formed a conspiracy against him, who were ready to destroy him, who have sent a deputation to the enemies of their native land. Here they lay, buried in the depths of the earth which now revenged their treachery. Iván forgot their offence, and his only thought was to save them.

Now that the ventilator had been set in motion, the work of rescue might begin; but it was still a terribly hard fight.

Iván divided his band of men into two divisions. Each man was to stay only an hour at the dangerous work of clearing away the rubbish. Everyone must cover his face with a cloth drenched in vinegar. As soon as he began to feel faint, he was to be carried off by his mates.

By daybreak, the wreck of the fallen entrance had been shifted, but the sun could not penetrate the pit. One side of the slate-clay vault had collapsed completely, so that Iván, when he had carried the line into the pit, found scarcely enough space to

286

push through the cracks. He had placed the end of the pipe where the vault had collapsed.

It was an almost superhuman undertaking. The work of weeks had to be done in a few days. And yet it must be done.

In their work of clearing away the rubbish Iván's men had very little assistance from the company's miners for the explosion had taken place just when the miners were relieved. In collieries it is usual to relieve men four times a day. The accident happened at the time of the midnight shift. One party of the miners had already gone down the shaft; they were probably suffocated. The other party were on their way out, and were killed at once by the explosion. There was another party who had just reached the resting-stage, where neither the flames nor the fragments could touch them. These men were buried alive. The result was that only twenty to thirty were available of all the company's miners.

The director forbade the men in the forge to help in the rescue work. In all the ovens the metal was in a liquid state; if it was not watched, it would turn into rammers. The workmen give the name of *ram*, or *rammer*, to a solid mass of iron, which, in consequence of faulty melting, cannot be removed from the oven, and it has to be thrown away together with the oven as useless lumber.

The metal was needed urgently. The rail sections had to be finished by a certain date, or a large fine would have to be paid. So Iván had to set his men to the task of clearing the pit almost unaided. The women helped to rescue their husbands.

What a terrible undertaking! As the arches collapsed, the roof had to be supported on plugs, at a distance of every six feet, and a sort of street made through the ruins, where at every corner a new enemy waited for the intrepid rescuers.

After the explosion the pit was flooded by water. The water pumps had to be set to work, and where these were not sufficient, the men had to empty out the black slime in buckets, standing for hours in stinking mud, breathing foul air, threatened with

287

death or injury by the constant fall of stones and wreckage. Undaunted, the men made their way step by step into the bowels of the earth.

In the afternoon Rauné arrived. He had heard the news in the middle of a convivial gathering. He was in a rage. He came down the shaft, and cursed the victims.

"The bastards! They have cost the company a million. What does it matter if they are all killed? Serves them right. Why should any of them be saved? Stuff and nonsense! Let them suffocate, the drunken dogs!"

The workers did not answer. First, because they could not waste time talking, and secondly, because every man's mouth was covered. The clearing of a mine is very silent work.

But in the midst of his curses Rauné encountered a workman, who stepped in front of him, and faced him with a hard look. He was covered in mud and coal, like the others, his face was tied up with a cloth, and only his eyes were visible; they, too, were blackened with coal-dust, but Rauné knew by their expression that it was Iván. No one who had ever looked into his eyes could forget him.

Rauné turned away without another word, and, together with his engineer, left the pit. He did not interfere any further with Iván's work.

Four days and four nights the men never stopped. They overcame every obstacle, and cut a path through every difficulty. During those four days Iván never left the mine. He ate his meals sitting on a stone, and snatched an hour's sleep in a corner.

On the fourth day the workmen found one of the missing men. A man—no, but a mass of flesh and bones, flattened against the wall, which had once been a man.

A little further another body lay on the ground, but the head was nowhere to be seen. They tried to get him on one of the wheelbarrows, but he was in fragments; the splinters and shreds of his body were sticking to everything.

Then they found the charred, blackened corpses of the men who had been burned. They were not recognizable.

Further on there was a group of fifteen men crushed by a huge weight of slate stratum. This could not be moved, so they were left. It was more important to look for the living than the dead. They found corpses everywhere; yet the number of the missing was not complete!

The miners employed by the company told Iván that if any were still alive they would be at the resting-stage where they left their knapsacks before work, and fetched them again as they went up. In the passages, however, there had been such total confusion that even the oldest hand could not find his way. In many places the explosion had torn down the partition wall, in other places the entrance was stopped up with rubbish, or the roof taken off the passages which led into the inner vaults. It was all in such a state that no one could find out where the large vault lay.

At last it struck Iván that underneath a mass of coal and slack he heard a faint whimpering sound. He said to the men, "Dig here."

They set to work at once to clear away the rubbish, and as they cleared, the company's men began to orientate.

"Yes, here is the door which leads to the resting-stage." The pressure of the air had shut the door close, the side walls had fallen in, and so those, who had been safe from the conflagration, had been buried alive.

The whimpering cry for help was heard more clearly now. The door, too, was visible, and as it was swung off its hinges, Iván took a lantern, and peered into the dark cave.

No cry of joy reached him; the rescued men had not enough strength to utter a sound. There were about a hundred men alive. They lay there, still, speechless. They had suffered the tortures of hunger and thirst, they had been suffocated by the foul air, broken-hearted, despairing. And now these human skeletons could hardly raise a finger to show they were alive.

A heartrending whimper, in which there was no human tone, rose from a hundred parched throats. They had been thrown on their faces when the explosion came. Their lamps had gone out, and it would have been madness to re-light them. They had remained in total darkness. After a while the danger of their situation increased. Soon they began to feel that the water was gradually filling the space which served them as a refuge and a grave, and this space was, they knew, a fathom below the pit. They tried to get hold of some boards and plugs that lay about, and out of these they made a sort of stage or platform, upon which they all clambered, and there waited for death—the death that might come either through hunger, foul air, or drowning. When their rescuers opened the door the water had reached the threshold, and touched the foot of the wooden stage.

Iván directed that the poor creatures should be carried carefully and silently from their living grave. Each man lay where he was, and waited until his turn came. The foretaste of death made every one tranquil. Some of them could not open their eyes at first, but all were alive, and Iván could not help thinking that the strength of human nature is wonderful.

He had saved them all, but the work was not yet finished. What if, beyond the breach mentioned by the engineer, there were others waiting for rescue? One thing they had to find out for certain: whether the explosion had finished the work begun by the engineer's men, and carried away the wall dividing one pit from the other. If this were so, it would lighten the work of the rescuers. At the opening of the tunnel a man's body lay; he was an unrecognizable charred, burnt mass. The dead man held his safety-lamp in his hand. It was open.

So this was the damned soul who had done hell's deed. It was human folly that had caused this infernal explosion.

The corpse was not recognizable, his clothes were burnt to ashes. However, on his belt they found a small steel box, and in this box there was a gold watch, with the portrait of a lovely woman in its enamelled back.

When the watch was brought to Iván, he recognized the portrait. It was Eveline. With the watch there was also a half burned hundred florin banknote with the written message:

'A year ago today I received this money; today I pay it back.'

What a fearful repayment!

Iván was now able to grasp the connection between the words and the deeds of this terrible man, whose recollection of his own act of eating human flesh had prompted him to this dreadful massacre. His threats after Evila's elopement, his entering into the company's service, the last occasion when he got drunk, and the breath he had blown into Iván's face. It was all clear now. This man had the character of an Antichrist. His soul and body were full of concealed demons, prompting him to revenge himself on those who had hurt him, ridiculed him, robbed him, scorned him, fooled him, insulted him with money, tempted him with luxuries, and took advantage of his simplicity to lead him by the nose.

All of them should fall. He would pull the foundation-stone from under their feet, even if he dug his own grave in so doing. They should fall from their high estate—the banker, the priest, the broker, the minister, and the actress.

In Hell, the demons could teach Péter nothing.

Iván stood before the unsightly corpse, deep in thought. In his heart a wild conflict of passions raged. He also had been robbed, oppressed by the wealth of his enemies, his heart wounded by a hundred poisoned arrows, and this by the same men on whom the vengeful hate of Péter Saffran had fallen.

Iván had come to their help. He had saved the lives and the property of his enemies; at least, what they called their property; the monstrous treasure which lies in the very bowels of the earth does not, in truth, belong to any man alone, but to all men; it is the treasure-trove of the State.

And yet a great dread, an unconquerable fear possessed Iván.

291

He dared not mention his fear to any one, for if he were to share his suspicion with any one of the workmen, who up to this had followed him obediently through every peril, they would without another word have turned their backs and fled for their lives.

The wire cylinder of Saffran's safety-lamp was filled to the top with a red flame. This was a warning that the atmosphere was still charged with one-third of hydrogen gas, and only two-thirds of air.

But there is an even greater danger than the pit-gas, whose fearful spirit had been laid, whose victims lay silent on the wheelbarrows. Yet another and a worse spirit lurks in ambush —a foe who goes about with closed eyes, whose presence is awful in its consequences; it is carbon monoxide.

When the men broke through to the tunnel, they found, just as the engineer had said, that the explosion had burst through the partition wall, and that the *débris* had only to be removed, and the passage between the east and the north pits would be established. Not one of the workmen could remain long at this work. After a few minutes, each returned coughing and complaining that in that place his safety-lamp would not burn.

In the pits the flame of the lamp filled the whole cylinder; this was not reassuring. But in the neighbourhood of the ruins it would hardly burn; this was a far more dangerous sign.

The last miner who returned said that as he removed a large lump of coal such a terrible stench had penetrated through his mouth-protector that he had almost fainted. The smell was like putrid vegetables.

The old hands knew what this putrid stench meant. Paul suggested to Iván that he should go and look where it came from. Let him cover his mouth very carefully, and come back as soon as possible.

Iván took his iron rod and his lamp, and went. Seizing the rod with both hands, he struck it with all his strength against a mass of coal. It rolled with a great noise into the vault on the other side. Then he fastened his lamp to the hook of his rod, and pushed it through the hole. The lamp went out at once, and as he looked from the darkness into the hole, he saw to his horror a red glow in the next vault, which lit up the vault. He knew that there was no time to lose. He did not stop to withdraw his rod, but rushed back to the men.

"The east pit is burning!" he cried.

No one answered, but they seized Iván, and carried him from the pit into the open air. Behind them came the horrible stench, not the foul air which accompanies 'choke-damp,' and is often fatal. This was the more insidious gas, which kindles pit-fires, baffles the ingenuity of man, respects neither the brave nor the scientific, and whose progress, once begun, can never be arrested. There is nothing to do but to run for life.

In a few minutes the pit was empty.

As they came into the light of day, they were surrounded by women and children, weeping and crying in joy at finding their lost ones still alive.

The engineer was also there. Iván went straight to him. Ripping off his masking cloth, he said:

"Do you know, sir, what is going on, down there in your mine? It is the end. The east pit is burning. It must have been alight for some days, for the whole pit is red-hot. I shall never forget the sight. Now let me tell you what this means. This is not the work of human evil, nor the avenging hand of God; it is caused entirely by the negligence of the overseer. You know as well as I do that collieries take fire when sulphur gets mixed with coal-dust, and is allowed to lie in heaps. It is always hot down there, and when the stuff is fanned by the air, it lights of itself. Your pit is full of this dangerous burning waste. And now both your pit and my mine are finished. Colliery fires can never be extinguished. You have heard of the burning mountain of Dutweiler? A hundred and twenty years ago that coal-mine caught fire; it is still burning. Here, we have another case of it. Good night, sir."

The engineer shrugged his shoulders. It did not concern him.

Iván left the God-forsaken colony. He and his men returned to his side of the mountain.

Meanwhile, what happened to his own mine? He had been absent four days and four nights, and had never given it a thought.

Chapter XXVI

FROM THE SUBLIME TO THE RIDICULOUS

To understand the meaning of the proverb, 'There is only one step from the sublime to the ridiculous,' one should gamble on the Stock Exchange.

Today you are a deity, tomorrow a beggar in the street. Today sixty brokers yell the name of your speculation; you are a king, and the other kings on the Exchange study how the wind shifts by your face. Today, as soon as one o'clock strikes, buyers swarm round you. Leaning against a broker's back, competitors enter the number of shares they want. Today all hands point to the dividends, the proof of your high estate. Today the crowd who are speculating on your credit fill the corridors; they scream, 'I sell,' 'I buy.' Outside the Stock Exchange, sweet creatures of the opposite sex, who like dabbling in stocks quite as much as the men, make their books. Women are prohibited from the Exchange; but they gamble all the same. Hundreds of ladies wait on the stockbroker, with a copy of the Exchange list in their hands; they have marked your shares. Still greater ladies sit outside the Exchange, in their grand carriages. In their eagerness they lean out of their carriage windows asking the first passer-by at what figure the shares —your shares—stand.

This is today. Tomorrow, you may not be found; your name is deleted from the Exchange list. Everyone knows that your affair has 'burst.' You are nowhere. You are nobody.

The firm of Kaulman stood at the summit of its triumph. Felix and his bosom friend, the Abbé Samuel, were enjoying their afternoon siesta. The room was full of smoke, and under its soothing influence the friends were building their castles in the air.

"Tomorrow," said Felix, "the Pope's loan on the Hungarian Church lands will be floated on the Exchange."

"Tomorrow I shall receive my appointment as Bishop of Transylvania from Vienna."

"The plutocrats are ready to plank down millions on the loan."

"The Pope gives it his blessing," murmured the abbé. "The cardinal's hat is ready for my head."

"The Monarchist financiers have shown a decided objection to my wife appearing on the stage. This may injure the loan, therefore tomorrow I intend to explain to her that she is not legally my wife."

"Is it true that Prince Waldemar has arrived in Paris?"

"Yes, he has followed Eveline."

"But his presence here will injure our speculation. He is our open enemy."

"He cannot hurt us now. Since he met such a total defeat in the matter of the Bondavára mine and the railway, his teeth have been drawn."

"Then it is Eveline who has brought him here?"

"He is mad about her; he follows her like a lap-dog, and is anxious to pick up any crumb she will give him."

"But she cannot stand him."

"So much the worse for her. It was greatly Prince Theobald's doing. That old chap is mad."

"Is it not the case that countess Angela's husband wants to put the prince's affairs into the hands of trustees?"

"There was some talk of it before we left Vienna."

"Will this affect the Bondavára shares in any way?"

"In no way. The only unmortgaged part of his capital is

made over to the company absolutely. I can assure you, the Bondavára speculation is built on a rock."

As he spoke, three telegrams were brought in by the servant. One of these was addressed to the abbé, under cover to the firm of Kaulman.

"*Lupus in fabula*," said Kaulman, as he handed the first telegram to the abbé. The abbé read:

"Prince Theobald declared incapable of managing his affairs."

"Poor Eveline, she will have time to repent!" remarked Felix, with a cynical smile.

As he was speaking, the abbé opened the telegram addressed to him. He handed it to Felix, saying:

"And I, too, shall have time to repent."

The telegram ran:

"The Minister resigned; Emperor accepted his resignation; Government will change."

"Good-bye to the bishop's mitre, to the cardinal's hat!"

And then, they both read the third telegram.

"Explosion in the Bondavára colliery. Entire mine on fire."

"This is indeed a blow," said Felix, as he let the telegram fall from his hand.

The three telegrams had come like three flashes of lightning. The last was the worst.

When the news reached Prince Waldemar he would let loose his vengeance. Something must be done to avert the imminent danger—but what?

If only there was time to float the Papal loan, such small things as the Bondavára shares and the burning mine would be of little consequence. But could the enemy be reduced to silence?

It was settled that the abbé should go to Eveline at once, and that Kaulman should speak to Prince Waldemar.

The faces of the two men now wore a more sombre look. They had only one card to play, only the smile of a woman could save them now.

Chapter XXVII

TWO CHILDREN

Eveline had arrived in Paris at a very important moment. Two great changes had come over the world of fashion; the Empress Eugénie had decreed that the crinoline should be laid aside, and Cardinal Chigi, the papal nuncio, had pronounced that dresses cut high at the throat should be worn at receptions. Piety had become the rage. It was considered good taste to go to church, and to wait for the sermon.

Piety being, therefore, the fashion, no better moment could have been chosen by Kaulman for floating the papal loan. He was pleased to find that Eveline was eager in the pursuit of piety because it matched the poor girl's frame of mind.

A few days after her arrival in Paris her crippled brother died. A celebrated surgeon had performed an operation which had put him out of pain for ever. Eveline grieved over her loss; now she felt alone in the world, she had no one to love, no one to live for. She kept the boy's useless crutches in her room, one on each side of her dressing-table, and twice a week she went to the cemetery to put fresh flowers on the little grave. The conventional fashions just suited her. She preferred to sing Mozart and Händel in church to Verdi at the opera.

One day she conceived the idea of giving a concert of sacred music in her own drawing-room; the price of the tickets should be high, and the proceeds would be for some good purpose—God knows what. She was busy planning her programme when

298

the door opened, and Árpád Belényi, unannounced, entered in his old unceremonious way.

Eveline was delighted. Throwing down her pen, she ran to meet him, holding out both her hands.

"Oh, you dear friend, what has brought you here?"

"My profession. I am looking for some place where I may strike the keys and give a concert."

"What a coincidence; you have come at the right moment. But how did you find me?"

"Without much difficulty. If I hadn't seen your name on the posters at the Opera, I couldn't avoid seeing it outside St. Eustache."

"Then you have heard me sing?"

"In both places—the theatre and the church. I must tell you I think the good fathers lay it on pretty strong. I heard you at the Opera for twelve francs but I didn't get out of the church so cheap. A beautiful lady took twenty francs from me."

"You are silly! What are your terms?"

"May I ask your reason for the question?"

"How stupid you are! What are your terms for playing the piano at an evening concert?"

"To you, merely thanks; to the public, five hundred francs."

"But if it is for a charitable purpose?"

"Then, neither for thanks, nor for money."

"You are a cynical creature! Don't you feel sympathy for any one? Would you do nothing for the poor?"

"I know a poor woman to whom I owe everything; that is, my mother. Every farthing which I give to anyone else is taken from her. When the world has given back to her all that she has lost, then I shall give the world all that I have; but until then, everything belongs to my mother."

"Very good; you shall pay your mother. You shall have the five hundred francs; but for this you must play something superlative—Liszt's Mass, or one of Händel's oratorios."

"What is the concert for? Is it to help the papal troops?"

"Yes. I am arranging it."

"Then I cannot do it."

"Why?"

"I shall not play for Garibaldi's enemies."

"Oh, how stupid you are. Who asks you to play for Garibaldi's enemies? You play for my friends."

But the young man kept insisting that no, he wouldn't. In his excitement he stood up from his chair and throwing back his waistcoat, showed her that he, too, wore a red shirt.

First Eveline laughed at him. "A red shirt! Does it mean that you have enlisted with Garibaldi?"

"I should have done so long ago, except for my mother."

"And what would you do if your hand was shot off?"

"Then I should become a pensioner to some fine lady, who would, I know, support me."

At this, Eveline burst into tears. His words had touched a chord in her tender heart. Árpád, however, could not understand what he had said to upset her; he tried to console her, and asked how he had offended her. Still sobbing, she said:

"My poor little brother is dead. There, by my table, I keep his crutches."

"I am sorry. I join in your grief with all my heart. He and I were good friends; we had a lot of fun together."

"Yes, you liked him. The world is quite dead to me. I listen for the sound of his crutches scratching along the floor, up the stairs. Ah, my little brother! I have no one now. I want some one to take care of. I should like to nurse some one—an artist who had lost his eyesight; a musician whose hand had been shot off; or a political hero, who, concealed himself in my room from his pursuers, and to whom I should be benefactress, protectress, breadwinner, everything."

She was laughing now. "You have heard me sing in public. What do you think of me?"

"I think you would be a great artist if you could sing for the devil as well as you do for the angels."

"I don't understand. What do you mean by the devil?"

"You surely have heard from the pulpit that the theatre is the devil's synagogue."

"You rude man! Don't you know that I belong to the theatre?"

"I beg a thousand pardons. I thought that you were a nun in the daytime, and an actress at night; that would be a fair bargain."

"You silly boy! Why do you think I am a nun?"

"Because you are dressed like one."

"This is only a penitential dress. You godless creature, you are making fun of religion!"

"No, Madame. I agree that it is a great mortification to wear grey silk, a great penance to play the coquette with downcast eyes, a real fast to eat crayfish at twenty francs the dish. I am also told that fashionable ladies of Paris have taken to wearing high dresses because they discipline the flesh so severely that their shoulders and necks are a mass of scars, and therefore the effects of their flagellations must be concealed."

"That is not true. We don't do anything of the kind."

"The world says so. I don't want to inquire; it is your secret."

"It is not true," Eveline repeated. "We do not flagellate ourselves: look!" And kneeling down before Árpád, she raised the lace collar which was round her neck, and made him look at her fair skin.

They were a pair of children.

Árpád took his hat and his leave. He left a card with his address, but he would not take part in her concert.

Eveline, however, started afresh to compose her programme.

Chapter XXVIII

UNTOUCHED

Eveline was still writing her programme when the Abbé Samuel was announced. In Paris it is not thought unusual for an abbé to visit an actress, and besides, the abbé was an old friend, well known to both husband and wife. He was very interested in the concert, and read the programme attentively.

"It would have been all so nice," said Eveline in a vexed tone, "only for that stupid Árpád. See, Father, just there between my song and the cello solo, he would have come in so well."

"Is Árpád in town?"

"Yes, he has only just left. I begged him to help my concert. My song from the Stabat Mater would have gone so much better with his accompaniment, but he has grown quite silly. He has become a heretic."

The priest shook with laughter, and then a sudden idea struck him. It was plain Eveline liked Árpád, which was only natural, for they were about the same age. He was twenty, she nineteen —a pair of children, and children like to amuse themselves. They don't care for serious things; that comes later. What if he made use of Árpád to introduce Waldemar?

"I should like to bet you that Árpád Belényi will play at your concert, and, moreover, that he will accompany your Stabat Mater on the harmonium. What will you give me if he does?"

"Oh, he won't do it; you may be sure of that. I know him well; he is very obstinate once he takes anything into his noddlecock, and if I have not been able to persuade him . . ."

Eveline had immense faith in the magic of her dark eyes.

"Well, you shall see. What will you give me if I succeed?" repeated the abbé.

Eveline answered this by another question:

"How do you mean to get round him?" She said nothing of what she would give in case he succeeded.

"Oh, there are many ways; for instance, I might say to him that if he played in your drawing-room, he may even be engaged by the Empress, and that then his fortune would be made, at least for this season. An artist would see at once what a chance this would be. Then I would offer him money."

"I have done that already—five hundred francs."

"Well, although a young man may turn up his nose at five hundred francs, an old woman will appreciate a hundred Napoleons at their true value. Árpád always obeys his mother, and what she promises for him, he must do. I know the circumstances."

"You are a very sensible man. I should have begun with the mother, but it never occurred to me. Well, manage it all for me. If you do it, I shall do whatever you ask."

She was in such good mood that the abbé saw he could ask her anything; still, it was with slight hesitation that he said:

"I want you to give an invitation for your charity concert to a friend of mine."

"You shall have ten," cried Eveline gaily.

"I only want one, but this invitation must be written in your own hand."

"Tell me the name of your friend, and I will write the card this minute."

As she spoke, she sat down at her writing-table, and took an invitation from the drawer.

"Now the name."

"Prince Waldemar Sondersheim."

When she heard the name, Eveline threw down her pen, and sprang to her feet.

"No," she said decidedly, "never!"

The abbé burst into a shrill laugh. "Your excitement is very becoming," he said. "You are a fine actress."

"I shall not invite Prince Sondersheim to my concert," returned Eveline, seating herself on the sofa with a defiant air.

"Is the prince disagreeable to you?"

"I loathe him."

"Do you imagine that the world consists only of simpletons like Árpád Belényi?"

Eveline got up from the sofa, went to the writing-table, and tore the programme she had been writing into little pieces.

"Árpád may stay at home, tied to his mother's apron-strings. I don't want him, nor any one. I'll give up the concert"; and she threw the fragments of her programme into the fire-place.

The abbé rose, and took the excited girl by the hand.

"Compose yourself, my dear young lady," he said. "I have come to you on a most urgent matter—a matter which is of great importance to you and your husband, and I do not deny that it is of great moment to me. I may, in fact, call it of vital importance to each one of us. If everything should turn out as badly as it now looks, your husband shall have to go to America, I must return to my monastery, and what will become of you, I do not know."

Eveline sat down again on the sofa. She listened attentively.

"You must know," the abbé said, "that the old Prince Theobald, after you gave back the palace in the Maximilian Strasse, which had been his present to you, took shares in your name in the Bondavára Company to the amount of a million."

"I never knew it," answered Eveline.

"That proves that you never thought of asking your husband how much this splendid hotel cost, to say nothing of your magnificent carriage and horses, your numerous servants."

"I thought that my salary added to what Kaulman . . ." She stopped suddenly; the incredulous smile on the abbé's lips made her silent.

"All this splendour is at an end," he continued. "A telegram, which came a few hours ago, brings the news that, at the suit of his son-in-law, Prince Theobald's affairs have been placed in the hands of trustees; the trustees will, without any doubt, seize the shares taken for you."

"They may do as they like," returned the girl indifferently.

"Oh, there may be a lawsuit. But there is worse to come. Another telegram brought the news that last week there was a fearful explosion at the Bondavára colliery."

At this Eveline gave a cry, then quickly asked:

"And Iván Berend, has his mine also exploded?"

The abbé looked somewhat surprised, but continued in his earnest manner:

"I believe not. The company's shares, however, have received a terrible blow. Especially as one of the collieries is still burning, with no chance of the fire being extinguished."

As he spoke he looked fixedly at her, and his penetrating eyes soon saw the truth: her joy at the escape of Berend's property outweighed her sorrow for her husband's loss.

"You can understand," continued the abbé, "that we are in danger of actual ruin; everything now depends on one thing. Of course, you know that, in consequence of the Bondavára Company, Kaulman's reputation is one of the highest in the financial world. Millions have been invested, and ten times as much floating on the Stock Exchange. Money is not a tangible thing. This catastrophe—which may still be averted after all, for it is possible that the fire may be extinguished—will be a terrible weapon in the hands of the company's enemies, who want, above all things, to ruin Kaulman. Today he is a king, hands full of gold are stretched out to him, a hundred millions are eagerly offered to him; tomorrow the same people will be clamouring to get back the money they have entrusted to him.

Whether the cry is raised or not depends entirely on one man, and this man is Prince Waldemar Sondersheim. He is here; he arrived today. Probably, he has had news of the explosion, earlier than Kaulman, whose director, Rauné, no doubt, hoped against hope to get the fire under control. Kaulman's fate lies in the hands of Prince Sondersheim, and so does my own. I admit it. I was the pivot of an enormous world-wide project. Tomorrow, Kaulman's proposal for the Church loan was to be offered to the financial world of Paris and Brussels; it is an important crisis, that may begin a new page in history. If Prince Waldemar makes use of the collapse of the Bondavára Company to raise a cry against us, then the whole venture will vanish like a dream. If he calls out on the Exchange that the Bondavára shares are sixty per cent, below par, we are lost. If he keeps silent, the loan will float, and then the Bondavára misfortune will sink into a matter of small importance, like so many in the money-market. Now you can understand what an effect a word from you may have, and what you can do, if you speak this word."

Eveline shook her head, and laid her finger on her lips; she looked the very genius of silence.

"What!" cried the abbé, his anger getting the better of him, "you refuse—you think more of one word that costs you nothing than of the consequences? The Holy See may be overthrown, the standard of heresy may be unfurled, the saints torn from their shrines—and all for a woman's caprice."

Eveline spread out her arms as if she were engaged in a combat with a giant. She said in a resolute voice:

"No! I cannot speak to that man."

The abbé grew even more angry. He felt that, if he could not persuade this stubborn woman, at least he would have the pleasure of wounding her.

He took his hat, and holding it behind his back, said in a cold, cutting voice:

"I neither understand your dislike of the prince nor your

extreme delicacy. Prince Sondersheim is in no way inferior to men you have accepted previously."

At this insult Eveline seized the abbé's hand, and suddenly abandoning her usual reserve, she cried:

"Father! I am still a maid!"

The abbé looked at her in unfeigned astonishment. He saw by her blush, her unconscious turn of the head, her childish sobs, that she was speaking the truth.

He sighed.

It had been his last stake, and he had lost. Good-bye to glory, to greatness. All had vanished into air at Eveline's words; they had scattered his dreams. He recognized that all the deeds which have made men famous were dust and ashes in comparison with the real nobility of soul possessed by this peasant girl, this girl who, in obedience to her husband's infamous commands, and because she had sworn to obey him, had worn the red shoes of a harlot, while she preserved the purity of a bride. He felt himself incapable of forcing her to descend from her pedestal.

"Eveline," he said in a voice shaken by emotion, "the words you have spoken banish me to my cell. My dreams of power and splendour lie in the dust—their fitting place. You said, 'I am still a maid'; my child, keep yourself so. The French law recognizes no marriage unless it has been contracted by the civil authorities. Your marriage with Felix Kaulman is null and void in this country; you are here Mademoiselle Eva Dirmák —nothing more. You can tell Kaulman that I have told you this. I have given him the same information, as he wished to free himself from his nominal tie to you. And now, fare you well; I shall return to my monastery, to reconcile myself with an offended God."

Eva Dirmák threw herself at the feet of the priest, and covered his hands with tears and kisses.

"Put your hand upon my head," she sobbed, "and bless me."

"My daughter," said the abbé, "the Invincible watches over you and protects you. May you ever be thus safely guarded."

With these words, the priest left the room. He did as he said; he sought no further interview with Kaulman, but went straight to the station, and journeyed back to bury himself in his monastery.

The world never heard of him again.

Chapter XXIX

MAN AND WIFE

Felix lost no time in seeking an interview with Prince Waldemar. He preferred to find him in his house to meeting him accidentally on the Bourse.

Waldemar did not keep him waiting long, neither did he treat him to a display of his rank. He received Kaulman in his study.

"Ah! Your Highness is occupied with business," said Felix, in the airy manner of an intimate friend; but he was secretly astonished to see that a man of the prince's position was actually cutting the pages of the pamphlet before him, and underlining with red and blue pencils the passages that pleased him.

The prince laid down the pamphlet, and asked Felix to sit down.

"I have only this moment heard," continued the banker, "that your Excellency has arrived, and I hastened to be the first to pay my respects."

"Strange! At this very moment I, too, was occupying myself with your affairs," returned the prince, with a peculiar smile, which Felix noted, and thought he understood. He tried to put on a jaunty air as he made answer:

"I have come as an envoy under a flag of truce into enemy country."

The prince thought that his flag of truce would be a handkerchief worked with the letter E.

"Powers greater than us," went on Felix, twirling his hat in

309

his embarrassment, "have co-operated in sudden emergencies, and from being enemies they have become friends, recognizing that it was to their mutual advantage to bury the hatchet."

"And may I inquire, what is our mutual advantage?"

"My projected loan."

The prince said nothing, but the smile that played on his thin lips was a sufficient and most irritating answer. Felix began to lose his poise. He rose from his chair, and in his earnestness leant over the table at which the prince was sitting.

"Prince," he said, "this loan is for the benefit of the Holy See. You are, I know, a good Catholic."

"Who has betrayed my secret?"

"Besides, you are a thorough aristocrat. It must go against Your Highness's feelings to see that, while in Hungary a bureaucratic minister pillages the Church, and pockets its revenues, a band of free-booters throws St. Peter's heritage to the mob. All this could be prevented by our striking one blow. You will do it, for you are a nobleman in the best sense of the word."

"What else am I?"

"Above all, you are a financier. It cannot escape your keen eye that this loan is one of the greatest, the soundest of speculations; for you are a prudent man, and you know how to add two and two."

"Have I any other qualifications?"

Waldemar's cold, sarcastic rejoinders did not put Felix out of countenance. His face assumed a still more amiable expression as he offered his hand to the prince, saying:

"I trust you will be the honoured friend of the house of Kaulman."

Such words could be met either by a warm shake of the hand, or by a box on the ear. He ran the risk, waiting breathlessly for the answer, which was different, and yet worse. The prince picked up the pamphlet which he had been busily marking with his red and blue pencils.

"Now, my excellent brother in the faith, my fellow aristocrat,

310

my comrade in finance, and my best friend, just you glance at this little brochure, for it contains my answer. I beg that you will take your time."

He handed the pamphlet to Felix, and while that gentleman cast his eye over it, the prince pared his nails.

Felix laid down the pamphlet. "This purports to be my biography."

"As I think the title-page indicates."

"Your Highness is, I presume, the writer?"

"I have supplied the facts."

"All kinds of affairs are mentioned here, in which I have thrown dust in the eyes of the public, leading finally to the Bondavára speculation, in which, it seems, I have announced a false balance and a feigned dividend, and drawn ten millions out of the capital, which capital is now irrecoverably lost with the catastrophe in the mine. It is a terrible indictment."

"Is it not true, then?"

"It is true! Your Highness is my faithful biographer; but allow me to fill out some details. Yesterday's unexpected misfortune can be repaired tomorrow; the unlucky speculation may be glossed over if a better takes its place; a small defeat is compensated by a great victory. What use does Your Highness intend to make of this brochure?"

"Frankly, I intend, as soon as you declare your new loan, to circulate this pamphlet freely on the Bourse. I shall then set the bears to work, so that your shares shall be driven out of the market in no time."

"I guessed as much, and to be frank, this is why I came here, to prevent, if I can, my ruin."

Felix tried by the continuous winking of his eyes to express his despair. He put his right hand into his vest, and in a low voice added:

"Perhaps when you see me stretched dead before you, your aim will then be accomplished."

Prince Waldemar broke into an irrepressible fit of laughter, and clapped Kaulman on the shoulder.

"I beg you not to play this farce for my benefit. You did not come here to blow your brains out. Nothing of the sort; you came to sell me something. You are a ruined speculator, but you still possess one jewel of value, a wonderful dark diamond which you found in a coal-mine, and polished smoothly, which you have sold once at a great profit, but which is now back on your hands. You are perfectly aware that I want to get this jewel if I can, that I am willing to offer all I have for it; and this is why you have come here today. Let us understand one another. I will treat with you. What is your price?"

The prince threw himself back in his chair, but without asking Kaulman to sit down again.

The banker abandoned his tragic manner, and resumed his customary cool, hard, matter-of-fact voice.

"First of all, this." And he laid his hand upon the pamphlet.

"Good. You shall have it—a thousand copies and the manuscript. You can burn it, unless you care to keep it as a souvenir."

"Secondly," went on Felix, "you must abandon your conspiracy against me. During the three days of raising the loan your bears are to keep quiet; there are to be no manoeuvres. Thirdly, your name must appear in the list of subscribers with a decent sum."

"Good. We shall understand one another. Now listen to my modifications of your proposal. On the first day when the shares of the new loan are drawn, I undertake to keep the bears quiet, but I shall take no shares. On the second day I shall also keep quiet, but I shall not give you a shove. On the third day I shall take one million shares, and from that time I undertake to push your speculation as if I were your best friend."

"And why not on the first two days?"

"I will tell you what is to happen on those days. This very day you must go to Madame, and tell her that Prince Theobald's fortune is sequestrated, and that she can no longer occupy his

Hotel. Madame was once generous enough to return to the prince his palace in the Maximilian Strasse, together with all it contained. She will have to repeat this act of renunciation, and return to her husband's roof. Her husband must celebrate this happy event by a splendid party, to which he will, as a matter of course, invite his best friend." Here the prince laid his little finger on his breast with a significant gesture. "The friend will take this opportunity to show Madame a photograph of his summer palace, which is situated on Lake Constance, and only waits for the presence of its mistress to be perfect, while she needs the lovely breezes of the lake to restore her."

"You are really very thoughtful."

"Do not praise me too soon. On the second day you must reach an understanding with Madame. You will tell her that in France a marriage, to be legal, must be contracted before a civil magistrate; therefore, you will go with her to the register, and be legally married."

"But, Prince," cried Felix, with a horrified expression upon his face, "why should I do that?"

"Why?" returned the prince, standing up in his turn, so as to be able to overawe his victim. "Because I want to defeat your little game. You took a wife in another country, knowing you could repudiate her here. It is my wish that Madame shall bear your name for ever; otherwise you would have it in your power, on the fourth day, to say, 'I gave you what was not mine to give.' I must have the diamond in its proper setting. I shall not remove the stone from your wedding-ring; but I shall wear it on my finger."

Kaulman could not conceal his embarrassment. "This whim is incomprehensible," he said.

"On the contrary," returned the other, with an evil sneer, "it is quite clear. I am desperately in love with a woman, and she detests me. She will not even look at me. But she is unaware that I know the reason of her abhorrence. Your wife is a pure woman. You look surprised—naturally. It is not your merit that she has remained so. Oh, you need not protest. Prince Theobald has told me her story. Amongst other things, he made her swear that she would never receive me. Poor old fool! He did not have much knowledge of human nature. If he had not interfered, it's very likely I should have tired of pursuing a woman who did not care for me; but the mystery that surrounded her has added to my interest. I adore her, not alone for her beauty, her charm, but for her innocence, her goodness. She requires nothing to raise her in my estimation; but she must take her fitting place in the world. She must have the shield of her husband's name, the right to his protection. Now you understand what I require of you."

"Prince, your ideas are devilish! You wish to bind me to my dishonour."

"To your dishonour!" and the prince laughed with scorn. "My good Kaulman, who asked you to come here and sell your honour? Ah, you cannot answer that! Never mind, we shall keep our secret; the world shall know nothing. In Society the head of the house of Kaulman shall be considered an honourable gentleman, an excellent husband, a good family man. In the commercial world he will be looked upon as a sound financier. Honours will crowd upon him; he will go far . . . His real position will only be known to three people. There, my good friend, don't feign so much virtuous indignation. You are over-acting, which always spoils the effect. I will take it all for granted. Time is short; you had better use it."

This was true. Every moment was precious. Felix abandoned his attempts to pretend outraged feelings of honour, and composing his agitated features, held out his hand to the prince. The latter, however, did not take it.

"There's no need to shake hands over our honourable compact. Take your note-book and write down the conditions, and be sure you put the dates correctly. If I receive by one o'clock the card of invitation to your entertainment tomorrow, I shall stay away from the Exchange. The next day I shall do the same;

that is, if I receive the official notification before one o'clock that your civil marriage has taken place. On the fourth day, if your solicitor brings me the news before one o'clock that you have set off for Brussels to negotiate the Papal loan, and hands me the key of your house, with the request that I look after the business in your absence, then I shall go down to the Exchange, and push your speculation like my own. Now you may go, sir, and indulge your outraged feelings in private."

Chapter XXX

EVA DIRMÁK

Felix Kaulman felt that he had made good use of his opportunity. All would go well now. The prince would no longer use the Bondavára catastrophe to ruin him; on the contrary, his influence would stem the panic which the news had, no doubt, already caused in the Vienna money-market, and when the Papal loan was concluded, everything would be all right. There was Eveline, of course; but a man such as Kaulman, whose conscience had long since withered with his heart, soon found excuses. No one could blame him for the prince's infatuation; only a fool wouldn't take advantage of it, especially in his situation. A drowning man catches at any straw; and as for Eveline, she owed him her gratitude. Had he not raised her from the dust of the coal-pit to her present situation, saved her from a brutal husband, the savage Saffran, educated her, made her a fit companion for a prince? Many a woman would be glad of the elevation that was awaiting her; and this reminded him that Abbé Samuel's talk with Eveline must have broached the matter.

He waited for a long while for the priest; when he did not come, Felix finally decided to go to Eveline's house, but she was not at home. She had gone to the theatre; it was one of her performances.

Felix drove to the Opera House. First he went to his wife's box, but only found her companion. He looked around the house. In the pit there were numerous *claqueurs*. In one of the front boxes he saw Prince Waldemar.

Then he went backstage; as he was known as the *prima donna's* husband he had access to her dressing-room.

Eveline was dressed for her part, and waiting to go on. When she saw Kaulman she turned away angrily. Why did he disturb her when she was busy in her work?

"I have only come to wish you good evening," he said.

"You might have waited until tomorrow."

"To wish you good evening? Ha! Ha!"

"No; but you know I am always so nervous before I go on . . ."

"I only wanted to tell you that the cream of Parisian Society are fighting for tickets for your concert. Have you reserved one for me?" Felix was full of amiability and admiration.

"I have reserved none."

"Ah! And why not?" He said this in a soft, complaining voice.

"Because I have cancelled the concert."

The face of her husband lengthened. "Will you kindly tell me the reason for this change?"

"After I come off. This is my scene. I must go." She left the room, and went to the wings.

Felix followed to a place where he could watch his wife on the stage, and have a general view of the house.

Eveline played badly and sang worse. Her voice trembled, and she was out of tune. She was evidently nervous. Nevertheless, she was applauded to the echo, the *claque* worked hard; and Prince Waldemar clapped as if he had been paid for it. When she had finished her last song, a shower of bouquets and wreaths came from the prince's box, and fell at her feet.

Eveline left them on the stage, and hurried away to her dressing-room. Kaulman followed her.

"Why didn't you pick up those lovely bouquets?" he asked.

"I didn't deserve any. I know I did badly tonight."

"But, surely, you should have taken one of the bouquets for the sake of the donor."

"Ah! You would like that."

"I?"

"Yes. All those flowers came from you—at least, so I always understood."

"Pardon me, *ma chère*. Didn't you notice that they all came from the side box? Didn't you recognize who was in that box?"

"I never looked."

"It was Prince Waldemar."

"The man who is your enemy—who wants to ruin you?"

"Oh no, that is not so. He has changed. He is now our best friend."

"Our friend? Whom do you include in 'our'?"

"You, as well as myself."

"Thanks; but I decline my share."

"I am afraid you will find it difficult to stand aloof, for I consider Prince Waldemar as my best friend, and my house will be open to him as to a brother."

"As you please. My door shall be shut in his face."

"I am sorry, but you are forcing me to break a disagreeable piece of news to you; but I see you are busy. You don't take any interest—"

"Go on talking," returned Eveline, who was standing before the mirror, taking off her grease paint. "I am listening."

"In the future, I regret, you will not have a house of your own. The fortune of your friend, Prince Theobald, has been sequestrated; his property is now in the hands of trustees. I need not tell you, for I am sure you have known all along that the hotel you occupy, together with all your expenses, was paid by him. This, naturally, is at an end. In my circumstances I could not afford to give you a separate establishment, and we will be obliged to live together. It follows naturally that I shall expect my wife to receive my friends, and to make them welcome."

Eveline had laid aside her queenly robes; she now took off her diadem, and as she slowly unfastened her bracelets, she turned and faced Felix.

"And you think," she said, "that when I leave my hotel I cannot get a garret somewhere, where there will be a door with a strong lock, to keep out unpleasant visitors?"

"I must call your attention to one thing," he said. "We are in Paris, and the French law is strict. A wife must live under her husband's roof. She must go where he goes. She must obey him."

Eveline was now busy undoing the gold sandals from her feet. She looked steadily at Kaulman.

"I must call your attention," she said, "to another thing. We are in Paris, and according to the French law, couples who have been married at the altar, and not by the civil authorities, are not considered legally married, and so, our marriage is null and void."

Kaulman sprang to his feet as if he had been bitten by a tarantula.

"What are you saying?" he cried in a voice that was almost a shriek.

Eveline had loosened the golden sandals. She stood before Felix in her bare feet, and threw him the sandals.

"These belong to you. I am once more Eva Dirmák. I belong to myself."

"Who told you this?" stammered the banker, pale with rage.

"The Abbé Samuel, who had first advised you to do this."

Kaulman felt the room was going around his head.

"And now," continued Eveline, with a dignified motion of her hand, "I must remind you that this is the dressing-room of a single girl."

Felix did not wait for her to repeat his dismissal, he took his hat and left without a word. He ran away, and he ran without noticing where he was going, till he stumbled and fell.

All was over; he had played his last card. Everything was lost; there was no more help. He had two alternatives: he might put a pistol to his head, or he might take all the money from his counting-house and fly.

He chose the latter.

Chapter XXXI

CRUSHED

Eveline felt that she had been given a new life after a wrong beginning. She was no longer married. And yet she was not a widow, who would shed tears over happiness that had vanished. Her heart was full of newly-awakened desires, hopes she hardly dared to confess to herself, dreams that delighted whilst they embarrassed her—delicious secrets she was afraid to guess. When she heard next day that Kaulman had absconded, and could never return, she recognized fully that her chains were broken for ever.

When the caged bird escapes into the open air of heaven, does he ever regret his gilded cage and all its luxuries, or the tender endearments of his owner? The bird only thinks to enjoy his freedom. It may be that wilder and stronger birds will tear him in pieces; that the frost and rain may freeze him. He does not care. He wings his flight still higher; he looks for a branch; he looks for a mate, he is happy.

Eveline never for one moment reflected that she was in any way implicated in Kaulman's fall and the shame of his ruin. She had no idea that her name was being bandied about. She who had been a queen, who had been admired, had such a *succès!* What was to become of her now? No one knew anything of her past; but it was pretty safe to prophesy her future. She would have another protector. Of course; but who will he be? Which of her many admirers?

Such was the talk of the clubs, and the gossip of Society. While Eveline sat in her room, rejoicing at her new life of freedom, a sudden idea came to her.

She looked for Árpád's visiting-card, ordered her carriage, and drove to visit the Belényis. They lived some little way from Paris, in the suburbs where rooms can still be had on the ground floor. Madame Belényi liked to live on the ground floor. The house she had lost was of this sort, and renting a similar one had the advantage that, with her own kitchen, she could cook for her son, and feel sure he was not dining at some tavern in bad company. Except on special occasions, Árpád invariably came home to dine with his mother; he would not have missed this for any feast. He thought there was nothing to compare with her way of cooking pig's trotters with beans.

Eveline's coachman found it hard to find the narrow street in the neighbourhood of the Montmartre, where the Belényis had established themselves. Eveline would not let the carriage go past the nearest corner; she got out, and, accompanied by her footman, walked up the street, looking for the right house. Madame Belényi had hired two rooms in an old-fashioned cottage, divided by a kitchen. A girl working in the garden showed Eveline where the young gentleman lived. As Eveline gently pushed open the kitchen door, she saw that the door of the inner room opened, and a woman looked out, probably Árpád's mother, who was curious to see who had come to visit her son.

Eveline tiptoed to the door opposite, and turned the handle noiselessly, she wanted to surprise Árpád.

His room was a picture of comfort and order. It was easy to see that it was kept neat by his mother. The table and walls were crowded with pictures and ornaments, gifts from patrons —cups, wood-carvings, antique weapons, classical paintings; there were flowers in the window-boxes; the bookcases were full of books. Everything was arranged well, with taste and comfort, and Árpád preferred being at home to being anywhere else.

322

The hired piano was from Erard's and was standing open. Árpád was sitting with his back to it, brush in hand; he was painting. The pianist was also a painter. Many artists indulge in these freaks. One of our most distinguished portrait-painters loves to torture his neighbours by scratching the strings of his violin; another well-known musician spends his time writing feeble verses; and a third, a real poet, produces excrescences in marble and ivory.

What was Árpád painting?

Eveline stepped behind him softly, but the rustle of her silk dress betrayed her presence.

Árpád turned scarlet, shoved the picture into a drawer, and getting up quickly, confronted his visitor, who had only time to see that he was painting a portrait.

"Ah, it is you," he stammered, in an embarrassed voice. "I thought it was my mother."

"Aha! You are doing something you should not. Your mother does not allow you to paint; is that it? Well, it is a silly thing, I must say, for a pianist to spend his time painting; and what is your subject?"

"Oh, nothing—a flower."

'What a lie!' thought Eveline; 'it was a portrait.'

"Then if it is a flower, give it to me."

"I should rather not."

"But if it is only a flower?"

"I am not going to give it to you."

"Don't be so cross. Won't you ask me to sit down?"

Árpád was annoyed with her. Why had she come to disturb him just at that moment? Any other time she would have been welcome.

This opening spoilt their meeting; for the picture was not Eveline's portrait.

"Sit near me, else I shall think you are afraid of me. I thought that you would have come to see me, to scold me for my performance last night. Tell me frankly, didn't I sing badly?"

"Very badly," returned Árpád peevishly. "You are going back instead of forwards; and you seem to forget all you learn. I was quite ashamed of you. And your acting! I thought I was in a puppet-theatre."

"To tell you the truth, I was in a miserable mood. I had domestic troubles. I have parted from Kaulman."

"That was no reason to sing flat. He wasn't worth risking your engagement, and playing in such a perfunctory manner —singing, all out of tune. You never troubled yourself much about him."

Árpád knew nothing of what had happened to Kaulman; the news had not penetrated to the Montmartre.

"And, at all events, you should have had the discretion not to order a shower of bouquets, when you were doing so badly; it doesn't look well."

Eveline was very much wounded by his unjust remark. She answered, almost crying:

"I assure you I have never ordered bouquets to be thrown to me."

"Well, it was one of your admirers, that crazy prince. It is all the same. To be pretty, to sing badly, and to receive flowers for it are three sins rolled into one. The world cannot distinguish between them."

"Very well; go on finding fault, go on scolding, my wonderful old master. What else have I done to displease you?"

Árpád began to laugh, and held out his hand to Eveline.

"Forgive me," he said. "My rudeness is only the anger of a teacher; it is over. Now we shall be young again, and talk. Shall I fetch the draught-board? Shall we play for love or for nothing?"

This tone warmed Eveline's heart. She laughed, and slapped Árpád's hand, which he did not like.

"What are you going to do now you have got rid of Kaulman?" he asked. "Will you marry again? Is another man ready

324

for the yoke? There are enough fish in the sea. Or are you going to hang on to your artistic freedom?"

Eveline cast down her eyes, and grew suddenly grave.

"I have no one," she said sadly.

"Ah, that does not mean that there aren't many you could have if you liked."

"It means the same thing. I shall belong to no one. I shall never take a husband who is above me. Do you see, a girl who walked barefoot in the coal-mine should stay in her own class. If I could give someone a place in my heart, it would be someone as free and independent as I am. He should owe nothing to great people; he should depend absolutely on his own genius; live absolutely by his own work. He should be esteemed not for money, or rank, but for his talent; he should glory in being an artist."

This was a frank confession for any one who understood. Árpád understood; he became even more peevish.

"H'm! Then I am afraid you are on a path that leads you away from a man such as you describe."

"What do you mean?"

Árpád stood up. "Artists have many strange ideas, inseparable from the artistic temperament. Do you see that antique goblet there on the table? It was a present to me from Count Demidoff at one of my concerts. It was an heirloom of his family. It is a wonderful relic. Princes, generals, rulers have drunk from it. I value it highly, and I keep my visitors' cards in it. But I never drink from it; I prefer an ordinary glass, for which I have paid ninepence, but no one has drunk from it except me."

Eveline flushed deeply at this cruel speech.

Árpád was, however, quite determined to make the matter even clearer.

"You say," he went on, "that you would like to find an artist, a genius, a proud, independent man; him you would choose for your husband! And you imagine that a man like this would submit to sit by your side as you drove in the Champs-Élysées, knowing that the people in other carriages, or walking along the path, were saying, 'There is the curled and scented Hyperion, but the horses that draw his carriage are not paid for by his muse, they are the thoroughbreds of Prince X or Y; his wife is not content with the glory of his name, she wears the diamonds provided by Marquis G.' How easily do you think you will find such a husband?"

Poor Eveline! She tried to defend herself against this cruel boy.

"But I am ready to throw away all riches—everything that is not earned by my own honest work. I want to live by my profession, to be what I am, an actress. I would work night and day to perfect myself. I do not want any other distinction but to be an artist."

Árpád then told her the one thing she had never heard before. Children and fools speak the truth, and in Árpád there was a mixture of both; he was a child in years, and a fool, as only an artist can afford to be.

"My dear Eveline, you are not an artist; you will never be an actress; you are one of the stepdaughters of the Muses. There are many such, who have great talents; one only is wanting—courage. You sing very well, you act with feeling, with humour —at home, for two or three people; but as soon as the proscenium lights are lit your voice grows weak, you sing flat, you see and hear nothing, and you act like a puppet. This is called stage-fright, and it can never be cured; it has ruined more brilliant careers than all critics put together. You shake your head, and quote your triumphs. Don't deceive yourself; I know the machinery of the stage, and how artificial thunder and lightning are manufactured. At every performance you triumph; you receive thunders of applause, mountains of flowers. The morning after your performance your breakfast-table is covered with newspapers full of praise. This is all gilt, and will last only while some rich admirer pays the piper. But try the experiment

326

of closing your doors to your wealthy patrons, and step on the stage with no help but your own talent; ask to be applauded for your own sake. Then you will learn the price of the entertainment, and that the critics' praise was bought."

Eveline's head sank. She knew that every word he said was true. Árpád viewed the matter not only from the artistic angle, but from his youthful ideals. He was indignant with the folly of the world; he was indignant that Eveline should have lent herself to such low intrigues, and taken the place of better artists, better musicians, better actresses; but in his heart he was sorry for her. She had been kind to him; she had never offended him. Why was he so cruel to her? It was the petulance of his boyish nature. Why had she disturbed him when he was happy at his painting? Why had she asked him questions? What was it to her whether it was a flower, and if it were a flower, why should she want it? And when he put out his hand, why should she slap it in that intimate manner?

The picture was not painted for her.

"What shall I do? What am I fit for?" asked Eveline, cast down by his words. Her beautiful eyes were full of tears; she felt crushed.

The young man considered his answer for a few minutes. As she had asked for his medicine she should drink it to the dregs.

"You have two alternatives, for I would not advise you to take a third and return to your husband. If I were a woman, I would prefer to be stretched out in the morgue than share that man's ill-gotten wealth. So we have only the two courses to consider. Either you continue on the stage as before, take the bought applause, and the flowers paid for by your noble patrons, or go back where you came from, and be content to shove wheelbarrows for the rest of your life."

Eveline rose from her chair, drew her wrap round her shoulders, and murmured in a low, constrained voice:

"Thank you." And she silently left the room.

Tears came into Árpád's eyes. But why had she come? Why

327

had she disturbed him when he was happy painting? The moment she had closed the door he returned to the table, and took from the drawer his flower, to see if it had sustained any injury. It was in one sense a flower—a fair child with blue eyes!

The door opened again; the picture was concealed quickly. No one, however, came in. Árpád's mother spoke through the half-opened door.

"Árpád, my son, who was that beautiful lady who was here just now? Was she a princess?"

"She was a poor woman who came to beg."

"H'm! It's wonderful, how fine the beggars are in this Paris here, dressed in silk. Did you give her anything, Árpád?"

"I had nothing to give her, mother."

"That's just as well, my son." And she shut the door, and went back to her own room, to stitching her son's shirt.

Chapter XXXII

COAL

Eveline made up her mind to a great effort. She knew that there was some truth in what Árpád had said; but he was wrong in one thing: the gulf between 'can' and 'must.'

Her resolution to succeed grew in proportion as her chances of success lessened. Many before her have found strength in the thought: 'If I have no one to care for me, at least, I am my own master.' She would shape her own future; she would be an actress. She would show the world what was in her. She would steel herself before the footlights. The circumstances which had deprived her of courage would now give her strength; she would sing in public as if she were alone. The crowd should not matter, except to share her triumph.

She spent a miserable night. The luxury which surrounded her, the works of art on her tables, in her cabinets, the costly vases, seemed to reproach her; goblets set with precious stones recalled Árpád's words. Better to be a ninepenny glass than a silver goblet!

At last sleep came to her, and she woke refreshed and full of fresh energy in the morning.

The opera in which she had sung the day before yesterday was to be repeated. There was a rehearsal scheduled for the morning. At this rehearsal, then, she would show what she could do; she would look at no one; she would sing like the blind nightingale.

329

She ordered her carriage. When she reached the theatre, she told the coachman to call for her in two hours.

As she reached the foyer, the stage-manager came to meet her, and told her that her part had been given to another singer.

Eveline flew into a passion. Why had it been taken away from her, and in such a way, without her permission? Such want of respect towards her!

The man regretted it, but he either could not or would not offer an explanation. Would she like to see the manager?

Eveline, in her excitement, went to look for him; but he was not in his office. His secretary, however, gave her a letter, which the manager had intended to send to her.

Eveline took the letter, and in the foyer she broke the seal and read it. It was a dismissal, immediate, uncourteous, on the grounds that she was unequal to the position of a *prima donna*.

She did not know how she got out of the theatre and into the street; she recollected herself when she saw the stares of the passers-by. She was walking like one dead; her body moved, but her mind was lifeless. It was strange to be thus annihilated.

Then it was true; the cruel boy was right. The clouds were gilded only while the sun shone. All her splendour had been on the surface. There was nothing tangible; nothing came from herself. The whole thing had been a conjuror's trick; it has now vanished for ever.

Eveline wandered on, she didn't know where. Eventually she found herself in front of her hotel. She would not have thought it strange if she had been told at the door that no one lived here, that she was dead and buried years ago. She thought she was too stunned to feel either surprise or pain, but one thing still had the power to shake her.

She went upstairs, still in a daze, and through her apartment until she reached her dressing-room. As she came in she saw, stretched in an armchair, Prince Waldemar.

He was faultlessly dressed, his hair carefully arranged, and his fair whiskers, cut in the day's fashion for muttonchops; his moustache was pointed and waxed.

Eveline's voice rose in fear mixed with anger:

"May I ask, sir, what are you doing here?"

"I was waiting to see you," said the prince, with well-bred nonchalance; but without rising from the chair, in which he lounged so comfortably.

"Who gave you permission to enter my room?"

"I did not ask for permission."

"What right have you to intrude here?"

Lazily, the prince put his hand into the pocket of his coat, and drew out a red paper like a bill; he handed it to Eveline with a slight motion of his head, which conveyed, 'This is why I am here.'

Eveline took the paper, which trembled in her hand.

"What is this? I do not understand it."

"It is quite clear," said the prince, rising at last from his chair. "Kaulman's creditors have seized your things. Kaulman was careless or thoughtless enough—I really cannot say which—to declare that what belonged to his wife was his, and so his creditors have seized everything here. During your absence this morning, the bailiffs broke open your door, to take possession. They fixed a notice outside, inviting people to come in, and inspect the things for sale. In consequence, I am here. I came in to look around. You will observe that there are government seals on everything. I am here as a purchaser."

Eveline looked round, and saw that it was all true.

"But, sir, it is impossible. Kaulman knew perfectly well that nothing here was his property."

The prince seemed to enjoy the situation.

"I am sure of it. It was gross negligence on your lawyer's side; he should have protected your interests better. People only know that Kaulman brought the stuff here; it was supposed that he had bought them. In any case he cannot testify for you. A misfortune overtook him. When he saw that the police were after him, he jumped from the railway carriage. Unfortunately, he broke his neck, and died at once."

Eveline fell back upon the sofa, and hid her face in her hands.

"If you wish to shed a few tears to the memory of Kaulman, I will withdraw to the window," remarked Prince Waldemar, with polite irony.

Eveline did not answer. Everything was confused in her mind; she could think of nothing. Let everything go; what did it matter? Should she start a law-suit to recover her property? Should she bring witnesses to prove that this ornament, these hangings, or rich carpets were not the property of her husband, but gifts from an old man—the most upright, the dearest of men, a Hungarian noble, who had adopted her, an actress, to be his own child, quite selflessly, not for sinful gratification, but out of pure affection? No one would believe her. She would never tell it. She would not subject the name of her benefactor to the jeers and laughter of the incredulous. She preferred to let everything go.

"I am not crying, sir," she said to the prince. "If you have anything further to say, I am ready to listen."

"I could recount some other unfortunate circumstances," answered Waldemar, leaning against the fireplace. "For one thing, Prince Theobald, your former patron, has been placed under legal restraint, by his family, and cannot take an active part in the affairs of the world."

"I know."

"The shares which he took, as a provision for you, in the Bondavára Company, have been sequestrated."

"I've been told that already."

"This loss, however, has its compensation; those shares are now almost worthless. Since the colliery explosion, and the impossibility of extinguishing the fire in the mine, they have fallen to nothing."

"That does not concern me."

"I have not quite finished. The priest, who was your friend, who dreamed of a bishopric, has returned to his monastery."

"I have known that for some time."

"You seem to have heard everything. Perhaps you know also that your manager has cancelled your engagement, and given your part to another actress?"

"Here is his letter," answered Eveline, drawing a crumpled paper from her pocket. And then she looked at the prince with proud contempt. She was very beautiful. "Have you taken the trouble to come here to tell me all this?" she asked, her eyes gleaming not with tears, but indignation.

"I did not come here for that," answered the prince, sitting down on the sofa and bending towards her. "I came to speak to you frankly. Do you not see that the whole fabric on which your golden dreams were built has crumbled? The Bondavára mine is on fire; the shares are falling; the prime minister is disgraced; the prince is under restraint; your husband is dead; your property will be sold by auction; you are dismissed from the theatre. The comedy is played out. Let us applaud, if you like, and let us begin again. I can return your shares. I can get you a palace in the Maximilian Strasse. I can buy you back all your things—your furniture, your diamonds, your horses. I can arrange matters with the manager of the theatre; you shall be reinstated as *prima donna* on better terms than before. I can give you a far better position than you have ever enjoyed, and I can offer you a truer, more self-sacrificing, more adoring lover than you have ever possessed. His name is Waldemar Sondersheim." He bowed low.

Eveline looked contemptuously at his boots.

Waldemar was now certain that he was master of the situation. He took a watch from his waistcoat pocket, and pressed it into her hand.

"My sweetest love, my time is precious. I am expected at the Stock Exchange. The Kaulman speculation has to be rushed. It is just twelve o'clock, I give you one hour to think over what

333

I have said, and to decide your fate. I am content to wait until then; it is only one word I ask for—yes or no."

Eveline gave him a shorter answer. She threw the timepiece which he had put into her hand with such force on the floor that it shattered into a hundred pieces.

Prince Waldemar laughed, put his hand in his left-hand waistcoat pocket, took out another watch, and said dryly:

"I expected just such an answer, and therefore I brought another watch. I beg you to break it if you like. I shall be only too happy to provide you with a third."

This time, however, Eveline did not take the watch. She sprang to her feet, and pointing to the door, cried out:

"If you have bought my things, take everything away; but the apartment is still mine. Go!"

Prince Waldemar looked at her haughtily, although he was still smiling.

"My dear lady, this is easily said; but reflect a moment. What will become of you if you reject me? You have no other resources."

"I have a place," returned the girl, bitterly, "where I can return: the coal-mine."

Prince Waldemar made a low bow, and without another word, took his hat and left her.

A woman who thinks of coal-mines does not need a rich man's friendship. Many poor wretches have found their last refuge there.

That evening Eveline visited her jeweller. She brought her last pair of diamond earrings. They were all she had; all her ornaments had been seized by the bailiffs. She sold these to the jeweller, and left the money in his care, to be spent annually on her little brother's grave in Père Lachaise, to have green grass planted round it, and fresh flowers placed there on All Souls Day. The jeweller promised, for she had been a good customer. She told him she was going away. Apparently it was a long journey, for the next morning a bundle was found on

334

the banks of the Seine by the police. It was tied in a cashmere shawl, which her maid recognized as belonging to the lost actress.

Prince Waldemar offered a large reward for finding the body. But it was never found; the bundle laid on the riverbank was a ruse, and while everyone was dragging the river, Eveline kept her word, and sought refuge in the coal-pit.

Prince Waldemar never heard of her again. He and his household wore mourning in her memory for six weeks.

Chapter XXXIII

CSANTA'S LAST WILL AND TESTAMENT

Before the crash came, and when the Bondavára Company shares stood at sixty over par, and looked as if they would go even higher, Csanta was satisfied to sell at sixty. There could be too much even of a good thing. One should not be too grasping, and sixty thousand is a nice profit for one year. He thought he would act as Spitzhase had often recommended, and sell his shares in small lots. It would add to his pleasure not to do it all at once.

For some time the quotations had stood at sixty. Every morning he went to the coffee-house, and read the financial column, and always saw the same, 'Bondavára, sixty above par.'

On the morning when Csanta had arranged to send the first instalment of his shares to Vienna, he went to his coffee-house, and while waiting to be served, took up the first newspaper that came to hand. As usual, he began to read it backwards, from the Exchange column on the back page. The first thing that caught his eye was 'Bondavára, sixty below par.'

A printer's error; and a very serious one! The printer must have been drunk. The fellow ought to be put in prison. If there is a policeman in Vienna, or justice in the government, it should not pass unpunished; it is enough to shake the nerves of the hardest man. If this is not a disturbance of the peace, I don't know what is.

Then he picked up another paper. The same mistake! He

went through all the daily papers, and found that all the printers must have chosen this day for a drinking bout. Each made the same mistake of printing below par.

Csanta was convinced that a great mistake had been made; but as he could not rest until it was cleared up, he wired Spitzhase.

A telegram from Spitzhase crossed his.

'Great misfortune. Bondavára mine on fire. Great panic. Shares sixty below par. Every one is selling.'

Csanta cursed and swore with rage. 'The devil! Sixty below par; a loss of sixty thousand! That means extinction. Where is a piece of rope and a nail? Let me hang myself! Six casks full of silver gone! I shall kill some one! I must go to Vienna. I shall knock the whole place down like a card-house if I don't get back my silver. I didn't take my money to Vienna to loose it.'

He foamed like a madman, and dragging his bonds from his safe, threw them on the floor and stamped over them.

'Villains! knaves! paper beggars! It is you who have eaten up my silver florins! You have swallowed my sixty thousand silver florins! I will tear you in pieces! I will cut my money out of your stomachs! I will kill you dead!'

Turning out his safe, he suddenly caught sight of an agreement. He looked at it closely. His mood changed.

'What a fool I have been. I won't lose a single hair. Here is my young friend's signature. How lucky that I didn't destroy this, or light my pipe with it. He binds himself, to take over a thousand shares at par at any time, should I wish it. Ah, well done, Csanta! You are a wise old bird, not easily caught. I am saved, thanks to my own sagacity, to my prudent nose which can smell danger ahead. This letter covers my loss. As far as I am concerned, the sky may fall, I am safe.'

He folded the shares tenderly, and locked them up with the precious guarantee in his safe. Then he sat down and wrote to his dear young friend in Paris.

Luckily he had the address. He asked him politely—seeing how matters stood—to send at once some accredited person to take over the bonds, according to their previous agreement, and to arrange how the money should be paid. As for the outstanding interest, some compromise or arrangement could be made.

A week passed, and no answer came; but, after all, it is more than a cat's jump from X to Paris.

During the week he received twice every day, morning and evening, a telegram from Spitzhase, pressing him to part with his shares, for they were falling ten per cent lower every day. By the end of the week they had dropped still further. The bears had won the day.

Csanta did not stir. He hugged himself in his safety; and as for the others, their shares might go to the bottom of the sea for all he cared. He had no shares. They were all Kaulman's. 'Take them away, and give me back my silver!' was his cry. 'Rogue! villain! I have you by the neck!'

The accounts that he read of the sudden collapse of the company and the ruin of the shareholders did not disturb him in the least. The losses of others could not affect him. On the ninth day, however, he started to worry. The morning's paper contained an account, wired from Paris, of the flight of the banker, Felix Kaulman, who left his affairs in the uttermost confusion. This was succeeded by a second telegram, announcing that the banker, Kaulman, seeing that the police were on his track, had thrown himself from the window of the railway carriage, and had been killed instantly.

Csanta narrowly missed a stroke. When he came to, he telegraphed to Spitzhase to sell all his shares for what they would fetch.

Spitzhase wrote by return post:

'Too late; they are quoted at seventy, but this is only nominal. There are neither buyers nor sellers. The mine is gone; the railway is gone; everything is gone. Why didn't you sell last

338

week, when I told you? Now you can put your shares in the fire, and roast chestnuts over them.'

'All is over for me!' sobbed Csanta. 'Let me go home; let me lie down and die! I cannot live. In three days I shall not be alive.'

He took leave of his acquaintances; he had no friends. He told them they need not be afraid, he would do himself no injury. He was simply dying of grief, just as a man might die of sickness.

All gone!

Some compassionate souls took pity on the old man, and escorted him home. If he had been alone, he would never have found his own house.

Once there, he insisted on going down to his cellar, to see with his own eyes if it were not some hideous dream, from which he would wake and find his beloved casks in their old places. When he saw that all were gone, he fell forward on his face.

They carried him upstairs, undressed him tenderly like a child, and put him to bed. Ha called for a priest, so they fetched him one. He made his confession, and received the last sacrament.

Then his lawyer came, and his will was written and duly signed. He had still something to leave. There were his houses, a whole street, he left them to the church into which no one came, on whose threshold the grass grew between the stones, in whose courtyard the schoolboys played ball on half-holidays.

The church, notwithstanding, should have a priest, a verger, and a bell-ringer. The priest should say mass, the bell-ringer should ring the bell, the verger should open the door every day; just as a hundred years ago, when many men passed through the church doors, with silver buttons on their jackets, and women with long silk veils. The old man now dying was the last descendant of the old Greek traders. The church should remain standing in their memory.

The house next door he bequeathed to the widow, who was

the daughter of the last Greek. This woman had quarrelled with him long ago. God alone knows the rights or wrongs of a quarrel about paper money, which today is worth a great deal, and tomorrow not a penny. Therefore, he bequeathed on her and her son the pile of cursed, worthless papers called shares in the Bondavára Company, which had caused his unexpected death. They should have these papers, whether for good or ill.

After he had made these depositions, and arranged his affairs, his will was sealed and signed. He divided amongst his neighbours and servants his few remaining possessions. He called the bell-ringer, and told him to toll the bell three times for two hours, and if any one asked why, he should answer: 'The Greek, Csanta, is dead.'

Then he sent everyone out of the room.

When they returned next morning, he was dead. He had died of grief, just as an aged husband will not survive the loss of his wife with whom he had grown old. A man with a strong will dies when he has said that he can no longer bear his life.

Chapter XXXIV

THE GROUND BURNS UNDER HIS FEET

Péter Saffran's curse seemed likely to be fulfilled: 'No grass shall ever grow again in this field.'

It was true that the green grass still grew in the field, but who could tell what was seething underneath, in the bowels of the earth?

The directors of the company's mine believed that when they closed all the entrances and openings to the shafts and vaults they had checked the conflagration; by preventing the flow of air, they felt sure the fire would soon die.

On the other hand, there was the irremediable evil of the gradually diminishing supply of coal, there was not enough even for keeping the forge heated. They tried to fire it with wood—there were plenty of trees in the forest—but without coal the furnace would not work, and much iron was lost in consequence. Instead of iron bars, many 'rammers' lay scattered about. It was soon obvious that, from all these causes, the company were not able to fulfil their contract with the railway contractors for iron rails. The guarantee was in danger, as was also that of the railway company, in case the railway could not be opened at the promised time.

The Bondavára Mine Company and Railway Company were glued to one another, so to speak; neither could take a step without dragging the other down the dangerous path headlong to ruin.

In their straits, the directors began to look for help to the other mine. Coal they must have. In Iván Berend's colliery there must be a large supply. He had sold none for a whole year. They must buy from him, even at a high price.

Rauné also thought of begging for coal from the same source. Surely no one could refuse to oblige an old friend and neighbour.

His letter, however, came back with the seal unbroken. Rauné was terribly hard pressed. He resolved to call on Iván, and make his request in person.

His visit was a short one. He spent less than two seconds in Iván's room, from which his hat issued first, followed promptly by his body. Then Iván's voice was heard:

"I do not talk to spies."

Rauné wrote the directors a long letter, in which he said that Berend was a boorish, selfish man, determined to profit by the misfortune of the Bondavára mine, and would not give his coal at any price; instead of selling, he was using it to manufacture iron rails, and speculating on the chance that the company would be forced to buy at any sum he asked.

The result of his letter was very different from his expectations. The railway board wrote to Iván at once with a good offer for his iron rails; and had he asked twice as much, they were prepared to accede to his demand.

The profit of Iván's faithful workmen was a handsome one. The deserters now begged to be taken on again; they had no work. A committee decided whom to take on. Their decision settled the matter, and Iván was forced to acknowledge it was just. Any new member was bound to work for a year as a common labourer, and it was not the committee who would decide whether he should be admitted to the rights of the colony, and entitled to a share of the profits: this should be put to the general vote.

Meantime the work went well. Each man looked on the mine as his own property, there were few mistakes, and their success was remarkable; neither labour nor time was grudged. Order was preserved, discipline maintained, and there was no necessity for harsh measures.

In all this fine weather, storms were gathering in the distance, evident to an experienced eye.

Iván knew the approaching danger, but he did not speak of it. It could not be averted. His mine was threatened; the fire consuming the neighbouring colliery might spread to his. This thought filled his mind day and night. The situation of the coal-stratum forced him to the conclusion that the fire would spread to his mine. It might take years, but in the end other pits would share the fate of their Bondavára neighbour, and be reduced to ashes.

The earth has buried many such wrecks. Yet, not only below, but above earth, too, the Bondavára misfortune ruined a great many people.

In the beginning the board of directors, who administered the shares, hit upon the idea that with the ready money at their command they would buy up all the shares in the market, with a double purpose. In the first place, they would secure the shares which had been issued at par, at a price far below par, and secondly, they would check a further fall.

The board, however, by this manoeuvre only effected a more rapid smash; their money dwindled, until at last there was nothing left for necessary expenses.

Prince Waldemar knew how to use the daily papers. He was always ready, and after the shares had fallen thirty per cent, he was resolved to send them still further down. The time was coming when they would stand at nil, and then any owner of such miserable shares would be glad to offer one per cent, to any one who would take them off his hands.

It was a wicked game. Thousands were beggared. Poorer people suffered most, those who a short year ago came with their little savings in their hands, clamouring to take shares. Poor souls! the high interest had tempted them to their ruin.

Ah! this is an old story, which repeats itself periodically; the clerk, the old man, the widow, the old maid, the governess, the teacher—they are the victims of this cruel Juggernaut. The cashier, who has gambled with his master's money, completes the picture. But there is no lack of others who suffer, but are not altogether ruined. Solid tradesmen are crippled, people who drove their carriages have to walk, lovers whose wedding-day was fixed have to wait, and sometimes pine away in single bliss.

But the Bondavára catastrophe had ruined not only the poor and the middling; its fall had dragged down the high and powerful family of Bondaváry, one of the oldest in Hungary.

The Marquis Salista had learned a severe lesson; he found that you cannot take away the centre-piece of a structure without endangering the whole. The sequestration of the prince's property had drawn the whole body of creditors on him. And so it came to pass that the large property of a great nobleman fell under the administration of his creditors; his heirs had, in fact, burned the ground under their own feet.

If the stewards and agents in the prince's time had been thieves, the administration of the property by creditors was the very picture of plunder on all sides.

The result was disastrous for countess Theudelinde; no one was responsible, it appeared, for her forty thousand florins. All the family charges and mortgages preceded it on the lists. Let her grasp hers—if she could.

The one who suffered most was countess Angela. Her husband, Marquis Salista, had from the first lived in the extravagant manner of a man who came into a fortune of twenty millions. It was impossible to induce him to change his ideas, which led to clashes between the married pair.

Then, Angela had shown him plainly that she had married him not from liking, but out of pique.

The marquis knew it—and so did Iván; but he had something else to think of. The ground was burning under his feet.

Chapter XXXV

CHILDREN AT PLAY

The concert season was in full swing when the Belényis heard that Csanta was dead, and that he had restored their former house to them in his will. Had Árpád been engaged to play in a quartet with Beethoven, Mozart, and Haydn, still he would have left Paris at once in order to see again the garden of his old home. His mother was just as eager and willing to forego the highest fees. They did not delay; they were off on next day's train.

On their arrival at X, the notary unlocked their old home, and gave Madame Belényi full possession. Everything was exactly as they had left it, with only the dust of years covering all their pretty things.

Árpád's first thought would have been to run down to the garden. The notary, however, detained him. He had another legacy to make over, a large iron chest fastened with three steel locks. It contained the Bondavára shares.

"The devil take his shares!" laughed Árpád. "It's still summer, so we don't even want a fire."

"They are down to nothing," said the notary. "They are quoted today below ten. That's what killed poor Csanta."

They had to take the shares, all the same. You do not look a gift-horse in the mouth.

Árpád slipped out of the room, and escaped to the garden. The fruit-trees were untouched, and in full bloom. The cherry-tree was a mass of rosy blossom. He remembered well that he didn't dare to touch a flower for pain of a good whipping. And the forget-me-nots on the bank of the stream, at the end of the garden, and the bluebells were ringing in chorus, though no one listened.

Everything was just as it had been, only somewhat overgrown. The long branches of the trees tangled with those on the other bank.

He stretched out on the green grass, among the cowslips. No one would beat him for it now. He might waste his time, and drink his fill of lazy enjoyment. Fame, paper gossip about his sudden disappearance, ladies who would regret him—what were they all, compared to this? In a hiding-place on the river-bank he sought for a little flute he had made secretly in those old days. To his joy it was still there, just where he had left it.

Árpád took from his pocket a newspaper full of his Parisian triumphs, with the announcement of his next performance. Where was Paris now? He made a large sailing-boat of the paper, big enough to carry cargo. He pulled off a cluster of cherry blossom; he set the vessel on the water, and as it danced over the little bubbles of the stream, he stretched out again among the forget-me-nots and began to play on his flute.

At the sound of his flute, another child appeared from the house opposite; a girl, about fifteen. She had a round, fair, laughing face, and beautiful blue eyes. Timidly, like a fawn, she took a few steps, then stopped and listened. By-and-by she drew nearer, then stood still again. She could not see the flute-player; she only heard his flute, and then she saw the paper-boat with the cherry blossom.

The girl approached without attracting Árpád's notice. He was made aware of he presence by her laugh. The laugh of a child is clear as a bell. Árpád looked up, surprised.

"Ah, is that you, Sophie? How pretty you have grown! Please, will you send me back my boat?"

Sophie did not wait to be asked twice. She picked up her

346

skirt with one hand, tucked it between her knees, and replacing the red cherry blossom with white flowers, she gave the little boat a heavy push to the opposite shore. Then their game began again. It was such fun!

Madame Belényi saw them from her window. She didn't disturb them, but let them amuse themselves until sunset, when the air took on a chill. Then the more prudent of the two—it was the girl, no doubt—suggested that the grass was damp with dew, and that it would be well to go indoors.

Árpád took his boat out of the water, and putting it with the flute back in its hiding-place, returned to his mother.

Madame Belényi did not scold him. She did not, however, kiss his forehead, as she was wont to do. She showed him all she had done to settle in the house while he had been amusing himself in the garden.

Árpád was very much pleased to find it so comfortable.

"Mother," he said, "we will live here for ever."

"I don't object to our living here, Árpád; but only on one condition. You must marry a good girl, and bring her here to help me."

"I, mother?" returned Árpád, half pleased, and yet surprised.

"Yes, you. Why not? You are a young man. I can't look after you for ever."

Árpád laughed again. "So, because I have grown into a young man, and because you cannot keep me tied to your apron-string any longer, I must take a wife who will keep me in better order than you can. Is that it, mother?"

"My son, it is in the natural order of things," Madame Belényi replied gravely as if there was nothing else for a young man but to have either a mother or a wife to look after him. It never entered her imagination that he could look after himself.

"Sooner or later I shall obey your wish; but just now, as we have got a house, I shall have enough to do to provide for the housekeeping, and I could not take a wife everywhere, when

I have to fulfil my professional engagements. This sort of Bohemian life, wandering from Paris to London, Petersburg to Vienna, is a bad thing for a woman, whether she goes with her husband or is left behind."

"But we have something to live on, Árpád. I have been very lucky with your earnings, and there is a nice nest-egg in the bank. Besides, there are the shares. Don't laugh, you silly boy! Although they are only worth ten florins, yet there are a thousand of them. If we sold them, that would be ten thousand. In a small town like this, that would be a fortune; and with it, you can afford to take a wife."

"Mother, you don't understand about these shares. One could be sold easily, but if, the next day, I went back with another one for sale, they would kick me out. Any one who would offer a thousand Bondavára shares in the money-market would be clapped up for mad. Put the shares away with those other important papers of Csanta's, and, if you like, you can hold on to the hope that one day they may be worth the paper they are printed on."

"Well, stranger things have happened. Did you ever think we could come back to this house? I am very sorry I did not keep those other papers. I burnt them. Who knows, but we may be lucky with those bonds? If, one day, they rise again, we shall make twice two hundred thousand . . ."

"I don't count on strokes of luck like that, mother. The worst compliment Providence can pay a man is to let him win a lottery. It is just as if God said to him, 'You ass! I cannot keep you in any other manner.' God would not allow a man who has any brains to win a lottery. To such a one he would say, 'Wilt thou cease to beg alms of Me so shamelessly? Is it not enough that I have endowed thee with talent? My consolation-prizes are reserved for the fools.'" Then he added: "Mother, don't be afraid; we shall live by my art. Wait a little, and you shall see; only give me time. In the meantime I shall

348

buy a doll with a china head as a toy for the little girl. You must take care of me for a little longer."

At these words, the widow tenderly embraced her son. She was happy; but later that evening Árpád went out and sat under the weeping willow in the moonlight, and played a melancholy air on his flute. Sometimes he stopped to listen to a soft silvery voice singing the same air, across the stream. However, when she no longer heard the flute, the singer knew that he was listening, and stopped her song. It is sweet to be young!

Chapter XXXVI

EUREKA!

Iván's fears about the danger to his own colliery increased day by day. One morning he found that the amount of hydrogen was scarcely perceptible; and yet there was water in the pit. This discovery made him thoughtful; he could not understand it. He descended to the cave where the lake had been. Not a single drop of water!

Iván stayed for three hours, watching anxiously whether the water would rise; but none came.

At the end of three hours he was relieved by the men, and they arranged to take turns during the night in watching the reservoir. As soon as the water began to rise, they were to call him. Iván went home, and fell into a deep sleep from which he did not wake until the sun was high. He wondered why no one had called him, as had been agreed.

Perhaps the men too, had been overcome by sleep. Poor wretches, they were just as exhausted. He hurried to the pit. The men told him they had kept watch all night, but there had been no sign of the water. He waited patiently another twenty-four hours. Not a sign of water!

Iván thought he could explain the absence of the water by a theory of periodic springs. He believed that the water-supply of the mine was worked by the pressure of air on such springs. If the water did not return, this could be from one of two causes: either the channel which brought the water from the

350

larger basin had collapsed suddenly, and was no longer subject to atmospheric pressure, which had kept it open; or some split or crevice had occurred in the rocks which protected the basin, and the force of the air had driven the water further down into the bowels of the earth, where, no doubt, another basin was forming. From the first, Iván had an idea that some such lower reservoir existed. But where?—that was the problem; and if the reservoirs were not found, what then?

The cave where Iván stood was empty. The black gates to the subterranean kingdom of Death stood open. He could enter the labyrinth; he could discover what he had long sought, the link between the upper and the lower water basins. There was only one difficulty. He must take someone else. He called the old miner, Paul.

"Paul, how old are you?"

"Sixty-nine."

"You would like, no doubt, to live till you are seventy."

"I should like to see the golden jubilee of the pit. Next year, it will be fifty years since it was opened."

"And if you die before then?"

"I should say, 'Bless the name of the Lord.' "

"Are your sons grown men?"

"Even my grandson can keep himself."

"Would you be ready to come on a dangerous expedition with me? The chances are we might never come back."

"I think I have run that chance often enough."

"You must understand, Paul, what the risk is, before you agree. We are going to look for the water that has left the basin. It is a matter of life and death to every one of us, and, therefore, I think God will help us; but it may not be so. The Almighty may say, 'Why should you mere worms of the Earth dare to interfere between me and the sentence I have passed against you and yours? I did not listen to the entreaties of Lot, and now the Dead Sea covers the ruins of his city. Ye men of Bonda-vára are no better than the men of Gomorrah.' Do you under-

351

stand? I have often looked for the spring through the narrow paths of these caves. These windings are so narrow that one can sometimes press through them only by force, or slide along on one's stomach. There are great chasms underneath: any slip would be fatal; we shall have to cling to the walls like spiders. We must go through stinking sewers, up to our waist in filth. These clefts and fissures have been made some time, God knows when, by an earthquake which uprooted the coal-bed. Now, it is quite likely that the explosion has now closed many of these tunnels, and opened others. If, as I think, the aperture which led between the pit beneath us, from the one above has been shut, then we have a lake full of water over our heads. If we come upon this aperture in our search and accidentally break a hole not bigger than a pin's head, the water in the basin over our heads could break through and drown us; if we hear its roar, we are lost. But, on the other hand, the explosion may have caused a rent in the upper cleft, and if so, the water has gone to the lower basin, under our feet. What we have to do is to find out where the water is, whether we die in the search or not."

"I have no idea what you mean; all I know is that I am ready to go with you."

"Then go home and take leave of your family, as if you were going on a long trip. Go to your priest, and make your peace with God. Then come back. Don't tell anyone where we are going."

Then Iván made his own preparations. He might never return from this adventure. He made his will, bequeathing his mine to his workmen, his money to Paul's family.

When this was done he went out, and took his leave of light and air before going into the blackness of perhaps everlasting night.

A letter was brought to him. It was from Árpád Belényi. It told him of the fall of Kaulman and the disappearance of Eveline, who was believed to have drowned herself. Iván's heart

352

was stirred by deep sorrow. The sky lost its brightness; the meadow was no longer green; the blackness of the pit would be welcome to him. The news braced him; his fears vanished. Life was now even more worthless than before.

He set about his preparations calmly. He collected the instruments needed for the strange search—the spirit level, the circumferentor, the plumb-line. He put them in a bag which he tied round his neck. Paul carried the pick, the iron rod, and a strong rope.

With this equipment, they descended, and vanished through the windings of the underground stream. They reappeared after six hours. This went on day after day.

Iván measured the windings of the labyrinth, and when he reached home, he compared them carefully. At night he retired into his laboratory, heating the deadly gasses, and forcing the mysterious elements to surrender long-concealed secrets. He fought with demons who refused to obey.

'Which of you is the spirit that can put out the fire? Come! come! Not with Alpha and Omega, not with Solomon's Seal, not in the name of Abraxas and Mithras do I conjure you; but by the force of knowledge and science, I bid you to come!'

But no spirit appeared.

This double battle, the one beneath the earth, and the one above it, this fight with the two great demons of the world's creation, went on day by day, in daylight and darkness. Iván took no rest.

One morning he was told that the water in the castle well was hot, and tasted of sulphur. He began to despair. The subterranean conflagration was closing in sooner than he had expected. The situation was lost; in one year, the whole place would be consumed.

When this became known, Rauné threw up his appointment, and took service with Prince Waldemar. He was commissioned by his employer to write—as an authentic witness—an account of the catastrophe, printed in the Vienna papers.

Iván threw himself into the search with the energy of despair; he penetrated further into the subterranean labyrinth. His old companion's very soul was steeped in terror, but he bravely stayed with his master.

One day, among the confusing different winding passages in the rock, they came to a place from which there seemed to be no exit. They struck the wall. It gave out a hollow sound; it seemed there was a cavern, or open space of some sort on the other side. The tumbled masses of slate fallen over one another was a proof that the blockage was recent.

"We must clear a passage here," said Iván, taking the pickaxe.

Paul cowered, clinging to the wall. He trembled at each blow of the pickaxe worked by Iván with terrible earnestness. So might a despairing soul beat against the gates of Hell, and challenge the devil to single combat.

At last the pick made a small hole. Iván pushed through the iron rod, and raised a mass of slate.

"Now, if the water is overhead, it will be the last of us."

The old man crossed himself, and recommended his soul to God.

Iván, however, shouted suddenly, with joy:

"Do you hear? The rubbish makes a splash as it falls. The lower basin is here, below us!"

But what if the one above is full? They waited while they counted a hundred beats of their pulses.

Never was a pulse felt under such terrible circumstances, not even when Iván had gone down into the burning mine. Not a sound was heard. In the bowels of the earth, all was quiet. Iván was trembling with happy excitement.

"Found at last!" he cried. "Now, tie the rope round me, and lower me into the cave."

It was done. The old miner, as he held the rope, prayed fervently to the Blessed Mother that she would forgive this heretic, who did not know what he was doing. Meanwhile the lamp sank lower and lower.

354

Suddenly Iván called out: "Pull me up."

His old comrade drew him out slowly. As he held out his hand to grasp him, Iván threw his arms round Paul and embraced him.

"We have found it," he said. "The plumb-line shows a very deep water."

Paul's brain began to clear. He had a dim idea of the point of their struggle for the first time.

"Now, let us get out of here."

When Iván got out of the pit, he went home as fast as he could. He compared his measurements, and was satisfied with his results. At night, he shut himself in his laboratory. He was flushed with his first triumph; ready for his second victory. He would conquer the demon which hitherto resisted his will. He had the pride of a victorious general who demands the surrender of the last stronghold.

God sometimes lends immortal gifts to his creatures, moments of creative power, when the indefinite takes shape, and the finite cries to the infinite, Eureka!

Iván poured out ten drops of the water he had brought from the well, no more. The laboratory suddenly darkened. The strong heat of the burning coal in the oven went out, as if by magic. All was dark; black as night. This darkness was the light which Iván had been seeking.

"I have found it!" he cried aloud. "I have found it!" he cried to his workmen, as he rushed out, half dressed, without his hat like a madman.

They did not know what he had found, but they were sure that any discovery considered so important by their guide and master must be a matter of joy, and so the miners cheered heartily.

Chapter XXXVII

AT PAR

The devil's comedy was being played on the Stock Exchange day by day. The Bondavára Company and the Bondavára Railway shares were tossed from hand to hand. The tragedy had turned to comedy; that is, for the few who found such a game amusing. The very word Bondavára made stockbrokers laugh. When some fool bought a share, no one could help laughing a little. The shares, in fact, were given away for anything, useful or not as, for instance, with an old umbrella for a new one. They were also presented to charitable institutions.

One witty man went to a fancy-dress ball in a coat made of Bondavára shares. The Exchange was the only field where a desultory fight was still kept up by the shareholders.

Prince Waldemar forced the shares lower each day. At last they fell to one and a half per cent, then to one and a quarter, and this quarter was to go lower, as the prince aimed to banish the shares from the list. The owners were fighting to prevent this; ineffectually, it seemed. They very nearly agreed to give up the forlorn fight.

How could they win against such odds? The day Rauné's report was published in the papers, they resolved to lay down their arms; there seemed no reason to protract the struggle. The report described the nature of the elements which, since the fire in the Bondavára mine, had been found mixed with the water in the lake of the castle; this caused a great sensation, and was the last straw to break the back of the luckless share-holders.

Prince Waldemar proclaimed on the Exchange that on settling day, he would sell his Bondavára Company shares at ten florins. Some people took up his gauntlet. These were shareholders who knew that they would lose by taking this risk, but hoped to prevent the shares from disappearing altogether from the share list. If, by the end of the month the shares went down to six florins, they must pay the other side the twenty thousand difference; if the shares went up, the other side must do the same.

About noon a broker came to the bank, and said, loud enough for all bystanders to hear, that a gentleman present would take five hundred Bondavára shares at par.

No greater whirr and whiz could have been heard in the country than now ran through the hall. Screams of laughter, exclamations of astonishment, howls of joy, curses and ejaculations of incredulity resounded in every corner. Who is he? A lunatic? At par! Bondavára shares! Where is the man?

The broker pointed him out. He was evidently a provincial, unassuming in his appearance. He was leaning against a pillar, calmly surveying the Olympian games.

"He is evidently a fool, making what he thinks is a joke," scoffed Prince Waldemar. "Go," he said to his agent, "and ask his name. We must know the name of any one who deals with us."

The agent returned in a few minutes saying that the gentleman gave his name as a Hundred Thousand Florins; and said money was the best surname. He showed a handful of banknotes, which he received from the stranger.

"Who sells five hundred Bondavára shares at par?"

This cry caused a revolution. Tranquillity was at an end; tumult, uproar and confusion reigned. Credulous and incred-ulous people surrounded the stranger; they pressed on him, overwhelming him with questions, stretching across each other to thrust their note-books into his hands. The unknown met

357

their noise with indifference, pointing out the crowd who were ready to do business with him.

Prince Waldemar now made his way through the mob to the newcomer. With refined impertinence he drew the brim of his hat over his eyes, and stuck his hand into the waistcoat pockets as he surveyed the other.

"Sir, your appearance has created a revolution. May I ask your name?"

"My name is Iván Berend," returned the stranger, without changing his own casual attitude.

"Ah!" said the prince, suddenly taking off his hat and bowing low. "I have had the honour of hearing about you. Are you not the famous shot, who can shoot a cigar from a man's mouth? I am nobody by comparison; I am only Prince Waldemar Sondersheim. I cannot shoot like you. But let us talk sensibly. You want to buy Bondavára shares at par? Have you inherited the fortune of an Indian nabob, on the condition that you should buy the shares at par?"

"No. I buy at that price because they are worth it."

"Don't you know that the Bondavára mine is on fire?"

"I happen to own the adjoining one, so I am quite aware of the fact."

"Then your mine will catch fire next."

"No. I have put out the fire in my mine a fortnight ago."

At these words the noise rose to an uproar, the shareholders pressed round Iván, and nearly suffocated him. There is a man here who can extinguish the fire! The mine will soon be working again. Bondavára stands once more at par.

Joyous shareholders surrounded Iván and carried him in triumph from the hall. That evening a large meeting was held, at which Iván declared to an enormous audience which filled the room that he had an infallible method which had been tried in his own mine, and had put out the conflagration. He invited every one present to see the experiment tested next day in open air, when it would be proved that he was not boasting.

In the morning he fulfilled his promise, in the presence of a large crowd. A funeral pile of coal and turf, over which petroleum had been poured, was set on fire, and at the height of the blaze was put out at once by a few drops from a small bottle.

The jubilant crowd escorted Iván back to the town in triumph, and at the next general meeting of shareholders it was resolved to offer him a reward of six hundred thousand florins if he would bring the Bondavára mine back into working order.

Opponents were not wanting, however. Foremost among them was Prince Waldemar, who, in spite of possessing the largest proportion of shares, nevertheless, offered the most determined opposition. He did everything to embarrass and obstruct Iván's scientific propositions.

"I grant," he said, "that you may be able to put out with a bucket of fluid six cubic feet of burning coal. But in the Bondavára pit, from the place where the explosion took place to the castle, there must be at least sixty thousand cubic feet of coal layers burning. To meet this, you must have ten thousand buckets of fluid ready. Have you a machine for such an operation as this?"

"I have not forgotten that a machine would be necessary," returned Iván, quietly.

"Let us suppose," continued the prince, "that you do succeed in getting a sufficient quantity of fluid into the blaze. Don't you perceive that this itself will develop a monstrous amount of gas, which would permeate the pit from top to bottom, and cause a second and worse explosion?"

"I have foreseen the danger."

"And, finally, if you possess any idea, which you evidently do, of the mechanism of machines and the expenditure necessary to procure the best, you must face the problem that a million is hardly sufficient to buy the materials which would make the experiment successful."

"I have drawn up an estimate of the probable cost."

The shareholders here shouted that they undertook all expenses, even if they amounted to a million; and it was agreed on the spot that Iván should receive full powers to do for the Bondavára mine what he considered necessary, at any price.

Prince Sondersheim saw that he could not stem the course of Iván's popularity; it must have its way. While the assembled shareholders were signing a deed of authorization, he took Iván aside, and said to him:

"Iván Berend, whether the undertaking you have engaged in succeeds or not—I do not believe that it will succeed—you will have taken out of my pocket a million—a net million. In addition, you have squandered five hundred of your own money, apart from what is still to be spent. Let that be. You have done this by fixing the quotation at par. True, shares will be neither bought nor sold, for both sides are still afraid, and will hold back; nevertheless, the quotation will stand at par, and I am obliged to pay the difference on this—that will cost me a million. But that is nothing; I have lost as much before now, and recovered it again. One has to play a waiting game. If, however, in a fortnight's time you find that you have miscalculated your powers, and that your experiment fails, you have only to let it be known, and I shall pay one million into your hand."

Iván answered this proposal with business-like composure.

"Prince Sondersheim, I am well aware that the Stock Exchange is a privileged place. A man can say things here without fear of consequences. Whatever a man says or does, whatever proposals he makes—everything is allowable, and ordinary rules, which govern the outside world, do not apply. Here a man may ask, 'How much do you ask for selling the honour of your company?' and if the answer is, 'It is not for sale,' that is enough. This is plain speaking; no one is offended when he is asked to take part in a robbery. It would not be a reflection on his character; he would not assume any airs of righteousness, but simply say, 'I really haven't the time.' If men quarrel, if they spit on each other, tear out one another's hair, it is nothing; it goes no further; no one turns to look. They wipe the spittle off their faces, pick up their hats, and in half an hour they may walk about arm in arm. No one remembers that they fought; only a little 'difference,' leading to an animated scene. And so there is only one answer to the proposal made by Sondersheim, the Bondavára coal-merchant, to Berend, the Bondavára coal-trader: 'Sir, I cannot entertain your offer.' Prince Waldemar Sondersheim would do well, however, to remember not to repeat such a proposal to Iván Berend outside the Stock Exchange."

The prince laughed. "I guessed as much. I have heard much about you, and you shall hear why I feel particularly friendly towards you. Once upon a time, you took my part forcefully, and to a very lovely woman. I do not know why you should have done so; it is sufficient for me that you did. Also, you withdrew your own claim to the favours of this very beautiful woman. But it was no good, she married a worthless fellow. Your inexplicable intervention in my favour, which could not have been a business manoeuvre, but must have sprung from your innate Puritanism, has placed me under a debt of gratitude. If the lady had listened to you, things would have been very different. No sulphur deposit would have been found in the Bondavára lake; the whole speculation would not have existed. Outside the Exchange, the subject will not recur. I was prompted to it from a sense of gratitude, and I shall note it in my book. If you succeed in putting out the fire you will get six hundred thousand florins from the company; if you fail, you shall have a million from me."

This long conversation between Iván and the prince alarmed the shareholders, and they tried to interrupt.

"Don't interfere, Prince. Let our man alone." They were afraid he would be bought.

"Don't be afraid," answered the prince. "We are talking of a lady we both courted."

But the shareholders' suspicions were not allayed. They chose a commission of three members, who should dog Iván every-

361

where, never leave him, eat with him, sleep outside his door, keep watch under his window, so that their enemy should not approach him without their knowledge. This was done under the pretence of assisting him to transfer his supplies of money.

Iván procured the machines and workmen, and took them and his three companions back to Bondavára.

These three commissioners were detailed to furnish the company with a daily report of the work's progress. One of the three was the clerk Spitzhase, who had the reputation of being the most circumspect, careful, and impudent employee of the company. This last epithet is not meant in the bad sense of the word. In money matters, modesty and meekness are counted as faults, and the opposite qualities are of infinite use. The word is, therefore, used here in praise. Iván chucked Spitzhase out at the door many times, but the clerk always returned by the window.

Chapter XXXVIII

THE UNDERGROUND WORLD

For the first week, the three commissioners had little to say; their report was meagre. Berend came to dine and sup with them daily at the village inn; the rest of the day, and the whole night, he spent underground. Whenever they asked him what he was doing he said curtly that everything was going well.

Things might be going well, but nothing was visible to the commissioners. And, moreover, there was one very suspicious circumstance, which struck Spitzhase in particular, and this was that Berend spent his time in his own colliery. All the expensive machines had been set up, and all the chemicals had been bestowed there. Not a single thing had been done to the company's mine, not one piece of rubbish had been cleared, not one entrance had been opened; in fact, a fortnight had slipped past, and no work was visible. It was undoubtedly true that the machines were always at work, and cart-loads of clay and stones were being wheeled away.

The whole thing was incomprehensible, and Berend would not give the slightest explanation.

At the beginning of the second week Spitzhase lost his patience.

"Sir," he said to Iván, with suppressed irritation, "you promised that in a fortnight the conflagration in our mine would be extinguished. One week elapsed, and I have not seen that anything has even been tried."

"That is quite likely," returned Iván, quietly.

"Do you still tell us that everything is going well?"

"I do."

"Can I see for myself what has been done?"

"It would be impossible for you to judge from where you are standing."

"Well, let me go where I can see something."

"Do you really want to go below? It's not a pleasant place."

"Where you go I can too; for my part, I don't care if it's hell itself."

"It is not unlike what hell must be like."

"Well, I am ready to visit it. I want to meet the devil; perhaps I could make an arrangement with him to supply us with coal."

"You may come on one condition; if you accompany me, you must understand that I cannot let you stand gaping about. There is no room for more than two people, and they must both work."

"I am not afraid of work. I am a devil for work."

"All right, then, come along," said Iván, "and if the other gentlemen would like to accompany us to the machines, they can follow us."

The others seized the opportunity.

Iván made them wear miners' outfits. They were then hoisted into the crane, and lowered into the shaft. Each one had a safety-lamp fastened to his belt, and wore a thick felt hat.

Iván led them through the various windings of the pit until they came to the iron door of the cavern, where, not long before, the lake used to ebb and flow. The middle of this space was now filled by a large engine, kept in motion by an endless conveyor belt worked from above. In this mill some substance was being ground, and, when reduced to fine powder, was carried, by a set of other conveyors, through a pipe and over a bridge, where it disappeared from view.

Iván led his guests through still more tortuous ways. They

364

descended the shaft of a well; then they climbed high ladders to a small chamber, measuring less than six feet round, in which two miners were waiting—one old and one young.

"Now," said Iván to Spitzhase, "here is our dressing-room; we must put on our costumes."

"What? Do we have another change of clothes?"

"Yes, we have to wear chain-mail for tournament in which we are going to take part; we need armour."

At a sign the miners came and began to prepare the two gentlemen. The equipment was similar to that of the fireman—a coat and stockings, the outer cover made of asbestos, the space between it and the lining filled with pulverized charcoal; the hands and arms were also covered with long gloves made of asbestos, with the fingers air-proof.

"We could pass for knights," joked Spitzhase.

"Wait until you see our helmets," answered Iván.

The miners brought two helmets of glass, each with an opening with twelve joints and three apertures. Iván explained the use of these.

"It is full of coal-gas down there. We must have an apparatus to enable us to pass through fire, and to dive under water."

Spitzhase began to repent that he had been so restless, but he was ashamed to turn back now.

"We need," continued Iván, "an apparatus which is a combination of the diver's and the fireman's dress. To the glass helmet, which will be attached to the coat-collar by means of airproof bakelite, two tubes will be fastened. Through one air will be conveyed to us, and through the other, the bad air will be expelled. The ends of both the tubes will remain here, while we drag them after us like the deep-sea diver. Although the bad air is led out from our helmets, we shall still find the air rather warmer than up here, and it will smell like vulcanized india-rubber; however, we will not choke. An elastic tube will be fixed to the third hole which unites our two helmets; so that we can hear what the other says, for the glass is too thick for sound to penetrate it. You will have difficulty to hear what I say."

Spitzhase was beginning to feel very uncomfortable as the miner adjusted the glass helmet to his head. When the tubes were fixed into the three apertures, he suddenly became stone deaf. He saw the lips of the two commissioners moving, without hearing a single word. He no longer belonged to the world. The only sound that reached him was the voice of the man to whose head he was fastened.

"Take the end of the hose on your arm," shouted the voice into his helmet; yet the sound seemed to come from a long way off, out of a tunnel.

Mechanically, he took the coil over his shoulder.

"Let us go," shouted Iván, taking the other end of the coil, and, opening a thick oak door, which had hitherto escaped Spitzhase's observation, they left.

The two commissioners had heard nothing that had passed between the two 'knights'; but when they saw the oak door open they hurriedly asked the miners whether the foul air would not come in. The older workman assured them that the carbon was heavier than oxygen, and even thicker than hydrogen. The foul air stayed below, where the two divers had gone. They were quite safe as long as their safety-lamps burned.

Meantime, the others had reached a large cave with walls which had not been made by men, but were a natural formation. Each part of the wall fitted into another, like the pieces of a puzzle, and each block was as smooth as a mirror. Masses of coal were set obliquely on one another. The cavern was bridged with thick, strong wooden planks. The gearing strap, which had made its way from the cavern like a serpent had set a wheel in motion, and the noise of the clapper could be heard under the bridge, sounding as if it were working in deep water. From this bridge a narrow path led up into the strata. Past the entrance of this dark path their lamps stopped burning; the coal-gas was too thick. An electric machine stood on the bridge whose brilliant light was shaded by a wire screen.

The old miner started the machine, and the light flashed into every corner of the subterranean cave. It lit up the narrow tunnel which Iván had been boring for the last month from his own mine to his neighbour's. He had told no one what he had been doing, but now it was almost finished; only a thin wall had to be broken through. This work, which would take another week to complete, needed to be done in diver's equipment. The length of the narrow tunnel was brightly lit by the electric machine, almost like sunlight. Where the tunnel turned, high-polished steel mirrors were positioned to reflect the light itself until it faded away to a faint glimmer. By now the two divers could hardly see anything.

"We shall soon be in darkness," said Spitzhase to Iván.

"We shall have enough light," Iván answered, as he led the way further into the tunnel.

Spitzhase was forced to follow, as his head was fastened to Iván's head. Wonderful pair of Siamese twins! If the tube that bound them were to break, both would die.

"Stop!" cried Iván. "Here is the pump. Give me a hose."

In the half-dark, a little machine, some three feet high, was discernible; it carried a spring wheel. This suction-pipe had been brought down on the previous day. Iván took the plastic coil from his companion's shoulder, and screwed the tube to the aperture of the machine; then he set the wheel in motion, and in a few seconds it was revolving with the heavy balls attached to it. Then he took the end of the tube, and gave the coil back to Spitzhase, but instead of putting it over his arm, he hung the hose over his neck. Spitzhase felt as if the tube were about a hundredweight heavier, and that it had grown suddenly stiff.

"Forward! Quick march!" shouted Iván into his helmet.

"It is as hot as hell itself," grumbled Spitzhase, who was suffering horribly.

"We are in that part of the mine where the fire has been put out."

Both the men wore glass slippers, otherwise they would have felt the ashes, through which they were wading, glowing with heat.

The rubber hose hung round Spitzhase's neck. It grew darker and darker.

"I can't see anything," shouted Spitzhase.

"You are safe if you follow me," returned Iván.

It began to grow a little lighter. The light, however, was a rose-colour; there was twilight, then, in the bowels of the earth.

Spitzhase complained he could hardly breathe.

"That will get better soon," Iván encouraged him.

They had now turned the corner of the tunnel, and the terrible tragedy, hell itself, lay before them. Yes, hell itself: a burning labyrinth, with the prismatic colours changed every moment in the glowing passages. The blue-green flames leaped from the ground, and blended with the brilliant scarlet flames which played on the burning wall, and faded into a deep purple in the far distance. Through the fissures and crevices sheets of white rays poured like molten silver. Amidst the glowing coals shapes seemed to rise, as of demons dancing, creatures with green hair and red beards, and from the red sulphate of the vaulting there fell a slow golden shower, a melting rain of sparks. From the clefts in the side walls the gas let loose hissed like serpents, and kindled flames of its own. Out of the depths of the pit fire spouted suddenly, showering sparks in every direction. Over the whole a milk-coloured cloud floated, which filled the vault with a nebulous vapour, threatening every moment to envelop the rash visitors. Spitzhase, alarmed out of control, pressed closer to the wall; fear was overcoming him.

"Let go the hose!" shouted Iván. The hose fell like a serpent unchained, wriggling back and forth. "Now follow me. Hold the tube on your arm," and he drew Spitzhase after him.

He was constrained to follow, although his heart was beating in his mouth; their heads were tied together. If he had the strength to free himself from this terrible bond, it would not have helped him, for the carbon gases would have killed him at once.

Mechanically, he allowed himself to be drawn on. Hell, with all its horrors, disclosed itself to his eyes. His companion seemed to fear nothing. Was he a human being, or a fiend, who was indeed possessed of power over the demons of hell? Iván dragged Spitzhase to the very edge of the burning lake. Then he took the hose, which lay in rings and coils, from his shoulder, and opening the stop-cock, directed it into the middle of the hell. The hose shot forth a flash like a diamond; the liquid fell into the glowing Hell.

"Hold tight!" shouted Iván.

And from the force which the jet exercised on the burning mass, the air was filled with dark clouds of smoke. It peopled the still brilliantly lit cave with strange, unearthly spectres, which, dissolving suddenly into steam, covered the two adventurous visitors with damp.

"Don't be afraid," called Iván, "we are quite safe here."

"It is suffocating; I am burning!" cried Spitzhase.

"Don't be afraid; follow me," said Iván, and drew his trembling companion over the wet rocks, over the charred, burning mounds. Wherever he saw the flames rising he directed his hose, and a shower of cool, refreshing water fell from the rubber pipe on the burning, seething flames.

The gas hissed, the hot steam bubbled round them, the flames, beaten in one place, sprang up in another, but they went on. He was afraid of nothing. "Come on! forward!" Mysterious clouds hovered over him.

"We are lost!" moaned the other poor mortal, whose fear began to be uncontrollable. He fell on his knees.

"You coward," said the conqueror of hell, "get up. Let us go back." And he lifted him up, as the Redeemer lifted Peter, on the stormy sea of Galilee.

Then he rolled the hose once more round his neck, and took it back to the suction-pump; he closed it down, and then led his companion back again to the little room where they had put on their equipment.

Spitzhase sunk back when he reached this haven. When his helmet was removed, he gasped as if he were suffocating. Iván looked at him with compassion.

The miners gave them a glass of fresh lemonade, and rubbed their temples with vinegar. They then undressed them, put them into a tub of cold water, took them out in a couple of seconds, and rubbed them down with coarse towels, until Spitzhase began to recover.

As they put on their own clothes Iván said to him:

"Well, sir, how did you like it down below?"

Spitzhase was no fool, but he answered good-humouredly:

"I wouldn't have missed going down for a hundred florins, but I would pay twice as much not to go there again."

"Now you know what to write to your board of directors. Paul, take this gentleman home. I must stay here and continue."

Spitzhase wrote a glowing account of what he called 'the fight with the world of spirits' to the Vienna papers.

The next day Iván said to the commissioners, "We have now laid pipes four inches in diameter to reach the very core of the fire. As soon as I am ready, we shall set a high-pressure machine at work. This will empty ten thousand buckets of fluid on the burning coal in four hours."

"The devil!" cried Spitzhase. "Will this farce never end, unless the escaped gas blows up the colliery, and makes it a new Pompeii?"

"Do not be afraid. I have thought of this. We have taken care to stop all outlets from the quarry with sand-bags. We have walled up every possible fissure, crevice, and exit. The entrance to the well-shaft has been barred with an iron door, with a thick bed of clay over it. If it should happen that in the gallery, where the fire is at its worst, and where most of the fluid must be poured, the gas should explode, the iron door would still save us. It will resist the explosion, and the force of the gas will be broken."

The members of the commission trembled with fear. This was a pleasant prospect indeed! Iván, however, had no time to spare on reassuring them; the crisis was at hand, and he had much to do. Great care and foresight were needed. At midday he returned to the quarry.

As the clock struck twelve, he signalled for the large suction-pump to be set going. From then on, he remained at his post, not leaving the machine until his work was done. Let it be said in their honour, the three commissioners stayed with him; they kept still in their places, without a word. During the awful time that followed, only Iván's voice could be heard. Soon after the signal was given, a rushing noise came from underground, faintly at first, but gradually growing louder. It sounded as if water was pouring through a sluice-gate in the distance.

At first the machine was worked at half speed only. After half an hour or so a strong din mingled with the rushing sound, as if bells were vibrating in the air. This noise did not die away; on the contrary, it grew stronger every moment.

The earth was in labour; the ground heaved and trembled, and those who felt it were also made to tremble. The sufferings of the earth were shared by her sons. Only one man was calm; only the leading spirit was not afraid.

Iván watched the pendulum and the thermometer of the machine with close attention; he marked the variations in the barometer, the ozonometer and electrometer, writing his observations in his notebook. After another hour, he signalled to the man working the machine to put on more pressure.

A terrible uproar rose from below; it was the battle of the Cyclops. The bowels of the earth sent up a roar like the rolling of thunder; periodically the ground shook, as in an earthquake. The houses began to rock, the tops of the trees and the cross

371

on the church spire tottered; its fall added to the fear of the entire valley. The underground fight grew fiercer every moment; the giants joined in battle. They howled, they raged, they put their gigantic shoulders against it, and shook the earth. The bellowing of the hurricane in the cave was the sound of their struggle.

Those who heard this fearful scene looked on with horror; they were speechless, but their eyes seemed to say, 'What have you done? Are you inciting spirits who live under the earth to wage war against each other?'

Iván answered with a calm look: 'Fear nothing; I have my foot on the head of the giant.'

The underground battle lasted for three hours. Even his own people were beside themselves with fright; they turned against Iván:

"Do you think you are God," they cried, "and can make an earthquake?"

Iván paid no attention to their fears; he gave another signal to the men at the machine.

"Turn it full on!"

At this, the machine, the product of man's wonderful inventive genius, stormed the gates of hell. The tremors followed one another rapidly underground, growing stronger and stronger; the groaning rose to a deafening roar.

"It is all over!" shrieked the people in the valley, and fell on their knees.

Then, a shrill whistling sound was heard in the air, like an engine suddenly letting off steam, and from the company's mine shaft there rose a white column of steam, which shot up into the sky, forming itself into a white cloud. Then this cloud suddenly broke into a deluge of rain. The underground convulsion soon ceased, and the shrill whistling died away in the distance.

Iván looked around and said: "Paul, please collect the rainwater; I must know what it contains." Then he gave the signal to stop the machine. There was not even a drop of perspiration on his forehead. He took the bottle of rain-water that Paul brought him, and put it in his pocket. "Now, gentlemen," he said, "you can have your supper. The work is done."

"Is the fire extinguished?" asked Spitzhase.

"Completely."

"And that pillar of steam over there?"

"That will go on till about midnight, and then slowly die away. Go and have your supper. I have something important to do at home."

But who could be bothered with supper?

The pillar of steam continued to rise from the shaft, forming a cloud, from which the rain fell continuously, interspersed with flashes of lightning; but no one thought of going indoors. The richer members of society wrapped themselves in mackintoshes, the workmen in their cloaks, and all continued to watch the strange apparition, until at last, towards ten o'clock, it began to diminish.

The whistling sound was interrupted now and again by a piercing shriek, and sometimes a flash of lightning illumined the shadow of the pillar—the white cloud.

The steam-giant then sank back; not all at once, but by degrees, into the pit from which it arose. Only from time to time did its head reappear for a second, but by then the whistling stopped, as did the heaving of the earth. The uproar was silenced. From the church the organ could be heard, and voices intoning 'Halleluia! Halleluia!' The people walked in procession, carrying lanterns and banners.

The commissioners made their way to the inn, where they found Iván eating his supper by himself. He could eat now; he remembered that he was mortal, and he was having meat and potatoes.

"I have finished my analysis," he said to the others with the indifference of a chemist, "and I am happy to tell you that 0.75 of carbonic acid is to be found in the residue."

Spitzhase did not understand. "What good is it," he asked, "if there is 0.75 of carbonic acid in the residue?"

"Tomorrow we can open both the entrances to the colliery, and when the air-pumps have been settled, after a little airing, we can go back to work."

Halleluia! Halleluia!

Chapter XXXIX

ANGELA'S REVENGE

Success brings fame, fortune, and universal esteem. Men worship success, and justly so.

He has saved a great treasure, restored their country to the people, their industry; he has overcome the calamity which threatened the whole region; he has restored livelihood to thousands on the verge of beggary, and dried the tears of the widows and the orphans—does he not, then, carry the divine spark within?

Honours and rewards were showered on Iván. The Government gave him a patent for his discovery in perpetuity. He was handsomely remunerated by the Joint-Stock Mining Company. A huge deputation forced him to accept a directorship. Scientific societies at home and abroad elected him as a member. His picture and life-story appeared in the illustrated papers of Europe and America. The simple villagers in Bondavára prayed for him morning and evening; and when the first train steamed out of the Bondavára station, the locomotive bore the name of 'Berend.' It was only the goodness of God which preserved him from receiving an order.

But among the many letters of thanks and congratulations, the one most valued by Iván was a letter from countess Angela.

The countess recounted honestly all that had happened to her since they last met; how she had married the Marquis Salista; how unhappy he had made her by the pressure he brought to bear on her grandfather, Prince Theobald, which ended in his property being sequestrated, and to the ruin of the whole family of Bondaváry. She had suffered much in consequence, and had learnt the meaning of privation; also, that countess Theudelinde's income was considerably lessened, and the old lady had been forced to reduce her household. Such circumstances had shown them their former friends in their true light—among others, her husband Salista, who had gone to Mexico, and left her to shift for herself.

Then Iván came to the rescue. Prince Waldemar's triumphant progress had been checked. The million invested in the Bondavára Company by Prince Theobald had regained its value. The prince had compounded with his creditors, and his affairs were once more settled. She had been reconciled to him, and lived with him. Countess Theudelinde likewise recovered her rents. The great family of Bondaváry, which had been so near ruin, was reinstated in its former position. And for its new lease of life it had to thank a certain beneficent, clever . . .

Here countess Angela's letter broke off. There was, however, a postscript.

'Answer this letter. I beg you for one line. Write: "I forgive you." '

Iván answered her immediately. He expressed his gratitude for her kind remembrance, but he could not imagine what he had to forgive. On the contrary, he had a lively recollection of the many kindnesses he had received from the countess.

His letter was evidently written with an effort to be cold, and polite. It was followed by a second letter from Angela:

'Do not answer me like this. I have sinned against you. You do not reproach me, but my own heart and conscience do. To quiet these, I must have your pardon. Answer me honestly. Can you ever forgive me? I should not have treated you as I did . . .'

Iván answered this by a long, confidential letter. He confessed to her those secrets of his heart which never before passed his

376

lips. The countess might feel confident that she had never offended him. She had never forfeited the place she held in his respect.

A third letter came from Angela.

"If you can do so from your heart, write on a piece of paper: 'Angela Bondaváry, I forgive you, from my heart.' Nothing else."

Iván wrote these words, and nothing else.

One evening, two carriages drove into the yard of Iván's house. He lived in a handsome residence provided by the company for the director. The porter spoke a few words to the person who sat in the first of the two carriages, and then brought Iván two visiting cards.

Iván, to his surprise, read the names

Countess Theudelinde Bondaváry
Countess Angela Bondaváry

These names disturbed Iván. What did they want? Why did they come to him? He told the porter to show the ladies in, and then taking up the cards again, it struck him as odd that the countess Angela's did not bear the name of her husband.

The door opened and only one lady entered. She was dressed in mourning, and her face was covered by a thick veil, concealing her features. It was the countess Theudelinde. She had on a long, double-caped black travelling-cloak. She came to Iván and held out to him the tips of her black glove, which he carried to his lips, while she murmured some words of greeting.

"Where is the Marquise?" asked Iván, anxiously.

"She will be here immediately; but it is very difficult to bring her in."

Iván led the lady to a sofa, and asked her to sit down.

"Do not go to meet her," continued the countess, "she will find her way. You will receive her kindly, won't you?"

"Oh, Countess," Iván began; but Theudelinde interrupted impatiently:

"No phrases, please. We have not come here for polite words, or to exchange compliments. We come to make a request; the answer is simple. Yes or no. Angela wants to stay here."

"Here!" repeated Iván, horrified.

"Yes, here! Do not be afraid; not in this house, but in the neighbourhood. She wishes to stay near you—never to leave you—that is her desire; and she has a right to have her wish granted."

Iván began to think he was dreaming; he did not know what to say, but his thoughts were diverted by a strange noise outside. Along the passage came the heavy tread of several men. The door opened, and four of his miners came in, carrying a metal coffin, on the lid of which lay a wrought silver wreath.

The wreath surrounded the arms of the Bondaváry family, and beneath it, carved in gold letters,

ANGELA BONDAVÁRY

They put the coffin on the oak table. Iván stood like one turned to stone, his eyes fixed on the wreath, and the name underneath.

Theudelinde got up and took his hand.

"This is the countess Angela Bondaváry, who begs you, the present lord of Bondavára, to find for her a small place in the family vault of the Castle, where she may wait for the coming of Jesus Christ—the bridegroom of desolate women who have suffered in their lives."

"How could she be dead?" asked Iván deeply moved.

"How? Very easily! When you throw a rose into the fire, in a minute you will only find its ashes. I had just heard her laugh. She was quite cheerful; then she went too near the grate; the next moment she screamed, and I saw her covered in flames!"

"She was burned to death!" cried Iván, covering his face

with his hands. Then, after a pause: "Was there no one near to save her?"

"Was there no one?" answered Theudelinde. "Were you, then, asleep at midnight? Did you not hear her call, 'Iván, help me!' Did you not see her standing beside your bed in flames—an angel with hell in her heart? Why were you not by her side to hold her in your arms, to stifle the flames, to snatch her from the jaws of death? Where were you, who should have saved her? Now she is here, and says to you, 'I am gone. I am no one. Let us be united.'"

Iván felt as if an iron grip had been laid on his heart.

"She lived," continued Theudelinde, "for two more days. She suffered terrible pain. When I think of all she went through, I feel that I shall go mad. To the last, she was conscious. She spoke—but no—why should I tell you what she said. Just before she died, she asked for a pencil, and she wrote something to you. Here it is, in this envelope. Do not break the seal, do not read it while I am here. I would not explain you anything, anyway. If you have anything to ask, ask her. Here is the key of the coffin; I give it to you."

Iván recoiled from receiving such a present.

"Why should you be afraid? Why do you object to opening the coffin? There is nothing to fear. The body is embalmed, and the flames did not touch her face. You will see that she smiles."

Iván forced himself to raise the coffin-lid, and to look at her face. There was no smile on her lips. She was calm and cold, she lay upon her white satin cushion as when she lay insensible in the wood, with her head on a cushion of moss. Iván felt that if she could open her eyes for one minute, she would look at him proudly and say: 'I want nothing,' and close them again. How beautiful she was, with her still, marble face, her immobile eyebrows. Iván could not disturb her calm loveliness by even one kiss. He would have felt it to be dishonourable, and yet, if she could have come to life again, who knows . . . ? Just as he had closed her dress with his tie-pin, he now shrouded her secret with the lid of the coffin. Her secret was safe with him.

"Keep the key," said Theudelinde. "The coffin, its key, and the treasure it holds are yours; that is settled. You are the lord of the vault; it is your duty to take her there. You cannot escape it."

With eyes that were hot and tearless, Theudelinde looked at Iván through her veil. He returned her look. If either of them had shed a tear, or even uttered a single sob they would both have broken down and wept. But both were resolved to show strength of mind in the other's presence. They could both command their emotions.

"Do you accept your duty?"

Iván nodded.

"Then you will perform it alone. I shall never enter our family vault alive. You know why."

Both were silent. Then Theudelinde burst out:

"Why was I not left in my Castle? Why was I undeceived when I imagined that my ancestors visited me? If I had not been shaken from my delusions, I would still be happy. I should never have gone into the world, where I have found so much misery; Angela would not have come to me; my brother Theobald would not have been ruined; hell would not have been let loose in the Bondavára mines; I should have never known you; all—all would have been different!" Then, after a brief silence, she went on: "There is no need for a priest; there is no need of ceremony. You can say some prayers. You are a Protestant —so was Angela. She changed so that she might be divorced from her worthless husband. Let them carry the coffin quietly and reverently to the family vault. There I shall leave you with it, for I shall not go inside—never, until I am dead. You will put the coffin in its place, and then I return whence I came, where I am wanted by no one."

Iván called the miners to take the coffin on their shoulders again, and told them to carry it through the vestibule and a

380

private door into the park which separated the director's house from the castle.

As they walked through the winding paths of the park, the trees were shedding golden leaves over the coffin, and the robins in the brushwood chanted a dirge.

Iván walked bareheaded behind the coffin, and behind him came countess Theudelinde.

When they reached the entrance of the vault, Iván told the bearers to put down the coffin, and kneeling down, he remained for a long time, perhaps praying. God hears us if we speak to Him in a whisper; nay, He hears us, even if we do not speak, but feel.

Theudelinde bent over Iván and kissed his forehead.

"Thank you. You walked behind her with your head uncovered. Now she is all yours." Then she returned by the winding path, as if she were afraid that Iván would make her take away that which she had brought.

Iván placed the coffin in its resting-place, and sent away the bearers; he remained by it for many hours. By the light of the torches he read Angela's last words to him:

'For whom shall I wait on the shores of the other world?'

Iván sighed deeply. 'Who will wait for me on the shores of the other world?'

Then he made his way back to the house. There was no trace of the countess's travelling carriage, nor of Angela's hearse.

Chapter XL

HOW IVÁN MOURNED

They were both gone, the high-born lady and the peasant girl —gone where there is no sorrow, and no sin. One was lost to him in the coal, the other by fire—two vengeful spirits.

Iván thought of both with bitter regret. He felt that now he was alone in the world. He would have given all his fame, all his money, all the good he had done, to have been able to save even one of the two. He mourned them not in black, nor with crape on his hat. What good are the signs of grief?

The European mourns in black, the Chinese in white, the Mussulman in green; the older generations in Hungary in purple; the Jew in rags; the philosopher in his heart. The wise man does not share his grief, only his joys.

In the meanwhile, peace and plenty reigned; in the Bondavára Valley where there had been a half-savage race, there was now a happy people.

Even the worst elements settled down; morality had grown fashionable.

Iván sent young men to factories abroad at his own expense, where they learnt the arts of civilization. He brought wood-carvers from Switzerland, and lace-workers from Holstein, to teach their trades to the women and children, so that they might unite artistic work with increased earnings. Where every-one, large or small, works either from necessity or for amuse-ment—those who look on work as their pleasure, and who do

382

not feel it a privation to be employed—such people are ennobled by work.

Iván looked after the schools. He liberated the state-employed teachers from the misery of their tyrant, the state; he rewarded students with scholarships, schoolboys with useful prizes; he established a library and a reading-room in every parish. He taught the people to put by the pence they could spare; he taught them how to help one another; he established a savings bank and a hospital in Bondavára.

His own colliery was a model one. The miners were joint owners, and shared his profits. Whoever was taken on in this colliery had to pass an examination, and work on trial for a year. This rule applied to women as well as men. This trial year was not always easy, particularly not for girls.

Nowhere was a girl so well looked after; not in her mother's house, nor in a convent was there more attention paid to manners and morals than in Iván Berend's colliery. Every word, every act was watched. If any one failed to reach the mark during his probation year, he was not mocked or despised. He was simply told to go and work in the company's colliery, where there was better pay; and the workman or woman could imagine that this was promotion, and not a degradation. In the company's colliery there was more freedom, and less strict rules.

If, however, at the end of the trial year, the applicant had fulfilled all requirements, he or she was received into the colony, and became a shareholder. In addition, a good-conduct prize was given once a year, on the anniversary of the great pit fire, to the most modest, well-behaved girl in the colony.

Iván spent fifty florins on this prize, and the miners promised the winner a handsome wedding present.

It was, of course, understood that no one applied for the prize. No one knew who was likely to get it. The elders took notes; it was their secret. There was no special ceremony to award this prize. It would be done on an ordinary working day, when all the miners would have their picks and shovels, so that every one could see that the reward was not for a pretty face, but for a good heart and industrious fingers. It was to be a day of quiet rejoicing to the people.

This was how Iván mourned.

Chapter XLI

EVILA

It was the anniversary of the great pit fire. Old Paul had gone to look for Iván at his house on the central settlement, but Iván had already started for the smaller colliery. He caught up with Paul on the road, and took the miner up in his carriage.

"This was a memorable day a year ago," said Paul.

"I remember it all too well," returned Iván. "But today, we have to award the good conduct prize. Have the jury settled who is to have it?"

"They have. It's a girl who has been with us for less than a year."

"And does she fulfil all the conditions?"

"In every way. The girl is most hard-working. She is always the first to come and the last to leave. She never complains about the work, as many of them do; she treats it as if it was fun for her. If her wheelbarrow is overloaded, she even tells the miner to put on more; then she runs away gaily with it and comes back singing as if she had been playing. At the end of each break she gets the other girls back to their work."

"Is she vain?"

"No; she wears the same Sunday best things she wore a year ago; of course, they are not quite as fresh-looking as they were. She has a little string of beads round her throat, and a narrow ribbon in her hair. She washes her clothes in the stream at night for she is peculiar that way, she wears clean linen every day; but she does it herself, so she has the trouble of it herself."

"Is she saving?"

"She has more in our bank than the other girls. She could have even more, only that on Sundays she gives a day's wages to the beggar at the church door."

"Does she go to church regularly?"

"Every Sunday; but she never sits with the other girls. She kneels at a side-altar, covers her face with her hands, and prays throughout Mass."

"Is she good-tempered?"

"She never offends anyone, and never lost her temper. Once a woman said something very nasty to her, for which we fined her: the woman was ready to pay, but the girl denied that she had been insulted. The same woman was taken ill; she had no one to nurse her, being alone and a widow, and this girl nursed her every night, and got her medicine from the chemist."

"Do you think she is a hypocrite?"

"She is too cheerful for that, and ready for a joke. Hypocrites are a gloomy lot. Our people would soon find her out if she wasn't on the level; but she is liked by every one. We don't choose our words exactly, but we can make a fair guess at the girl who respects herself. We like one that gives a good slap to a fellow who would make too free. Ready at hand, but soft-tongued, that's our sort. But I have watched her in a different mood, too: for instance, on Sunday afternoons, when we sit under the mulberries, they all come and make me tell—God knows how many times—the story of how you carried the hose of the air-pump into the Bondavára mine, and how we all thought you were dead. The women and children hold their breath while I talk of it. I think I do tell that story well, for they all know it by heart, and they still listen. They take it in different ways; but this girl, I have noticed her, she covers her face, and cries the whole time."

386

"And is she a modest girl?"

"To make sure, we had to call a jury of married women. They couldn't accuse her of anything. Then we got the girls together, and we pressed them to say if there was anything with any young man, but they all said—no. And there was no need for them to deny it for a peasant girl would be well mated with a miner, and if he wants her, he can have her."

They had now reached the colliery, and went into the station building which stood at the corner of the branch line. There was now another railway, running underground, which connected the two collieries. Here Iván found a great many of the miners. He sent for the rest, and told them to stop work for the day.

The men and women assembled slowly. Only a group of the girls went on working: they had agreed to go on until they had pushed their load to the hill between the entrance to the quarry and the station, where Iván sat waiting. He could not see the girls; he could only hear their clear voices as they called to one another to hurry and get the work done.

One of them began to sing. The melody was familiar to Iván—one of those sad Slav airs in which the singer seems on the brink of tears; and the voice was sweet and melodious; full, too, of feeling.

> 'Say, when I smoothed your hair,
> Showed I not tender care?
> Say, when I dressed my child,
> Was I not fond and mild?'

Iván's face clouded over. Why do they have to sing this? Why should it be on anybody's lips? Why not let it be forgotten?

"The girl is coming," said old Paul. "I hear her singing; she is now coming down the hill with her wheelbarrow."

The girl appeared at the top of the mound. With a run, she

shoved her wheelbarrow ahead, and tipped it with unusual skill; big lumps of coal rolled down the hill slowly. She was a young, well-developed girl in a blue jacket and a short petticoat; but her red petticoat was not tucked up, it fell over her ankles, and only showed her feet. The coloured handkerchief on her head had slipped back a little, and her thick plaits could be seen wound round her head.

Her face was smudged with coal-dust, and was beaming with good humour—the dirt of the earth, and the glory of the spirit. But what the coal-dust could not conceal were the two large black eyes shining like diamonds—the darkness illumined by dazzling stars.

The girl stood still on the top of the coal, then looked down in surprise on the crowd.

The next moment Iván was at her side. In his joy he had leapt from the station across the rails, and had rushed up the coal tip.

"Eveline!" he cried, taking the girl's hand in his.

She shook her head, smiling at him. "No, sir," she said, "Evila."

"You are here! You have come back here!"

"I have been here, sir, for almost a year, and if you will keep me on, I should like to stay."

"You can stay, but only on one condition—as my wife," cried Iván, pressing her hand to his heart.

All who were at the foot of the hill saw his gesture; they could almost hear his words.

Evila shook her head, and drew away her hand. "No, no. Let me be your servant, a maid in your house, your wife's maid. I shall be quite happy; I want nothing more."

"But I want more. You have come back to me; you are mine. How could you be so cruel as to be so near me for almost a year, and never tell me?"

"Oh, sir," said Evila, with a sad yet dignified look. "If you knew all, you would never forgive me."

"I know everything, and I can forgive everything."

His words proved that Iván knew nothing. If he had known the truth, he would have known that there was nothing, nothing to forgive. As it was, he pressed his love to his heart, while she murmured:

"You may forgive me, but the world will never pardon you."

"The world!" cried Iván, raising his head proudly. "My world is here," laying his hand on his breast. "The world! Look around from this hill. Everything in this valley owes its life to me; every blade of grass has to thank me that it is now green. Hill and valley know that, with God's help, I have saved them from destruction! I have made a million, and I have not ruined any one. With every penny, I am blessed. In the prince's palace and in the widow's cottage I have averted despair; I have saved my enemies from a living grave, and I have saved their wives and children from being widows and orphans. My name is known all over the world, and yet I have hidden myself here, not to be troubled with their praises.

I do not care for the world. The loveliest of women has smiled on me and loved me, but she was not of my world. She is dead, and the key of her coffin is my reminder that her whole world has passed away. My world is within me, and into that inner world of mine no one has ever entered, no one will ever enter, except you! Speak, Evila; answer me. Will you try to love me?"

The girl's eyes closed under the ardent gaze of her lover. Many men had sworn their love to her, but no one like this one, whose face shone on her like a god's.

"Oh, sir," she whispered, "if I do not die, I shall always love you, but I feel that I shall die."

As she spoke she fell back in a faint. Her brilliant colour faded to a wax pallor, her flashing eyes closed; and her body, which a moment before was like a blooming rose, crumpled lifeless, like an autumn leaf.

Iván held her lifeless body in his arms.

The woman whom he had loved for so long, for whom he had suffered so much, was his, just as her pulse ceased to beat, just as she said, "I shall always love you, but I feel that I shall die."

But she did not die.

A diamond is a diamond for ever.

Printed in Hugary 1978

Franklin Printing House, Budapest

CO 1682 – h – 7880